# ESCAPE . . . AND LOVE

It was just at dusk when they heard the roar of the stream flowing fast and deep. Dynna had not thought the water would be running this high.

Brage studied the banks on either side, trying to pick the safest place to ford the stream. The current looked fast and dangerous. "Follow me," he said, as he slid down the bank. "Here, take my hand and I will help you."

As she reached for his hand, juggling her bundles of food and clothing, she slipped and lost her footing.

Brage reacted instinctively, sweeping her up into his arms and clasping her to his chest. "Are you all right?" he asked.

Dynna gazed into his eyes. "Yes." She was breathless from his rescue . . . and more.

He stood there, the cold stream rushing around him, unaware of anything save the precious weight of Dynna in his arms. He looked into her eyes and could see the longing there that matched his own, and he could not stop—not this time.

He bent his head to her, his lips seeking and finding hers in a passionate claiming.

# TODAY'S HOTTEST READS
# ARE TOMORROW'S SUPERSTARS

**VICTORY'S WOMAN** (4484, $4.50)
by Gretchen Genet
Andrew—the carefree soldier who sought glory on the battlefield, and returned a shattered man . . . Niall—the legandary frontiersman and a former Shawnee captive, tormented by his past . . . Roger—the troubled youth, who would rise up to claim a shocking legacy . . . and Clarice—the passionate beauty bound by one man, and hopelessly in love with another. Set against the backdrop of the American revolution, three men fight for their heritage—and one woman is destined to change all their lives forever!

**FORBIDDEN** (4488, $4.99)
by Jo Beverley
While fleeing from her brothers, who are attempting to sell her into a loveless marriage, Serena Riverton accepts a carriage ride from a stranger—who is the handsomest man she has ever seen. Lord Middlethorpe, himself, is actually contemplating marriage to a dull daughter of the aristocracy, when he encounters the breathtaking Serena. She arouses him as no woman ever has. And after a night of thrilling intimacy—a forbidden liaison—Serena must choose between a lady's place and a woman's passion!

**WINDS OF DESTINY** (4489, $4.99)
by Victoria Thompson
Becky Tate is a half-breed outcast—branded by her Comanche heritage. Then she meets a rugged stranger who awakens her heart to the magic and mystery of passion. Hiding a desperate past, Texas Ranger Clint Masterson has ridden into cattle country to bring peace to a divided land. But a greater battle rages inside him when he dares to desire the beautiful Becky!

**WILDEST HEART** (4456, $4.99)
by Virginia Brown
Maggie Malone had come to cattle country to forge her future as a healer. Now she was faced by Devon Conrad, an outlaw wounded body and soul by his shadowy past . . . whose eyes blazed with fury even as his burning caress sent her spiraling with desire. They came together in a Texas town about to explode in sin and scandal. Danger was their destiny—and there was nothing they wouldn't dare for love!

*Available wherever paperbacks are sold, or order direct from the Publisher. Send cover price plus 50¢ per copy for mailing and handling to Penguin USA, P.O. Box 999, c/o Dept. 17109, Bergenfield, NJ 07621. Residents of New York and Tennessee must include sales tax. DO NOT SEND CASH.*

# BOBBI SMITH

# PASSION

**ZEBRA BOOKS**
**KENSINGTON PUBLISHING CORP.**

ZEBRA BOOKS are published by

Kensington Publishing Corp.
850 Third Avenue
New York, NY 10022

Copyright © 1995 by Bobbi Smith

All rights reserved. No part of this book may be reproduced in any form or by any means without the prior written consent of the Publisher, excepting brief quotes used in reviews.

If you purchased this book without a cover, you should be aware that this book is stolen property. It was reported as "unsold and destroyed" to the Publisher and neither the Author nor the Publisher has received any payment for this "stripped book."

Zebra and the Z logo Reg. U.S. Pat. & TM Off.

First Printing: October, 1995

Printed in the United States of America

*This book is dedicated to four ladies whose knowledge of the book business is phenomenal. They are a joy to work with and exciting to watch in action: Lynn Brown, Kathryn Falk, Laura Shatzkin, and Joan Schulhafer.*

*I'd also like to thank the Pinnacle Lake Gang for their constant support: Marilee Poulter, Paul Poulter and Louis Reuther.*

*A special note of thanks to Mr. Tom Pearson, History Librarian of the St. Louis Public Library.*

## Prologue

*Norway, 838*

Lightning flashed across the night sky, and thunder, deep and ominous, rumbled across the land.

Standing in the doorway of her small home, the old woman stared out into the darkness, waiting. He would be coming soon, just as he had in the past. She was sure of it.

The rain began then, pelting the earth with a stormswept violence that sent her seeking a seat by the fire in the center of the main room. Though the night was not cold, she felt chilled—a chill of the soul. Her gnarled hands clutched her wrap more tightly around her. She closed her eyes to her surroundings and sought peace from the storm of nature outside and from the storm the gift of foresight had created within her.

"I have come." His voice was deep.

The old woman opened her eyes and looked up to find the tall, dark-haired warrior standing over her. Her expression revealed no surprise at his presence. "You would have me read the runes for you?"

"I sail with the new moon."

She nodded, then rose slowly to go to a small table with two benches nearby. She sat on one bench and motioned for him to sit on the other opposite her. She then paused to study him for a moment. He was a handsome one, this Viking whose black hair, a trait inherited from his Irish mother who had died giving birth to him, had set him apart from the others and earned him the name of the Black Hawk. His eyes were blue, as pale as his Nordic father's. His features were chiseled and strong, his shoulders broad and powerful. He was a magnificent warrior, his reputation for courage and honor unmatched by any other . . . save his sire.

After a moment, the old woman turned her attention to the runes. She spread a white cloth over the tabletop and then took out the prophetic stones. Holding them in her hands, she chanted two verses from the *Runatál* to invoke the powers.

> "I know I hung upon a windswept tree,
> Its roots to the wise unknown;
> Spear-pierced, for nine long nights,
> To Odin pledged, self offered to self.
>
> They gave no bread, nor drinking horn;
> Down to the depths I gazed:
> Crying aloud I took up the runes,
> Then finally I fell."

As she spoke the last, she cast the runes on the cloth before her. She chose three very carefully, then studied their inscriptions.

"What do they say, old woman?" the Black Hawk asked, wondering at her lengthy silence. "Will my raid succeed? Will I claim the prize I seek?"

Her blue eyes were glittering with the secrets of the ages as she lifted her gaze to him. She stared at the warrior for a moment, measuring, judging, then looked down again at the stones she held in her hand. Finally, she answered him. "You will get far more than you bargained for, my handsome one. Oh, yes, far more . . ."

Relief showed in his expression. "Good. And what of my men? Will the fighting be fierce?"

"There will be danger. Blood will be shed. False words will be spoken. But a treasure of great value awaits you at the end of your journey."

As she made the last pronouncement, lightning once more ripped across the heavens. The ground trembled and a heavy roll of thunder followed in its wake.

The sense of unease that had gripped the warrior lessened at her words. "So we will be successful." He smiled as he got to his feet. "The prize is a glorious one?"

"More precious than any you have claimed before."

He nodded, satisfied, then paid the woman and left.

She watched him go, knowing that danger surrounded him and wondering if he would survive the treachery. She had not told him everything she had seen. There was a path he had to walk and a danger he had to face alone.

Lord Alfrick, roused from his sleep by his servant, was disgruntled at being disturbed. He pinned the man with an icy glare as he sat up in bed to speak to him.

"What is it of such importance that you would wake me in the middle of the night?" he demanded.

"I am sorry to disturb you, my lord, but a stranger from the Viking lands has come to the tower demanding an audience."

"A Viking?" Lord Alfrick was now fully alert.

"Yes, my lord. He insists that he must speak to you and no other. He claims it is a matter of life or death."

"Whose life? Whose death?" he asked. "I do not trust any Norseman."

"Yours."

"Mine?" He scowled blackly as anger filled him. "Who is this messenger who dares to approach my tower and threaten my life?"

"Not threaten, my lord. He says he is here to warn you of danger to come."

Lord Alfrick frowned as he considered his words. "Rouse Sir Thomas. Tell him to meet me belowstairs with several guards in my private chamber off the Great Hall. I will speak with this mysterious one from the north, but I will have him slain in an instant should this prove some kind of devilish trick."

Lord Alfrick rose and prepared for his audience with the stranger. He dressed quickly and strapped on his sword. His mood was cautious and wary now. He had ruled this land for more than twenty-five years and had suffered at the hands of the raiders more times than he cared to remember. Never before had any Viking sought him out to talk. He wondered what this man was about. Ready to meet the midnight visitor, he quit the room.

A short time later, Lord Alfrick faced the mysterious man with Sir Thomas and several other of his armed guards by his side. Sir Thomas was a tall, battle-hardened man of some thirty years. His dedication to Alfrick was known throughout the land, and he was trusted above all others. It was Sir Thomas's counsel Alfrick sought when making important decisions, for he was a good judge of character and often offered insights overlooked by the other advisers. Alfrick was glad he was with him now.

"Tell me why I should not kill you where you stand, Viking?" Lord Alfrick demanded. The Norsemen were his sworn enemies. He held no love for them.

"Because I have news that could save your life."

"Why should I believe anything you say?" the lord asked as he peered into the heavy gloom, trying, but failing, to make out the man's features.

The stranger deliberately stepped farther back into the shadows. He kept the hood of his dark cloak up, shielding his identity even more from the probing gaze of the Saxon lord. He shrugged as he answered, "It is your choice to accept my warning or not. I am here to tell you what is to come.

The Black Hawk and his men will attack your land soon after the new moon."

As if in prophetic emphasis of his words, lightning flashed and thunder rumbled around them.

"The Black Hawk!" Lord Alfrick went rigid at the information. He exchanged quick glances with Sir Thomas, his dark-eyed gaze mirroring his disbelief. The Viking known as the Black Hawk was a powerful raider who plundered towns at will, stripping them of their wealth and making captives of their men and women. "Why would you tell me this? Why would you betray one of your own?"

"Because I want him dead!" the traitor hissed, his voice full of venom. "I cannot raise my hand against another of my kind, but I can give you the sword to do it."

"What payment do you demand of me for this knowledge you have shared?"

"Only that you see the Black Hawk slain."

"If the attack does come as you've said, how will we know which man is the Black Hawk?"

"The sail of his ship is blood-red and bears the crest of a Black Hawk in its center, as does his shield and helm."

Still, knowing how cunning Vikings could be, Lord Alfrick harbored doubts. "Is this some trick? Some ruse to distract us, while your warriors attack us from another direction?"

"If I had wanted to attack you, I could have done so this night. You and all your men would have been slain in your beds," the conspirator pointed out. "You have heard my warning. I have given you time to prepare. If you do nothing, this tower and all its treasure will belong to the Black Hawk."

"And if I do prepare?"

"You may defeat the mightiest of all the Viking raiders and save yourself and your subjects."

"How many will come?"

"He will sail with at least three ships of warriors. You must amass a powerful force if you are to prevail against them. His men are the fiercest of fighters."

"Will you sail with him?" Lord Alfrick asked, a sneer sounding in his voice. He felt great disgust at this man's betrayal of one of his own and wondered if this traitor considered himself a fine warrior.

"I will know all that transpires," he replied. "But be warned. The Black Hawk will not be stopped easily. No man yet has matched him for strength, courage, and bravery. You must be clever or you will lose all."

"You need not worry. We will prepare," Lord Alfrick answered. "I will see the Black Hawk dead, and, by doing so, I will bring a blessing upon the lands made safe from his pillaging."

The betrayer nodded, then turned to leave. One of the guards accompanied him in order to see him from the tower grounds.

Lord Alfrick watched until they had disappeared from sight, then spoke to Sir Thomas as they started upstairs.

"What do you think, Sir Thomas? Do we believe this man's warning?" Lord Alfrick's expression was grim as he awaited his friend's answer.

"I would like to believe that his words were all lies, but I know it would be a fool's game to doubt him. Far better that we are prepared for an attack that never comes than to be caught unarmed by the Black Hawk and his men."

"I agree. We must be ready. I will send word to the neighboring kingdoms. With our combined strength, we can mount a force large enough to repel the raiders."

"Shall I ride with the news in the morning, my lord?"

"Yes. The sooner we begin to plan, the better our defenses."

Lord Alfrick went on to his bedchamber, while Sir Thomas retired to his own quarters. Both men knew they would sleep no more that night.

Meanwhile, outside in the yard, a lone figure emerged from a darkened hiding place and silently followed the guard and the traitor into the night.

## One

The wind filled the sails of the three Viking longships and sent the vessels slicing through the water. The ship with the scarlet sail marked with the sign of the Black Hawk led the way, as its master guided it unerringly to the south and west. They had sailed from their homeland just three days before and were now closing on their goal—the Saxon coast.

"How much longer until we make landfall?" Seger, a brawny warrior aboard the lead ship, asked as he stared out to sea.

"If the wind remains strong in our sails, we should see the coast in another two days," Neils replied.

"Good." Seger grinned wolfishly as he thought of the battle to come. "It will be good to be raiding again. I have been wintering too long and my sword arm needs practice!"

"I believe the Black Hawk feels the same way," Neils remarked with a laugh as he nodded toward their leader, Brage Nordwald, also known as the Black Hawk. The tall, powerfully built Viking was standing on the small deck at the front of the ship, his sword already in hand. "That is probably why we sailed two weeks ahead of the others."

"He always strives to have the element of surprise on his side. No one will be expecting us. He is a great warrior, and it is my privilege to serve him."

"He is a clever man. I pledged myself to him three years ago, and I've never regretted it. My share of treasure has grown every season."

"When it comes to raiding, no one can match him. He strikes without warning, claims his prize and then quickly disappears."

"My father followed Brage's father, Anslak, and now I will follow him wherever he leads."

"And if everything I have heard is true, he is leading us now to one of the wealthiest kingdoms on the coast."

They both smiled as they thought of the riches that would soon be theirs. They glanced once more to their leader who stood brave and proud before them. They felt invincible knowing he was the one who would lead them into battle.

"No one can conquer the Black Hawk."


Brage had planned this raid very carefully, and he was eager for the fight. As he studied the horizon and thought of the battle to come, he tightened his grip on the golden hilt of his sword. Lord Alfrick would not be an easy opponent. That was why he'd sailed early. He wanted to catch the Saxons unprepared. He'd learned long ago to make use of every weapon he could, and surprise was one of the most effective tools of raiding.

"Well, my brother, are you ready to add even more wealth to your already bulging coffers?" Ulf asked as he joined Brage.

"As always," he answered with a smile as he slid his sword back into its scabbard.

Ulf was Brage's older half brother by their father's mistress. Other than their height and blue eyes, though, they bore little physical resemblance to each other. The blond-haired Ulf was a bear of a man, barrel-chested and heavily muscled. Many a foe had thought him slow because of his size, and their judgment had proven a fatal mistake. Brage, on the other hand, was lean yet muscular. His hair was dark in contrast to Ulf's fairer coloring. As children they had been ardent rivals, each constantly seeking to best the other, to prove their worth to their warrior father. As they'd grown to manhood, however, they had set aside their rivalry and had begun to raid together, earning accolades for their bravery from all who fought with them.

"Have caution," Ulf warned. "Do not be overly confident."

"My confidence is in my men, and the fact that Lord Alfrick will not be expecting us. While his tower is sturdy, it should present no great challenge to us since he has had no time to prepare for our attack. Once we make landfall, we should lay claim to the sizable treasure within a few days. The element of surprise will be with us."

"Let us hope for all our sakes that it goes as you say."

"It is my responsibility to make sure that it does. I took great care in the planning."

"Ah, but for a few words spoken before the gods, I could be the one leading this raid. Instead, I am relegated by our father to protect your back," Ulf remarked with a laugh and a rueful shake of his head, as if he accepted his fate.

"And a fine job you do." Brage clapped his brother on the shoulder. "Without you, I would have been long dead. You bear the scars to prove your faithfulness."

A long, jagged scar marred Ulf's right cheek, stopping just below his eye. It was a trophy from a particularly hard battle, fought years before when the two had first sailed together.

"Which is why I caution you now. I need no more marks upon me to further ruin my beauty."

"Fear not. The runes have predicted our claiming a great treasure on this raid."

"The stones are never known to lie."

"Besides, no Saxon can match any of my men. When the raid comes, the day will be ours." Brage looked down at his warriors, some fifty strong in his lead ship alone. They were the finest fighting force ever assembled and had never tasted defeat.

"We will show them the full strength of the Black Hawk's power," Ulf agreed.

Brage was smiling as he lifted his gaze once more to the horizon. It felt good to be at sea again. The future held promise.

Lady Dynna's mood was unsettled as she paced in her bedchamber. Since the death of her husband, Sir Warren, some six months before in a tragic hunting accident, the circumstances of which still haunted her to this day, she'd elected to take her meals in her room. She had pleaded the need for solitude during her mourning as her reason to want to eat alone, and her wishes had been respected by her husband's family. As of yesterday, however, that had all changed.

Dynna cast a quick glance in the large bronze mirror mounted on the wall and took the time to study her own reflection. A mane of raven hair framed her face. She was a trifle wan, but the paleness was to be expected, since she'd confined herself to her chamber most of the time since Warren's untimely passing. Dark brows arched delicately over wide gray eyes that stared back at her with a haunted, desperate expression. Her mouth was set and unsmiling, and that troubled her, for there had been a time when she'd loved to laugh and had enjoyed life. But no more. There was little to be happy about now, especially since she'd received the summons yesterday from her father-in-law, Lord Alfrick.

The memory of Lord Alfrick's command that she marry Sir Edmund, her dead husband's younger brother, left her shuddering in revulsion. She fought down the reaction, struggling for control over her runaway emotions. Lord Alfrick might insist she marry Sir Edmund, but the marriage hadn't taken place yet. There was still time. She could cling to a slim hope that somehow she would find a way to escape that dreaded fate . . .

Dynna was as ready as she would ever be to go belowstairs

and dine with the family. She was determined to hold herself aloof, regally distant. She didn't want anyone to suspect that she was frantic to flee the terrible destiny that the powerful men in her life had declared would be hers.

Knowing she could delay no longer, Lady Dynna left her bedchamber and headed for the stone staircase that led to the Great Hall. She had just reached the top of the steps when she came face-to-face with Sir Edmund on his way up. It took a major effort on her part not to panic.

Dynna knew many women in the tower thought that Edmund was extraordinarily handsome, with his fair hair and dark eyes, but Dynna was not fooled by his good looks. She had seen into his soul and knew the blackness of his heart. Where Warren had been kind and gentle, Edmund took pleasure in causing others pain. Where Warren had put others' needs before his own, Edmund satisfied his own desires and gave not a passing thought to anyone other than himself. He was a self-serving man of little character and even less faith. Dynna hated to admit that he frightened her, but there was little doubt he did.

As Edmund stopped before her, he gave her a slow, confident smile that spoke of victory and ultimate possession.

"Good evening, my lady," he said, his voice heavy with implied intimacy, his gaze hungry upon her.

"I'm not 'your' anything," Dynna said as haughtily as she could, drawing upon her anger to use as a defense against her fear of him. His salacious look suggested that he knew what she looked like without her clothing, and the thought unnerved her.

"Ah, but you soon will be mine," he said softly as he took a step nearer and reached up to touch her cheek. "Father has stated his wishes in the matter, so it is decided. It will not be long before I take you for my wife."

"I am still in mourning for your brother."

"My brother is gone, my sweet, but I am here."

"Does it not test your loyalty and honor to speak of your brother so? Does not his death leave an ache in your heart?"

Despite her protestations and her talk of Warren, Edmund was certain that she wanted him as much as he wanted her. No woman had ever refused him. "You have been alone long enough. You need a real man to warm your blood and erase forever the memories of one now dead."

Dynna felt color rise to her face at his bold words. She took a step backward, distancing herself from him. "It is not proper that you should say such things to me."

Sir Edmund's smile broadened. "Be careful, my dear Dynna. I am not a man to be easily put off."

He had wanted her since the first time he saw her, two years before when she arrived in their kingdom to marry Warren. He'd been more than patient in waiting to claim her for his own, but the time of waiting was almost over. By his father's decree, she would be his—along with her bounteous dowry.

"I am Warren's wife." Dynna held herself rigidly as she spoke with disdain. Yet even as she said the words, her heart was beating a frantic rhythm. Edmund had power over her, and they both knew it. Now that he was his father's only son, Lord Alfrick would give him whatever he wanted.

"You are Warren's *widow*," Edmund ground out, his eyes narrowing as he bristled at her censure. "You are a woman without protection." She had no right to rebuke him. She was, after all, only a female, mere chattel to be bargained at a man's pleasure. "My brother is dead and buried. As of this moment, your mourning is done."

The color that moments before had stained her cheeks faded before his cold dictate. Dynna felt intimidated and helpless, yet she knew she must not show fear or betray weakness. She met his regard with a look as steely as his own.

Sir Edmund saw the glint of defiance in her eye and the aristocratic way she held herself. He found himself excited by the challenge she presented. His gaze never left hers as he reached out and caressed her upper arm. "Once we are wed, my Dynna, I am going to explore the depths of your pride. I will take great pleasure in bringing you under my domination."

"I will never surrender to you."

"Ah, but you will. Make no mistake. Now, come, let me escort you downstairs. My father awaits your fair presence."

It was all Dynna could do not to flinch away from his touch as she muttered her resentful thanks.

She wanted to tell him that she would gladly die before surrendering to him, but she held her tongue. Without a husband's protection, she was a pawn in a game played by powerful men. Her wishes did not matter to Lord Alfrick or Sir Edmund. She only wanted to return to her parents' home and live out the rest of her life in peace and solitude. Lord Alfrick, however, wanted her dowry, and a fine one it was, too—consisting of the rent from some of her father's tenant farms! He would never allow those monies to slip away. He would keep her and her dowry under his control by marrying her to Edmund.

Sir Edmund linked her arm through his and drew her close to his side as he started down the stairs. She felt small and very feminine to him, and it filled him with an incredible sense of power to finally be able to touch her so. When they reached a small landing, he maneuvered her into the shadows.

"Edmund, what are you . . . ?"

Dynna got no further in her questioning. He boldly cut off her protest with a hot kiss. He pressed himself fervidly against her.

Dynna was stunned, but only for a moment. She reacted with outrage at his violation of her and struck him with all her might. His grunt of pain pleased her, but only for a moment. He did not end the embrace, but tightened his grip on her even more and deepened the kiss. With all the force she could muster, Dynna pushed against his shoulders to dislodge him.

"You villain! How dare you touch me?!"

Sir Edmund saw the fire of anger in her eyes and thought she had never looked more beautiful. He smiled knowingly. "I would dare much with you, Dynna."

Frightened by his naked lust Dynna tried to move away, to escape his vile nearness, but he grabbed her arm to stop her. His fingers dug into her soft flesh and he merely laughed as he pulled her back to him.

"We will descend together."

Gritting her teeth, Dynna managed a tight nod of agreement.

The Great Hall was noisy and crowded with men. Extra forces had arrived from two neighboring kingdoms to bolster the tower's defenses in case of a possible Viking attack, and they were now gathered to partake of the evening meal. Seated at the trestle tables, the men consumed much ale and mead with their meals. Their conversations were loud and boisterous as they bragged about their readiness to face the dreaded Norsemen.

Sir Edmund escorted Dynna to her seat beside Lord Alfrick at the raised table at the front of the room. She took her place and while she managed to smile politely at everyone, she felt like a bird caught in a snare.

"I am glad you have chosen to join us, Dynna," Lord Alfrick welcomed her. "We have missed your lovely presence at our table."

"I am afraid that until now, you would not have found me suitable company, my lord. The loss of my beloved Warren has sorely grieved me."

Lord Alfrick's eyes darkened with pain at the thought of his dead oldest son. "I, too, miss Warren, but we must continue our lives. He would want that."

"Yes, my lord." Dynna gave the proper outward appearance of acquiescence and respect, but she did not feel it in her heart. She knew Lord Alfrick was a cold, calculating man who cared only about her dowry. He certainly cared nothing for her happiness. If he did, he would have realized that she was not ready to remarry, and that even if she chose to marry again, she would certainly not choose Edmund.

As they were served and began to eat Dynna managed to make some small conversation. After a while, the talk turned to the Viking warrior known as the Black Hawk, who was rumored to be about to attack. Dynna wondered how word of the impending attack had reached Lord Alfrick.

"We are more than prepared for him," Edmund told his father with full confidence. He had been training with the men for several weeks and knew their battle-worthiness.

"What about you, Sir Thomas? You have seen more raids than my son. What do you think?" Lord Alfrick asked his friend who was seated at the table with them. "Is Edmund right? Will we defeat the Black Hawk?"

Edmund grew furious that his father didn't trust his own assessment of their situation. Still, he betrayed none of his anger as he listened to the older man's opinion.

Sir Thomas thought quietly for a moment, his expression serious, then concurred with Edmund's assessment. "Yes, my lord. I believe we will defeat the raider should he dare to attack. We are ready for him."

Lord Alfrick nodded, then stood and spoke to all in the Great Hall, "The Black Hawk has been a threat to us and our neighbors long enough. It's time to rid the world of the heathen raider from the north who would loot my land and take my subjects hostage. If he attacks, we shall slay him!"

Led by Sir Edmund, the men roared their approval.

Dynna only half listened to their heated, bloodthirsty talk. She had heard all the terrible tales of the Vikings, of how they plundered and pillaged, kidnapped and killed. She could not help but wonder if a fate at their hands would be any worse than being forced to wed Edmund. At that thought, her mood grew even more grim. Neither choice offered her a chance for a happy life.

Glancing over at Edmund, seeing his eagerness for battle mirrored in his dark eyes, she vowed that she would never marry him. Where once this tower had been a loving home to her, now it had become a virtual prison. Somehow, some way, she would escape! She would return to the safe haven of her parents' home.

When the meal was finished and Edmund moved off to talk to the men, Dynna managed a stealthy escape. Her steps were unhurried as she left the hall so she would not draw attention to herself; though, the instant she was far enough up the stairs to be out of sight, she quickened her pace. She didn't stop until she was safely locked inside her bedchamber.

Alone at last, Dynna waited for the feeling of comfort and security that usually surrounded her there, but there was no respite from her tortured thoughts. The longer she waited, replaying in her mind all that had transpired that night, the more she feared she would never again know a moment's peace as long as she remained in the tower.

A soft knock at the door caused her to jump nervously; was Edmund coming after her?

"Yes? Who is it?" she asked.

"It is I, my lady, Matilda. I thought you might be needing help preparing for bed."

Dynna relaxed at the sound of her trusted companion's voice, and quickly opened the door to admit her. Matilda had been but thirteen when she became her servant, and Dynna only five. When, years later, Dynna had come to this kingdom to marry Sir Warren, Matilda had traveled with her. Since Warren's demise, the slender, red-haired Matilda had proven her only true friend and her fierce protector. Dynna was desperate to confide in her.

"My lady! What is it? What is wrong?" Matilda saw how pale Dynna appeared and how haunted her expression was.

Dynna locked the door behind her, then dragged Matilda away from the portal for fear that someone passing by might overhear what she was about to say. "Sir Edmund escorted me down to the hall and . . ."

"And what?"

"And he insists that he is going to marry me . . . soon." She emphasized the last word.

"No. You cannot even think of marrying him." Matilda was horrified.

"He is the last man I would ever marry!" Dynna said with great emotion. "How can he think I would be ready to wed again so soon after Warren's death? It has been less than a year." Tears welled up in her eyes and she dashed them away. This was no time for weakness.

"I am afraid for you. Sir Edmund doesn't care about his brother's death or your mourning period. He has had his eye on your dowry all along, but that is not all he wants," Matilda pointed out bluntly.

"I know," Lady Dynna agreed. "He wants to control everything and everyone. I have seen the way he looks at me." She paused, shivering at the thought of his hands upon her. "I must go home to my mother and father," she said. "It's the only way. I'll be safe from him there."

"Will Lord Alfrick let you leave?" Matilda knew how greedy he was, and she doubted Lady Dynna would be able to leave the kingdom.

"No, and that's why I need your help."

"What can I do, my lady?"

"I must escape before I'm forced into this marriage. I must get back home. I must think of something clever . . ."

"You mean sneak out?" Matilda frowned.

"It is the only way. If I have to disguise myself to do it, I will."

A light shone in Matilda's dark eyes, and she smiled for the first time since coming into the room. "I could get some of the servants' old clothing . . ." she offered.

Dynna felt a ray of hope as she met her friend's gaze. "Will you come with me?"

"Of course, my lady! Heaven only knows what kind of danger you might encounter. You will need me to take care of you."

Dynna gave her an impulsive hug. "How soon can you get the clothing?"

"I'll find something for you to wear. When you are so dressed, no one will ever suspect it is you."

"It must be soon, Matilda. From Sir Edmund's actions, I do not think he will be put off much longer. He is determined to make me his wife."

"We are not going to give him the chance, my lady."

Dynna's mood brightened at her servant's supporting words. "We are going home, Matilda."

The days at sea had passed quickly for Brage. He loved the freedom of being aboard his ship again. The openness and wildness of the untamed waters matched his restless soul. When the craft was racing across the sea and the wind was in his face, he felt as though he were soaring, like his namesake—the hawk.

Brage had been pleased that the winds had been with them. By his calculations, they would be sighting the coast that very day. Since dawn, he had been at the helm, keeping watch.

"So, today is the day," Ulf stated as he came to stand beside his brother.

Brage nodded, his gaze trained on the horizon. "We should be dividing Lord Alfrick's treasure by tomorrow night."

It was then that Brage caught sight of the first faint outline of land in the distance. He called out to his men, and a cheer rose among them. At last! They would be raiding soon!

Kristoffer, son of Anslak and his second wife, Tove, heard his older brother's call and hurried to the fore to join him and Ulf. At nineteen, he was eager for adventure and ready to match Brage in laying claim to the riches of the world. One day, he was determined, he would be as renowned as the Black Hawk.

"Soon we will fight again." Kristoffer's expression was avid as he watched the coast come into clear view.

"The pup is feisty today," Ulf said.

"I spent many a cold winter night waiting just for this."

"Ah, Kris, you should have found yourself a willing wench and warmed up the night." Brage chuckled.

"I can get a woman any night. The heat of a fight is much more exciting! I am more than ready for this battle."

"By the morn, you will have your wish," Brage stated.

Brage turned his full attention to the coastline. He recognized their location and knew that the deserted landing site he wanted was farther to the south, close enough to Lord Alfrick's tower to make it an easy march for the men, yet shielded enough from view to save them from being discovered. He directed the ships onward, and finally sighted the landmark he had been searching for.

Issuing orders tight and fast before they lost all daylight, Brage directed the ships closer to shore. With speed and expertise, the Vikings maneuvered their craft into a protected area where they wouldn't be readily observed. The other two ships drew in close to them. They would wait out the night on board and go ashore at first light.

The days following her decision to flee the tower had passed at a snail's pace for Dynna. There seemed to be no getting away from Edmund's oppressive presence, except when he was gone from the tower, training for battle with his men. The rest of the time, no matter where she went, he was always nearby, watching her with a hungry, hooded gaze. His watchful, predatory manner unnerved her, but it also made her that much more determined in her effort to get away.

"I've got them!" Matilda declared excitedly as she rushed into Dynna's room late in the afternoon three days after their initial conversation. She stopped long enough to secure the door behind her, then hurried to Dynna and handed her the parcel she carried. "Your disguise, my lady."

Dynna quickly unwrapped the package. She felt a surge of hope as she stared down at the assortment of villagers' clothes.

"You did it!" she breathed in excitement and relief. "We will go this very night!"

"You are sure you want to do this?"

"I have never been more sure of anything in my life," Dynna affirmed, the memory of Edmund's kiss fueling her need to flee.

"We can leave the tower the way the servants do. If luck is on our side—"

"No, not luck—God. If God is on our side, we will be blessed and safely make our escape," she corrected.

They shared a long look of mutual understanding, then set about finalizing their plans.

While Dynna hated every minute she was forced to spend with Lord Alfrick and Sir Edmund at the evening meal, on this particular night the dinner seemed more interminable than ever. Once again, seated beside Edmund, Dynna tried to ignore the heat of his gaze upon her and the occasional "accidental" touch of his hand upon hers.

As had happened every night of late, the conversation was centered on the threat of the Viking attack. The more Edmund talked about war, the less attention he paid to her, and that pleased Dynna immensely. When they spoke of battles and weapons, his manner became excited and his eyes glowed with an inner fervor. While he had made it plain that he desired her, she knew that to him she was only an object to be won, like a battle. Once claimed, he would not stop until he had dominated her completely, and once he had conquered her spirit, she would be set aside, another trophy to be displayed.

The knowledge of what the future held for her as his wife only made waiting the few short hours to the time of her planned escape all the more difficult. Dynna had to keep her eagerness to be done with the meal from showing. Each minute seemed an eternity until the hour came for her to retire.

When Sir Edmund moved off to discuss strategies with Sir Thomas, Dynna rose to return to her bedchamber. She had hoped to make her exit unnoticed, but to her dismay, Edmund looked up just as she was leaving the table. He saw that Dynna was leaving, and he quickly excused himself from the men and moved to intercept her.

# Two

"Retiring already?" Sir Edmund asked as he closed on Dynna like a hunter on its prey.

"I am a bit tired." She hoped she sounded convincingly weary.

"Please, allow me to escort you to your room." He took her arm with possessive familiarity.

Dynna's flesh crawled where he touched her, but she did not jerk away. "There really is no need."

Edmund bent his head toward her in an intimate gesture as he led her to the stone stairs. "One night very soon, my sweet, we will be mounting these steps together, and when we reach your room we will be seeking more than just sleep."

"Edmund, it is wicked for you to say such things to me. I have told you that my heart and my love still belong to Warren. Your brother is my husband and—"

*"Was* your husband!" he snarled, sick of hearing about her feelings for his older brother. Warren had been such a paragon of virtue that living in his shadow had been a source of constant torment for Edmund. He was finally rid of Warren, and he didn't miss him. In fact, he was enjoying his absence tremendously. His brother's untimely demise had left him heir to his father's lands, and he was about to lay claim to both his brother's widow and her dowry. Yes, he was truly enjoying life now.

"Warren will always live in my heart."

"You speak nonsense. You are free to marry again, and you will, Dynna. You will marry me . . . and soon!"

Dynna stiffened.

He felt her resistance and tightened his hold on her. "Do not fight me. It will do you no good."

They had reached her chamber as he spoke, and he stopped outside the door.

"You should realize, sweet Dynna, that I always get what I want."

"Good night, Edmund." Dynna's words were cold as she reached out to open the door.

Her curt tone fired his temper, and he grabbed her hand. He had just started to drag her back into his arms when suddenly the door opened from the inside.

"Lady Dynna? Is that you, my lady?" Matilda asked in a perfectly timed rescue.

"Yes, it is I, Matilda." She took advantage of Edmund's surprise at being interrupted and fled into the shelter of her room. "Good night, Edmund."

With a great show of bravery she shut the door firmly in his face.

Edmund stared at the closed portal, torn between rage and reluctant admiration for her daring. He wanted to smash the door in and take her right then and there in front of her arrogant servant. Her continued defiance stirred his blood as no other woman ever had. Dynna was a fine-looking female, and he greatly anticipated having her beneath him in his bed. He smiled at the thought as he started back down to the hall to rejoin the men.

"He's gone, my lady!" Matilda whispered, her ear to the door as she listened to his receding footsteps.

"Thank God! As angry as he was, I was worried he might try to break down the door."

"But he did not."

"You are right. We are safe for now. Let us get ready!"

Dynna began her transformation from royal lady to peasant woman.

"The hardest part will be getting through the Great Hall, but within another hour or so, most of the men will either be asleep or well on their way to becoming sotted. With luck we will not be noticed, and then once we are out of the tower, it should be simple enough. Of course, the whole trek would go faster if we had horses."

"There are no mounts we dare take," Dynna pointed out. "They would be missed immediately. It will be wiser to travel on foot; we will be less likely to be noticed that way. We can pass through the villages, and no one will think anything unusual about the presence of two peasants."

"How long do you suppose it will take to reach your parents' home?" Matilda was pleased to be going back.

"I think we can make the journey within two weeks. That is, if everything goes as planned."

"It will be fine," Matilda assured her, then held up a small sack. "I have some bread and cheese. We will not go hungry."

Matilda helped Dynna don the plain clothing. She laid aside her fine woolen gunna and tunic and helped her into the crudely made, rough brown linen garment so common to the village women. When Dynna was finally dressed, Matilda stood for a moment in total silence, staring at her. Even wearing these poorest of clothes, there was no hiding her regal beauty or her elegant bearing. She was going to have to instruct her how to act like a peasant.

"How do I look?" Dynna asked, having not yet checked her appearance in the mirror.

"You are dressed like a villager, but you must not stand so straight."

"Why?"

"Your manner is too elegant for one of the lower class, my lady. If you are to pass for a serving wench, you must keep your eyes downcast and mumble your words a little.

And when you walk you need to slump more. Anyone who even caught a glimpse of you standing as you are now would know you're no ordinary villager."

"You must show me everything I need to know. Our escape depends on it. I cannot risk making any mistakes."

"Yes, my . . ."

"Yes, 'my' what?" Dynna challenged.

"Yes, madam."

"That is better. A slip of the tongue could betray us, just as easily as my own manner. We have to be careful."

After Matilda quickly showed her how to move as if she had the weight of the world upon her shoulders, Dynna moved to the mirror. She did indeed look very different in the dark, unadorned tunic, and shoes of plain, soft leather. Still, her hair was loose and fell freely about her shoulders in a thick tumble of soft ebony curls.

"We must braid my hair and pin it up. I don't want to take any chance of being recognized."

Matilda agreed, and braided the lustrous tresses into a single plait.

"Soon it will be late enough so we can finally leave," Dynna said.

"I am ready," the loyal maid responded.

Dynna went to the narrow window and stared out for the last time at the night-shrouded countryside that had been her home for two years. She thought of Warren and the love they had shared. At his side, she had felt an affinity for the land and its people, but now, all she felt was loneliness. It would be good to go back to her real home, to a place where she was loved for who she was and not merely wanted for the riches of her dowry.

The thought of returning to her parents made her smile gently. Any hardship she might endure in these next days would be worth it to be safely back with them again.

Dynna smiled at her maid as she took the cloak Matilda was holding out to her. She drew the hood up and then pulled it low over her face to hide her features from any who might look her way. Matilda did the same with her own. Dynna slipped her small jeweled dagger into her belt; after taking one last look around the chamber, she was ready.

The two women crept quietly from the room and made their way cautiously down the stairs. Dynna was careful to keep her eyes downcast and to walk as if she'd worked a hard day of physical labor.

There was still some activity in the Great Hall, and the fear of discovery struck terror in them both as they moved through the torch-lit room. The deep rumble of the men's voices around them magnified their terror. It was all they could do not to charge headlong out of the place. When at last they had crossed the hall and slipped across the drawbridge, unnoticed by the few men who stood guard, their hearts were pounding.

Staying close together, Dynna and Matilda moved down the road toward the village. The darkness that swallowed them was a welcoming, safe embrace.

As the eastern horizon brightened, Brage roused his men and ordered the longships in to the shore. The shallow draft of the boats allowed them easy access, and the oars were put in to help guide them.

As the ships landed silently and unseen on foreign soil, Brage turned to Ulf. "Take Seger and Neils," he directed, "they both speak some of the Saxon language as you do, and see what awaits us. We should be just an hour's march to the tower. Check the area and report if we're going to meet any resistance."

Ulf called to the other two men, then strapped on his sword, donned his helmet and picked up his battle-ax. He always prepared himself for the worst; that way he was never taken by surprise. Ulf did not like surprises.

Seger and Neils hurriedly prepared to accompany him.

After fetching their weapons and donning their helmets, too, they joined Ulf on shore. The three headed inland to scout the area.

While they were gone, Brage and the rest of his nearly 150 warriors prepared for battle. They worked in silence, not wanting anyone to know they were there. Brage pulled his padded leather vest on over his wool tunic and trousers. He fastened his scabbard, enjoying the weight of the sword at his side. After putting on his helmet, he picked up his shield with the crest of the Black Hawk emblazoned on it and left the ship to wait on the shore for the others.

As the Vikings finished preparing for the fight to come, they took up their weapons and shields and went to join their leader. The bigger, stronger men carried battle-axes. Their massive strength would enable them to cut their way through the enemy resistance. Others, less endowed, were armed with bows and arrows; still others carried spears and swords. Together, they were a formidable force. All were committed to complete victory and to the spoils of war.

Brage was proud of his men. He knew they would fight well in the coming attack. The runes' prophecy had said he would claim a treasure more precious than any he'd ever won before, and he was eagerly looking forward to it.

As they waited for Ulf, Seger, and Neils to return, the Norsemen offered up prayers to Odin asking for his help in the coming battle. They were strong and confident, accustomed to victory through power and might, and untouched as yet by the terrible cunning of deceit and betrayal.

Lady Dynna and Matilda had spoken but little since fleeing from the tower the night before. They kept their cloaks clutched protectively around them as they moved along the road until they came to the outskirts of the village. Determined to circle around the small town, they headed down a path in the woods, Matilda in the lead. There was little celestial light to help them, but the maid knew the way. They made it past the village and then returned to the road.

They walked through the night, never stopping, wanting to put as much distance between themselves and the tower as they could. Dynna did not want to be anywhere near when the discovery was made that she was missing.

Near dawn they sought refuge in a thick grove of trees and took time to eat. The two women had no doubt that within the next few hours, Sir Edmund would learn that Dynna had run away and would begin searching for her. If they could elude him and his men for the next twenty-four hours, they had a good chance of making it all the way to the safe haven of her parents' protection.

They settled in, meaning to rest for a while; neither Dynna nor Matilda planned to fall asleep. They expected only to nap for a minute or two, but when they closed their eyes their energy drained away, leaving them exhausted. They slept.

Ulf, Seger, and Neils stayed within sight of one another as they explored the area for Brage. As he topped a low rise, Ulf caught a glimpse of some slight movement in a grove of trees in the distance. He silently signaled his two companions to move in that direction and then approached the hiding place with his battle-ax at ready.

"Matilda! Wake up!" Dynna commanded as she opened her eyes and saw that it was fully morn. "We must have..."

She never finished her sentence. She looked up to find the most hulking, ferocious-looking man she had ever seen standing at the edge of the trees. No Saxon looked like this!

"Matilda!" she gasped, grabbing her maid's arm.

Matilda jerked upright, and at her first sight of a Viking she let out a scream.

Ulf was silently cursing his luck at being found out before he could get any closer to them. He started forward, determined to trap them before they could get away.

"Run!" Dynna urged frantically as he came toward them.

The two women scrambled to their feet and fled in different directions.

Ulf swore loudly as they managed to elude him. Forced to give chase, he bellowed orders to Seger and Neils, telling them to circle around and trap the pair. They could not be allowed to escape and alert others.

Moving with a speed unusual for a man his size, Ulf gave chase. Neils was in a good position to trap Matilda, and the servant let out a cry of abject terror as his massive arm snared her around the waist. She was slammed back up against the iron width of his chest.

"I got one of them!" Neils called out to Ulf and Seger.

"Let me go!" Matilda shrieked, twisting and fighting to be free of his hold.

He laughed at her futile resistance. Against his strength she was little more than a pesky annoyance. Holding his prize, he watched as Ulf and Seger closed in on the other woman.

"Seger!" Ulf called out. "She ran into the brush."

Dynna knew it was the Nordic language she was hearing, having learned it from a servant in her parents' home, and she knew at least one of them was chasing her. She dove even deeper into the thicket of spiny bushes. Like a rabbit caught in a hunter's sight, she remained totally silent and still in the depths of her hiding place.

The rustle of the brush close by set her nerves on edge as she fought to keep her fear under control. The footsteps moving ever nearer were heavy and intimidating, and she had to clench her hands into fists to contain her terror.

"She is in here somewhere . . ." Ulf growled as he searched through the thorny thicket. "I will see that she pays for the trouble she's causing me!"

Hearing his voice so close filled Dynna with panic. Her hand closed on the jeweled dagger at her waist. Finally, when it seemed the Viking was right on top of her, Dynna could stand the tension no longer. She tore from her hiding place like a game bird flushed from its nest. The briars tore at her, scratching her flesh and snagging her clothes, but she did not care. She ran blindly, seeking freedom even as she knew it was hopeless.

"I've got her!" Ulf called as he followed his frightened quarry. Undaunted by the thorns and brush, he caught her easily.

Dynna cried out in outrage as he grabbed her and yanked her back to him. He turned her forcefully around so he could get a good look at her.

Dynna stared up at her captor and went cold with terror. He looked savage and ferocious. The helmet he wore had a guard for his eyes and nose and kept his face largely hidden. His beard was wild and untamed, and a long, ugly scar marred his cheek. Every terrible thing she had ever heard about the Vikings came back to her. She was sure she was going to die!

"And a pretty one she is!" Ulf shouted back to the others, grinning.

The grin horrified her, and she struggled even more wildly against him. He had little patience with her and gave her a fierce shake.

"Be still, woman!" he ordered in her language.

Dynna was not about to give up so easily. The dagger was still in her hand, and knowing this might be her only chance to save herself, she struck out at her attacker. She heard him grunt in pain as she made contact with his arm, and she felt a moment of pride at her effort. The moment was immediately lost, though as he knocked the weapon from her grasp in a numbing blow.

"You little fool . . ." Ulf snarled, again in her own tongue as he held her in a bruising grip.

Dynna saw the murderous expression on his face and renewed her desperate efforts to break free. It proved no use, however. His hands on her were like bands of iron. There would be no breaking away from him. In that moment, she realized she faced her doom.

"Ah, she *is* sweet looking," Seger remarked as he caught up with him.

"She is far from sweet. She is a dangerous little thing." Ulf bent down to retrieve her dagger. He showed it to him.

"She attacked you?" Seger laughed, finding humor in the fact that the woman had challenged the giant beside him.

Ulf grunted in disgust as he showed him the bloody gash on his arm.

"Perhaps the Saxons should set their women to fighting us instead of their men. It seems she is a far more formidable foe."

Ulf agreed as he studied the small, jeweled dagger with interest. He thought it odd that a peasant woman would have such a prize in her possession. He looked from the knife to her, seeing the glint of defiance and anger in her eyes, and wondered at her daring. Dragging Dynna with him, he started back to where Neils waited with the other female.

"Take one last look around and make sure there aren't any more of them," he ordered Seger.

Matilda was still struggling with Neils when Ulf and his captive reached them.

"Be still!" Neils commanded in their tongue.

Matilda ceased her struggle when she saw that her lady was unharmed.

As the men began to talk in their own language, Matilda whispered tearfully to Dynna that she was sorry for their situation.

"Save your tears. There was no escaping them. We would have been caught no matter what."

"Silence!" Ulf ordered gruffly as Seger rejoined them and told them that there were no others.

"What are we going to do with these two?" Neils asked.

"We can't let them go," Seger said.

In that moment, as Dynna listened to their discussion, she believed her life and Matilda's were over. These were the dreaded Norse invaders. They were known as the scourge of the coast for good reason.

Dynna glanced at Matilda. Of everything they had worried about when they had planned their escape, being caught by newly landed Viking raiders had never been one of them. And now . . .

"True, we cannot free them," Ulf was saying. "If we do that, they will spread the word of our landing." He paused as he let his gaze rest upon the two. Outwardly, they appeared to be mere village women, and yet something about the jeweled dagger bothered him. "We'll take them back with us and let the Black Hawk decide what to do with them." He was not pleased with the prospect of taking them along, but there was no other way.

Neils grabbed the unsuspecting Matilda and threw her over his shoulder. She let out a grunt as she landed painfully on her stomach on Neils's shoulder, and she pounded on his back in outrage at being so manhandled. The Viking only laughed at her. He rested his hand familiarly on her hip to hold her still as he moved off. His touch shocked her, and she squirmed wildly, trying to get away. Neils gave her a warning spank to still her.

Matilda wanted to keep kicking and fighting and biting and scratching, but she realized it was useless. There would be no escaping this man. He was ruthless. It tortured her to know that there was nothing she could do to help her lady. She only hoped Dynna would bear up well under the warriors' abuse and that they would not learn her true identity.

When Dynna heard that they were going to be taken along with the warriors, relief rushed through her. They were not going to be killed! Tears threatened, but she refused to shed them. She would be strong, for herself and for Matilda, and, somehow, she would survive.

Ulf bound her wrists with a leather strap and ordered her to start walking. He looked none too pleased as he led the way back to the landing site. He had expected to encounter Saxons to fight, not two sleeping women whom he had to herd back to the ships.

Glancing down at the raven-haired beauty walking beside him, Ulf once again found it hard to believe she was a peasant woman. There was something about her . . . a beauty, grace, and pride not usually found in commoners. And to think she'd been brave enough to attack him with her dagger . . . Had she been a Viking woman, he would have been proud of her exploits. As an enemy, she would bear watching. He would not give her a second chance to maim him.

They had walked a goodly distance before topping a rise near the shore. Dynna stopped dead still in her tracks to stare at the scene below. Three Viking longships had put ashore, and over a hundred men were waiting, armed and ready, to begin an invasion. At the sight of the one ship's scarlet sail, marked with the sign of the hawk, she began to tremble. It had all been true! The Black Hawk was going to raid the tower!

"Move!" Ulf ordered, giving her a push in the direction of the others.

Dynna started down the incline, holding her head high. She watched as one separated himself from the group and came forward to meet them. He was tall and bearded, his coloring as dark as her captors' were fair. Dynna found herself mesmerized by the sheer, brutal force he exuded. He was powerfully built, with broad shoulders and heavily muscled arms. He wore a padded leather vest over his tunic, tight trousers, and leather boots. A lethal-looking sword was strapped at his side, and he carried a large, round battle shield. The shield was red with a hawk painted on it, and she realized in horror that this was the infamous Black Hawk.

She tried to make out his features, but couldn't see his face clearly, for the beard and intimidating helmet he wore shielded him from her scrutiny.

Dynna tried to remember everything she had heard about the man. For the last five years, it seemed, he had been invincible—raiding, kidnapping, and plundering the coast at will. No kingdom had been safe from his swift and vicious attacks.

Staring at him now and seeing his power, she understood why he had been so victorious. The Norseman looked primitive and frightening. She thought of the Saxons at the tower, and though Sir Edmund had bragged about how prepared they were for the possible attack, she wondered if, even with their superior numbers, they would be any match for this man and his invading force.

She stopped before the Viking leader. Taking care to remember Matilda's admonitions to keep her eyes downcast and her shoulders a little slumped, she played the serving wench.

Ulf was at her side. "We found these two sleeping in a grove of trees."

Neils had been following close behind, and he dumped Matilda unceremoniously on her feet as Ulf explained how they had discovered and captured them.

"These two women were alone, sleeping in the countryside?" Brage glanced at the females standing before him. He had thought they might be village women who had been caught trying to run ahead and warn Lord Alfrick of their pending attack.

"Yes, and look at this." Ulf handed him Dynna's jeweled dagger. "Once again, I've been wounded protecting you," he said with a grin, showing him the cut on his arm.

Brage took the knife and studied it, then looked at the two women. "Which one did this to you?"

"This one." He pulled Dynna forward so Brage could get a better look at her.

"Lucky she did not have a bigger blade," Brage taunted in good humor. "Yet odd that she should have such a fine dagger."

When Dynna did not respond to his statement or look up, Brage cupped her chin in his hand and tilted her head so she was forced to look straight at him.

For an instant, as Brage gazed upon her features for the first time, he could only stare in wonderment. Her beauty was uncommon, from her raven-black hair to her fair and flawless complexion. As he met her gaze, he saw that her gray eyes fairly sparkled with intelligence, and that intrigued him. Dull-witted wenches had never appealed to him. He let his gaze drift lower, studying her body disguised beneath the coarse garment, and knew that she was a woman full-grown. Her breasts seemed ripe where they swelled beneath the gown, and her hips were pleasantly rounded. It was then that he noticed her hands and saw that they were soft and well cared for. This woman was no mere peasant. His curiosity was piqued by the mystery of her.

"Tell me, wench, where did you find such a fine weapon?" he asked as he held the dagger out to her.

"I stole it," Dynna said, surprising herself at her ability to lie. As she gazed up at him, she found herself almost hypnotized by his blue-eyed gaze.

"Perhaps . . ." Brage replied thoughtfully, watching her intently for a moment longer. "But I do not think so."

He dropped his hand away from her chin and grasped her hand, drawing it up to study her palm. His thumb was resting across her wrist, and he could feel the rapid beat of her pulse beneath his touch.

"These are not the hands of a serving wench," he observed.

The touch of his hand on hers was gentle, surprising Dynna. When he lifted his gaze to hers again, she forced her eyes to remain level with his, trying to brazen it out. But his piercing, somehow knowing, regard unnerved her; it seemed he could see into the very heart of her.

"What shall we do with them?" Ulf asked, wondering at his brother's unusual interest in the woman. When they raided, females were the last thing on his mind.

Ulf's question forced Brage's attention back to their real reason for being there. He released Dynna's hand and turned to his brother.

"Bind them both and bring them along with us. Just make sure to keep them to the rear, out of my way. I want no distractions for my men."

Ulf signaled to one of the waiting warriors, and the man rushed forward.

"Take the women and see that they cause no trouble."

"Will we share them later?" the man asked eagerly.

Dynna saw the hunger in the Viking's face and felt a shaft of fear.

Brage looked back at Dynna and Matilda. There was something about the gray-eyed one . . . something special that he wanted to look into once the fighting was over.

"No," he answered. "No one is to touch them."

Dynna's knees almost buckled in relief at his answer, but her relief was short-lived.

"Keep them out of harm's way. They'll bring a better price in the slave market if they're untouched." Brage glanced down at the dagger she had carried once more and then tucked it into his own waistband. He would have liked to find out more about her, but there was no time to think of females now. He was a warrior, ready to do battle. He had to lead his men.

Still, even as Brage turned his attention to the tower and their attack strategy, he glanced over and watched the women being led away.

Dynna's fury and frustration were boundless as she was drawn along with the other man. The future looked hopeless and threatening. She did not know which was worse—to be used as a whore by the Vikings here or to be sold into slavery and never heard from again. She wondered if her life would ever change. It seemed she was forever to be mere chattel to some man.

When the women were gone from sight, Brage, with Kristoffer by his side, spoke quietly with Ulf, Seger, and Neils, finding out all they had learned while they'd been scouring the countryside. The knowledge that they had observed no resistance and the march was clear to the tower encouraged him. He called the men together in preparation to move out.

"We attack Lord Alfrick's tower!" Brage told them as they gathered around. "When we have breached that, the land and all its riches will be ours!"

The warriors shouted their approval, eager for a fight.

"Remember! Captives bring us gold; the dead are worthless to us," Brage reminded them.

The men understood. While they had often faced death on their raids, it was the treasure they were after. Killing served no purpose unless in self-defense. Healthy slaves brought wealth.

Brage invoked Odin and Thor to aid them in their quest, and then led the way inland.

The Black Hawk's warriors were more than ready for the excitement of battle as they climbed the hill and started on the trek to the tower. With Brage, Ulf, and Kristoffer in the fore, they moved quickly and quietly, heading relentlessly toward the riches they believed would soon be theirs.

# Three

"What do you mean she is not in her chamber?" Edmund roared at the female servant.

"Her room is empty, Sir Edmund."

Edmund had left the tower early that morning to train with the men. He returned just past noon, wanting to see Dynna. He had searched below for her, and when she was nowhere to be found, he set the servant off to her room to fetch her and bring her to him. "When was the last time you saw her?"

"Now that I think about it, Sir Edmund, I have not seen her all morning."

Edmund brushed past the woman and mounted the stairs two at a time to Dynna's chamber. He threw the door wide and stared about the empty room. His gaze went first to her bed. It had not been slept in, he saw, and the clothes she had worn the night before were tossed haphazardly upon it.

"Where is the servant who cleans this room?"

"That would be her maid, Matilda, Sir Edmund, and I have not seen her today, either," the servant answered.

"Inquire of the others. I want to know if anyone has seen her today. Report back to me immediately," Edmund ordered, suspicion coiling hot and ugly within him.

The servant rushed off to do as she had been ordered, leaving Edmund alone in Dynna's room. He gazed about, then moved to the bed to pick up Dynna's crumpled gown. His hands caressed the soft fabric, and he imagined it on her slender body. As he stared down at the bed an image of her, warm and willing, holding her arms out to him in invitation, flooded his mind. Heat surged through his body. He was still holding the garment when the servant returned long minutes later.

"No one has seen either of them."

Edmund growled at the servant to leave the chamber. After the woman had scurried away, he remained standing among Dynna's things, cursing her even as he desired her. Finally, in anger, he cast the gown aside and strode from the room. He sought his father to tell him of Dynna's disappearance.

"You think she's run away?" Lord Alfrick was genuinely surprised. He was not accustomed to anyone, male or female, contradicting him in any way.

"What else am I to think? No one has seen her today, and her bed was not slept in."

"Find her."

"I will, and once I do, I will bring her back, and our plans to wed will be announced."

"The priest will be returning within four weeks. The ceremony can be performed as soon as he arrives."

"I will speak to you again when I return with my betrothed."

After leaving his father, Sir Edmund gathered a small group of his men to ride with him. They charged from the stable ready to search the countryside for the errant Lady Dynna and her maid.

It took them several hours to comb the area near the tower. After no success, they spread out farther across the countryside. Sir Edmund knew if Dynna were trying to escape marriage to him, she would attempt to reach her family home and seek her father's protection. With that in mind, he widened the search in the direction of the lands of her father, Lord Garman.

They rode like the wind, checking along the roads and byways, seeking some clue to the missing women, but to no avail. They were just starting through a narrow part of the road that was bordered on both side by trees when they caught sight of a distraught-looking villager racing toward them. The man appeared near exhaustion, yet he kept running, waving his arms frantically at them to stop. Edmund urged his mount forward and met the man.

"Sir Edmund! I saw them!" he blurted out as he gasped for breath.

"You saw who?" he asked, looking up past the man in the direction he'd come, thinking Dynna was just beyond the hill.

"The Black Hawk, Sir Edmund! He is coming and he has brought hundreds of Vikings with him! They are going to kill us all!"

Caught off-guard and stunned by the news that the raiders had landed, Edmund could only stare at the man in disbelief.

"They are here, I tell you! I was in the woods when they passed by. I cut through the back path to reach the tower first. Thank God I found you, so I could warn you in time!"

"How do you know it is the Black Hawk?"

"I saw his shield! Everyone knows his emblem!"

The declaration jarred Edmund into action. Turning to his men, he called out, "Bring this man with us. We must ride quickly. Our trap must be set at once or all will be lost!"

He ordered a return to the tower, though his thoughts remained on Dynna. He wanted to find her, teach her she should never have run from him, but there was no time to think of her now. The battle he had been preparing for was about to begin. He would deal with the Vikings first. A mere woman could wait. Wheeling his horse about, he put his heels to his mount's flanks and raced back to tell his father of the invasion.


"The warning the stranger gave us that night was true, Father," Sir Edmund advised Lord Alfrick. "Viking ships have landed and the Black Hawk is approaching on foot from the east with at least a hundred warriors."

"You are certain of this?"

"One of the villagers has seen his shield. It is the Black Hawk all right."

Lord Alfrick smiled, but it was not a smile of pleasure. It was a smile of grim determination. They were as ready as they would ever be to defeat the Vikings. He was thankful they had had time to prepare. "We will attack as planned, my son."

Edmund hurried from his father's chamber to summon Sir Thomas and call the men to action. The Saxons were ready. They took up their arms and raced to assume their designated positions along the only road leading to the tower. There, hidden among the foliage, the heavily armed Saxons awaited the invaders.

Brage led his men on the trek to Lord Alfrick's tower. Ulf stayed near the rear, watching out for trouble at the same time as he kept an eye on the two women and guarding Brage's back. Kristoffer marched in the middle. There was little talk as they trudged silently onward, each man concentrating on the battle to come. They saw a farmer in the distance and watched with obvious pleasure as he fled in terror at the sight of them. Having a terrible reputation had its benefits. Sometimes fear could bring about a capitulation without any use of force or bloodletting at all. The Vikings were hoping the Saxons in the tower would be as easily cowed.

Brage realized that Lord Alfrick had surely been alerted by now, but he was not worried. The Saxon lord had no time to call for extra men, so the fight would be a relatively simple one. The worst that could happen, he reasoned, would be that they might be forced to resort to a siege. But even if that came to pass, the siege would not last long, for the Saxons would not have prepared the needed supplies to wait it out.

As they rounded a curve in the road, Brage spotted the stronghold for the first time.

"There's the tower!" Brage called out.

A rumble of excitement stirred through his men. Brage paused to survey the peaceful scene before him. The final distance to the tower crossed open ground for the last half-mile, then the road curved through a forest before reaching the clearing where the stronghold stood.

"May the day be ours!" Brage drew his sword and started forward at a quickened pace. The men followed eagerly. As he drew near the trees, he caught sight of a glimmer in their depths. The instincts that had kept him alive through many a savage battle screamed a violent warning that all was not as peaceful as it seemed.

Brage paused, ready to call out a warning to his men, but before the words could pass his lips, the surprise attack came. A storm of arrows rained death and destruction upon the raiders as the Saxon archers, hidden in the woods, took careful aim.

At the rear of the column of Vikings, Dynna and Matilda were shoved ruthlessly aside as the men prepared to go into combat. Dynna fell to the ground. With her hands tied behind her, she had trouble getting back up, but finally she managed. She and Matilda stumbled away from the ambush. The blood-curdling sounds of battle seemed to follow them as they ran. They stopped a short distance away only long enough to untie each other.

"What are we going to do?" Matilda asked. She was as pale as a ghost, and her eyes were wide with terror from the deadly scene she had just witnessed.

"There is nothing we can do but run. I just wish I still had my dagger," Dynna said, knowing she would feel better if she had it in hand. "We have to keep moving, otherwise we might get caught in the fighting."

"They're going to find us again . . . I know they will!" the maid cried, nearly hysterical.

"Matilda!" Dynna's tone was deliberately harsh. "Hush! This is no time for hysteria. We have to save ourselves!"

"But where can we flee?" Matilda asked in a tear-choked voice as she followed Dynna.

"I wish I knew," Dynna answered. "I only know we must escape before the Vikings come after us."

Chaos erupted as Lord Alfrick's men, led by Sir Thomas, charged forth from their hiding places in the forest to do battle with the hated Vikings.

The invaders were momentarily taken by surprise, but disciplined as they were, they quickly recovered and took action. Norsemen bearing battle-axes ran to the fore, mowing down those Saxons who advanced upon them armed only with swords. Brutal hand-to-hand combat ensued as lethal sword met deadly axe.

The ferocity of the Saxon attack startled Brage, and he found himself quickly engulfed in the thick of the fray. Wielding his sword with accuracy and power, he cut his way through a mass of opponents as his men around him did the same. They fought hard and took losses, but Brage never wavered in the belief that his side would prevail.

The battle seemed to be going their way. Brage remembered the prophecy of the runes and felt the moment was close at hand when they would breach the outer wall of the tower. When Ulf suddenly bellowed a warning, Brage looked up in his direction. The sight of mounted Saxons attacking them from the rear filled him with rage and doubt. Lord Alfrick had never had so many men at his disposal. There was only one way they could have been so well prepared for their raid. Somehow, Lord Alfrick learned about their attack ahead of time!

The knowledge that they had been betrayed fired Brage's blood. A roar of fury erupted from him. There was a traitor in their midst!

Shouting orders, he rallied his warriors. They were now severely outnumbered and at a distinct disadvantage because they were on foot. Still they continued to fight.

Sir Edmund had been waiting weeks for this moment. Leading the mounted defenders, he circled behind the initial fighting and attacked the Viking rear. His plan was a simple one. He had divided his fighting force in two, trapping the unsuspecting Vikings between them. The battle sprawled out bloody and violent before him. Sword in hand, he urged his horse into the midst of the mayhem. He began killing with savage enjoyment.

Brage was sickened by the number of his men he saw falling around him, yet he could not let himself be distracted. Striking out at those who attacked him, he continued to battle until an unseen blow from behind staggered him. Pain lanced through his right shoulder, and his sword dropped from numb fingers. He struggled to stay on his feet, knowing his men needed him, but without his sword, he was unprotected. Another blow knocked his shield from his grasp as an attacker struck him on the head from behind, knocking his helmet off and taking him down.

Brage collapsed on the bloodied Saxon soil he had sought to conquer. The warring raged on around him, and as the blackness of unconsciousness engulfed him, he wondered why the runes had failed him this time.

From across the field of battle, Ulf saw Brage collapse.

"Brage!" he roared in violent protest, swinging his battle-ax with even greater fervor as he tried to cut a swath to his half-brother's side. For every Saxon he felled, though, it seemed another was immediately there to take his place. He fought on, valiantly, desperately.

Kristoffer heard Ulf's cry and looked toward Brage. He saw his older brother cut down. "No!"

"Try to get to him!" Ulf ordered as he continued to fight.

Kristoffer battled even harder, trying to reach Brage, but even with Brage's greatest warriors beside him, fighting with all their strength and ability, they could not turn the tide of the battle. The Saxons numbered too many. There could be no victory this day.

Sir Edmund was in the thick of the battle when he glanced up to see two women fleeing in the distance. He recognized one of them immediately as Dynna. He did not stop to question why she was there; he only knew he had to go after her. Withdrawing from the fighting, he rode after the fleeing women at breakneck speed, bloodied sword still in hand.

Dynna and Matilda heard the sound of a horse giving chase. They had no idea who was coming after them, and they were not going to stop to find out. Terror drove them as they ran even faster.

Sir Edmund was furious as he closed on the two women. He slid his sword back into its scabbard, then bent low and in one move, grabbed Dynna around the waist and hauled her up against him on the horse's back.

"No!" she screamed as she found herself once again in the possession of the very man she sought to escape.

"No? Be very glad that you are still alive, Dynna." Edmund's face was contorted with fury as he stared down at her.

It was obvious from the peasant's clothing she was wearing that she had been running away. Edmund kept a deliberately painful tight hold on her while he turned his horse toward the nearby trees. He left Matilda to follow on foot. He did not release Dynna when he reined in, but kept a hold on her as he dismounted. Grabbing a piece of rope from his saddle, he pulled her over to one of the trees.

"What are you going to do?" Dynna asked.

"What I want to do to you and what I'm going to do are two different things," he threatened. "Be warned, my lady, if you dress like a serving woman, I will treat you like one." He boldly reached out and fondled her openly.

Shame flooded through Dynna, but she stood proudly before him, refusing to cower in the face of his indignity.

Sir Edmund would have liked to stay there and teach Dynna a lesson in obedience, but the battle was still raging. The Vikings were proving to be as fierce as rumor had it. He was anxious to get back to the fighting.

"I am going to make certain that you are still here after the battle." His voice was harsh.

"Stay away from Lady Dynna!" Matilda shouted.

Sir Edmund had had enough of these two. He backhanded the maid, knocking her to the ground, then made short order of tying Dynna to the tree. When he was sure she was securely bound, he jerked Matilda to her feet and bound her there, as well.

"I will be back," he warned darkly as he mounted his steed and drew his sword once more.

The women could only watch helplessly as he rode away. From their vantage point, they could see all that was happening. It was obvious that the Vikings were being driven back by the overwhelming numbers of Lord Alfrick's men. Dynna and Matilda looked on in horror as men on both sides were struck down. The invaders fought bravely, constantly shifting their defensive positions to protect themselves and each other.

It seemed the battle raged for hours. The women were unsure how long they were forced to observe the bloody scene. When at last the fighting had ended and the Vikings had escaped to the sea, an eerie silence fell over the battlefield. Only the strangled cries of the wounded and dying disturbed the deadly quiet.

"The Vikings have lost. Sir Edmund has defeated the Black Hawk!" Dynna said to her maid as she stared down at the hellish scene.

"Perhaps God heard our prayers, and Sir Edmund died a glorious death on the battlefield . . ." Though there was no one but Dynna to hear, Matilda spoke in a hushed tone, fearful of saying her heart's wish out loud.

As Dynna allowed herself the faint hope that such a fate might have befallen Edmund, she saw a rider separate himself from the others and come their way. There could be no mistaking Sir Edmund even at this distance.

"I have won the day!" Sir Edmund announced as he dismounted before them, his weapon still in hand. Blood was splattered on his clothing and his sword bore gory testament to the havoc it had just wreaked.

Edmund sliced through the ropes that bound the women. His cunning had defeated the Black Hawk! No one could deny what a fine fight he had waged. The world and all that was in it belonged to him.

He turned to Matilda. "You must walk back," he ordered her.

The maid looked questioningly to her mistress, and when Dynna would have accompanied her, Sir Edmund grasped her arm, preventing her from leaving. He stared at the servant with a cold, dismissive gaze until she had moved off, then pulled Dynna against him.

"I know what you were about, Dynna. But understand this. You are mine. You will never escape me. We will be married as soon as the priest returns to the tower."

"I am a lady in my own right! Have I no say in my future?"

"You may say 'yes' when the time comes, my dear. That is all the say you have. Until then . . . perhaps, a kiss would soothe the savage beast that rages within me and demands that I punish you for daring to try to defy me." His mouth took hers in a devouring kiss.

Dynna did not struggle. She knew it was pointless to try to refuse him. Still, she remained unresponsive in his arms.

Her sense of helplessness made Dynna furious. If she gave up and accepted the fate that Lord Alfrick and Edmund had planned for her, she knew her very existence would be meaningless. But she did not know what she could do. Complete and utter despair threatened as Edmund ended the embrace.

"Let us return home. There is much to celebrate—my victory and our coming wedding," he said with a triumphant laugh as he lifted her to his horse's back and mounted behind her. Even as he was smiling, though, her lack of response to his kiss bothered him. He vowed that, one way or the other, he would force her to his will.

Dynna remained silent on the ride back. She held herself rigidly before him and suffered without protest his hands upon her. For now, she would make a valiant attempt to tolerate what she could not change.

As they crossed the battle ground she saw, up close, the death and devastation that had been wrought. Her heart ached for all the injured and slain.

"Sir Edmund, when we reach the tower, I must go to the people and help them. They will be needing me now," she told him firmly. Her talent as a healer, learned from her mother, had earned her much respect in the village.

He nodded. "It is good that you think of the people, but do not assume for a moment that I will ever trust you to go out alone again. From now on, there will always be someone watching you when you leave the tower."

His words only confirmed what she had feared. Never again would she know happiness. Never again would she know freedom. Never again would she know love.

Ulf and Kristoffer took command of what was left of Brage's warriors. Many had been slain in the fighting and many more had been grievously wounded. Their dreams of glory had turned into a deadly nightmare, but the slain warriors would be in Valhalla this very night, for they had died with honor.

Once they reached the ships, Ulf and Kristoffer boarded Brage's vessel and ordered the men to put out to sea. They rowed away from the coast as quickly as they could. Though the Saxons had not followed them all the way to the shore, they would take no chances.

Once they were a safe distance away, Ulf ordered the men to stop.

"We will wait here until nightfall and then return," Ulf announced.

Kristoffer stared at his older half-brother in total shock. "Have you lost your mind? They outnumbered us at least three to one! It would be suicide to return!"

"We cannot leave. I must find Brage."

"We *must* leave. Brage would expect us to. Anyone who tried to go back would be killed," Kristoffer said.

"Brage may be alive. I cannot leave him here!"

"I saw Brage felled, Ulf. Our brother is dead," Kristoffer argued.

"All the more reason to find him. He must be given a proper Viking burial."

"It is a fool's plan to return there! Do you really think you would be able to find his body?"

"I must try."

"Have you given any thought to the cost in other lives? Brage died a warrior's death. He has gone to Valhalla."

"If you will not go with me, I will go alone."

"You would risk your life and the lives of the men just to bring back his body?" Kristoffer countered angrily. "Brage would call you a fool if he were alive."

"Stay or go. It does not matter to me. You are young, Kris. You have been taught to do as you are told. I am a man. I do what I believe is right. I can do no less for my brother than to try to find him and bring him back."


Lord Alfrick stood with Sir Edmund and Sir Thomas surveying the death and destruction on the road. Mangled bodies were strewn everywhere. The losses had been tragic, but their defense had held. The tower had been saved. The Black Hawk had been defeated and his force pushed back into the sea.

"Is the Black Hawk dead?" Lord Alfrick demanded to know.

"We found his shield, my lord," Sir Thomas showed him the scarlet shield marked with the sign of the Hawk. "But there are so many felled, we are not certain which body is his."

"Did the Vikings take any of their dead with them when they retreated?"

"No, my lord."

"Will they return for them?"

"We had men follow them at a distance all the way to the sea to make certain that they sailed. Their losses were severe. I doubt they will be back soon," Sir Edmund said with pride.

"Our losses were heavy, too." Lord Alfrick could see the bodies of his men along the road.

"Ah, but we won, Father! We protected our lands."

"Your reputation as a fierce and mighty lord will be known by all," Sir Thomas told him.

Lord Alfrick smiled. "The cost was worth it, if the Norsemen never return."

"I hope Sir Edmund is right," Sir Thomas said thoughtfully. "I hope they never again land upon our shore. Still, I wonder if they might not descend on us again and in an even greater number."

"Without the Black Hawk to lead them? I think not," Edmund scoffed.

"Revenge is a good reason to fight," Sir Thomas warned.

Lord Alfrick's lips curled in contempt. "We shall keep watch for a time," he directed. "For now, Sir Thomas, see that our dead are given proper burials."

"Yes, my lord. And what of the Vikings?"

"Burn their bodies."

"What shall we do if we find any survivors?"

"Bring them to me. I will deal with them personally."

Sir Thomas moved to direct his men while Lord Alfrick and Edmund returned to the tower.

"This one is dead!"

The sound of the man's shout close at hand cut through the blackness that surrounded Brage and forced him back to consciousness.

Blinding, searing pain wracked him as he swam up from the depths of oblivion. His head throbbed and his right shoulder burned as if on fire. The pain in his body, though, was nothing compared to the agony of his soul. Memories of the battle were seared into his mind, and they replayed before him, bloody and deadly.

Slowly, Brage opened his eyes. He struggled to focus his blurred vision, and when he finally did, he found himself staring up at a red-streaked sky. Brage decided that the color was a testimony from the gods. He believed they were spilling their blood across the heavens to match the horror of that day.

Brage was jarred to action by memories of those of his men who had suffered and the ones who had died. Trying to ignore the pain that stabbed at him, he started to rise. He would continue the fight. He would find his sword and shield and battle to the death. Death with honor was infinitely preferable to life without it. As he struggled to stand, though, the man who had called out before appeared over him and viciously shoved him back to the ground.

The Saxon brought his sword to bear on the Norseman. "Lie still or die, you Viking pig!"

Brage glared up at the man with open hatred, wishing he had his own sword. Weak or not, he would have given him a fair battle.

"This one is alive!" the man called out to the others nearby who were also checking the dead.

"Lord Alfrick will be glad you found one, Henry. He wanted any survivors brought to him."

Brage heard the exchange between them. He refused to be taken prisoner. While the man's attention was momentarily distracted, Brage made his move. With all the strength he could muster, he pushed himself upward and tried to grab the man's sword at the same time, but his effort was for naught. Weakened as he was by his wounds and loss of blood, he had not the strength or agility to overpower his opponent. A well-aimed booted kick sent him sprawling backward, and he found the Saxon's sword point pressing at the base of his throat.

"I know you prefer death, Viking, but know this: death is not to be yours—just yet. Our lord will be pleased to have a captive," Henry sneered. "Now, since you're so eager to stand—get up! You can walk to the tower." He stepped back and motioned with the sword for him to rise.

Brage got slowly to his feet. His right arm seemed almost useless and his head was pounding. He looked around at the carnage and saw Neils and Seger lying dead nearby, along with many more of his faithful warriors.

Rage greater than anything he had ever felt before erupted within him. He was more certain than ever that they had been betrayed! A traitor had caused their deaths. The knowledge that there could be such a man among his own people pained him more than any blade ever could.

Brage noted with empty satisfaction that the Saxon dead greatly outnumbered the Viking. He saw no sign of Ulf or Kristoffer among the bodies, and offered silent thanks to the gods for that much. Knowing they were alive gave him a faint hope that they might return with a greater force and raid again.

"What is your name, Viking?"

Brage decided to pretend that he did not know the language, and so remained silent.

Frustrated by his captive's arrogance, Henry shoved him

hard. "Talk or not, it matters little to me. Get moving. Lord Alfrick will want to see you. He will find a way to make you speak."

Brage began the trek toward the tower. Each step was agonizing. Blood oozed from the wound that went deep in his shoulder. He tried to use his right hand, but it felt leaden. His head ached beyond description. His captor dogged his every step, taunting him and forcing him along when he would have slowed his pace.

They were nearing the drawbridge that permitted entry to the tower when they met some of Lord Alfrick's guards. Sir Edmund was with them.

"What have you here?" Edmund asked, eyeing the captive with open interest.

"I found this one alive, Sir Edmund," the guard called Henry informed him.

"You can leave him with me. I will take care of him for my father."

"I would like to, but I cannot. Your father has decreed that he would deal with any survivors personally."

Sir Edmund's eyes were cold as he looked at Brage. "Pity."

Brage stood before Edmund as straight and proud as he could. He met his enemy's hate-filled regard with equal contempt, refusing to show him any fear. He could tell by looking at him that he was like others he had known—men who took pleasure in inflicting pain on those in their power. When faced down by someone of equal strength, such men usually proved to be weak and cowardly, but when they were in complete control, they were vicious.

This Viking looked very arrogant, and Edmund would have preferred to see the man dead by his own hand. But maybe his father was right. The captive might know something about future raids. If he did, Edmund would certainly enjoy being the one to convince him to part with the information.

"Move on." Henry shoved Brage forward once more, deliberately prodding him near his wounded shoulder.

Brage bit back a groan as he made his way across the drawbridge and into the tower. He had planned to be entering the Great Hall with his men in triumph at this hour. Instead, he was entering the hall as a prisoner and many of those who had trusted in his leadership were dead.

Ignoring the excruciating agony of his wounds, Brage concentrated on trying to figure out who had betrayed him. He hoped the anger of thinking about the traitor would help sustain him. He made a silent vow that somehow, some way, he would escape this place and avenge his dead warriors.

In this he would not fail.

## Four

The Great Hall was crowded with men. In spite of the loss of life among their ranks, their mood was joyous. They had successfully defended the stronghold against the fierce Black Hawk and his warriors. Food and drink were flowing freely as each man loudly recounted tales of his own heroic deeds during the battle.

Henry noticed that Lord Alfrick was seated at the high table in the front of the room with Sir Thomas. He forced his prisoner on before him as he made his way through the crowd.

Sir Thomas had seen them enter the hall, and he spoke to Lord Alfrick, directing his attention to the captive. "My lord."

Lord Alfrick glanced up to watch one of his soldiers bringing a prisoner to stand before him. Even injured as he was, this tall, powerfully built Norseman in his blood-soaked tunic impressed him as a warrior to be reckoned with. Dried blood matted the prisoner's hair and stained his face and beard, making him appear even more savage. Lord Alfrick's lips thinned as he contemplated the punishment he would order for this man.

"What have we here?" he demanded in a booming voice.

All those in the hall turned to watch the display.

"A Viking who has survived, my lord. He was left for dead on the battlefield. I have brought him to you as you ordered."

"He certainly looks more dead than alive," Lord Alfrick observed. "I think perhaps he would prefer to be dead than standing here before me."

Brage was reeling from loss of blood, but he steeled himself, struggling to maintain a show of strength before his enemy. He would never grovel.

"What is your name, Viking?"

"He has not said a word since I found him," Henry put in quickly. "It is possible he does not understand our language, my lord."

"That, or he's deaf and dumb." Sir Edmund laughed cruelly as he approached. He had come to see what his father would do with the Viking.

Brage's jaw tensed at Sir Edmund's words. He ignored the jeers of those surrounding him as he concentrated on Lord Alfrick, the man he had planned to defeat that day. He thought of the runes' prediction and cursed the old woman for her lies. True, she had told him that false words would be spoken, but she had also told him of a great prize he would claim. There was no prize here. Only misery and eventually a tortured death.

"My name is Brage," he finally answered tersely.

"Ah, so he does know our tongue." Lord Alfrick was thoughtful as he considered what a gift this captive was to him. One of the Black Hawk's men was now in his power. There were many questions he wanted to ask him. He studied the dark-haired Viking intently for a moment. "Tell me, how is it that you came to sail with the Black Hawk? You look no Norseman to me with your dark hair. Were you a slave? Where did you come from?"

"Make no mistake. I am a Viking."

"It seems we have a proud one here, my lord. What shall we do with him?"

All eyes turned to the bloodied captive. Hatred for all things Viking ran hot among the Saxons. Though they had driven the invaders back into the sea, the desire to spill more Norse blood hung heavy in the air.

"Kill him, Father," Sir Edmund urged as he stepped forward. "He is wounded and of little use to us. Slay him and be done with it." He drew his sword, ready to end the prisoner's life before all who looked on.

"You are very eager to kill, my son," Lord Alfrick remarked. "What glory is there in slaying a half-dead man?"

"Many of *my* men lost their lives today, Father, yet this heathen lives. Is there glory in allowing him to live?"

"Have forbearance, my son. He surely must know something about the raiding plans that might help us." Lord Alfrick turned his attention back to Brage. "Tell us, Viking, we have the Black Hawk's shield and his sword. Was that person killed in the battle today?"

Brage looked at Lord Alfrick and answered coldly, "The Black Hawk was felled."

Again a roar of approval and excitement swept the hall as the crowd took his answer to mean that the Black Hawk had died.

"Good, good," Lord Alfrick said with great satisfaction. "In celebration of this good news, I might let you live for a while. What better trophy could I have to display to those who come to our tower than one of the Black Hawk's own men!"

Edmund was furious over his father's decision to let the captive live, but he could not contradict him. "Father, this man should be cowering before you, begging for his life! Not standing here so arrogantly, showing no remorse for the terror he has wrought upon us. Beg, Viking! On your knees before Lord Alfrick!"

Brage was weak, but he refused to debase himself. "I kneel to no Saxon."

At the Viking's insolence, Edmund backhanded him full force.

Brage had already unsteady on his feet, and the power of

the blow sent him to one knee. He shook his head to clear it as he struggled to stand again, determined to reveal no weakness to his enemies.

Edmund moved quickly to grab the staggering Brage and hold his blade to his throat. "Shall I rid our land of this vermin, Father? Shall I kill him here and now?"

The men crowded in closer, watching avidly. Lord Alfrick looked at the sea of faces turned to him, each man waiting for his decision on the prisoner's fate. He stared at the Norseman and saw the infuriating glint of defiance in the Viking's gaze. He was just about to make his pronouncement of death for the captive when Lady Dynna's voice rang out in horror from the entrance to the hall.

"No!"

A stunned hush fell over the crowd, and all eyes turned to the woman who had dared to interrupt.

Dynna stood frozen in the entry, her gaze fixed on the terrible scene before her. She had heard all that had been said, and from across the hall, she recognized the Viking. There could be no mistaking his identity, even as bloodied and injured as he was. It was the Black Hawk. The leader of the Vikings. She had almost blurted out his name, but had stopped herself in time. She knew what Edmund would do to him if he learned his true identity, and she would not be responsible for a man's death—even if he was a Viking.

Brage heard the woman's voice and thought it somehow sounded familiar. He lifted his gaze and surprise ran through him. It was the woman Ulf had captured before the raid! She no longer wore the clothing of a peasant, but was dressed in the fine garments of royalty. She knew his identity, and he wondered if she would betray him.

"Lady Dynna," Sir Edmund was saying in a tightly controlled voice as he kept his stranglehold on the invader, "surely you don't want to interfere in matters that do not concern you."

Brage heard him call her Lady Dynna, and his gaze narrowed suspiciously as he studied her across the room. It gave him no pleasure to discover that he had been right about her. She was no ordinary peasant woman. She was a lady—beautiful, elegant and . . . deadly.

He waited tensely, pain wracking him, for her to announce his true identity and seal his fate.

"I have just come from hours of nursing the wounded and dying in the village. There has been enough death in the land this day." Her words were spoken with quiet dignity as she moved forward to Lord Alfrick. Dropping down on her knees before him, she beseeched him for clemency. "My lord, you have the power to restore peace and bring healing to our land. Let there be no more killing."

Dynna's words were heartfelt as she pleaded for the Viking's life, though she did not fully understand why his fate mattered to her. She realized that Lord Alfrick and Sir Edmund were unaware of the identity of their captive. If he was calling himself Brage, then she would keep his secret.

"What care you for this Viking?" Edmund asked. "He is one of those responsible for the carnage wrought on us this day. There can be no denying his sword cut a path of death and destruction through our people. Why should I not slay him?"

Dynna slowly rose and turned to Edmund. She could feel both his gaze and Brage's upon her, yet she did not waver in her determination to save this man. "Because I pray you are a better man than he is, Sir Edmund."

He bristled. "Revenge is not a bad thing. Does not our God call for an eye for an eye?"

"Does not our Holy Book also instruct us to turn the other cheek?"

Sir Edmund scowled. He was a firm believer that women should be seen and not heard. Lady Dynna's opinion should have absolutely no influence here, and he wondered why his father had not silenced her.

"Think you, my lady, that the wives and children of the

men slain today would be as forgiving? He is no Christian, but a heathen, a pagan animal, who kills and loots for his very existence. Even knowing this, you would plead for his life?" Edmund tightened his grip on Brage.

Dynna looked over at Brage, and for the first time their gazes met. Edmund's blade was at his throat. He was facing death. Yet she saw no fear in his regard, only a proud defiance. She turned away from him as she answered, "After what I witnessed on the battlefield today and what I saw just now while helping in the village, I would willingly plead for any man's life."

Dynna spoke her true feelings, for she was haunted still by the memories of the carnage she had witnessed. Her healing abilities had not been able to save their lives, but she could stop this death.

Edmund believed that no female had the right to publicly voice an opinion contrary to a man's, and his disapproval of her outspokenness showed in his expression. He promised himself that once they were wed, she would change much in her manner. Obviously, Warren had been far too soft on her. It was time she learned her place and was taught to stay in it.

"Dynna is right," Lord Alfrick pronounced slowly, thoughtfully. "The battle is over and we have won. In our victory, we shall be generous. Let there be no more bloodshed."

Dynna bowed her head and said a silent prayer of thanks. "I celebrate your wisdom, my lord."

Edmund thrust Brage from him as he struggled to mask his fury at being so thwarted. "As you wish, Father." He stalked off to join some of the other men in their drinking.

"And what of his wounds, my lord? Shall I tend them?" Dynna asked, seeing how badly the Viking was injured.

"No, Dynna. Spare his life though I have, I care not about his suffering. Sir Thomas, chain our captive with the dogs," Lord Alfrick directed. "Perhaps in time he will prove of some worth to us. Until then, let him live as a Viking should—in chains."

Sir Thomas quickly moved to obey his command. He prodded Brage toward the corner where the hounds lay amidst dirty rushes and rotting food scraps.

"Lady Dynna, sit beside me and share this repast while you speak to me of the villagers," Lord Alfrick said.

"I would be pleased to, my lord." Dynna smiled gently. As she settled in beside him, her gaze remained on the captive as Sir Thomas led him across the room. She could not help but notice how proudly he carried himself in spite of his weakened condition.

"How fare my people?" Lord Alfrick asked.

"Many were killed, and many more were seriously injured," she said. Tears burned in her eyes, yet she managed to control them. "I helped where I could, but there were some . . ." Her voice became choked as she thought of some of the horrors she had seen.

Lord Alfrick patted her hand. Seeing the pain in her expression, he spoke kindly. "War is not for innocents like you. But lest you forget, we were the defenders today, not the attackers. Had we not fought today, our lives would have been forfeit. The Vikings are ruthless."

Dynna ached to tell him that Edmund was as ruthless as any Viking they had seen today, but she wisely did not. "After today, I am no innocent to the brutal ways of men. Death has ravaged our land, and I fear more have yet to die. I must go back to the village in a little while to see if there is any more I can do for the wounded."

Dynna's eyes were upon Sir Thomas as he shackled the Black Hawk. She could almost feel the bite of the chains on her own flesh. Even across the width of the Great Hall, she could see that Brage's features were grim, and by the rigid way he was holding himself, she could tell he was in great pain. She found his courage impressive, and she had to fight the urge to go to him and treat his wounds. With an effort, she forced her attention back to what Lord Alfrick was saying.

"It is good that you use your gift of healing to help our people."

"If I can somehow ease their suffering, I must."

"You will make a fine wife for Edmund," Lord Alfrick told her. He lowered his voice as he spoke, "It is hoped that despite your momentary attempt to flee, you have come to understand that your future is here, as Edmund's wife."

"I understand that, my lord." Dynna answered politely, trying to avoid any discussion of her misadventure.

"I trust that you have learned your lesson and will not put yourself at risk in such a way again. Should you leave my protection, I fear for you. It pleases me to know that you are safely ensconced here at the tower where no harm can come to you."

"Yes, my lord."

"You will be happy with my youngest son." Lord Alfrick was more than satisfied with the way things had turned out. The Black Hawk was dead. The Vikings no longer threatened his land, and now, Dynna would marry Edmund. Things were going very well, indeed.

"As you say, my lord," she said, lowering her eyes to hide her true feelings.

Her answer was quiet and submissive, and he smiled, pleased that she was finally behaving the way a lady should.

As Dynna returned his smile, she pretended a contentment that she was far from feeling. The whole day had been nothing but turmoil for her. When Edmund brought her back to the tower, she had taken only enough time to change clothes before going out to help the people. As Edmund vowed he would, he had sent one of his men to follow her about her duties. She had found his presence maddening, but realized it was the price she had to pay for having dared to try to escape.

Listening to Lord Alfrick now, Dynna supposed it could

have been worse. The priest could have already arrived at the tower and Lord Alfrick could have insisted she marry Edmund immediately. As it was, she had at least a fortnight until the holy man returned and sealed her future for her.

"Make yourself comfortable, Norseman," Sir Thomas said to Brage as he finished chaining him. "Your meal is whatever the dogs will share with you."

As Sir Thomas straightened, he happened to glance at Brage, and for the first time their eyes met. In that moment, he saw the deadly strength of the Viking's anger mirrored in his gaze, and it sent a chill down his spine. In all his years of service to Lord Alfrick, he had fought many enemies, but none had seemed as fierce as this man. He was glad he wasn't facing him on the battlefield.

As Sir Thomas thought of the battle that day, he reluctantly admired the Vikings. Even as outnumbered as they had been, they had continued to fight with unbelievable fury. He could well imagine how the raid would have turned out had the Saxons not been forewarned about the attack, for the Vikings had certainly been the superior fighting force.

Sir Edmund stopped Sir Thomas as the older man passed him. "What shall we do with the prisoner?" he asked.

"Your father has already decided his fate. Perhaps the Viking will prove helpful with information about raids, or perhaps your father will just display him as a trophy. Certainly, he is a prize. Is he not one of the Black Hawk's warriors?"

"Indeed." Sir Edmund agreed. He was seething because Sir Thomas had credited his father with the victory. It was he, himself, who had fought and defeated the Vikings! It had been his plan that had trapped them. Yet as the tale was repeated, the glory would belong to his father.

"My only regret is that we could not identify the body of the Viking leader," Sir Thomas said.

"We have his shield and sword," Sir Edmund pointed out.

"And since the Vikings did not take their dead, we can assume the Black Hawk's body will rot on Saxon soil."

"Let us drink to Lord Alfrick's victory!" Sir Thomas called out as he grabbed up a mug of ale and lifted it high.

"Rather let us drink to the death of the Black Hawk!" Sir Edmund amended, joining Sir Thomas in his salute. The others in the hall followed, and Lord Alfrick stood, drawing Dynna to her feet as the battle-weary soldiers cheered their victory.

"We have slain the most powerful Viking leader! We have triumphed!"

Dynna managed a covert glance at Brage, who was sitting on the floor, his uninjured shoulder braced against the wall. His expression was inscrutable as he watched the Saxons pass his shield and sword around the hall in celebration of his "death." Suddenly, his gaze found hers. It unnerved her that he was staring at her, yet she managed to maintain her outward composure.

Dynna was relieved when one of the women servants approached her to explain that she was needed in the village.

"My lord, I must return to the people. Will you give me leave?" she implored.

"Of course. If they need you, you must go to them. It is our duty to see to the well-being of our people."

She tried not to reveal her eagerness to be gone from them. Though the duty that awaited her was bloody, she would find the villagers' company infinitely preferable to the domineering presence of Lord Alfrick and Sir Edmund.

Dynna had to pass Brage on her way out. This near to him, she could see the tightness around his mouth and the grayness of his skin. The bloody condition of his clothing was not lost on her, either. Sympathy welled up within her. She paused, hoping to ease his suffering, no matter that Lord Alfrick had said otherwise, but Sir Edmund blocked her way.

"Do not bother with this one. Your talents are better served in the village."

"But he is in pain."

"I care not. He deserves no better, and if he dies in agony, so be it. No one here will mourn his passing."

"You treat him worse than you would any animal. Even the lowest servant is cared for when he is ill."

"Our servants are worthy. They tend to my needs. This one is just a Viking."

"I cannot bear to see anyone suffer so."

"Then do not look," he told her sharply.

Dynna's hatred for Sir Edmund grew even stronger. She had the ability to ease Brage's pain, yet he had forbidden her to help. Thwarted for the moment, yet not giving up, she turned and left without another word.

Brage had watched and listened to the exchange between them. He ached to meet Sir Edmund on a battlefield free of his chains, sword in hand. He tried to shift positions, and pain shrieked through his body. The only solace he could cling to was that one day he would find the traitor who had delivered him into the hands of his enemies.

Edmund watched Dynna leave, then glanced down at the captive. Brage returned his regard.

"Had I my way, you would be dead, cur." He smiled thinly. "I will find pleasure in extracting information from you." His statement was accompanied by a sharp kick to Brage's side.

Brage could not suppress the groan of pain that escaped him. He railed silently against the fate that had brought him here and left him trapped and at this man's mercy. He tried to move again, but the chains cut into his legs.

Brage thought of his men. He wondered how they had fared in their escape, if they thought him dead or if they would regroup and come back for him. He wondered, too, if he would be alive if they did return.

Brage let his gaze follow Sir Edmund around the room, and swore to himself that he would not die this way—helpless before his enemies. He would not give his tormentor the satisfaction. He would die a warrior's death.

Brage clung to the thought as he tried to ignore the agony that ate at him like a living thing. Seeking what little comfort he could find against the cold wall, he closed his eyes against the torment of his situation.

As darkness fell, Ulf directed the longship back to the Saxon soil. The two half brothers had argued heatedly over what was to be done. Kristoffer had finally agreed to the landing, when Ulf had conceded that only the two of them would return to the site of the battle. No other Viking life would be risked on this mission; only their own.

It was late when they left the ship and made their way inland. They took extreme care, for they knew there would be no escape were they discovered.

"I am still uncertain how I allowed you to convince me to do this," Kristoffer said under his breath as they followed the road toward the tower, staying hidden in the brush alongside.

"I will not believe Brage is dead without seeing his body, and if he was killed, he deserves a Viking burial," Ulf insisted.

The two men crept through the darkness until they neared the scene of the fighting. It was then that they saw the eerie light of the burning pyres and watched as the Saxons threw the bodies of their dead comrades on the blaze.

"There will be no finding him now," Kristoffer said.

"I should never have left him when we retreated." Guilt sounded in Ulf's voice.

"It could not be helped. There was nothing else you or any of us could have done. Brage would have done the same had he been in our situation."

"Perhaps . . ." he said slowly.

In silence, the two withdrew. Brage was dead, forever lost

to his family, killed in this hated land. They slipped away into the night, heading back to the ship.

Once Ulf had boarded, he immediately ordered the men to set sail for home. Complete quiet reigned as they rowed away from shore. Their losses had been great, and the men were still shocked. No one had expected the resistance to be that heavy. No one had expected the Saxons to be armed and waiting for them.

Ulf assumed the leader's position, standing at the front of the vessel. He stared off into the blackness of the night, going over in his thoughts all that had transpired.

"We must go together to tell our father of Brage's death," Kristoffer said as he came to stand with Ulf.

"Yes. It will not be easy, but it must be done."

Silence lay upon them like a heavy mantle. Hours before, they had been confident and cheering, ready for battle. The horror of their crushing defeat had stripped them of their belief in themselves and their pride. Hatred grew within them, as did the need for revenge. Each surviving Viking swore that the day would come when they would return to Lord Alfrick's land and claim vengeance for their losses.

The Black Hawk's longships sailed north away from the Saxon coast and toward home, bearing the news of defeat and death.

Lady Dynna applied the poultice to the gaping wound on the man's side and managed a smile. "That will draw some of the pain away," she explained in a soft, soothing voice.

"Thank you, my lady" came the hoarse reply. The injured man was very pale and had a glazed, distant look in his eyes.

Dynna doubted he would live the night, and her heart was heavy, for she knew him. He was married and the father of two young sons. She stayed longer, watching until some of the pain had eased from his face. Only Matilda's touch on her arm drew her from his side.

"Come, Lady Dynna," Matilda coaxed gently. "There is little more you can do for him." She had joined Dynna earlier in the evening to help her with her healing.

Dynna slowly rose to follow her maid from the small hut. The night sky was cloudless and the stars sparkled in the black heavens. As she gazed upward, she marveled at the sky's eternal beauty. "How can the world sometimes seem such a beautiful place, and yet at the same time be so ugly?" she mused.

"It is not the world that is ugly," Matilda offered. "It is the people in it."

"That is true. There is so much hatred and fighting. I often wish that there was more I could do to change things."

Matilda looked at her in surprise. "More, my lady? You have given of yourself to the people. You tend their ills and watch over them. How much more could you do? You cannot change men's hearts, and until their hearts are changed, there will be killing and war."

Dynna's mood was solemn. She felt as if the weight of the world was upon her shoulders. She could heal, but she could not raise the dead. Her gift was good only if there was hope.

All evening her thoughts kept returning to the injured Viking leader, and again she wondered how he was faring.

"You are tired and need to rest," Matilda advised her. "You fought a battle of your own this day."

"And I lost," she added wearily, not allowing herself to think about what might have happened if the Vikings had not landed.

They started back to the tower, dreading the prospect of returning, but knowing they had nowhere else to go. There had been no time for Dynna and Matilda to speak openly all evening, for Edmund's man had always been hovering close. For the first time tonight, he lagged a short distance behind, and they felt free to take advantage of the moment.

"Why did you keep the full truth from Lord Alfrick about the Viking's identity?" Matilda asked.

"Had I named him, they would have murdered him on the spot."

"But he is the Black Hawk. His reputation alone . . ." She shuddered.

"He brought no harm to us when we were in his power. I could do no less for him."

"His wounds looked serious."

"I would have gone to him, but Edmund refused to let me near him."

"Perhaps he was right to do so. He is our enemy."

The guard closed on them, then, and they could say no more. They entered the Great Hall to find that drunken men were sleeping on the benches, others were passed out under the tables, and others were still drinking and eating. The victory celebration would go on for days.

Dynna led the way through the room, treading quietly. Sir Edmund's guard had left them after seeing them safely inside. There was no avoiding the area where the dogs lay, and Dynna stopped before Brage.

"Lady Dynna . . . it is not the time . . ." Matilda started to protest.

Dynna shot her a silencing look as she studied him. Brage was slumped against the wall and appeared to be sleeping.

"You must not do this . . ." Matilda whispered. "Sir Edmund—"

"Should I not help him because Sir Edmund has deemed it so? He is injured," she retorted in a hushed voice. "Help me or go. It matters not to me. You have the choice."

"Don't you know how dangerous he is?"

"Chained?"

"Even chained!"

"He will not harm me," she said with certainty. She did not know how she knew that it was true.

Dynna knelt before him, intending to examine his injuries.

The moment she reached out to touch his shoulder, though, his eyes flew open, and she found herself impaled by his icy, blue-eyed gaze. Though he was bloodied and restrained, there was a fierce resolve in his eyes, and Dynna knew he had not been defeated. He snared her wrists in an iron grip as he glared at her.

"What do you want?" he demanded.

"I am a healer."

"Leave me." He growled the words.

"I can help you."

"I want no Saxon hands upon me!" Brage thrust her from him as if touching her was vile to him. He was a strong man. He had healed on his own before, he would heal on his own now.

"Lady Dynna!" Matilda could not prevent her cry of alarm when the Viking pushed Dynna from him, and her cry brought some of the men running to their aid.

"What has happened?" Sir Thomas was the first one there, his expression dark with concern for his lady. He had drawn his weapon and was ready to run the captive through if he had harmed Dynna in any way.

"He . . ." The maid started to explain, but Dynna silenced her with a look.

"He is a Viking, and my maid thinks he is not worthy of my help."

Sir Thomas visibly relaxed as he slid his weapon back into its scabbard. "That is true enough. I would caution you to stay away from him, my lady. I fear he would not hesitate to take your life should he get the chance."

Dynna started to argue with him. She had been in Brage's power and he had chosen to save her life, not end it. He could easily have harmed her right then, too, but he had only chosen to push her from him. She knew it was pointless to argue with Sir Thomas. He was a good man, and she knew he was only protecting her. It was better that he did not know that the man had laid hands on her. Even injured as he was, there had been no mistaking the power in the Black Hawk's touch.

"Come, Lady Dynna. You should retire for the night," Matilda encouraged. "It has been a long day. There is nothing more for us to do here."

Lady Dynna followed Matilda up the stairs to her bedchamber, pausing once to glance back toward the Black Hawk. When she did, she found his gaze still upon her. He seemed to look into the very heart of her, and she turned away from the power of his gaze and hurried into her room.

Brage watched Dynna climb the stairs, and he wondered why he could not seem to look away from her. Something about her had haunted him ever since the first time he had seen her with Ulf. He remembered Ulf boasting of her bravery in attacking him when he'd tried to capture her. Beauty and courage were not what Brage expected to find in a Saxon woman.

When Dynna had disappeared from sight, he settled back against the cold wall. The pain in his back was unrelenting, yet he tried to ignore it. He sought what comfort he could among the hounds and kept a wary eye on the Saxons who still were drinking and celebrating in the Great Hall.

# Five

When Dynna reached her room, Matilda prepared a bath for her. It was heavenly to shed her bloodstained clothes and step into the tub of hot water. Though the tub was not large and its hard surface did not encourage lounging, she sank down into the heat of the water and closed her eyes. For a moment, embraced by the soothing warmth, she was almost able to forget the horrors of the day, but as always there could be no avoiding reality for long. The sorrow and pain returned.

Dynna sighed heavily. She had seen much death in her lifetime—a beloved younger brother when she'd been but a child, her grandparents, then Warren . . . With time, she had found ways to deal with the fact of death, but she had never become used to it.

Dynna understood that in old age, death was sometimes a joyous release from the bondage of living in a frail, failing body. Thus, she had been able to accept her grandparents' passing. But the wantonness of death wreaked through war battered her soul and left her reeling. She wondered why man in all his years of existence had not found ways to pursue peace rather than wage war.

An image of Edmund suddenly formed in her mind, and she had her answer: As long as men like Edmund walked in this world, there would be fighting and savagery.

The thought of Edmund and the remembrance of his hands upon her that day set her to scrubbing herself. It was easy to wash her body and her hair physically clean. She only wished there was some way to cleanse the sorrows from her heart and erase the scenes of death from her memories.

When she finished, Dynna rose from the tub in dripping splendor. Matilda brought her a linen towel. She dried herself, donned a nightdress and climbed into bed. Matilda extinguished the candle and left her to her rest.

Dynna lay on the softness of her clean bed, exhausted. As weary as she was, though, sleep would not come. Every time she started to drift off, a haunting vision of the wounded Brage invaded her consciousness. She tossed and turned for hours, seeking rest but finding it elusive. Finally, unable to ignore her worry that the Viking would die without help, Dynna left her bed, dressed in a simple tunic, and gathered up her basket of healing herbs and ointments.

Creeping from her chamber, Dynna let caution dictate her every move as she made her way silently down the steps.

There was little sound coming from below. The only noises were of the men snoring as they slept off the effects of their drunken celebrating. A few torches were still burning, so there was just enough light to see by. With a measured tread, she descended to the gloomy Great Hall, her gaze fixed on the dank, shadowed corner where the captive was chained.

Brage had needed to sleep, but the pain of his wounds, coupled with the knowledge that he was a prisoner of Lord Alfrick, had left him restless and angry. All night, he had suffered the taunts and jibes of the Saxons. Once they grew tired of him and fell into drunken stupors, Brage took the time to try to find some way to escape. He worked the chains at his legs, but they were fastened securely and would remain so until unlocked. He studied the links where they were attached to the wall and knew they could not be worked loose.

There was nothing he could do to save himself. Until now, despair had been unknown to him. He had never before been trapped. The feeling of helplessness ate at him. He was sitting there in the predawn darkness, silently raging over his situation, when he noticed a movement on the stairs.

At first, Brage thought it was one of the servants, but then Dynna passed beneath one of the torches. He recognized her immediately from the sleek beauty of her raven hair, unbound now and tumbling down her back in a cascade of curls.

He could not imagine what she was doing moving about the tower at this time of night. It puzzled him that she seemed to be looking his way. When he had sent her from him earlier, he had meant it. He did not want or need the help of a Saxon woman. Dynna's maid had been right to caution her about him. He could be a very dangerous man. His hands were not restrained, and she was a fragile little thing. Her wrists, when he had grabbed them earlier, had felt delicate enough to snap had he applied enough pressure. He watched as she reached the bottom of the stairs and started across the room toward him. Why had she returned?

It did not surprise Dynna to find the captive awake and watchful as she made her way to him. She imagined that his wounds were too grievous to give him much peace. Knowing this, she grew even more determined to do what she could to ease his pain.

Brage was concentrating on her approach, watching the graceful way she moved and thinking how lovely she looked. In the unadorned gown she wore, he was able to see just a hint of the sweet, womanly curves of her body. Had his men won the battle that day, and had she still been his captive, he doubted that he would have sold her away at the slave market.

The next moment, Sir Edmund stepped out of the shadows before her, blocking her way.

Dynna gasped at the sight of him, her heart in her throat. "Sir Edmund . . ."

Brage was just as shocked as Dynna by the nobleman's unexpected appearance. He silently cursed the chains that held him fast as he watched her bravely face the man he had already come to despise.

"Ah, so I have taken you by surprise, my lady. That is good. Surprises are nice," Sir Edmund said drunkenly as he leered at her in the half-light. "Dynna, my dear, you look lovely. Did you come down here seeking out my company tonight to join in the celebration of my bravery and daring?"

"I . . ." she began nervously.

She did not get to finish her sentence, for at that moment Edmund saw the basket in her hand and realized her plan. Moments before, he had been ready to seduce her with soft words and kisses. Now, he knew she had come down only to help the Viking, and it infuriated him.

"Dare you help our prisoner after I told you to let him suffer?" he asked, glancing over his shoulder at Brage and wishing his father had let him kill the man earlier so they could have been done with him. "As my wife, you will learn that when I issue an order, it is to be obeyed." His voice was full of rage as he grabbed her by the upper arms.

"I am not your wife yet!" she protested, trying to jerk free of his hold.

Brage was shocked by the news that she was to marry this cur, and he fumed at Edmund's brutal treatment of her. None of the men he knew treated their women this way. Wives were to be cherished and adored, not abused and hurt. Even as he tried to convince himself that Lady Dynna was a Saxon woman and meant nothing to him, he realized that he did care what happened to her. The knowledge troubled and confused him.

Hatred glowed in Brage's eyes. He wished he were free to go to Dynna's aid. It enraged him to know there was nothing he could do. His jaw clenched in anger, but he held his silence.

"It is only a matter of time, my sweet—a few weeks at

most. Then you will be my wife, and once you are, you will do what I tell you to do, when I tell you to do it. As my future queen, you must grant my every desire . . . fulfill my every wish . . ."

He pulled her closer. As she fought him harder, she dropped her basket, spilling her remedies about the dirty floor.

"Release me! The Vikings you so feared would never have manhandled me so!"

"But I have the right. You are mine!"

He laughed again, and then he kissed her, his mouth claiming hers in a possessive exchange that almost gagged her. She turned her head to the side to try to escape him, but he held her still and forced her to accept his kiss.

Dynna wanted to scream. His touch was vile, and yet try as she might, she could not break free. When at last he released her, she stumbled back away from him, wiping her mouth with the back of her hand.

"How dare you?" she demanded, trying to maintain a haughty demeanor when she felt like running in terror.

"I would dare anything with you, Dynna," Edmund told her, his eyes burning with the fire of his need. The way she avoided him and acted as if she were uninterested in him presented a challenge. But he knew better. It was just a game. In the end, he would win. She would be under his control, and she would submit to his will.

He had never been denied by a woman before, and while her actions did stir his passion, there was also a limit to what he would take from her. Tonight, with her open defiance of his order, she had pushed him close to that limit.

"You are despicable! I do not know how Warren could have been such a good, kind man, and you could be so . . ."

The mention of Warren was the final insult, and he closed on her threateningly. "Speak not his name to me again, Dynna."

"Warren was my husband. I chose him! I did not choose you!"

"What would your fine husband think of you if he knew you were sneaking off in the night to whore for the enemy?"

"Your words are as vile as you yourself, Edmund!"

"Sneaking about the castle in the middle of the night, using your healing powers as an excuse to come down here . . . What was it you really wanted tonight, Dynna?"

At his insult, Brage's anger turned to fury. Had he the strength, he would have ripped his chains from the walls and used them to thrash this hated Saxon.

Dynna was white-faced as she listened to his words. "It is difficult for me to fathom that you were born to the same parents who bore Warren."

At the mention of his brother's name again, the fire that had shone in Edmund's eyes turned to ice. His heart hardened, and he raised his hand to strike her.

"No . . ." she cried.

"What is this?"

Sir Thomas appeared out of the gloom of the hall, a worried, questioning look on his rugged face as he glanced from Sir Edmund to Dynna and back. Edmund lowered his hand, frustrated for the moment.

Sir Thomas's expression remained serious, his demeanor threatening. He would allow no harm to come to her. He had cared greatly for Sir Warren and had approved his choice of Lady Dynna for a wife. Upon Warren's death, he had quietly appointed himself to watch over her, and he would not tolerate anyone hurting her. When she had run away earlier, he had almost hoped that she would make it to her family home. He did not believe Sir Edmund would be a good husband to her, and he wanted to see her happy again. She had not laughed since Warren's death.

"Lady Dynna? Is something wrong?" he asked.

"Sir Thomas . . ." Dynna had never been so glad to see

him. Somehow, he always seemed to know when she needed him. "No, no, nothing is wrong."

"You are sure? You sounded as if you needed help, as if you were troubled . . ." He looked pointedly at her basket, its contents strewn on the floor. "I see you were about another mercy mission."

"Yes, but I was just finishing here and was on my way back to my room."

"Then, please, allow me to escort you. I would see that no harm befalls you tonight."

"Thank you."

"Sir Edmund?" He awaited some response from him, some explanation for the scene he'd just witnessed.

Sir Edmund chose to ignore Sir Thomas's inquiry and spoke directly to his betrothed. "Good night, Dynna. I count the days . . . and nights . . . till you will be mine."

Dynna percieved the threat in his words, and she quickly gathered up her things. Not bidding him good night, she turned her back on him and hurried away in the company of her protector.

Sir Edmund cursed low under his breath as he watched Sir Thomas escort her to the stairs. She had outmaneuvered him again, but the day would come when he would win. She was going to pledge herself to be his wife, and he was going to enjoy the part of the wedding ceremony where she professed to obey. And obey she would—in every way.

Brage remained silent in his anger as Lady Dynna walked away with Sir Thomas. He was tremendously relieved that the older man had interceded. He did not know what he would have done had Edmund struck her.

Sir Thomas stood with Dynna at the foot of the stairs. "Are you all right, my lady?"

"Yes, Sir Thomas. Good night." She managed a smile for him.

He watched until she had disappeared safely up the steps, then returned to Sir Edmund.

Edmund saw him coming and wondered in drunken annoyance what the interfering fool wanted now.

"Sir Edmund, may I speak my mind with you?"

"Have you ever not, Sir Thomas?"

"Have no doubt that Lady Dynna is well honored here in your father's court. Many would look askance on any harm coming to her or anything being forced upon her against her will."

"I had no intention of harming her," Sir Edmund sneered. He was seething, but said nothing more as he glared at the man who was his father's favorite son.

"It did not look that way to me. You are clearly drunk and would be better off abed."

Sir Edmund turned a baleful, demeaning glare on him. "I shall tend to my own affairs without any advice from you."

"As you wish, but know that I will protect Lady Dynna—even from you," Sir Thomas replied.

Then Sir Thomas was gone, and Edmund was furious. He turned to look at the cause of all the trouble . . . the Viking. It outraged him to find that the Norseman had been watching all that had transpired and was now daring to smile at him.

"Smile while you still can, Viking. I am going to enjoy watching you suffer in the coming weeks."

Brage said nothing in response to his taunt. Brage had no respect for Sir Edmund as an enemy or as a man. He did not flinch from him as he drew near.

"She would have treated your wounds, but it is better that you suffer slowly."

"Death does not frighten me," Brage replied calmly.

"What does frighten you, Viking?" Edmund closed on him, his expression cunningly savage.

"Very little, Saxon."

Sir Edmund drew his knife and looked from the finely honed blade to the captive and back. "It would be a shame if you tried to escape tonight and were slain in the attempt."

"Free me from these chains, and I will escape—using your knife," he answered.

Edmund smiled. "Had my father not plans for you, I would do it in an instant, just to have the pleasure of hunting you down. As it is, you must languish where you are. The chains suit you. Animals should be restrained."

"I am not the animal here tonight. I do not have to use force on women."

Edmund's jealousy flared hotly, and he quickly held the blade up before Brage's eyes, then touched it to his cheek. "A slip of the blade here or . . ." He lowered the knife until the point was resting high up on his thigh. "Here . . . would certainly end any attraction the women might feel for you."

Edmund grew even more angry when the Viking met his regard coolly, without emotion. As much as he would have liked to torture him to relieve his own frustration, Edmund remembered his father had ordered that this man be kept alive. He slowly withdrew.

"Beware, Viking. Your days are numbered."

With that, he disappeared into the shadows, leaving Brage alone with the sleeping dogs.

Brage did not allow himself to relax until Edmund had been gone for many minutes. Then, slowly and carefully, he leaned back against the wall again. The wound in his shoulder was hurting worse than before.

As he sat there, he went over in his mind all he had overheard in the conversation between Sir Edmund and Lady Dynna. Brage now understood more of her situation. She was Edmund's brother's widow and not a virginal lady promised in marriage to Sir Edmund. It was obvious that she was being forced to marry Edmund against her will. He was convinced that marriage had something to do with Ulf's finding her and her maid dressed as commoners, sleeping in the countryside. He did not doubt that she had tried to escape the fate of being Sir Edmund's bride.

Brage wondered again why Lady Dynna and her maid had not revealed his true identity to Lord Alfrick. Certainly, if Alfrick had known that the infamous Black Hawk was his captive, he would have designed some fascinating torment for him. As it was, he was merely a Viking, and as such, a prize, but not one as noteworthy as the Black Hawk himself would be. He was greatly puzzled. She had had much to gain and nothing to lose by telling them who he was.

Exhaustion plagued Brage. He let his eyes drift shut as he sought mindless peace. He tried to let his mind go blank, but a vision of a brave, dark-haired woman played in his thoughts.

What rest he got in those late hours of the night was uneasy and heated.

In her room, Dynna lay wide awake. She had double-locked her door against the possibility that Edmund might follow her upstairs in spite of Sir Thomas's gallant interference. As she lay huddled beneath her blankets, she searched frantically for some way to avoid her upcoming marriage, but no idea came to her. Dawn was brightening the sky before she finally fell into a tormented sleep. When she awoke a few hours later, she felt as if she had not slept at all. She spent the day in her room, so she would not have to see Edmund again, but her thoughts were on the Viking below and how he was faring.

"Here is your breakfast, Norseman. See if the dogs will share with you!" a servant called to Brage as he tossed a platter of scraps in his general direction the second morning after the battle.

The dogs were used to this ritual. At the first sight of the servant, they had all jumped up. Now that he had tossed the food their way, they began to fight over it, snarling, snapping and biting each other to get their share.

The servant gave a shrug of indifference when Brage made no attempt to challenge the hounds for their food. Turning away, the man disappeared toward the kitchen and returned a few minutes later with a good-sized bucket of water. He ventured forth, yet stayed far enough back so he would not go too near the murderous invader. When he put the bucket down, Brage lifted his head and pinned the man with a deadly glare. The servant froze and then hurriedly moved away. He did not trust this captive. He believed the Vikings were capable of anything, even when they were locked up in chains.

Had he the strength, Brage would have smiled over the man's fear. As it was, he made no move toward him as he watched him go. Brage stared at the spoiled scraps of meat the dogs were still fighting over and felt no hunger. He was, however, desperately in need of water. The bucket was just out of reach, so he attempted to rise. The pain in his shoulder was excruciating, growing ever worse by the hour. When he finally got to his feet, he swayed uncertainly until he got his balance.

It puzzled him that he was having difficulty standing. He staggered as he made his way to the bucket, but he dismissed that as a reaction to being in chains. He reached the bucket and dropped down beside it to drink thirstily. Though the water was cool, it did little to relieve the heat that filled him. He splashed water on his face and neck and finally breathed a little easier. When he moved back to his place against the wall, he dragged the bucket with him. There was no telling when—or even if—they would bring more water and he could see no reason to share with the hounds.

He felt somewhat refreshed as he settled back in. Once more he let his gaze sweep the hall, trying to devise some plan to flee this place of his imprisonment. He conjured no

## PASSION

possible solution, though, and he slumped down in defeat, trying to ignore the agony that sliced through him, both body and soul.

He realized miserably that his only hope was that his brothers would realize he was alive and mount a counterattack. He worried, remembering the seriousness of their losses, that the attack might not be coming. More than likely they thought him dead upon the field of battle. It would be weeks, maybe even months before they would mount another powerful force and seek revenge against Lord Alfrick.

Defeat settled over Brage in a crushing weight. Never before had he been at another's mercy, his freedom lost, his power stripped from him. Surely, Valhalla would be infinitely preferable to living like this. Glorious, honorable death would be better. It had to be. Only Brage's burning need to find the one who had betrayed him kept him from surrendering to the ever-growing, feverish weakness that threatened him.

Much later in the afternoon, Sir Roland, one of Lord Alfrick's men, met up with Hereld, a traveling merchant newly arrived at the tower, and informed him about the battle the day before.

"We defeated the Black Hawk's warriors and chased them back into the sea!" he boasted.

"Do not be too sure of yourselves," Hereld said, having dealt with the Vikings and knowing how fierce they were. "How can you be sure they will not return?"

"Their losses were too great. They will not be back any time soon."

"But the Black Hawk is not one to give up easily."

"The Black Hawk is dead," Sir Roland told him. "Our land is safe from his raiding forever."

"Dead?" Hereld was shocked. He had seen the Black

Hawk several times and knew he was a magnificent warrior. He was completely stunned to find that these Englishmen had killed him. "How can that be? How could you have defeated him?"

"We were warned ahead of time of his raid. No one is sure of the man's identity, but he came to Lord Alfrick in the middle of the night and told him of the raid. We had time to prepare, so when the Black Hawk attacked, we were ready for him."

"And you are certain he was killed?"

"His shield and sword were found, and the Vikings in retreat took no dead with them."

"This is truly a feat of great acclaim. Send my compliments to your lord."

"You can tell him yourself."

"Indeed, I will. I will spread the word of his brave victory from village to town."

Sir Roland was pleased, and he knew his lord would be, too. "We do have one trophy of the battle."

"Oh?"

"We found one seriously wounded Viking who was left for dead on the battlefield."

"Is he still alive?" The trader's eyes glowed at the prospect. Ransoming captives was a very gainful trade, and he was not above making a tidy profit if he could convince Lord Alfrick to let him do it.

"So far he has survived, although Sir Edmund would like to see him dead for all the misery he has caused. Come, take a look at our prize."

Sir Roland led the trader into the Great Hall and over to where Brage was chained. Several of the dogs growled as they approached. Sir Roland kicked at them, and they crawled away. He was surprised when the captive did not look up or pay attention to them. In fact, the Viking seemed to be asleep, for his head was hanging down on his chest.

"Here he is. I do not know what plans Lord Alfrick has for him, but we will keep him here until it has been decided."

When the hounds had cleared away, Hereld approached. As he saw the dark-haired prisoner for the first time, he went still. "You claim this one is a Viking? One of the Black Hawk's men?"

"Yes. He said his name was Brage. That was all we got out of him." Sir Roland booted Brage roughly in the thigh. "Wake up, Norseman. You have a visitor."

Hereld watched as the captive slowly raised his head. When he found himself staring into a pair of blue eyes he had seen before, he could not believe his luck. The Black Hawk himself was their prisoner! Excitement coursed through him. These Saxon fools had no idea of the treasure they held.

At that moment, someone across the hall called out to Sir Roland, and he went to see what the man wanted.

Hereld stood alone, staring down at Brage, a smile of pure delight on his face. "This is wonderful!" he mused out loud. "Anslak will pay a fortune to have his son returned. I will be wealthy beyond my wildest dreams . . ."

Brage wondered what the two men wanted other than just to torment him. Brage thought he heard the wiry little man speak his father's name when he started to follow after Sir Roland. He wanted to call out to the man, to find out what he knew about his father, but for some reason he could not think of what to say. He felt awkward and confused. His one coherent thought was that this man with the shifty dark eyes knew who he was, and he was heading off to tell Lord Alfrick . . .

"Wait . . ." Brage finally managed in a harsh rasp.

Hereld heard him speak and turned to look at him. "Be patient, my friend. I will have you out of here in no time!"

He did not understand.

"You are going to make me very rich. All I have to do is talk Lord Alfrick into giving you to me and then I'll make myself a tidy profit when I sell you back to your father. Do not go anywhere," he said with an almost evil chuckle. "I will return shortly." He hurried away, laughing in delight at the good fortune that had been handed to him. Now if he could only convince Lord Alfrick to release the prisoner to him . . .

Hereld sought out Sir Roland and found him with several of the other men. He requested to meet with Lord Alfrick, and Sir Roland left to seek the lord's permission.

Hereld was forced to wait the better part of an hour. The trader was finally taken to a small chamber off the main hall. Lord Alfrick was there with Sir Edmund.

"You wished to speak with me," Lord Alfrick said in greeting.

"Yes, my lord. I just arrived at the tower today and have heard of your great battle against the Black Hawk. You are truly a magnificent lord to have defeated the hated Viking so decisively."

"My people fought valiantly. It was not an easy fight, but it had to be won to preserve our land."

"Indeed, my lord. You have proven your mastery of strategy. I will tell everyone of your marvelous deed."

Lord Alfrick was pleased with this, for he knew Hereld was a well-traveled merchant and trader who knew many people. It would be a good thing for him to have a reputation as a fearless leader. Respect for his prowess in battle might prevent others from attacking them. "That is good. Now what is it you want of me, Hereld?"

"I want nothing, my lord, except to buy something I hope you are willing to sell."

Alfrick looked puzzled. "I do not know of what you speak."

"You have something I think I can sell elsewhere, my lord, and I would bargain with you for it."

"And what is it that I have that so interests you?"

"Your Viking captive, my lord. Sir Roland has told me

that you have no use for the man. I, however, would be willing to pay you for him."

"What use could a Norse prisoner be to you?"

"I know many who would buy him from me for a goodly sum. He is worth much at the market. Usually, it is the Viking selling slaves. This time it would be me, selling a Viking."

"How much is he worth to you?"

Hereld quoted him a figure that was not outlandishly high, but certainly substantial. "Well, my lord?" he pressed eagerly. "Do we strike a bargain?"

Edmund was looking on, saying nothing at first. He grew slowly angry as he listened to the man and spoke up. He did not want to see the warrior sold away. He wanted to see him dead. "I think perhaps our good merchant should stick to dealing in goods."

The trader turned to him. "But, Sir Edmund, does seeing him dead mean more to you than making money? I am offering you a good price for him."

"Why do you think that he would bring such a good price?"

"He sailed with the Black Hawk. Many would pay to have him."

Lord Alfrick heard the greed in the voice and wondered at it. There was some money to be made here, but certainly not enough to make this man so excited. "The Viking attacked our land and murdered our people. I think we will just leave things as they are. It pleases me to keep this one." He saw the flash of hungry desperation in the man's eyes and knew his intuition had been right. There was more to this than the man was revealing.

"My lord! I will give you more for him. Name a price and I will try to meet it."

Lord Alfrick's eyes narrowed suspiciously as he regarded the overeager little man. "Tell me, Hereld. Why is this particular one so important to you?"

Hereld realized he had revealed too much. "It is not he

who is important, my lord. I just saw the chance to make some money easily, that is all."

Sir Edmund saw his nervousness, and asked, "Hereld, is there truly that much to be made on a mere warrior? Or is there more to this than you have told us?"

"No . . . No, there is not more." He tried to hide his sudden feeling of unease at being caught in a conniving scheme. "If you have no wish to sell him to me, so be it. I will stick with my merchant goods and leave slave trading to others."

Hereld started to back away from the room. His mind was racing, trying to come up with another plan to make money off the Black Hawk's misfortune. He was certain Anslak would pay a high price to learn that his son was alive and being kept prisoner here. All he had to do was travel to the Viking leader and deliver the news.

Already mentally preparing to set sail northward, Hereld kept backing away from Lord Alfrick and Sir Edmund. He had just about reached the door when he came up against the solid barrier of Sir Thomas standing in his way.

"Sir Thomas," Sir Edmund called out. "Bring our friend back to us, please. I believe he knows more about our Viking than he is telling us. Something seems amiss."

The big man ushered him forward to face Lord Alfrick and Sir Edmund once more.

"Is this true, Hereld? Do you know more than you are telling my lord?" Sir Thomas demanded. He rested a heavy hand on Hereld's shoulder. "Was there something more you had to tell Lord Alfrick?"

Hereld glanced up at Alfrick's huge protector. He saw the steel in his expression and knew his own greed had given him away. Thinking quickly, he decided to tell the truth—for now. Later, he would see what else he could devise.

"More, Sir Thomas?" Hereld tried to sound innocent.

"More, Hereld." Sir Thomas's voice was a deep, threatening boom as he put his other hand on the dagger he wore at his waist.

"There might have been one other small thing I neglected to mention . . ."

"And what is that one other small thing, trader?" Lord Alfrick asked imperiously.

"Your prisoner, my lord. He is worth much gold to the Vikings."

"So you have said. I ask you once more, why is he so valuable to you?"

Hereld realized there was no way out of his situation; he must speak the truth. "The man you hold, called Brage, is also known by another name . . ."

"Yes?" Sir Edmund was impatient.

"He is the Black Hawk."

# Six

A stunned silence gripped the three Saxons as they stared at the trader.

"The Viking leader?" Sir Edmund said, smiling broadly, his eyes aglow with a renewed fervor. "All the more reason to kill him and be done with it!"

Lord Alfrick was incredulous. "You say we have the Black Hawk?"

"Yes, my lord."

"And you know this for certain?"

"I saw him at the market a year or so ago, and I have never forgotten him. His dark hair and beard set him apart from the others, and those eyes . . ." He shuddered as he remembered the barely leashed power and cold fury he had seen in the other man's gaze. "It is the Black Hawk, my lord. There is no mistake."

Lord Alfrick smiled cynically. "And you were going to sell him into slavery?"

"I was going to sell him, my lord . . ."

"To his people?"

"I am a businessman, my lord," Hereld said. "They would certainly pay the highest price for him . . ." He let the sentence fade.

Lord Alfrick was thoughtful for a moment. The trader's greed had stirred an interest of his own. "I think there may be a way here to use our prisoner to our own advantage. I had thought of him as a mere trophy, but now I see he is much more."

"What are you planning, Father?" Edmund asked. He was thrilled that they had captured the Black Hawk for, once again, it proved just how good his plan had been.

Ever thinking of ways to make a profit, Hereld spoke up. "If I may be so bold as to offer my services, Lord Alfrick, I would be more than willing to help if you want to arrange a trade of some kind with Anslak. I have access to his village and could deliver any messages you would like to send."

"For a price, of course," Alfrick said.

Hereld bowed low. "My lord, I make my very living by my wits. My ability to barter is my best talent."

"Very well. Leave us for now, but wait in the Great Hall."

"Yes, my lord."

Lord Alfrick waited until the man had left the room.

"It would seem we have been given a rare opportunity, Father," Sir Edmund began.

"What would you do, my son?"

"I know you are always searching for ways to increase our treasure, and this man is worth much gold to his people."

"Do you mean you would ransom him back?"

"I would," Sir Edmund answered, "but I would make certain that he never had the chance to attack our land again. I would claim the gold and then destroy the prize."

"There would be war."

"We would be ready, just as we were yesterday."

Lord Alfrick looked to Sir Thomas. "And you, Sir Thomas? What do you think?"

"As Sir Edmund says, we were prepared for the Black Hawk's invasion and we defeated him." He looked at the younger man and saw the conniving weakness in him. With each passing day, his opinion of Edmund sank lower and lower. Edmund was no man of honor or character.

"I hear a note of hesitation in your voice," Alfrick said. "What is it that troubles you?"

"Deception is cowardly. Would you give your word that an exchange was to take place, and then kill those who had come in good faith to complete the bargain? Your reputation as a courageous leader and just lord would suffer for it."

Alfrick had been momentarily blinded by the thought of defeating the Vikings again, but Sir Thomas's words blunted his enthusiasm for an ambush.

"What shall we do about Hereld, my lord?" Sir Thomas asked.

"He has offered to help us in this, and we shall accept. Bring him to me."

Within moments, Hereld was once again before Lord Alfrick. "Travel to Anslak and tell the Viking leader that I hold his son," the trader was instructed. "Tell him I will return the Black Hawk to him for five hundred pounds of gold and their pledge to never raid our land again."

"Five hundred pounds of gold, my lord?" Hereld's eyes widened in shock at the high amount.

"That is my price if he wants his son back."

"Yes, my lord."

"We will await word from you."

"See to it that no harm comes to your captive while I am gone. It would not be good to tell his father that he lives, only to have Anslak find him dead when he comes to pay the ransom. Anslak is not a forgiving man."

"Anslak will see his son alive again," Lord Alfrick said.

"He is also a doubting man, my lord. Is there some proof I can take with me to show him that I speak the truth?"

"I will see that you are given one of his garments to take along. That should be proof enough for the Viking."

"That is good. And what of my reward, my lord?" he asked boldly.

"I will pay you handsomely for your effort, once the exchange has been made."

"Then I travel north to do your bidding as soon as you

have given me the garment, my lord." Hereld's eyes were gleaming with avarice as he hurried away.

"How long do you suppose it will be before he returns?" Sir Edmund asked, anger dripping from his words.

"A fortnight, I am sure. We have time to prepare," Sir Thomas said.

Lord Alfrick was pleased. "Now, let us pay our 'guest' a visit. I would speak to the fearless Black Hawk." He thought back over the previous conversation he had had with the prisoner. "Let me see . . . How did he answer me when I asked him if the Black Hawk had been slain?"

"I believe he said the Black Hawk was felled," Sir Thomas reminded him.

"Clever man, this one. We will be wise to watch him carefully."

Edmund did not join in their discussion, but silently seethed at being so overruled. Had he not devised the plan that had won the battle? Why would his father and Sir Thomas not listen to him and agree to ambush the Vikings? It would be no great loss if all Norsemen were wiped from the face of the earth. He began to plot a strategy of his own. His father might voice an objection now, but when the time came, he would be proud of his daring.

Brage had been watching for the little man, waiting for him to return. He did not know what the stranger planned to do to get him released, but he had presented Brage's first ray of hope.

For a while after the man had left him, Brage's spirits had soared. As time passed, though, and there had been no sign of him returning, his despair returned. He began to wonder if he had imagined the whole thing. Certainly it seemed possible. The pain from his wounds was near to maddening, and he was finding it more and more difficult to think straight.

Brage felt hot. He kept splashing water from the bucket

on his face and neck, but each movement brought more agony, and after a while he ceased. The water seemed to have little lasting cooling effect anyway.

Brage suddenly saw some men coming toward him from across the Great Hall. His vision was hazy, and he struggled to focus on them, thinking it might be the stranger returning to free him. As they loomed closer, though, he saw that it was Lord Alfrick, Sir Edmund, and Sir Thomas. The one who had promised him freedom was nowhere to be seen.

"Well, well, well. What have we here?" Lord Alfrick gloated as he stood over his prisoner. "Could it be the bravest of all the Viking raiders?"

"Yes, Father, it is, but from the looks of things, he will not be doing any more raiding." Sir Edmund walked to the wall and tested the strength of the chains that held Brage. He smiled in approval when they would not budge.

"Good, good." Lord Alfrick's words were harsh as he stood over his captive. "It pleases me to see you in bondage."

"It is important that you are pleased," Brage said sarcastically. He struggled to rise, to face his enemy squarely.

"Indeed it is, and I am very pleased today."

Brage was gritting his teeth against the pain as he fought to stand. He finally got to his feet, but his legs would barely support him. He stayed upright, but slumped back against the wall, exhausted from the effort. His head was spinning. He heard Lord Alfrick talking, but it seemed as if from a great distance.

"I have recently learned that you are the Black Hawk himself, not just one of his warriors."

At the sound of his battle name, Brage lifted his head. He wondered vaguely how they had learned of his true identity. "It is as you say, I am the Black Hawk."

Lord Alfrick and Sir Edmund exchanged smiles as the trader's story was confirmed. Sir Thomas watched his worthy adversary struggle to maintain his dignity before Lord Alfrick, and he felt a deep admiration for him. He doubted he would have been able to keep such fine control had he been caught in a similar situation.

Brage did not show any emotion as he awaited Lord Alfrick's pronouncement. He expected death—and in fact was almost ready to welcome it. The world seemed to be spinning around him and his knees were threatening to buckle. He held himself upright, though, determined not to collapse before them.

Lord Alfrick had been studying him with interest. He saw how gray his features were, how glazed his eyes. He frowned. "Sir Thomas, take our prisoner to the tower room."

"Yes, my lord." Sir Thomas felt relief at his order. The man called the Black Hawk was obviously in great pain, and he remembered Hereld's warning that the prisoner must be kept alive.

"The Black Hawk seems weak, but do not trust him. He is known for his strength and fearlessness."

"Yes, my lord."

Brage was trying to focus on what was being discussed, but everything seemed to get farther and farther away, moving ever downward in a spiral.

"Edmund, accompany me." Lord Alfrick moved off toward his chambers with his son, leaving Sir Thomas to take charge of the prisoner.

Sir Thomas removed the chains from Brage. He had seen seriously injured men before, and he knew this man's display was no act. He could see the feverish look in his eyes. Sir Thomas only hoped Lord Alfrick realized it and ordered that he be treated soon.

"Move!" he directed, pointing the way toward the tower stairs.

Brage was pleased to be unshackled, but he could summon no strength to try an escape. He was not sure whether they were going to kill him or let him go, but either would have been a release.

He started off in the direction Sir Thomas had pointed.

The Great Hall tilted crazily around him and all noise seemed magnified. He fought to keep his focus on putting one foot in front of the other, but his legs did not seem willing to cooperate. Only the sheer force of his will kept him upright and drove him onward. When suddenly he felt himself grow even dizzier, he swayed and reached out to brace himself against a table.

Sir Thomas saw him stagger and barked orders to the others in the hall. Two men came running to help.

"Take him to the tower room," he ordered.

The two lifted Brage's arms around their shoulders and started toward the steps. Brage groaned as pain from his shoulder wound knifed through him. He sagged weakly between the Saxons. Slumped as he was, the two were forced to half carry, half drag him up the stairs.

"I do not understand why you did not leave him with the dogs," Sir Edmund complained to his father. "The Black Hawk is hated throughout the land. Why should he be taken out of chains?"

"Put your bloodlust aside and think of the fortune that will be ours when he is returned to his people. He is worth nothing to us dead. Now bring Lady Dynna to me. I will send her to tend to him."

"Why Dynna? Why not send one of the old women to nurse him? I do not want my betrothed healing that cur."

"My son, you make no sense. Dynna is the best of our healers. If the Black Hawk dies, we will have nothing. She has worked wonders before our very eyes with her talent. She has the ability to keep this man alive."

"I will not have it!" He was furious over his father's dictates.

Lord Alfrick's voice turned icy. "I say to you, my son, I am lord here. My word is law. The Black Hawk must be alive when Anslak arrives with the gold. I will do whatever

I must do to see that he survives. After the gold is in our hands, I do not care what happens to him, but until then, Lady Dynna will care for him."

Edmund ground his teeth in frustration as he bowed to his father's wishes. "I will find her and bring her to you."

He was fuming as he mounted the steps to Dynna's chamber, then pounded on the door. When it opened, he found himself confronted by Matilda. His frustration grew even more, for the maid's expression turned suspicious and sullen when she saw who stood there.

"I must speak with Dynna," he stated.

"One moment." Matilda closed the door again before he could walk into the room. Lady Dynna had told her what had happened between them at their meeting, and she wanted to give her a moment of privacy to prepare herself before facing him.

Dynna had been embroidering a gown when the knock came. She was staring at the door now, her color pale. "It is Sir Edmund, is it not?"

"Yes, my lady."

Dynna had stayed closeted in her room, trying to avoid just such an encounter. She did not want to speak to Edmund ever again if she could help it. Yet now, here he was at her chamber door.

"He says he must speak to you right away."

Dynna put aside her sewing and rose slowly, mentally girding herself for the confrontation to come. She had known there could be no hiding from him. She had just hoped he would stay away a while longer. It pained her to have to see him after his threats. Her mood was dark, and she felt very isolated as she readied herself to face him.

"Thank you, Matilda. Please stay close by me, unless I dismiss you."

"Yes, my lady."

When she had her courage up, Dynna opened the door to

face her intended. "Yes, Sir Edmund? Matilda said you wanted to see me."

He stood in the hall waiting for her to come to him. There was no denying that he was handsome. It wasn't the physical part of him that repelled her. It was the evilness and cruelty in him. She kept her physical distance from him. He was looking at her with a heated hunger that left her feeling almost sullied.

"My father wants to see you. He is waiting below to speak with you."

"Is something wrong?"

"No, nothing is wrong. Is it so unusual for him to summon you?"

"He is a busy man who has little time during the course of his day to concern himself with me. It is a rare moment when he wants to see me other than at meal time."

"I, however, want to see you all the time," Edmund told her in a lower voice as he took a step closer. "And I concern myself with you all the time."

Dynna stepped back away from him. "Your father awaits me, Sir Edmund. Matilda? I believe we should go belowstairs."

The maid came to her, and together they moved past him. He followed close behind them, enjoying the movement of Dynna's hips beneath the soft wool of her slim-fitting gown. The night would come when he would have the right to strip that garment from her and take her. He was counting the days until the priest returned to the tower. In just a few weeks, she would be his—in all ways.

Dynna did not speak on the way down to the Great Hall. She wondered what Lord Alfrick wanted of her and knew it had to be important. As she reached the last curve in the steps, her gaze went to the area where the Viking should have been chained. She was startled to find he was gone, the chains hanging empty from the wall.

Fear struck Dynna's heart. Brage had not looked well the

night before when she had tried to go to him. It horrified her to think that he might have died from his injuries overnight, or worse yet, to imagine that Edmund had slain him.

"Where is the Viking? What has happened to him?" she asked.

"Do not concern yourself with him."

"Has he died?" She had to know.

"Your worry for him is touching, my sweet," he sneered.

"He was feverish last night. Has he died of his wounds?"

Edmund was wishing it was that easy. "You will know his fate soon enough." His answer was curt, for he was not pleased that she showed such concern for the man.

Dynna feared the worst. She practically ran the rest of the way to Lord Alfrick. "Yes, Lord Alfrick. Sir Edmund said that you wanted to see me."

"I have learned important information today." At her puzzled look, he continued. "It seems our prisoner is no ordinary Viking warrior after all. We have discovered that he is the Black Hawk, the leader of the raid against us."

"He is the Black Hawk?" she gasped. Her surprise was real, for she did not know how he could have learned of the Norseman's true identity. "How did you discover this?"

"Hereld, the merchant trader, had seen the Black Hawk before. He identified him. Once we learned who he was—"

"Is he dead? Have you had him killed?" Pain stabbed at her heart as she imagined the fierce warrior murdered while in chains, helpless to defend himself.

Her reaction again annoyed Edmund.

"No, the Black Hawk is yet alive. I have had him taken to one of the tower rooms so he can be more comfortable while we await a response to the ransom demand I have sent to his people."

At the news that he was still alive, she had to fight back a sigh of relief.

"However, I am concerned about his physical condition," Lord Alfrick continued. "I fear it is not good. His father,

Anslak, will pay a large sum to have him returned, so we must see that he is healed, and quickly. That is why I called you here. I want you to get your healing basket and tend him. You are our most gifted healer. If anyone can save him, it is you."

Dynna bowed her head at his words. Lord Alfrick thought by her posture that she was pleased by his compliment. In fact, Dynna was giving thanks that the Viking was still alive. She did not question why she was so pleased to hear the news.

"I shall do your bidding, my lord."

"Edmund, take Lady Dynna to our prisoner and see that she has everything she needs.

"I still disagree with your decision to send Dynna to him, Father. Surely there is some other healer who could do this," Edmund argued.

"Dynna will do this," he dictated.

"Yes, Father."

Edmund escorted Dynna and Matilda to the top of the tower and into the secluded chamber where the Black Hawk was being kept. This particular room had been chosen because its location was isolated and it could be easily guarded. As they reached the door, Edmund grasped Dynna's arm to prevent her from entering.

"Had I my way, I would not have sent you to tend him. I do not want your hands upon him."

"Your father has commanded that I heal him. I can do no less," she answered. She was pretending to submit to her future father-in-law's wishes, but she was really anxious to get to the wounded man quickly and ease his suffering.

Matilda wished she had the power to make Sir Edmund leave Dynna alone. She shifted her position as a reminder to him that she was standing there with them, and was pleased when he let her go.

Edmund knocked on the door, and when Sir Thomas

opened it to them, he announced that he had brought Lady Dynna and her maid.

"My lady, it is good that you have come." Sir Thomas smiled warmly at Dynna.

She glanced across the room toward the bed where the Viking lay.

"He is not well. Two of the men had to help bring him up here," Sir Thomas explained.

"Is it the fever?" she asked, her expression clouded with worry.

"Aye."

"I had feared as much last evening. It is good that I am here now. He has lost much blood and will only grow worse without help."

"I had the men undress him so you could tend his wound." Sir Thomas stood back to allow them to enter. He had had one of the men take Brage's vest to Lord Alfrick, so he could give it to Hereld to take with him and prove to Anslak that Brage was their captive.

Dynna's gaze swept the chamber, and she found it little better than a prison cell. The windows were slits in the thick tower walls, suitable for defense with a bow and arrow but not for admitting much light or breeze. It was dark and dank and unfurnished save for the hard bed Brage lay upon and the small table beside it.

Dynna's breath caught in her throat at the sight of the Viking lying on the bed on his stomach, stripped of his clothing with only a sheet covering him to his waist. His broad back and powerful shoulders were laid bare to her gaze. It was then that she saw the wound for the first time and truly feared for his life. It was an ugly gash that was swollen and festering. She crossed the room to his side, expecting some movement, some recognition that she was there, but he was strangely still. His face was turned toward the wall. She did not know if he was conscious.

Edmund remained back by the door with Sir Thomas. She

still found his presence stifling, but was resigned to the fact that there was nothing she could do about it. He would leave her alone when he was ready to, and not before.

"Viking . . ." she said softly as she knelt beside the bed. "I have come to help you."

Brage heard Dynna's voice and turned his head to look at her. He wanted to get up, to face her as a warrior from a position of strength, but he could not summon the energy to do more than stare at her. "Why?" he asked hoarsely.

"I know you are in pain. I will do what I can to ease it." Dynna could see the hatred and distrust mirrored in his eyes, but what troubled her more was his weakened condition and the inflammation of his wound. His face was flushed with the heat of his fever and he was bloodstained and filthy from the days in battle and then in chains.

"I prefer death to endless torment, *my lady.*" Brage's voice was weak, but his sarcasm unmistakable.

"No one will torture you here," Dynna promised, reaching out to touch his shoulder, wanting to examine him.

Brage shifted away, trying to avoid her hands, but when he moved, pain slashed though him. The agony was so great that he moaned, weakened even more by the effort.

Dynna saw his distress and stood, returning to Sir Thomas and Matilda who were still standing by the open door. "Matilda, go to our chamber and bring my basket—quickly. Sir Thomas, I need water, hot water, and much of it."

"Yes, my lady." They both hurried away.

"Will he survive?" Edmund asked.

"I do not know. He has lost so much blood . . . and his wound is infected."

Dynna returned to Brage. His eyes were closed, his expression one of rigid control. She laid a hand upon his arm, and the heat emanating from him was almost scorching. She could not stifle a gasp as she looked closely at the ugly wound.

"It amazes me that you are this seriously injured and are

still alert. A lesser man would have been laid low by this," she said.

She remained by his side, talking to him in soft, comforting tones even though he did not respond. Edmund stood silently in the background, looking on in anger.

Sir Thomas returned, followed by two female servants carrying buckets of water. Edmund directed the women to bathe the prisoner. They were afraid of the Viking at first, but Sir Thomas told them he would stand guard while they washed him. Brage offered no resistance to their ministrations, uttering only a guttural sound when he was forced to move. The women hurriedly performed their duty, then covered him again and left the room.

Dynna met Matilda in the hall as she returned with her medicines. When the servants had gone, Dynna went back into the chamber to treat his injury. Sir Thomas remained there with her, standing back with Edmund to watch.

With a light and gentle touch, Dynna washed the festering wound.

Excruciating pain sliced through Brage as she cleansed the infected area, and he closed his eyes against the agony of it. He had thought he would not be tortured here. Sweat beaded his brow. He lay, his jaw locked, his every muscle rigid as she probed the gash. As harrowing as it was, though, he did not try to avoid her touch. His control over his body was complete. He remained still as she sought to help him.

"I am sorry," she told him in a low voice, knowing how much it had to hurt.

"Do what you must," he answered tightly.

"I am almost done with the washing."

She finished cleaning the wound, then quickly turned her attention to making the poultice that would both draw the poisons out and ease his pain. She mixed the herbs and a yellow powder made from roots into a thick paste.

"This will hurt when I put it on," she cautioned.

Brage nodded once and waited in tense anticipation for her to finish.

Dynna leaned over Brage and very carefully applied the healing plaster to the injury. A slight shudder wracked him as the medicine touched his damaged flesh, but other than that he did not move. She was amazed by the discipline he had over himself and knew this was just an example of his strength.

After binding the shoulder wound, Dynna turned her attention to the cut on the side of his head. Blood from that injury had dried and matted in his hair. As she started to wash it away, she felt Brage's gaze upon her. He watched her intently as she doctored the cut, applying the necessary medicine.

"You are very brave," she said, letting her hand rest on his arm.

Brage did not know why, but he found comfort in that simple touch. He told himself it was the fever that was making him weak.

Edmund saw the touch and was annoyed. "Have you finished?" he demanded of Dynna.

"For now."

"Then come with me. I will take you to my father, and we can tell him of the Viking's condition."

"I will go with you for a moment, but I must return and sit with him tonight. If his fever worsens, someone has to be here who knows how to help." She stood up and put away her medicines.

"I will stay until you return," Sir Thomas offered. "Then for the rest of the night, I will leave a guard outside the door."

"Thank you, Sir Thomas," Dynna said. "Also, could you have a chair and a cot brought in here. Matilda will be staying with me, and there is no reason why we cannot take turns resting while we watch his progress."

"As you wish, my lady."

Brage watched silently as Dynna left the room at Sir Edmund's side. He did not understand why the Saxons were suddenly concerned about his health. Now that they knew who he was, it seemed more logical to keep torturing him, to leave him hanging in the chains until he was dead.

The dizziness that had assailed him earlier was still with him, clouding his thinking, but he had to admit that the poultice she had used on his back was working. Already he could feel a blessed numbness in the wound, where before it had felt as if he were on fire. As the pain eased, a terrible weariness overtook Brage and he slept.

Lord Alfrick listened to Dynna's description of the Black Hawk's wounds. "Will he survive?"

"I cannot say for certain, my lord. It would have been far better if I had been allowed to treat him that first day. I could have prevented the infection. Now . . ." The seriousness of her concern showed clearly on her features. "It will be several days before I know. His fever is high."

"You will stay with him and do whatever is necessary to make sure he does not die. If there is anything you need, you have only to ask."

"Yes, my lord."

Dynna was pleased when she left the room and Sir Edmund remained behind to speak with his father. She hurried back up the steps to the chamber where Sir Thomas and a fierce-looking guard stood outside the door.

She immediately informed Sir Thomas of Lord Alfrick's dictate. "I will be taking all of my meals here," she told him. "Also, I will need food and drink for the captive. We cannot allow him to grow any weaker."

"I will speak to the servants right away."

Sir Thomas opened the door for her, and they went inside together to find that Brage was asleep.

"What of your safety, Lady Dynna? Shall I remain in here

with you to protect you from him? Or will Sir Edmund be returning to stay by your side?"

Dynna grimaced inwardly at the thought of Edmund's constant presence. She glanced from the sick Viking to Sir Thomas. "There is no reason for you to fear for my well-being. Matilda will be with me, and your man will be right outside the door. If you feel safer, you can lock the door from the outside to make certain he does not escape, but I believe we have nothing to fear from him."

"Do not be so sure. Never forget he is a warrior first."

"He will not harm me," she replied with certainty. "Matilda and I will be safe with him."

"Very well, but I will tell my man to stay alert."

"I appreciate your concern for us." She touched the older man's arm in a gesture of genuine friendship. It seemed no one else in the whole world cared about her safety except her parents, and they were far away and would never know of her desperation.

"You are my lady," he answered, feeling honored that she looked so benevolently upon him. She was one of the kindest, most unselfish people he knew.

"Since my husband died, you have been my one true friend here. My life here would have been totally barren without you and your strength and goodness."

"I will do whatever is necessary to keep you safe."

"Thank you." Her voice was almost a whisper, and she forced herself to look away from the tall, powerful man who had become her self-appointed protector.

"Is there anything else you need?"

"No. The most important thing is seeing that our captive lives through the night."

"My man will be near should you need him, and if you need me, just send word."

With that he left her.

Dynna returned to Brage's bedside and touched his arm again. The heat was still burning within him.

"Matilda, bring me a bucket of cold water and a cloth. I am going to bathe him again and attempt to get his fever down."

Matilda brought her the water and rag begrudgingly. "Why are you so concerned with saving this one's life? He is a warrior who would have slain all those in the tower had he not been struck down during the battle."

"I know you are probably right, Matilda, but . . ." Dynna paused, realizing the question was valid. She was not there solely because she had been ordered so by Lord Alfrick. She was there because she was truly worried about this man called the Black Hawk . . . this man who was known far and wide as the most fearless Norse raider to ever set sail.

"Why do you care so much about what happens to him?"

Dynna fell silent for a moment as she tried to put into words what she was feeling. When she finally spoke, Matilda could hear the confusion in her voice.

"I am not sure, Matilda, but ever since I first saw him when we were trying to escape, I have known he was special. He is a powerful man, but it is not his power that intrigues me. My father is a powerful man and so was Warren. And while he is handsome, Warren, too, was very appealing. No, this is different . . . There is something about him, Matilda . . . something exceptional. I cannot let him die."

Matilda was frowning. "Take care not to let Sir Edmund know how you feel, or he will not allow him to survive to be ransomed back to his family."

"We will have to keep careful watch over him. Will you help me?"

"I will do whatever I can for you."

Dynna's eyes met hers. "Thank you. This night will be a long one. I do not know if he will live through it."

"He has you to nurse him. He will live."

Dynna looked down at the feverish Viking and prayed that her gifts were powerful enough to save him.

# Seven

Time passed slowly for Dynna and Matilda as they took turns bathing Brage with cool water. They would start at his neck and, taking care to avoid his injured shoulder, would work their way down his back to the edge of the sheet at his waist. It was near midnight when Dynna realized Matilda could barely keep her eyes open.

"Go ahead to bed. You can sleep on the cot," Dynna encouraged.

"No, my lady. I cannot sleep when I know you are exhausted, too."

"One of us must rest while we can."

"Are you sure?"

Dynna nodded. "He is quiet. I will wake you if I need you. Now I have to keep watch over him. I will sleep later, I promise."

Matilda did as she was told, and she quickly fell asleep.

Dynna stayed beside the Viking's bed. She was exhausted, but she did not have time to worry about herself. It was Brage who worried her. All her efforts to cool him had proven of little value. His fever was raging even higher now.

Putting a hand to his brow, Dynna felt the dry, consuming heat and knew she should bathe him again. She got up with her empty bowl and went to the water bucket near the door. As she was dipping some out to take back to the bedside with her, she heard Brage moan and rushed back to his side.

"Traitor . . ." he mumbled, his eyes still closed, his tone slurred in his delirium. "They knew . . ."

"Shh . . . Easy . . . It will be all right," Dynna whispered, stroking his back with long, easy soothing strokes of the wet cloth she'd dipped in the water.

He seemed unaffected by her ministrations, and he did not seem to hear her words.

"Find them . . . I must find them . . ."

He began to move restlessly on the bed, and Dynna feared that he might dislodge the poultice.

"Easy, my Viking," she repeated softly. "Later, you can find whoever it is you seek. Right now, you must stay still and get well."

She continued to bathe him, trying to think of him only as someone who was hurt and in need of her help. But as she touched him again and again, running her hands over his hard-muscled flesh, she could not fail to notice the masculine beauty in the lean, sculpted power of his back and shoulders. He was strongly built, and though she was used to clean-shaven men, she found him handsome, even with his heavy beard. She wondered how he would look without the beard and decided that as soon as he was past this crisis she would see him cleaned up even more—with a shave and a trim of his hair.

"Ulf!"

The name was a shout coming from him, and Dynna was startled from her reverie.

"Again he protects my back . . ." It was half laugh, half harsh cry. "It is hot . . . Too hot . . . Kristoffer! No!"

In a fit of feverish panic, Brage tried to rise, his eyes wide and wild. Dynna was immediately at his side, speaking to him calmly, pressing him back down as she began to caress him again with her cooling massage.

Brage looked up at the woman who stood over him. In the semidarkness of the candlelit room, she looked ethereal . . . dream-like. She was a vision, floating gently before him in the mist of his fever. She was beautiful—her dark hair, her flowing gown, her lovely features. He managed a twisted smile as he tried to ignore his pain.

"Ah, Valkyrie . . . So, you have come for me at last."

"I am no Valkyrie. I have no wish to see you in Valhalla, Viking. Drink this." Dynna pressed a cup to his lips filled with a potion she hoped would help him.

Brage drank what he could, then collapsed back down on the bed, his eyes closed once more. "The legends are true," he said in a groan. "The Valkyries are the most beautiful of women . . ."

Dynna found she was trembling when he finally fell into his feverish slumber again. She feared that his delirium would worsen and he might reinjure himself by thrashing around. For a moment, she thought of restraining him, but was immediately repelled by the idea. He had been chained long enough. Besides, she reasoned, he had quieted when she had spoken to him. She prayed he would continue to listen to her, for he was a very strong man, and if he decided to get up, she doubted she would have the strength to stop him, even as sick as he was.

For two days and two nights, Dynna remained by Brage's side, fighting death. His condition worsened instead of improving, and his burning fever tested her healing abilities to the limits. She slept little, dozing only occasionally in the chair.

Dynna suffered through Sir Edmund's daily visits. Every time she saw him she was reminded that each passing day brought her that much closer to marrying him. The thought destroyed what little peace she had.

It was near midnight of the third night that Dynna and Matilda sat together in the room that had become a torture chamber for them.

"Will he live the night?" Matilda asked.

"I do not know," Dynna answered truthfully, lifting her worried gaze to her maid's. "He has not had anything to drink for hours."

"There is nothing more you can do, my lady. You have tried everything."

"All there is left for us to do is pray," she said solemnly as she gazed down at his flushed features.

Brage smiled. He was home with his father and brothers, hunting, riding, and enjoying life. The mountains were snow-capped, and the waters were cool and inviting. Home . . .

A myriad of images played through his thoughts. In the distance, he could see the lovely Inger waving to him and calling his name. He thought of the sweet good-bye the blond beauty had given him. Her kisses had promised much for his return, and he knew she would be waiting. Odd that the knowledge did not excite him, for he knew his father would be most pleased if they were to wed.

Suddenly, he felt hot. Strangely so. He longed to be higher up in the mountains where the air was cold and pure. Heat pulsed through him, throbbing and burning. Brage shifted, seeking the coolness of the mountain breeze, wanting the chill of it to sweep over him, but there was no relief. He began to move restlessly, needing to escape the smothering, oppressive heat.

He tried to rise, but pain shot through him, shattering the images of home and the bliss of being with his family. There was only pain and fire and agony throughout his body. He groaned, unable to suffer in silence and deny the torment any longer.

"Quiet, my Viking," a soft, feminine voice called to him through the mist of his consciousness. "Lie still, let me help you."

"Help me?" he repeated, his tone deep and hoarse from lack of use.

It was quiet for a moment, and then the cooling motions started. He was vaguely aware that there was an almost sensuous rhythm to the cool water being stroked upon him. It chilled him and he shivered.

"That is better," the woman said. "Much better."

The caressing continued, each touch of the wet cloth dampening the fire that consumed him.

Brage fought his way up from the pain-seared depths, and he finally managed to open his eyes. Above him was a beautiful woman. He thought she seemed familiar, but he could not recall where he had met her.

"You are still here . . ."

"I will not leave you until your fever has broken." She touched his shoulder.

Her hand upon him was cool, and he closed his eyes again. Peace was close. If only he could find it . . .

His mind wandered to memories of the battle. The peace he had sought vanished as a vision of his dead men haunted him.

"Ulf! Beware! They know . . . Who could have told Lord Alfrick? Why would anyone have betrayed us?"

"Do not worry so, Viking. It is all past. Just rest and let your body heal," the woman called to him through the haze of his pain.

"Cannot forget . . ." he mumbled, knowing there was a traitor in his father's midst, knowing he had to find him and reveal him before he cost more Vikings their lives. The traitor had to be punished for his unfaithfulness. "Will not forget."

He tried to get up, but gentle hands settled him back down.

"Do not resist me. Rest for now. There will be time later for your battles, but this is not the hour."

Brage wanted to rise and seek out the man who had brought death and destruction to him and his men. His rage was as hot as his fever.

"You have no strength, warrior. What good would you be in a fight? You do not have the power to lift your sword.

Rest. Get your strength back. You risk your own life when you move so violently."

The voice and hands that quieted him worked on his body, but all the wisdom and kindness in the world could not ease the torment that filled him. His men had died, and, as their leader, he was responsible.

"Drink this."

Brage felt a cup pressed to his lips, and, at the woman's urging, he drank thirstily of the bitter brew. Moments after he lay back down, forgetfulness began to edge his mind. A short time later he was once again asleep, the medicinal tonic having given him at least that much peace.

The sighting of Brage's longships by Anslak's lookout was heralded by the sounding of the horns. The haunting call echoed through the fjords and announced to the people of Anslak's village that some of their own were returning from their ventures afar.

As always when a ship came home, the people hurried to watch. They had expected another of their men, one of the traders who had been gone to the east for many months.

Anslak had been riding the fields, encouraging those who tended the crops, when he heard the call. Pleased that one of his men had returned, he put his heels to his mount and raced for the water's edge. He thought it would be a trader, and he was eager to see what riches they were bringing back from their travels and to hear tales of their adventures.

When Anslak reached the summit of the hill overlooking the fjord, he reined in abruptly. There, far below, he could see the ships pulling in, and he went still as he saw the sail of the Black Hawk. Brage was back . . .

The Viking leader was elated by his son's quick return. He believed it meant that their raid had met with success. They must have attacked and looted quickly and then made their escape. He was proud of his son, and he urged his horse down the hillside toward the longships, eager to hear all about the raid.

Tove, Anslak's second wife and Kristoffer's mother, heard the call and hurried to join the others in welcome. She, too, was surprised to find Brage's ships had returned so soon. They had been gone less than two weeks. She stood with the villagers expecting wonderful news.

Anslak reached the welcoming group and, seeing his wife among them, left his horse and went to her.

"No one fights like the Black Hawk's warriors." He was near to bursting with pride. "I am sure they lived up to their reputations. Why else would they be back already?"

"Can you see Kristoffer?" Tove stared hard at the closing crafts, searching for some sign of her only son.

Anslak lifted a hand to shield the sun from his eyes as he studied the lead ship, trying to recognize the men onboard. "I see Ulf . . ."

Tove waited excitedly for him to say more.

"And our son," he finished.

She smiled. "He returns safely. That is good. I had begun to miss him already."

"And to think you are a Viking's wife . . ." Anslak teased her. She never seemed to grow accustomed to Kristoffer's going raiding. Even though he was a man full grown, she still doted on him as if he were a babe.

"I miss you, too, when you are gone. I am always thrilled when you return," she told him, slipping an arm about his waist.

"I know," he said with a sensuous chuckle that brought a blush to her cheeks.

He turned his attention back to the ships and watched as they were brought in. As the men started to come ashore, a cheer went up to celebrate their return. But the cheering waned as many of those expecting loved ones did not see their men among the warriors.

"Where is my Seger?" Marta, his wife, asked the woman standing next to her.

"I do not see him or my Neils, either. And where is Brage? Usually the Black Hawk is the first one ashore."

Ulf and Kristoffer climbed from Brage's lead ship and walked toward the waiting crowd. Their expressions were somber, reflecting the grave news they brought.

"Kristoffer . . . Ulf . . . Where is Brage?" Anslak asked immediately, his expression growing worried as he glanced from them, back to the ship.

"The news is not good, Father," Kristoffer offered. He had been dreading this moment throughout the whole voyage. How could they tell their father that Brage was gone . . . dead . . .

"What happened?" he demanded. "And where is Brage? It is not like him not to come ashore right away."

The onlookers crowded closer to hear what was being said. Those who saw their relatives ran to meet them. Those who missed their kin wanted to know what had happened to them.

"There was an ambush on the way to Lord Alfrick's tower. It was as if the Saxons had known ahead of time that we were coming. Many men were lost . . ." Ulf explained, his eyes were dark with pain.

"And Brage? What of Brage?" Anslak demanded, his expression hardening as he anticipated what was about to be told him. "Where is my son?"

"He is dead, Father." Kristoffer said. "He was killed in the fighting."

Cries of horror went up from all who heard the news.

"Brage is dead?" Anslak was shocked.

Kristoffer explained all that had led to this tragedy.

"He was so certain he would surprise Lord Alfrick," Anslak said this as statement. "How could this have happened?"

Ulf and Kristoffer shared a look. Then Ulf answered, "We

can only think the Saxons somehow knew of our plans. Their numbers were great and they were fully armed. It was as if they had prepared for our attack."

"How many were lost?" Anslak asked, his gaze sweeping over those coming ashore.

"More than fifty," Kristoffer told him.

The villagers realized then that their loved ones were not among the surviving warriors, and they wept in sorrow.

"You are certain Brage is dead?" Anslak repeated.

"I saw him fall," Ulf stared at the ground, unable to meet his father's searching gaze.

"Ulf and I went back after dark to try to find him, but the Saxons had burned the bodies. There was nothing left . . ." Kristoffer explained in a voice heavy with sorrow.

The death of his son left Anslak numb. Brage. His beloved child dead.

Images of Brage swam before him. He saw Brage returning triumphantly from his first raid; Brage gaining stature among his peers until he was their unchallenged leader; Brage confident and ready as he prepared to sail for the Saxon coast.

Anslak's thoughts drifted back even further in time then, and he remembered Brage's birth and how Mira, his beloved first wife, had died presenting him with a son. Mira . . . At the thought of her, pain knifed through the protective armor of his stunned grief. Brage had been his only connection to his adored Mira, and now he was gone . . . dead, too, just as she was. The twisting agony in his chest was almost too much for him to bear.

Tove was staring up at her husband, her eyes wide and filled with disbelief. "Brage cannot be dead. He was the finest of warriors. How could this have happened?"

"We were outnumbered and almost surrounded. There was no chance to take the tower," Ulf continued. "When Brage was killed, the men knew the battle was lost. We withdrew to the ships and, after trying to find Brage that night, we headed here."

"Oh, Anslak . . ." Tove clung to her husband, trying to comfort him. "I am so sorry."

Pain seared every fiber of Anslak's being as he spoke to Ulf and Kristoffer. "We will talk of this more later."

He kept an arm around Tove as he turned away from the sight of Brage's longships and the bloodred sail that bore the mark of the Black Hawk.

That night the men gathered in the main room of Anslak's house to speak of the voyage. Their mood was solemn. Death had touched them, and those who had survived knew they were lucky to be alive.

Each man mourned the Black Hawk in his own way. As the wine and beer were served, many a mug and drinking horn were raised in his honor. All knew the Black Hawk had gone to Valhalla. He was a brave and fearless leader who had died in battle. There were no others who could match him and he would be sorely missed by his followers.

Anslak was devastated. His faith in his son's abilities had never allowed him to consider that Brage might not return from a raid. He sat in mourning that evening, drinking wine and regretting the fact that he never had the chance to tell Brage good-bye.

"To my son," Anslak said, his voice choked with emotion, his eyes filled with tears. He stood and lifted his drinking horn high. "To the Black Hawk!" He took a deep drink.

Cheers went up from his men as they, too, drank to Brage.

Ulf was standing nearby, and at the gesture, he drank deeply, too, then set his mug aside and strode from the room. His expression was taut.

Anslak sat back down at the table. Across from him, Kristoffer watched him in his sorrow and wished there was something he could do to ease his torment.

"How could this have happened, Kristoffer? Brage planned the raid with care. And the runes . . . they promised him a great treasure, one greater than any he had ever won before." Anslak made a scoffing sound as he remembered the prophecy. "What great treasure has he claimed? Valhalla? I would have preferred he gain gold and remain here." His words were bitter.

"I do not know how this happened to us," he answered. "I only know that it seemed they knew our plan as well as we did."

"But how?"

"A traitor, perhaps? How else could Lord Alfrick have been so well armed?"

Anslak's gaze was sharp as it rested upon him. "Who would betray their leader? Only family and his best warriors knew of the plan. Who would turn traitor?"

"Who, indeed?" Kristoffer returned. "I have been thinking on this since the battle. Who had the most to gain if Brage was dead? Who wanted everything he had and more? Who would seek his honor and place as leader of the men?"

Anslak glanced around the room at the warriors who sat there with him. Of all those who had returned, only Ulf was not present. He wondered where he had gone. "I do not know, but I will find out, even if it's the last thing I do."

Anslak fell silent, thinking of Brage. His son had been a careful warrior. He had been as smart as he was powerful. For this terrible thing to have happened, the traitor had to have been someone Brage trusted. Infuriated by the possibility that someone in that very room had set Brage up to be killed, Anslak rose and slammed a mug down on the table to get their attention.

"Heed my words! It is rumored that a betrayal is suspected in the raid that has cost my son and his men their lives." He paused while the undercurrent traversed the room. "If one of you did betray Brage, know this! I will hunt you down to the ends of the earth to make you pay for his death!"

Another roar went up, for the men who had lost friends

in the battle were more than anxious to find the one responsible.

Anslak wished with all his might that he could identify the man who had caused Brage's death. He tried to guess who it could have been. He doubted that it was any of those who had sailed with him. Only a fool would have betrayed his leader and then joined him in the attack. It had to have been someone who had overheard their plans being made and had alerted the Saxons. But who? It frustrated him to think that he might never learn the traitor's identity. The man was as much a coward as a murderer, and Anslak firmly believed he deserved to be cast into eternal agony.

It was almost dark as Ulf strode away from the house. He could hear the sound of his father's voice as he vowed to find the traitor, and his mood turned even more grim. He was heading toward the water, hoping to seek some peace there, when he heard a woman call out to him.

"Ulf! Wait! I must talk to you!"

Looking around, Ulf found Inger running toward him. As she drew near, he could see the look of stricken desperation on her face and knew that she had heard the news of Brage's death.

Ulf knew that she had always held high hopes that she would one day marry his half-brother, but he was not so sure that Brage had shared her feelings. Pretty though she was with her silver-blond hair, pale-blue eyes, and slender form, he had not sensed that Brage loved her. His brother had never spoken of her except in passing, and when he did, there had been no great passion voiced on his part.

"Ulf . . . tell me it is not true!" Inger cried as she stopped before him. Her face was tear-ravaged and her hands were trembling as she reached out frantically to him. "Brage cannot be dead! He just cannot!"

Ulf's expression softened as he stared down at her and saw her heartbreak. Her emotions were very real. He felt awkward being the one to confirm the bad news, yet there was no way to soften the pain. "I am sorry, Inger."

Her hands on his arm gripped him tightly as she asked in a tormented, "Sorry? Sorry, for what?"

"What you have heard is true. Brage was killed in the raid, as were many of his men."

"But they said you did not bring his body back. He could still be alive. You could go back for him . . ." she pleaded, not wanting to accept the truth and the pain that came with it.

"Inger," he went on gently, "Kristoffer and I both saw him fall. He did not get up. We even went back later that night after the fighting was done to search for him. But all we found were the funeral pyres. My brother did not survive."

"But he could just have been . . ."

"Enough." Ulf's tone was commanding. "Do you not think that Kristoffer and I would go anywhere and do anything in our power if it would mean bringing Brage back to us? But it was too late, Inger. He was slain, struck down from behind. There will be no rescue. His body was burned by our enemies. We will not see him again."

A sob tore from her as the terrible truth settled in. She swayed weakly, and thinking she was about to faint, Ulf moved quickly to lift her into his arms.

"Inger . . ." He said her name a little fearfully, not quite sure what to do with her.

"I am sorry, Ulf," she managed weakly as she cried, "but I cannot believe he is dead . . ." Inger had always realized raiding was dangerous, but Brage had seemed invincible.

"You must try to accept that he will never return. We must all try."


Brage came awake slowly. He ached all over. Not an inch of his body was safe from the nagging discomfort. But somehow, this pain was different from the agony he had been suffering. He lifted his head a little to look around and was amazed to find Lady Dynna sitting in a chair next to the bed.

Brage had faint, fever-clouded memories of her trying to help him when he was in chains and a distant recollection of her nursing him once he had been brought up to this room.

He braced himself up on one elbow, expecting her to notice him moving. It was then, when she remained quiet and unmoving, that he realized she was asleep. He took the time to study her and saw that she looked exhausted. There were dark circles under her eyes and a weary slump to her shoulders as she dozed, and he wondered why she was so tired.

Lying flat on the bed suddenly seemed torturous to him. Brage pushed himself up and struggled to sit. He felt the stabbing reminder of his shoulder wound and gave a small grunt in pained acknowledgment that he would have to move more slowly.

Dynna had not meant to nap, but the long endless hours of keeping vigil at Brage's bedside had taken their toll on her. Matilda had gone off to tend to other duties, and Dynna had remained alone with the Viking, save for the guard outside the door. She had bathed him yet another time, wanting to wash the hated fever from his body, yet all her efforts seemed for naught. Nothing she had tried in the past few days had had any real effect on the fever that was burning the very life from him. Weary beyond measure, she had all but collapsed into the chair after trying to get him to drink another dose of her healing potion.

His groan woke her instantly. She expected him to be worse and was prepared to do whatever was necessary for him. At the sight of Brage sitting up, she almost panicked.

"Stay where you are. Be careful. Do not move . . ." she cautioned, thinking he was delirious and might harm himself. "Please, just stay still. I will bathe you again and then . . ."

"Bathe me?" he asked.

The sanity of his words brought her up short.

"You are better?" she gasped, really looking into his eyes for the first time. She hurried to touch first his shoulder and then his brow. Dynna expected him to still be feverish, and she was thrilled to find he felt cool. Her relief was tremendous.

"It would seem so."

"You are improved . . ." She smiled, her first in days. "You had better lie back down."

"I cannot. I have to sit up. I have been still too long." As he said it, he knew it was true, for he felt lethargic and weak, and the room seemed to spin dizzily around him.

"You have been very ill. Your fever was high, and I have been afraid for the last two days that you would not survive," she explained.

"Why would you care whether I lived or died, my lady? Why did you work so hard to save me?" His eyes bored into hers, demanding the truth.

Dynna had known the power of Brage's blue-eyed gaze from the first time she met him. And in that moment, as their gazes locked, she felt as if he could see into her very soul. She turned half away from him, blushing. "I would do the same for any wounded animal."

Her words stung him, and he reached out to snare her arm. He turned her to face him.

Dynna stared down at his hand on her arm, amazed by the unsettling sensations that were sweeping through her at his touch.

"Somehow, I do not believe that."

"Believe what you will." She tried to sound indifferent.

"I believe what I know, and I know the Saxons never do anything without a reason. So tell me, my lady, what is your plan? What do you want from me?"

"I want nothing from you," Dynna insisted.

"Then why did you save me?" His gaze held hers in challenge. "Why did you not let me die?"

"When your men found Matilda and me and brought us before you that morning of the battle, you could have had us killed, but you did not. I could not let any more harm befall you."

Brage regarded her without speaking for a long moment, not sure whether to believe her or not. He sensed there was far more to it than she was revealing, but he decided not to force the issue right then. He would go along with her for now, and just give thanks that he was still alive. He released her.

"Then I thank you for your help. You obviously are a very skilled healer. I do feel better," he finally said, giving a hesitant lift of his shoulder to test it. He only grimaced slightly.

Dynna was glad when he let her go. There was something about the touch of his hands upon her, restraining yet not painful, that disturbed her. She busied herself with bringing him a cup of her healing potion, so she would not have to think about the confusing feelings he aroused within her. "Drink this."

"What is it?"

"A tonic that will help rebuild your strength. I will send for some food for you, too. You have not eaten for days, and you will not really begin to feel better until you have had something solid."

Brage was in agreement. He wanted his strength back—and fast. He did not know what these Saxons wanted from him, but he wanted to be strong enough to deal with it when the time came. "There is one other thing." At her questioning look, he went on. "A pair of pants would be good."

Dynna could not prevent the high color that stained her cheeks. "Of course."

For now, Brage decided he would play the invalid a while longer and let Dynna think that he was weaker than he was. He did not want to be put back into the chains. Here in this room he could move around a little bit and possibly find a way to escape. Chained to the wall in the Great Hall again, he would be totally without hope.

Brage watched as Dynna opened the door and spoke to the guard outside. It would not be easy to get out of there, but when the first opportunity to escape came, he would take it.

# Eight

Knowing that Brage was finally out of danger, Dynna was able to relax her vigil. For several days, she remained abed much later than usual in the morning. When she finally did awaken, she enjoyed a bath and then a leisurely breakfast in her room. She visited Brage regularly and she was pleased with the progress he seemed to be making. On this particular morning, three days later, she was feeling quite refreshed as she made her way up to the tower room and greeted Perkin, the guard at the door.

"Good morning, Lady Dynna. The servant you sent to tend to the prisoner is with him now," Perkin said, smiling at her in welcome.

"Good." She returned his smile, pleased to learn that the morning was going so smoothly.

She was just about to enter the room when the portal flew open and the maid came running out.

"Anny . . . ? Is something wrong?" Dynna was startled by the look of fright on the girl's face. She wondered what Brage could have done to send the poor young woman fleeing in such terror.

"Lady Dynna . . ." the maid gasped. "That . . . that Viking . . . He is a demon!"

"A demon? What are you talking about? Did you shave him and cut his hair as I ordered?" Dynna glanced past the servant into the room, but she could not see Brage from where she stood.

Anny gulped nervously, her eyes wide with fright as she kept moving forward, out of the room, away from the prisoner. "I tried, my lady, honest I did, but he would not let me near him. He threatened me, he did! Said he would toss me out the window if I even came near him with the knife . . . and he meant it, too! I could see the meanness in his eyes! Oh, that Black Hawk is a dangerous one! It will be a fine day for us all when he is either dead or gone!"

"You had a guard right outside. All you had to do was call for help," she reminded her.

"Please, Lady Dynna, do not make me go back in there with him again! He scares me with those cold blue eyes of his! I know he is a monster!"

"He is no monster, Anny." She tried to calm her.

"He is a *Viking!*" The loathing in the word described her feelings perfectly.

"All right." Dynna sighed in frustration. "Go back to your chores in the kitchen."

"Yes, my lady. Here!" Anny held out the knife to her, ready to get away from there as quickly as she could.

Dynna struggled to keep from smiling as she took the blade from her. She remembered her first encounter with Brage and could understand how Anny could be so intimidated. With the longer hair and full beard, not to mention just the size of him, he was an impressive specimen of a man, even weak as he was.

"Do you want me to go in with you, my lady? If you are afraid, I can stay with you," Perkin offered after Anny had fled down the stairs to the safety of the kitchen. He had seen the other woman's fear and was not about to let anything happen to Lady Dynna.

"No, there is no need. I will be fine."

He looked skeptical as he stood back to allow her entry to the room. Despite her assurances otherwise, he was determined he would keep careful watch to make sure she was not harmed.

Dynna was ready for whatever battle of wills Brage wanted to wage. He had to be in a fine mood if he could frighten Anny so badly. When she had checked on his shoulder wound late the day before it had appeared to be coming along nicely. Still, his injuries had been serious and the fever fierce. It would take him some time to fully recover, and it was important to that recovery to clean him up. That was why she had sent Anny to him, and now, that was why she was going to do the job herself, no matter what his protest.

Dynna knew she was in for an argument when she found Brage sitting up on the side of the bed, scowling blackly, stroking his beard. She went to stand before him, her expression as serious as she could make it.

"You terrified the poor servant girl," she said.

"She came at me with a knife," he growled.

"You know very well that she was here at my bidding."

"To slay me?" He glanced up at her mockingly.

"Slay you? Hardly. She was sent to shave you."

"Slay or shave, it does not matter. Either way, as badly as her hand was shaking, I thought my life in jeopardy. One slip of her hand at my throat and—"

"Had you not intimidated her so fiercely, she would have been fine."

"There is no need for the beard to be shaved."

"It will go," she stated firmly.

"I have worn a beard since I was old enough to grow one." He raised one thick brow mockingly, his gaze challenging as it met hers.

"You are still not fully recovered and must stay abed for a while longer. You will not be so fond of your long hair and beard if it gets infested with lice. It will be much easier to keep you clean while you are recuperating if you are clean-shaven and your hair is shorter."

"And if I refuse?"

"You cannot. You are my patient."

"I am your prisoner," Brage stated flatly.

"Either way," she said with a grin she could not hide, "you are at my mercy. If you do not agree to let me shave you..."

"You will shave me?" he asked quickly.

"I will shave you," she repeated with emphasis. "But if you resist, I will call in the guard and have him hold you down till the task is done. Either way, by the midday meal, you will be clean-shaven and your hair will be trimmed. Which will it be, Viking? Will you fight me or surrender?"

Once again, Brage had to admire her courage. She did not flinch before him as the silly maid had done. It had been a simple thing to send the maid running from the room with one threatening look. Dynna, however, was made of sterner stuff. His reluctant admiration for her grew. "I find the thought of you taking a blade to me far more appealing than trusting the wench who just fled here in terror."

"If I were you, I would be more worried."

"If you had wanted to see me dead, my lady, it would have been a simple matter to let me die from the fever. I doubt my life is in danger from your hand."

"Only your hair and beard will suffer a cruel fate from me, unless, of course, you are foolish enough to move while I work. Come, sit on the chair, so I can reach you easily."

Brage mumbled something unintelligible, frustrated that there was no escaping this new torture she had devised. He took the seat and then gritted his teeth as she closed in on him.

Dynna tried to comb some semblance of order to his thick hair. Then with great care, for the blade was sharp, she began to lift sections of his dark mane and trim it short.

Brage sat perfectly still as she moved quietly about him, gently tugging his hair in her effort to shear him. He despised the idea of being made to look like his captors, yet he realized in a way she was doing him a favor. Should the opportunity to escape present itself, he would be far less likely to stand out among the people clean-shaven and with shorter hair.

Dynna's hands upon him were soft, and the perfumed scent of her was heady and teased him whenever she leaned near. He reminded himself that this woman was his enemy, and yet . . . Brage found himself frowning at nothing in particular.

Dynna was trying to be gentle as she trimmed away his long locks. His hair was thick, and it took her a while to finish with the heavy mane. When at last she was done trimming, she stepped back to survey her handiwork. Though his unruly beard still dominated his face, his hair lay neat and tamed.

"Better. Much better."

"I am glad you think so," he told her, staring down at the hair on the floor.

"Now, for your beard."

He said nothing, but met her eyes as she came to stand before him. He knew there was no escaping the fate she had set for him, and he set his jaw against the degradation of his position. He, the Black Hawk, had been reduced to this—being shorn by a woman, and a Saxon woman at that. Still, he had to admit as she began to trim away the longest part of the growth, that she was one fine-looking Saxon woman.

On several occasions as Dynna labored at her self-appointed duty, Brage was tempted to squirm. It was not an entirely painless ritual, but somehow he maintained his control and did not move. When at last the heaviest part had been cut away, she stood back to look at him.

"Are you done?" he asked hopefully, rubbing his chin to discover that there was still a stiff growth remaining on his jaw.

"No. Not yet."

Dynna got a bowl of water and soap and rubbed a lather to apply to his cheeks to soften the rest of the bristle. He growled as she turned and came toward him.

"Surely you will not give me trouble now. The guard is

but a call away," she reminded him, feeling quite powerful as she stood over him ready to lather him, knife still in hand.

"In truth, my lady, a knife in your hand when you are angry would give me more pause than any threat from the weakling guard," he countered.

Dynna could not help but smile as she leaned closer to put the soap to his cheeks and then scrape the last of the offending growth from his face.

Brage could have finished the task himself—if she would have trusted him with the blade. But they were enemies, and he knew she would not hand it over.

As she moved about him, her breath was sweet upon his cheek and her body brushed against his as she strove to shave him cleanly. The touch of her against him stirred him, and that surprised him. He told himself she was merely a woman, a lovely one, but still just a woman. It was normal that he would find her attractive, even if she was the enemy. It was then the realization came to him that he didn't think of Dynna as an enemy. What foe would have tried to save him, not once but several times, in spite of his own near violent rebuff? What adversary would have stayed by his side night and day to nurse him, when it would have been far easier to let him die? She was not his enemy. But if not that, then what?

Dynna would never have admitted it openly, but she was enjoying the intimacy of shaving Brage. It had been one thing to think of him as an attractive man while she had nursed him, but now that he was up and recovering, she felt an attraction to him that both frightened and excited her. She told herself that even though he had kept her and Matilda from harm, he was not her friend. As Anny had pointed out, he was a *Viking*. And yet, there was something there that drew her to him, and she knew she had to fight it.

Brage was feeling more and more naked as she finished shaving him. When she moved in front of him to scrape the last remaining whiskers from his chin, the look on his face was thunderous. She paused, fearing she had truly hurt him in some way.

"Are you in pain?"

"The only pain I suffer is that of being made to look like the Saxons," he told her, grimacing as he ran a hand across the bare nape of his neck.

"It is an improvement, I say." And she meant it. The shorter hair brought more emphasis to his eyes and their penetrating, blue intensity. His jaw, bared to her gaze now, was firm and strong. He had been intriguing before, but now, seeing his face clearly for the first time, she found the hard, masculine lines of his face mesmerizing.

He grunted as he rubbed his jaw again and found it smooth.

"I think perhaps having you at my mercy is not such a bad thing."

"You do hold the blade." He glanced down at the weapon she held, knowing he could take it from her in an instant—if he wanted to. But even as he considered it, he also knew that this was not the time. He needed to regain more strength, so that when he did make his escape he could travel far and fast.

"And there is the guard," she reminded him almost sweetly.

"It would seem that fate has decreed that I am to be in your power. But I wonder, Lady Dynna, how you expect me to remain this clean-shaven? Would you shave me every day or leave me the knife so that I might do the deed myself?"

"I think, perhaps, one of the servants will tend to it from now on."

He smiled slightly, remembering how easy it had been to intimidate the one woman. If Dynna was not wont to shave him, he might have his beard back sooner than he thought.

"The men are well versed in shaving," she went on, after seeing the look in his eyes. "I am sure there are any number of Sir Thomas's guards who would derive pleasure in taking a knife to you. Now I will be back later to look in on you."

His smile faded as she left him. He heard the door being barred after she had gone, and he was reminded once again of his situation. For a moment, while she had been there, he had managed to think of other things besides his captivity, but alone again, he knew he had to start planning. He forced himself to stand and tried to walk around the room. The sooner he got his strength back, the better.

Hereld traveled as quickly as he could, but there was no fast or easy way to Anslak's village. It had been several years since he had last met the Viking leader, and while Hereld knew the general location, he was not certain of the exact site. It took him two extra days, but he finally located the fjord that led to the secluded and protected settlement.

Hereld could almost smell the gold that would soon be his. It would not be long now. All he had to do was meet with Anslak, get him to agree to the ransom, and then set up the meeting place so the exchange could be made. He would soon be a very well-to-do merchant. He mentally rubbed his hands together in delight over the idea as he sailed toward the village landing area.

The horns sounded his coming, and the people came down to meet the ship. Hereld was welcomed cautiously into their midst.

"What brings you to our village?" Lynsey, one of the men, asked as Hereld climbed from his craft and walked up the bank toward those gathered there.

"I am Hereld, trader and merchant by profession. I have come seeking Anslak. This is his village, is it not?"

"Aye, you have found the right place. What do you wish to see him about?"

"It is an important matter, so it would be best if I spoke to him directly."

"Very well. I will take you to his house."

Hereld left his small crew behind on the ship as he followed the villager up the rocky hillside toward the town. They reached Anslak's home, and Lynsey called out for him.

Tove emerged from inside.

"We have a visitor, Tove," Lynsey informed her. "He wishes to talk to Anslak."

"My husband is not here right now." She turned to look at the stranger. "What is it you needed of him? I am his wife. Perhaps I can help you."

Hereld thought for a moment, and then decided to tell her of his mission. Certainly, word of his coming might reach the Viking leader faster if he knew how crucial the matter was.

"I have come bearing news from Lord Alfrick's land."

Ulf had seen the stranger speaking to Tove and approached curiously. When he heard him mention the Saxon lord, he interrupted.

"What of Lord Alfrick?" His manner was tense and threatening as he loomed over the smaller man.

Tove was glad Ulf had joined the conversation, for she was not quite sure what to make of this man.

"Who are you?" Hereld demanded.

"I am Ulf. Anslak is my father. What news do you bring about Lord Alfrick?"

"Tell your father that Lord Alfrick has sent a message for him. Tell him that after your raid, something very valuable was left behind. Tell him that Lord Alfrick wants a ransom for the return . . ."

Ulf's eyes narrowed suspiciously. "What are you talking about? Do not speak in riddles. Tell me straight out what it is you know."

Hereld decided to blurt out everything. "I have come bearing news that Lord Alfrick holds the Black Hawk prisoner. He knows that the Black Hawk is the son of Anslak, and he will ransom him back to his father for six hundred pounds of gold."

"You lie!" Ulf exploded, snatching the man up by the front of his tunic, giving him a violent shake. Fear lanced Ulf's heart. Brage could not be alive. They had seen him slain. They had searched for him.

"Lie?" Hereld protested. "Why would I lie?"

"For gold, of course." His icy gaze pinned the man with contempt. "I have dealt with your kind before. You will get no fool's gold from us. Be gone, before my father thrashes you himself."

"I will not leave! Lord Alfrick has sent me here to tell Anslak that the Black Hawk lives, and I have proof to back up my words!"

"Proof?" Kristoffer had heard Ulf's exclamations and had come out of the house to learn more. "What proof could there be? We saw him killed. You dare to give us hope that our brother survived!?"

"You saw him wounded, and wounded he was—severely. But Lord Alfrick has seen to it that he was healed. He holds him now for the ransom. Will you pay? Or shall I return and tell him he was mistaken, that the Black Hawk's life is of no importance to you?"

His challenge increased Ulf's fury. "What proof do you have?"

"His vest . . ." Hereld dug into his pouch and drew out Brage's vest. "See the rend and the bloodstains? The wound was serious, but it was not fatal. Your brother is alive and a captive of Lord Alfrick."

Ulf snatched the garment from his hands and knew immediately that it was his brother's. "How did you come by this?"

"It was taken from him when they treated his wounds. Once they discovered who he was, they could not let him die. They will take fine care of him until you pay the ransom."

"Lynsey, go find my father. Kristoffer, ride with him," Ulf ordered brusquely as he crushed the garment in his hands. Doubt raged through him. This man had to be a liar—an opportunist who had come on his own to stake a false claim to riches. He had to be, and yet, if Brage were alive . . . They would have to proceed, but they would have to be careful.

Tove invited the trader in and served him a drink as they waited for Anslak's return. As they sat in the Viking leader's home, Ulf wondered how his father would respond to the news, if he would believe this man. The whole village had been grieving since learning of the deaths of Brage and his men. He hoped this was not a scheme invented by a greedy merchant to fatten his coffers.

More than an hour passed before Lynsey and Kristoffer arrived back at the house with Anslak.

"Tove! Ulf! What is this story that Lynsey and Kris have brought me?" Anslak bellowed as he stormed inside. "Where is this merchant, that I may look in his eye as he speaks and see the truth of his words?"

Since hearing the tale, a fragile bud of hope had been planted in Anslak's breast. He was trying with all his might to temper it. He had accepted, albeit painfully, the news of his son's death, and now . . . It would be cruel to nurture hope, if these were lies the man was telling. It was Anslak's dream, his heart's wish, his one and only hope that Brage would be alive. If this man could show him real proof that his son lived, he would pay any price to have Brage back.

"Anslak, it is good to see you again. I am Hereld. We dealt together some time ago in Birka."

"I remember our meeting," he said, recalling their encounter at that trade center and eyeing him cautiously. He knew the man to be a shrewd bargainer. "What is this news you bring of my son Brage? All who sailed with him believed him to be dead, and yet you bring news that he lives?"

"I do, and I have proof to show you." He gestured toward Ulf, who still had the vest.

Ulf held it up for his father to see.

"That is his," Kristoffer confirmed.

"But it is no proof that he lives," Ulf argued. "This is only proof that you found his body on the battlefield."

"He was found, wounded but alive, at the scene of the fighting. He was taken before Lord Alfrick, and when he was recognized as the Black Hawk, Lord Alfrick decided to ransom him back to you."

Anslak went to Ulf and took the garment from him. He studied the slash across the back and the dried blood upon it. "It was indeed a grievous wound," he said in a harsh voice.

"Alfrick knew he was valuable, so he saw to it that a healer nursed him. The Black Hawk is recovering."

Anslak was still staring down at the vest. His son might be alive . . . Brage might be alive!! His hope was growing, and his heart swelled to near bursting with the good news. His eyes burned with tears he could never shed. "How much does Lord Alfrick demand for my son's life?"

"Six hundred pounds of gold." Hereld complimented himself on being so cagey.

"And what is your part in all of this?"

"I am to return with your answer and one hundred pounds of gold as proof of your intent. I am to arrange the time and place where the meeting is to be held so the exchange can be made."

Anslak nodded. "Leave us, Hereld. I must speak with my sons." He waved the man from the room.

Tove took Hereld outside, leaving Anslak, Ulf, and Kristoffer alone to talk.

"Does he lie, my sons?" he asked them, valuing their counsel.

"It is hard for me to believe a word of what he says," Kristoffer said.

"I do not trust the Saxons. But this trader . . ." Ulf was skeptical.

"I have had dealings with him," Anslak explained. "I know he is a sly one when it comes to turning a profit, but I do not think he would needlessly put his own life at stake. There is truth to his words, but how much truth, I am not certain. Even so, dare we risk that Brage is alive and we do nothing to save him?"

"No. We must rescue him. We must pay the ransom." Ulf was firm.

"We must save him from the Saxons," Kristoffer agreed.

"It is settled then. For Hereld's purpose, we agree to Alfrick's demand. For our own purpose, we will talk more after the merchant sets sail."

The two sons nodded in assent, and the trader was brought back to them.

"We will pay the ransom for my son's freedom."

Hereld's eyes lit up at the knowledge that by adding the extra hundred pounds to the ransom, he had just made himself a fine purse. He was pleased. "When do I sail with the first payment of the gold?"

"It will take a day to gather the ransom. You will sail day after tomorrow with the news of our agreement. Until then, you are considered a guest in my home."

"Thank you for your hospitality, Anslak."

"And thank you for bringing us this news of my son."

Hereld was thrilled. He was going to be rich. The trip had been worth it.

Later that night, Ulf, Anslak, and Kristoffer went alone to the top of a nearby hill overlooking the fjord to talk in private.

"There is much to plan and little time," Anslak told them. "How many men can be raised to sail with us, Ulf?"

"Two hundred."

"Good. Send word to them. Start tonight. We will sail

soon after the merchant. We must find my son and bring him home."

"Where shall we make the exchange?" Ulf asked.

"There is a landing site far to the north of Lord Alfrick's tower that is near a level and open field. It would be a safe place to make the exchange. We will be able to see if there are any surprises awaiting us from the Saxons."

"I pray Brage is well," Kristoffer said solemnly.

"*I* pray that this is not a trap. We will take one hundred warriors with us, and leave the other hundred on board their longships waiting just off the coast. Should we feel there might be trouble, we will be ready to defend ourselves," Anslak said.

Ulf and Kristoffer knew their father was right. They were ready to leave immediately to save their brother, but would have to do things according to the Saxon plan. That did not sit well with them, but they accepted it as the only way to rescue Brage.

"I still do not trust them," Anslak was saying. "We will remain alert until we are away from the coast with Brage safe. Only then will I believe that there is no treachery involved in their plan."

The following day, Anslak gathered his treasure. Late that evening, he called Hereld to him. The trader had been preparing his own ship to sail, but came at once upon hearing that Anslak wanted him.

"I have the hundred pounds of gold for you," the older Viking announced, his expression grave as he faced him.

"Good. I'm sure Lord Alfrick will be happy that you agreed to the terms."

"I am sure he will be, too." Anslak's tone was sarcastic. "Tell your lord that I will meet him at the field a day's march north of his tower in eight days. Tell him that as long as my son is returned to me alive and well, there will be no bloodshed. I will come forward with the gold, and I expect Brage to be there to meet me. If all goes as planned, we will leave immediately."

"I will relay your message to him, Anslak."

"I am trusting you to do so, but be warned, Hereld. Any betrayal will be repaid in kind."

Hereld saw the fierce look on his face and knew he was not a man to cross. "I will tell Lord Alfrick all you have said."

Anslak nodded and said nothing more as the other man left. He was glad the trader was leaving that morning. It meant they were that much closer to saving Brage from the hands of the Saxon lord . . . if he really was still alive.

Hereld was quite amazed at how well everything had gone. Except for his momentary scare with the big man named Ulf, all had gone just as he had hoped it would. He would stow away the gold, return to Lord Alfrick, tell him the news and then pocket the fee he had promised him. With any luck at all, he could be far away before the exchange took place, and that would be fine with him.


Dynna was just finishing her noon meal when Sir Edmund entered the room. Every time she saw him she was painfully and vividly reminded that her days of freedom were numbered. While she had been nursing Brage, she had been able to concentrate on keeping him alive and not be overwhelmed by the reality of what was about to happen to her. But now, as the Viking regained his health, she had little else to focus on, and so could no longer deny the chilling specter of her impending marriage. The priest could be arriving at any time, and when he did, her life would be over. She trembled at the thought of wha existence would become. Desperate to get away fro mund, she stood up to leave.

Sir Edmund saw her getting ready to go, and

in her direction. He caught her by the arm as she would have slipped out one of the side entrances.

"Do not be so hasty to leave, my lady," Sir Edmund said as he drew her back to him. "Come join me in my midday meal."

"I have already eaten and have need to go." She tried to put him off as she stared pointedly at his hand on her arm.

"Where are you bound that is more important than spending time with your betrothed? Surely you can keep me company while I eat," he said, sounding blandly entreating, but letting her know by the pressure on her arm that he was serious.

"If only I could, Sir Edmund, but I must see to my patient."

Edmund's expression hardened. "It is my understanding that the Viking's fever has broken, and he is recovering nicely."

"Indeed, he is much improved from when last you saw him, but he is still weak and in need of my help."

"I bid you to join me." His tone brooked no refusal.

"I must decline, for I have things to do that are more important than my being at your call."

"I said stay, my lady."

His grip was bruising.

"Your father has bid that I tend to the Viking. You have no power to say otherwise. Your father rules here, not you, Sir Edmund." Her eyes were flashing fire as she pulled away from him.

Edmund's hands clenched into fists as he watched her walk away. The desire to throttle her within an inch of her life was strong within him, and he wondered just how much longer it would be before the priest would come.

Dynna appeared to be calm and collected as she moved off. In truth, she wanted to scream. Was there no way for her to avoid the fate that would surely be worse than death? Is there to be no escape? She had tried to run that one time and had been caught. As desperate as she was, dare she try again?

Dynna reached up to brush away the tears that were falling and realized then just how badly her hands were shaking. It infuriated her that she was this terrified. She had always thought of herself as a strong person. It angered her to be trapped, and she desperately sought some way—any way—to save herself.

## Nine

On the way up the tower steps, Dynna actually found herself looking forward to going to the Viking's room. At least when she was with Brage, she was safe from Edmund.

The thought of Edmund upset her again, and Dynna grew agitated. No matter how much she wanted to fool herself into believing that she was out of harm's way when she was in the tower, there was no place really safe from Sir Edmund. Confronted again by her own helpless state, her anger grew. She was just as much a prisoner as the Viking, except hers was a more insidious kind of captivity. There were no bars on her windows and her door was not locked from the outside. It was the unspoken threat of what he could do to her and the persistent surveillance that left her thwarted at every turn.

Dynna forced a smile as she approached Perkin. "How is he doing this afternoon?"

"He has been quiet, my lady," he said as he started to open the door for her.

Brage had been using every moment to build himself back up. He had regained almost all the physical movement of his arm and shoulder, and he was able to bear the pain, severe though it still was. When he heard Dynna outside the door speaking to the guard, he quickly ceased his strengthening movements and half-reclined on the bed. He did not want her to find out how much he had improved.

Brage planned to escape the tower at the first opportunity.

He was not yet sure how he was going to do it, but he knew he could not stay imprisoned. Death in an escape attempt was far more appealing than remaining here indefinitely—a trophy for Lord Alfrick's pleasure. The longer his captors thought him weak, the better. They would not be expecting him to try to run if they thought he was still suffering.

Dynna entered the room. "It is good that you are trying to get up. Are you feeling a little better?"

"Some of the dizziness has left me," Brage answered. He watched her walk toward him, and again was struck by the graceful way she moved. She was wearing her hair down this day, and the thick, shiny mane was glorious to behold. It was then that he noticed a flush to her cheeks and a certain fierce glitter in her eyes. He wondered at her mood. Usually she was the picture of serenity, but he could tell that was not so today.

"Are you angry with me or some other?"

"I am not angry with anyone." She denied the truth. "But since you say you are feeling stronger, perhaps it is time for you to start moving. You have been lying down too long."

"There was a time when I would have loved to have spent time abed with a lovely woman watching over me," he remarked, a gleam in his eyes. A slight smile played about his lips as he saw her color heighten even more. "But lying in bed in a prison cell was not what I had in mind. You are right. It will be good to get around again." He started to stand.

"No . . . wait! Let me help you." Dynna insisted, reaching for him and slipping a supporting arm about his waist. She feared he would harm himself if he could not support his own weight. "I do not want to risk you taking a fall."

Brage chuckled, and Dynna shot him a questioning look.

"Why are you laughing? If you fell, you very well might injure yourself again."

"Lady Dynna, if I were to lean my whole weight on you,

I would break you. Then neither one of us would be walking."

"But this is your first time up. You are still weak, and you are going to be unsteady."

Brage said nothing. He could think of worse tortures than having her arm around him. The curve of her body, very feminine and lush, fit softly against his, and the touch and scent of her sent a fierce, unexpected surge of heat through him. He rested an arm about her shoulders for extra support, his hand curving about her arm.

Dynna tensed, almost flinching at his touch. It had been a long time since a man had touched her in gentleness and affection. Sir Edmund's pawings had left her nervous and unsure of herself. She hated Edmund's hands upon her, and at the thought of it, she trembled.

"Is something wrong, my lady?" he asked as he felt her shiver.

"No. Nothing is wrong. See if you can take a few steps," she encouraged quickly, wanting to distract herself.

Brage did as she suggested, taking care not to move too easily. He did not want her to know that he had already mastered crossing the room under his own power.

Dynna could not relax as they walked at a snail's pace around the chamber. Brage could feel the tenseness in her, and it puzzled him. Stopping, he looked down at her and asked, "Are you sure there is nothing troubling you? If you would rather not do this, I can sit back down."

It surprised her to find out that he could interpret her mood. Few men she had known gave any consideration to what a woman was thinking or feeling. Warren had valued her thoughts and opinions, but she considered him the exception. Edmund crept unwanted into her thoughts then. "There are many times in life when we are forced to do things we do not want to do."

Brage frowned, seeing for just a fleeting moment a

glimpse of pain in her expression. "Do you want to do this? I can walk on my own if need be."

"This I have chosen to do. But do not think that you are the only prisoner in this tower." Dynna knew Brage would eventually be freed to return home to his family, while she would be forced into a marriage to Sir Edmund that she would have to endure until death parted them.

He was amazed by her statement. He turned to face her, her supportive arm slipping from around him. His eyes were shadowed with anger as he spoke. "You speak foolishness. I hardly see a comparison. You have the freedom to go wherever you want. I, however, have been chained to a wall and am now locked in this room."

"Some chains are invisible."

"You still have the power to dictate your own future. You can leave if you choose to do so."

She lifted her gaze to his as she gave a brittle laugh, and for the first time he could see the torment within her.

"That is what I was doing when your men caught me." There was a catch of raw emotion in her voice.

Brage frowned at her confession. "You were running away that day . . . I had wondered at your disguise. Was it a situation you were running from or a man?"

"A man. Sir Edmund. I am promised by order of Lord Alfrick to marry him soon."

"You are too good a woman to be wife to a man like that," Brage said.

Their gazes locked. His regard was as solemn as hers was troubled. With utmost tenderness, he lifted his hand and touched her cheek.

"I am sorry that my taking you captive ended your bid for freedom. I would never want to hurt you in any way."

Dynna stared up at him, seeing him as a man and not a Viking prisoner. Desire flared in his gaze; and she knew Brage was about to kiss her. She told herself to move away from him, to escape the magnetic pull of his attraction, but she didn't.

Brage gazed down at her, thinking her the most beautiful woman in the world. He saw the uncertainty in her gaze and wanted to be gentle with her. With the utmost care, Brage bent to Dynna and brushed her lips with his in a tender-soft kiss.

Dynna gasped at the sensations that swept through her at the touch of his mouth on hers. She was no stranger to desire. She had enjoyed the gentle lovemaking she had shared with Warren. But this . . . this was different. This feeling was like nothing she had ever experienced before, and it was all from that one simple touch of his lips on hers.

When Brage drew back, Dynna stared up at him. From the dark slash of his brows over his brilliant blue eyes, to the hard masculine line of his jaw, Brage was the most strikingly handsome man she had ever known. She had thought him intimidating when she had first seen him, with his full beard, wearing his helmet. But now, clean-shaven, hair trimmed, healthy, he was not only powerful but devastatingly handsome. She cautioned herself that Brage was a danger to her; yet, she could see no threat in him.

A sense of her own vulnerability overcame Dynna as she realized the power of her feelings. She took a step back, needing to put a distance between them.

Her deliberate movement away from him forced Brage to give himself a mental shake. He would never have dreamed that one chaste kiss could have ignited so many fires within him. Lady Dynna was the most beautiful woman he had ever seen. He had known she was brave from the beginning, and now he knew she was one of the kindest and most generous women he had ever encountered. Her kiss had stirred him as no other before. He stared down at her, trying to judge her mood and read her thoughts.

Dynna stood before him, unnerved by the feelings that were overwhelming her. "I think you must be regaining your health quite nicely, Sir Viking. It seems quite obvious that you are feeling better."

"I *am* feeling much better," he replied in a low voice, but there was laughter in his eyes.

Dynna saw his amusement and took another step away from him. "Then I think you can walk better than I suspected. Perhaps you should try to go lie down under your own power."

Brage was smiling as he turned and walked to the bed. The inviting look he gave her as he sat down spoke volumes.

Dynna had an instant image of herself on the bed with him—touching him, not in healing, but in passion; caressing him, not to cool him, but to heat his desire. She turned and fled toward the door with all the dignity she could muster. As she escaped into the hall, she could hear Brage chuckling behind her.

Dynna exited the room calmly, for she could not betray anything to Perkin. She headed back down the stairs, even more confused and upset than she had been when she had climbed them earlier. Everywhere she looked she was surrounded by trouble. First, there was Edmund, and now Brage . . .

Dynna longed to be home, where her mother would counsel her and help her. But there was no returning to those days of love and family. Her future stretched before her bleak and cold.

Dynna knew there was only one source for help now. She passed her own chamber on her way downstairs and hurried to the chapel to pray. God was her only hope.

The chapel was plain and darkly shadowed. Only a few candles on the small altar offered any light. She knelt in fervent prayer, begging for divine guidance, pleading for rescue from her doomed fate as Edmund's bride.

Dynna remained on her knees for a long time. This attraction to Brage unsettled her. She had never known such promise in a kiss . . . Was it to be her destiny to marry a man she despised? Was there to be no peace in her life? She had hoped for some divine insight to help her decide her future. To her heartbreak and dismay, all she got was silence in answer to her eloquent pleas.

When she finally got up to leave the room, Dynna felt as abandoned as she had when she had first entered. It was as she had suspected all along—she was alone. She would have to save herself, if she was to be saved at all.

As she was reaching for the door handle, she heard voices outside in the passageway. She recognized one as Edmund's and stopped cold. She desperately wanted to avoid him. Seeing him once that day had already been too much. She stepped back into the shadows and waited for him and his companion to pass. She could hear his voice clearly as he strode by the door.

"Things are working out almost too perfectly, my friend," Edmund was saying.

"How so?"

"Both Father Corwin and Father Osmar have just arrived in the village. Now that they have returned, my marriage to the princess will take place. I have already spoken to Father Corwin, and he has agreed to perform the ceremony within the week."

"She is a lovely one, your brother's widow. I understand your eagerness to make her your bride."

"When I am made lord here, she will make a beautiful lady for our people."

Dynna's stomach lurched at what she had just overheard. The priests were back! The wedding would be within the week! She had thought prayers would help her, but it seemed her fate had only been sealed. She started to tremble at the news.

"What is happening with the Black Hawk?"

"That is the other part of my good news. Hereld should be returning any day with word of the exchange. My father will be very pleased when the ransom is paid, for as soon as we have the gold in our possession, I am going to personally see the Viking and those who come to ransom him slain."

"Another trap?"

"What fool would think us lackwitted enough to release the very raider who has terrorized our lands? I am surprised my father has let him live this long, but from what understand, Anslak will insist on seeing him alive before the gold will be given over to us. I will have archers hidden nearby with their arrows trained on the Black Hawk's back. He will be dead along with the others. Then we will reclaim some of the gold they have looted from us in the past."

"Yours is a brilliant plan, Sir Edmund, and not unlike the one you created after learning from the Viking traitor that the Black Hawk would be attacking. Once this is done, you will have satisfied them all—you will have gained gold for your kingdom and killed the Black Hawk, and that is what the informer wanted from you in the first place, was it not?"

"That was the only thing he wanted for the information he gave—details of the Black Hawk's raid for the Black Hawk's death. Once our arrows have found their marks, I will have kept our part of the bargain."

"You have a talent for deception."

"I have yet to fail when I plan my rivals' downfall," Edmund said, giving a confident laugh. "I do love outwitting the enemy, and I will have done it when I see the Black Hawk fall dead on Saxon soil."

With that, Edmund and the other man moved out of earshot.

Dynna remained where she was, shocked by all she had heard. Dear God! She had known Sir Edmund was a cold man, but now . . . She thought of Warren's untimely death and could not help but wonder now if his brother had had something to do with his "accident." She shuddered at the possibility. It frightened her that she would never know the truth for sure.

Thoughts of her dead husband brought thoughts of Brage. Sir Edmund had already planned his death. Her hands were shaking and her heart was pounding as she considered what she should do. She had to take some action to save Brage. She could not let him be slaughtered.

Opening the chapel door a crack, Dynna checked to make sure the passageway was safe, and then crept from the room. She hurried back to her chamber and began to pace nervously, trying to figure out how to rescue Brage from the certain death that awaited him.

Finally, as Dynna strode back and forth her gaze dropped to her healing basket, and the glimmer of an idea was born. If she was to save Brage's life, she had to get him out of the tower and back to his own land. If she was to save herself from becoming Edmund's wife, she had to go to her parents. They would protect her. As she had told Brage earlier, they were both captives. Now, they would have to escape together.

The most difficult part would be getting Brage out of the tower. Picking up her basket, Dynna went to her small table and began to mix some herbs and medicines. She made a large batch, taking extra care to ensure its extra strength. Her hands were still trembling as she worked, but she knew she had no choice. She could not let Brage die. She would do whatever was necessary to rescue him from Edmund's evil plot.

The knock at her door momentarily shattered her confidence, and she nervously called out. "Who is it?"

"It is Matilda, my lady. I must speak with you right away." There was an urgency to her voice.

Dynna heard the tone of concern and wondered what was wrong. After covering her mixture with a cloth, she went to unlock the door. She had no time to say a word as the servant rushed in.

"I came to you as quickly as I could. Have you heard the news?" She saw Dynna's expression and had her answer. "You have heard that the—"

"Priests have returned? Yes. I have heard."

"What are we going to do? Sir Edmund has publicly announced that the wedding will take place next week!"

"We are going to do nothing," she stated.

"But, my lady . . ." Matilda was shocked. Lady Dynna just could not marry this man. She just could not! He was nothing like Prince Warren. Sir Edmund was cruel and vicious.

"I, however . . ."

"You have a plan? What can I do to help?" She saw the cloth covering a bowl on the table. "You are making a potion of some kind? How will you use it? To poison Edmund and solve all our problems?" she suggested hopefully.

"No," she replied. "But there is more to the need of this potion than just the news of the priests' arrival."

"What else has happened?"

She revealed to her maid the conversation she had overheard between Edmund and the other man.

Matilda gasped.

Dynna paused to draw a deep, steadying breath, girding herself for what she was about to undertake. "I cannot stand by and let them kill him."

"I will do whatever I can to help you."

"No. I do not want you involved this time. I cannot take you with me."

"But, my lady!"

Dynna would not be swayed. "And you cannot know more than have already told you."

"But why? I want to stay with you. Who will protect you? Who will keep you from harm?"

"You know how closely Sir Edmund's men are keeping watch over us. That is why I will need your help. If we were both to disappear again at the same time, they would suspect us right away. This way, I have a better chance of slipping away unnoticed."

Matilda had no choice but to agree. "I will do whatever

you want me to do, but know that I would rather be with you to help you."

Dynna smiled at her faithful companion. "You are not only my servant, Matilda. You are my friend. There is no one, save my parents, I trust more than I do you. That is why you must stay behind and plead ignorance of my plans. It will be no lie, and they will not hurt you."

"If that is how I can best help you, then I will do it."

Dynna expressed her gratitude. "When the time comes for our escape, I will need the Black Hawk's sword and shield hidden outside the tower gate," she instructed. "I know it will not be an easy task, but I hope you can find a way."

"I will."

The two women's eyes met, and Matilda could see the hard look of determination in Dynna's regard. She hoped with all her heart that she would succeed.

Dynna bided her time. If she were to return to Brage's room so soon, questions might be asked, for she had no reason to go there again until the next day.

Dynna was not surprised when Sir Edmund sent a message to her "inviting" her to join him for the evening meal. She had a very good idea of what was to come. Not wanting to give him any reason to doubt or criticize her, she donned a pale-blue undergown with a contrasting darker blue embroidered overgown held at each shoulder by golden brooches. She had Matilda pull her hair back away from her face and braid it.

"Will you be all right, my lady?" Matilda asked worriedly as Dynna prepared to go down to the Great Hall to join Sir Edmund.

Dynna assured her she would be fine. "Now that I know what I am up against and what I am going to do about it, I feel more confident."

"Be careful."

"You do not have to worry about that. I will be more than careful. Sir Edmund will have no reason to suspect me tonight."

Practicing a pleasant smile one last time as she stared at her reflection in the mirror, Dynna knew she was ready to face Lord Alfrick, Sir Edmund, and the priests. She hoped Sir Thomas would be present so she would know there was someone in the room she could count on.

Sir Edmund was drinking a cup of ale with his father when he saw Dynna appear at the top of the steps. He made a great display of setting his cup aside and going to escort her to the table.

"You look lovely, my dear," he complimented her as he took her hand. His dark eyes glowed with approval as his gaze raked over her in a bold caress.

It was all she could do to not show her distaste at the predatory look. She gave him the well-practiced smile.

"Have you heard that we have guests this evening?"

"Matilda brought me word of the good priests' return. It will be a pleasure to see them again."

"I am glad that you are as pleased as I am," he said casually, then lowered his voice for her to hear alone. "I have spoken with Father Corwin and he has agreed to marry us. In one week, we shall be man and wife."

"That is what I was told." Dynna kept her gaze fixed on Father Corwin. Across the room, his eyes met hers and for a brief moment, she seemed to see something more in the holy man's regard than just polite kindness.

"We will make the official announcement tonight."

She nodded her acquiescence as they reached the table.

"Good evening, Father Corwin. Father Osmar," Dynna greeted the priests warmly.

"It is good to see you, my lady. Have you been well?" Father Corwin asked. He had married Sir Warren and Lady Dynna and had long been fond of her. He had been greatly saddened by Warren's untimely death.

"I have been very well," she replied by rote.

"Congratulations on your coming wedding."

Her reply of thanks was stiff and formal as she tried to hide the truth of her feelings from him.

They made general conversation, discussing his and Father Osmar's travels about the countryside ministering to the people. When Edmund interrupted them, drawing Dynna's attention away to greet someone else, Father Corwin had the time to study the two of them together. When he had first heard of this betrothal, he had been concerned. He had known Edmund all his life and had always disliked him. Where Warren had been good and kind and had made Dynna a loving husband; Edmund would be nothing of the sort.

Observing them now, Father Corwin could tell that this union was not her choice, just as he had suspected from the beginning. He would make sure to speak with Lady Dynna privately this week. He wanted her happiness and would do all he could to help her.

Lord Alfrick announced that the meal was to begin, and Father Corwin was called upon to say the blessing. A veritable feast had been prepared in honor of the announcement that would be made. When everyone had finished eating, Lord Alfrick rose. All those in the hall fell quiet as they awaited his words.

"Let it be known that a wedding will take place in seven days between my son, Sir Edmund, and Lady Dynna," he said with great pride.

The hall erupted in cheers of good will. Dynna managed to smile graciously through all the toasts, when in reality all she wanted to do was run screaming from the hall. She counted the minutes until she would make her escape. There was only one moment when her composure might have cracked—when she accidentally met Sir Thomas's gaze. She could see the older man's concern for her in his expression, and it was almost her undoing. She looked away as quickly as she could, lest he see her carefully camouflaged distress.

It was late when she pleaded the need to retire, and to her amazement, Sir Edmund was most solicitous of her.

"I will escort you to your room," he told her.

Dynna knew better than to argue the point and simply took his offered arm. When they reached her chamber, he stopped for a moment to stare down at her.

"We will make a handsome pair, we two," he said thickly. "I will be proud to have you by my side."

"I only hope that you find me worthy of you."

He smiled drunkenly. She was less than her usual feisty self tonight, and he was pleased. "It is good that the priests' arrival has helped you to realize the way of things. Perhaps you will not need as much taming as I thought."

She gritted her teeth. "A wife's duty is to please her husband."

"And I will be your husband very soon, Dynna. Very soon . . ." His face lowered, taking her lips in a passionate kiss as his arms came around her and crushed her to him.

Summoning all of her willpower, Dynna suffered his touch and kiss without trying to break free.

When at last he ended the embrace, he was frowning. "You are a little cold, but that is all right." His expression changed to one of hunger as he stared down at her. "It will be a challenge to teach you to respond to me."

"Good night," she said quietly.

"Good night, my bride."

He waited until she was safely inside and the door was closed before he returned to the Great Hall. He was pleased by Dynna's compliance, and glad she had not mentioned his dead brother all evening. He would wipe all memories of Warren from her mind once she was his. The next few days were going to pass very slowly, but the wait would be worth it.

Dynna was nearly ready to scream, but she could not for fear that someone would hear her. She tore off her clothes and washed herself to remove any trace of Edmund's touch. After donning her nightdress, she climbed in bed, but she knew she would not sleep. Somehow, she had to come up with a plan to get Brage out of the tower.

Dynna began to explore different ways that she could sneak the Viking out. It would be simple to drug the guard and get past him. But the biggest difficulty in their escape would be crossing the Great Hall unnoticed, just as it had been for her and Matilda when they had tried.

For a moment, Dynna thought of enlisting Sir Thomas's help, but she quickly dismissed the idea. He was pledged in honor to Lord Alfrick. He could not do anything that would compromise his word. No, she was on her own. Whatever plan she concocted would be hers.

Dynna's thoughts went to Brage as she lay there trying to devise a plan to save him. The memory of his kiss was emblazoned on her heart. His kiss had been gentle and warm; Edmund's had been torture.

Dynna wondered how he would react to what she had to say to him the next day. She was not sure if he would believe her or not, but she had to try. Somehow, she had to convince him to escape with her. They needed each other. She needed his strength, and he would need her knowledge of the tower and the surrounding land and people.

Together, they could make a run toward freedom.

# Ten

Brage passed an uneasy night. Thoughts of Lady Dynna and the kiss they had shared kept him awake until the early morning hours. He had not meant for the kiss to happen, but even as he told himself all the reasons it had been the wrong thing to do, he could not forget the wonder of it.

Brage tried to put memories of her out of his mind, but it was pointless. He had seen her bravery. She had more courage than some warriors he knew. She was a skilled healer and had fought to save him when the rest would have let him die. Dynna was a remarkable woman, and she did not deserve the fate that was being thrust upon her. Marriage to Sir Edmund was a cruelty he would not inflict on his most hated rival. He wondered if there was any way to help her, but realized it was pointless to even consider it. He was a prisoner. He was powerless to help anyone.

Brage turned his musings to the possibility of his own escape. When the time finally came, he believed it would be a simple matter, once the door was open, for him to overpower the guard and take his weapon. Armed with the guard's sword, he would feel confident about his chance of escaping the tower alive.

Thoughts of Dynna intruded on his planning then, but he immediately dismissed the idea of taking her along. He had no idea what he would do with her, and it would be far too dangerous for her. He wanted to escape alone. If Lady Dynna were with him . . .

Brage gave himself a mental shake. It was impossible. It would not work. Still unable to sleep, he got up from the bed and went to stand at the small window. Staring out at the night-shrouded countryside, he wondered when he should make his move.

Morning could not come soon enough for Dynna. She did not bother with breakfast. She gathered what she needed to shave Brage and went straight to the tower room as early as she could without seeming too eager. She greeted Clive, the man standing guard that day, with a casualness she was not feeling. Entering the room, she found Brage sitting on the side of the bed, much as she had left him the day before.

Brage looked up at the sound of her voice. As her gaze met his across the room, Dynna was struck again by how handsome he was. The shorter cut of his dark hair emphasized his eyes, and the shadow of growth on his jaw gave him a daring and dangerous look. He seemed to be holding his shoulders more squarely this morning, and she hoped it meant his wound was less painful. For what she had planned, he needed to be in good condition.

"You are early this morning, my lady," Brage remarked. Thoughts of her had haunted him most of the night, and now seeing her first thing, he thought her even more lovely than he had remembered.

She approached him, wanting to be close to him so Clive could not overhear. "I have to talk with you, but we must do so quietly. We will speak as I shave you."

Brage could tell she was tense. He wondered what secret information she had to tell him. He gave her a half-smile as he leaned back on the bed on one elbow. "If you would like, we could just talk and forget the shave."

"I must have a reason to come here. Shaving you is the reason."

"If I were given a choice, I would prefer we practice walking again." His gaze held hers.

"Prisoners do not choose. They are told what they are going to do and when they are going to do it," she said, the bitterness that filled her sounding in her words.

His smile disappeared and his gaze darkened at her blunt reminder of his position. "Of course, Lady Dynna. I had forgotten my place. I am a captive here and at your mercy." His words were cold. He wondered if the kiss they had shared was imagined.

"That is what I have to talk to you about."

"What is there to talk about? Nothing has changed. As you said, I am Lord Alfrick's prisoner."

*"For now,* you are his prisoner," she said.

"What do you mean?"

"I learned late yesterday that very soon you will not be a prisoner anymore; you will be dead." In case Clive looked in on them, she was trying to act as if they were having a casual conversation as she mixed the lather to soften his beard, but she did not miss the sharp glance he shot her way.

"What exactly is it you heard?"

"Sir Edmund plans to kill you regardless of his father's plans . . ."

"What plan does Lord Alfrick have?"

Dynna applied the lather and then began to shave him as she spoke. "Lord Alfrick has sent an envoy to your father offering to ransom you back to him for five hundred pounds of gold."

Brage was shocked at this news.

"Once they learned you were the Black Hawk, they knew you would be worth much to your people."

"So that is why you were allowed to heal me," he remarked thoughtfully.

"The envoy is due back any day now with your father's answer. Lord Alfrick is certain he will agree to his terms."

Brage grew furious. He wanted his freedom more than

anything, but it enraged him that his father would be forced to buy him back for gold. The news only reinforced his determination to escape as soon as possible. He would save himself, and he would save his father the ransom.

Dynna continued to explain all she had heard as she worked with a gentle touch to scrape the whiskers from his cheeks. "Edmund, however, has another idea. As soon as they get the gold from your people, they will kill you and all those who came to ransom you."

Brage stiffened at her description of his deceit. "Why are you telling me this?"

"I have a bargain to offer you."

"What kind of bargain?"

"As I told you, I am as much a prisoner here as you are, and just as I learned your life was about to end, I know that mine will soon be over, too. My situation is desperate. Father Corwin and Father Osmar have returned to the village earlier than expected. Last night, Lord Alfrick announced that Edmund and I would be married in one week."

"What does this have to do with a bargain between us?"

"I will not marry Edmund." The words were forcefully said, and her chin tilted in open defiance of the very idea. "I am leaving here before the day of the wedding. My offer to you is this: I will see you freed from this tower, if you travel with me as my guard to my parents' home. Once I am safely there, I will guarantee you safe passage home."

Brage stared at her in disbelief. He understood her need to flee Edmund, but he could not entangle his own escape with hers. Her plan was too dangerous. "Do you not realize how quickly they will miss you and how thoroughly Sir Edmund will search for you once he finds out that you have gone?"

"That is why I need you with me. Together, we can escape the fates that are about to be forced upon us."

"I will not attempt this with you."

She was shocked and angered by his refusal. "How else

will you save yourself? I am offering you freedom. If you do not come with me, you will be slaughtered."

"I have no intention of waiting here to be slaughtered. I was already planning an escape, but I have no intention of taking you with me."

"Why not? I know the land and the people."

"If we go together, Sir Edmund would chase us twice as hard. You are a female. You would only slow me down."

"I will match you step for step, Viking," she told him, her gray eyes glittering with the challenge.

"It would be too dangerous. If I am alone, I can fight freely. If you are there, I would worry about you."

"I will fight by your side."

"You could be killed," he warned.

"I do not care. I would rather die now, trying to reach my parents, than marry Edmund and spend the rest of my days in endless torment. What safe haven would I have? What love would I find in his arms?" She gave a harsh laugh at the thought.

Her impassioned declaration gave him pause. He remembered his own desperation a short time before, and how he would have welcomed death rather than the chains and humiliation of being Lord Alfrick's captive.

She finished shaving Brage and stood up.

Brage stared at her, seeing how proud and beautiful she was. He gritted his teeth against the image of her married to Edmund, forever in his power, forced to do his bidding, forced to bed him. He did not believe Sir Edmund knew anything of gentleness. Brage wanted to help her, but he did not want to endanger her. If something happened to her while she was with him . . . "Lady Dynna, you do not know what you are saying."

"I will not marry Sir Edmund. I am leaving this tower and traveling to my parents' home where I will be safe. I am offering you the chance to go with me and earn your freedom. I have a potion I can use to drug the guard; I can get your sword and shield for you; and I have the means for us to get out of the tower. Without me, you will never escape."

"When I go, I will go alone," Brage repeated, torn by the terrible thought of leaving her to Edmund's mercy.

Dynna was desperate. She hated coercing Brage into accompanying her, but she had no alternative. The look on her face was one of fierce resolve. "If you refuse to go with me, I will see to it that you will never escape this tower. I will have the guard take you right now and put you back in the chains with the dogs."

Brage's anger at being backed into a corner was barely leashed. "You drive a hard bargain, my lady," he ground out.

"Only because you have forced me to it. I will do whatever I have to, to get away from here."

Their gazes met and locked. Brage saw the unrelenting determination in her regard. She had forced him to her way, and he could not decide whether to admire her courage in confronting him so in her desperation or to be furious at being so manipulated.

"So, tell me Viking, is our bargain sealed? Do you agree to my terms? You will ultimately benefit from the bargain. All you have to do is see me safely to my family, then you will be free to go."

Brage had no choice. "I agree. Now, what are the rest of your plans? When do we go?"

"Tonight, when Perkin is at guard, I will come back. I will tell him that I am to help you exercise. I have a potion that will put him to sleep. Once he is asleep, it will be a simple matter to free you from this room."

"And what of the Great Hall? How do we cross it without being discovered?"

"By tonight, I will have it planned."

Brage resigned himself to the fact that they were going to escape the tower together. He wondered when it was that they had ceased to be enemies, and if they were not enemies, then what were they?

"I am to trust you in this?"

"Do not worry. By tomorrow morning, we will both be free of Lord Alfrick and Sir Edmund."

Brage was worried, but there was little he could do. This was her scheme. He had had no part in planning it. He only had to carry it out. He did not like it, he did not like it at all.

Dynna saw the strained look on his face and asked, "You are strong enough to make the attempt, are you not?"

"Just the thought of regaining my freedom gives me the strength of five warriors." At least, Brage was pleased that his act of being weaker than he was had worked.

"I will be back later, after dark."

Brage watched her walk from the room, her head held high, her bearing regal. Had he not been so angry over being forced to follow her plan, he would have thought her magnificent.


"Can you get them for me and see them hidden?" Dynna asked Matilda later that afternoon as they sat in her room sharing a moment of tense understanding.

"Once it is dark, I should be able to take them from the tower. I will hide them in the brush near the trees at the first turn in the road. But what of you, my lady? How are you going to get the Viking out of the tower without being found out? What shall I say in the morning when they discover you have gone?"

"I want you to take a small draught of the sleeping potion tonight when you go to bed. That way, you can say I gave you a dose and that you were sleeping soundly and knew nothing of what transpired. It will help to convince them of your innocence in the matter."

Matilda nodded, but she was not pleased. She wanted to be going with Lady Dynna. "You will be careful?"

Dynna assured her. "This will be the last chance I ever get to return home. I *have* to be careful."

"And what of Brage? Do not trust him overmuch. It might prove dangerous."

"I know he is savage by nature, but that is what makes him valuable to me. He wants his freedom as much as I want mine, and that is why I trust him."

The worry Matilda was feeling shone in her eyes. "My prayers will be with you."

"I fear that I will need them." Her words were spoken quietly.

Long after dinner, Dynna returned to the tower room. She carried her medicine basket with her, along with a full mug of ale for Perkin. Perkin had a particular love for ale, and she had already doctored the brew with enough of her sleeping potion to fell an ox for hours. She was not certain how quickly it would work on Perkin, but once it took effect, she and Brage would have the time they needed to slip away.

Perkin had been sitting in the hall beyond the tower room, bored. The day had been a long one, and when he went upstairs to relieve the other man from his duty, he had realized the night would seem even longer. He was settled comfortably in his chair near the door when he heard footsteps. He rose and went to investigate, for it was not common, now that the Black Hawk was feeling better, for anyone to check on him overnight.

Moving to the top of the stairs, Perkin peered down into the gloom below to see Lady Dynna coming toward him. "Good evening, my lady. It is a pleasure to see you this lonely night."

Dynna graced him with her most beguiling smile. "Good evening, Perkin. I have brought you some ale. I thought you might be needing a drink this evening."

"Thank you, my lady. It certainly would be refreshing,"

he agreed as he took the proffered mug. It was just like Lady Dynna to think of others and see to their needs. Here, she had no reason to be nice to him, and yet she had brought him a drink just out of the kindness of her heart.

"Please enjoy it with my blessing," she said. "How is our prisoner tonight?"

"Have heard not a word out of him since I took over, but then that is not unusual for him. He is a quiet one. Thing that bothers me, though, is that sometimes it is the quiet ones who are the most dangerous."

"I know. I will be very glad when he is back with his own people." She meant every word of it, too.

"Do you want to go in?"

"Yes. I was worried about him. He seemed a little weak when I was with him earlier this afternoon, so I thought I had better check back, just in case his fever had recurred."

"Let me get the door for you, my lady." Perkin set the mug aside and hurried to admit her to the tower room. "Would you like me to stay with you?"

"No. I should be all right. I will call if I need you."

He watched until she was inside, then closed and locked the door behind her. He was still smiling as he settled back on his stool and picked up the mug to take a deep drink. Lady Dynna was a fine one, thinking of him as she had. The ale was refreshing, and he enjoyed every drop of the brew.

"You are as good as your word," Brage said, once Dynna was inside and the door was closed soundly behind her.

"You had doubts?"

"Not a one," he replied with a slight smile as he saw the fierceness in her expression.

"I told the guard how weak you were feeling this afternoon, and that is why I'm here to check on you so late. Shall we get you up and see if you can walk?" she suggested, wanting to talk about their plans but needing to do so in low tones so they would not be overheard.

"You are the healer."

Dynna went to Brage as he stood. She put her arm about his waist. The contact of her arm against his bare skin was again electric, but Dynna knew she had to ignore the attraction. This was no time to think about such things. She could only think about their escape. As they started to move around the room, she could feel the play of his powerful muscles beneath her touch.

"Can you do this? Can you make it once around the room?" she asked, playing the role of concerned nurse.

Brage could not stop himself from smiling broadly down at her as he answered quietly, "With your help, princess, I think I could walk from this tower."

She returned his smile a little nervously. The time of their escape was almost upon them, and she could not prevent the worries from consuming her.

"We need a distraction," she whispered to him as they moved slowly, and seemingly painfully, around the room. "I slipped the potion into the mug of ale I gave Perkin. If he drinks it quickly, he should be falling asleep right away."

"I could pretend to fall."

"I do not think we have to be that dramatic. Just pretend to be too weak to make it back across the room. Perkin will come to help as soon as I call him, but let us wait a minute more. I want to give him time to drink all the ale."

Brage was anxious to be gone from the tower. In the hours since she had left him, he had thought of nothing else. Now that the time was upon them, he was more than eager to make their move, but he knew he had to be patient just a few minutes more. "Just let me know when you want my strength to fail me, my lady."

They circled the room twice more, moving slowly, before she spoke. "I think enough time has passed. Are you ready?" She looked up at him questioningly.

"More than ready." Brage stared down at her. Her gray eyes were shining silver with the determination that filled her. She was a force to be reckoned with. He pitied any man who tried to stop her tonight.

He deliberately sagged against her, causing them both to stagger.

"Are you all right?" Dynna asked, her voice loud to draw Perkin's attention.

Brage swayed and then slumped fully against her. "I cannot seem to stay upright . . ."

"Perkin!" she called out in real panic as his weight became almost more than she could bear.

The guard immediately came charging through the door, his sword in hand.

"Yes, my lady? What is the . . . ?" He saw how she was frantically fighting to keep the Viking upright.

Dynna thought that Perkin seemed to be moving about just fine, and she grew annoyed. She had hoped he would down the ale right away and save her the trouble of stalling. But if he had not finished it off yet, there was no hope that they could escape now.

"He suddenly went weak . . . I am having trouble holding him . . ." Dynna explained, realizing ruefully that Brage had been right when he had told her that they would both fall if he truly leaned on her with his full weight. She had always known he was a big, powerful man, but she had never realized just how big and powerful.

Perkin set his weapon aside and went to rescue his princess. Taking Brage on his uninjured side, he drew his arm over his shoulders and helped maneuver the tall Viking toward the bed.

Brage gave a very realistic groan as he was hauled across the room.

"He sounds as if he is in pain, my lady."

"I know. Lord Alfrick will not be pleased if he grows worse. It is important that he be healthy."

Perkin staggered a few times under the weight of the man, and he wondered at his own weakness. When he finally managed to help Brage lie on the bed, he felt strangely light-headed.

Dynna smiled at the guard as he turned to her. "Thank you for your help. I do not know what I would have done without you."

"Will it be all right now?" he asked, finding himself suddenly incredibly sleepy. "Do you want me to get anything for you?"

"No. It will be fine now."

Perkin started from the room, thinking what a brave woman Lady Dynna was. He had just about reached the door, his thoughts focused on Lady Dynna's finer points when a wave of faintness swelled over him and he swayed. He braced himself against the wall, turning a bewildered look to Dynna.

"My lady . . . ?" He slumped then and fell, letting out one low moan before he lay still.

Dynna had watched, fascinated, as the medicine took effect. She hoped Perkin had not hurt himself when he had fallen, and she hurried to his side to make sure he was just sleeping, and not injured.

"Perkin?" she said his name as she touched his shoulder. "Perkin, can you hear me?"

But the man didn't stir.

"Well?" Brage asked as he watched her tend to the man.

Dynna looked back over her shoulder at Brage. "He must have downed the whole thing to be this soundly asleep. He will be all right when he comes around. He did not injure himself."

She tried to lift Perkin, but found she could not budge him.

"Could you help me? I want to put him on the bed."

Brage went to her side and, kneeling beside the prone figure, lifted him by his arms. When Dynna would have helped, he brushed her aside.

Dynna watched in stunned disbelief as Brage carried the heavy guard to the bed. The knowledge that he was that well healed and that strong unnerved her. All this time when she had been worried about him, he had been almost back to full strength. He had been playing with her all along. The trust she had begun to feel toward him was shaken. If he had fooled her about being physically ready to make the escape, what else had he deceived her about? The thought of fleeing the chamber now, alone, while she still could occurred to her, but she held firm on her plan out of necessity. Together, she would have a much better chance of reaching her haven.

Brage stood up straight and turned to her. It was then that he saw the look on her face. "I told you the thought of freedom would give me the strength of five Vikings."

"I can see that."

Across the room, their gazes met. Brage could see the fire in her eyes and knew that she was angry. "Let us bind and gag him. That way if he awakens early, he will not be able to sound the alarm right away."

"Just do not hurt him. Perkin is a kind man. He has done us no harm."

Brage used the blanket to gag and tie the guard, ripping it into strips that could serve as bonds. Perkin did not even stir. While Brage worked at his wrists and ankles, Dynna opened her medicine basket and drew out the tunic and soft boots Matilda had gotten for him to wear.

She handed him the clothing.

He donned the tunic, but found it was tight, fitting snugly across the width of his chest. The boots fit comfortably. Once dressed, he strode purposefully across the room and seized Perkin's sword. He held it up, relishing the feeling of being armed again. It was not a poor weapon, and he was glad. If he had to fight, he wanted to be as well armed as possible. Short of having his own sword, this one would do.

Dynna had watched him as he had picked up the weapon, and she saw the same fierce, hungry gleam in his eyes that had been there the first time she had seen him. He no longer appeared the captive to her, but was once again the Viking warrior. She swallowed nervously against the realization of what she had done.

Brage felt her gaze upon him and turned to look at her. They stood in silence, staring at each other, recognizing that the daring adventure they were about to undertake could be deadly.

"You are sure you want to go with me?" Brage demanded.

"I am sure," she stated without hesitation.

They regarded each other for a moment longer, knowing that their fates were sealed.

"Let us go."

They slipped from the room and locked the door behind them before starting down the stairs on the first leg of their run for freedom.

They crept along silently, taking care to keep to the shadows. They were nearing the chapel when they heard footsteps coming their way. Dynna knew a moment of panic, for there was nowhere to hide. Frantic, she grabbed Brage's arm and pointed toward the door to the chapel. Together, they darted into the darkened room and stood there, waiting and listening as the footsteps neared and then passed them by.

A sigh escaped Dynna as quiet once again reigned. It was only then that she realized how badly her hands were shaking and that Brage was standing close behind her, the sword at ready. She looked from the blade to him and back.

"I will not go back to that room or the chains."

"I am worried . . . I did not think anyone would be around this late at night. I thought . . ."

"Lady Dynna? Are you in need of help?" Father Corwin had been at prayer when the door had opened and Dynna entered with the stranger. It took him only a moment to figure out who he was and why he was with her.

Father Corwin's question cut through the silence of the room. She gasped and Brage turned on the man, ready to fight.

"Father . . . Brage . . . no . . . " She grabbed him by the arm to stop him from advancing on the priest.

"Father, I did not know anyone would be here . . ."

Father Corwin heard the frantic note in her voice, and understood. He had wondered at her easy acceptance of Edmund's proposal. "Fear not, Lady Dynna, I pose no threat to you." He was kneeling at prayer and kept his eyes closed as he spoke.

"Father Corwin, I must leave this place. I cannot stay here any longer. I cannot marry Edmund."

"Do not fear. I have seen nothing unusual this night."

Dynna was sorely relieved. He had the power to end their flight right then and there, and he had chosen not to. "Thank you."

"Dynna?" Brage was still ready to attack. He did not take his eyes off the priest as he spoke to her.

"It is all right. Father Corwin is a friend."

Brage doubted that, but said nothing. Still, he remained ready for anything as he waited to see what they would do.

Father Corwin sensed the ferociousness in the man at her sided and, in a way, he was glad that the man was with Lady Dynna to protect her. She was going to need a champion. Care for Dynna as he did, he was glad she was daring enough to defy Sir Edmund. "Be careful as you cross the main hall. Eyes will be watching. However, if I were to leave at this hour, I would not be stopped or questioned."

"You would go with us?"

"I cannot, but search and see if you can find what is within God's power to save you." He gestured about the chapel and toward the door that led to the small room where he slept.

She was puzzled by his words and knew a hidden meaning lay beneath them. She moved about the chapel looking for something, anything that might help them, while Brage maintained vigil by the door. As she paused before the portal to Father Corwin's private room, she saw two of his brown robes folded on his narrow bed.

"This is what you meant!" she whispered, snatching them up.

"Peace be with you, my child," he said when he heard her statement. He kept his eyes closed and continued his prayers.

Dynna raced back to Brage who was confused by her actions.

"Here! Put this on."

"What is it?"

"A priest's robe. Put up the hood, and if anyone speaks to you, just nod and keep walking. Act like you are praying."

Brage donned the long, dark hooded robe.

"Good . . . I will wear the other one. That way anyone who sees us will think we're Father Corwin and Father Osmar. As long as we do not speak, no on will suspect."

Brage hid Perkin's sword in the folds of the robe as Dynna drew on the other robe. They were ready to try to escape again.

"Father, is there anything I can do for you?" Dynna implored. "Anything at all?"

"Be safe and be happy, Lady Dynna. God wants you to be so."

"Thank you, Father . . ."

She and Brage shared one last look before she opened the door and led the way toward the main hall.

## Eleven

Brage and Dynna were both thinking of the good priest's promise to pray for them as they continued down the steps. Dynna added her own pleas, while Brage offered up a prayer to Odin, beseeching him to guide them safely from the tower. He was certain he could hold his own in battle once they were in the countryside.

"We are almost there," Dynna whispered as they reached the last turn in the stairs.

Drawing a deep breath to steady himself, Brage tightened his grip on the sword he held hidden in the folds of the robe, ready for trouble as he descended the final steps. He did not remember a lot about the Great Hall, for his memories had been dimmed by the fever. He kept pace with Dynna, following her lead through this critical part of their escape attempt.

Dynna wanted to rush from the hall, but she knew she could not do anything that would draw attention to them. She moved at a deliberate, slow pace, much as Father Corwin and Father Osmar would.

As they began to cross the hall, she peeped from beneath the hood to see five or six men lounging about. Her trembling increased as they passed within ten feet of them, and she held her breath in terrified expectation.

"Good evening, Father Corwin and Father Osmar," one of the men called out.

Dynna could see Brage shift his hold on his hidden

weapon, and she came close to panic, fearing a bloody confrontation, but she held on to her daring, nodding silently in the man's direction. Brage did the same, and they continued on. She waited for the man to come after them or to question their disguise. Each step closer to the gate was torture; each second that passed was fraught with painful anticipation. She did not breathe a sigh of relief until she heard the men's conversation turn back to the mundane.

Both Dynna and Brage knew the worst test was yet to come. They would have to pass the guard at the gate, and if anyone was going to get a close look at them, it would be that one.

Brage did not relax his grip on the hilt of the sword. Having passed through the first test without incident and now being within sight of freedom, he was ready to silence anyone who challenged him. His jaw was locked in fierce determination, his body rigid in self-control as he stayed alert and ready for any sign of trouble.

Dynna could see the dark of night through the gate and knew that salvation was just that close. Just a hundred more feet and they would be away from the horror of the tower. Just another hundred feet . . . She ducked her head, making sure no one could see her face, and she checked that her hands were covered by the long, wide sleeves of the robe.

Each stride they took brought them closer and closer to the most difficult part of their passage. If they made it through the gate, Dynna believed they would make it to her parents' house.

"Good evening, Father Corwin, Father Osmar," the guard greeted them as they approached.

They nodded and continued on—waiting, hoping, praying.

"Trouble in the village, Father?" he asked, not thinking it odd at all that the two priests were going into the village this late. They often went out at all hours to tend to their flock, whenever the need arose.

Both Brage and Dynna tensed even more, knowing they

had to respond. Dynna, of course, could not speak; to do so would be the end to any hope they had. She prayed harder than she ever had in her life, hoping that Brage would know what and how to answer.

"We received word that there is an illness, so we must go and pray with the family."

Brage paused as he spoke in a voice that was as deep as Father Corwin's and just as authoritative. Dynna waited, breathlessly, to see what his reaction would be. She expected to be confronted, but to her surprise, the guard waved them on.

"I hope everything is all right."

"As do we. Good night."

They stepped outside beneath the night sky's canopy of stars and were just about to quicken their pace to distance themselves from the tower as fast as they could, when the guard called out to them.

"Father Corwin?!"

They stopped dead still. Brage kept his back to the tower as he freed the sword from the folds of the robe and stood prepared to slay anyone who attempted to stop him at this point. He waited.

"Yes?"

"Will you be hearing confessions tomorrow?"

Brage had no idea what he was talking about, and he cast a sidelong glance at Dynna in hopes that she could give him a hint of what to say. Dynna had gone pale at the sound of his call. Her heart was in her throat as she believed the end was near. She glanced over at Brage to find him looking at her for guidance. Desperate, she gave a curt nod in answer to the question.

"We will be hearing them tomorrow. Come see me in the morning."

"Thank you, Father. I will."

Brage gave Dynna a crooked, half-smile as he slid the sword back within the folds of the robe.

"Are you ready to go into the village, Father?"

Dynna nodded, returning his smile with a strained one of her own.

Together, they made their escape complete and tasted freedom. The sensation was heady for both of them, but especially for Brage. He wanted to stop where he was and shout his joy, but he did not. He continued on at the measured pace.

"Which way, my lady?"

Dynna still hesitated to speak and so pointed in the direction of the village. Her heart was pounding a frenzied rhythm, and her spirits were soaring as they moved farther and farther away from the tower. This time there would be no Viking invaders to kidnap her and foil her plan! This time she would make it to safety! She would survive by her wits, doing everything in her power to avoid Sir Edmund when he came looking for her the next day—and she knew he would come. But there was no way she was going back with him. She was free, and she was going to stay that way. Dynna did not run, though she wanted to. She walked on calmly into the night, leaving the guard to tell the tale that both priests had gone into the village late that night and had not returned during the span of his watch.

Neither Brage nor Dynna spoke again until they had reached the first turn in the road.

"Here! We need to look in here," Dynna said when she saw the brush and trees where Matilda had promised she would hide his shield and sword. She did not know how, or even if, the maid had managed to sneak them from the tower, but she had every faith in her that she had. Matilda had never failed Dynna when she had needed her.

"For what?" he asked.

At her words of explanation, he charged through the brush, looking for his most precious possessions. When he saw the big bundle wrapped in cloth hidden back behind a tree, he almost let out a shout of joy to Odin. He cast Perkin's weapon aside as he tore the wrapping off. A fire burned within him as he grasped the golden-hilt sword in his hand once more. There had been a time when he had despaired of ever holding it again! He picked up the shield, throwing his head back as he gazed up at the heavens, then he held both the shield and sword up to the sky in praise and offering to his gods who had watched over him and granted him his freedom. After a moment of silent contemplation, Brage felt alive and strong and ready for battle. He stripped off the priest's robe and stood before Dynna, the proud Viking warrior she had met the first time.

Dynna did not say a word as she watched Brage. Silvered by the moonlight, he appeared the powerful, invincible warrior, and she understood how he had come by his fearsome reputation. He was magnificent to gaze upon, and she found herself mesmerized by the strength and beauty of him.

Something stirred deep within her, yet she denied the attraction. Brage cared nothing for her. He had only joined her in the escape because she had forced him to and not for any other reason.

As she considered the thought, though, it occurred to her that now that he was armed and free, he no longer needed her for anything. Should he decide to strike out on his own, there was no way she could stop him. Not even the threat of telling Sir Edmund that he had escaped would matter, for he knew she would never go back to the tower herself.

Brage looked at Dynna then, standing in the moonlight still wearing the priestly robe. He thought she had never looked more lovely. She had the nerve of a dozen Viking warriors and the wits to outsmart the strongest of enemies, yet she was a mere slip of a woman. She looked delicate; he knew she was strong. She looked fragile; he knew she had the determination of a lioness. He remembered her kiss and knew she had the power to entice even the strongest warrior from his purpose. He was there, wasn't he?

Brage had a strong desire to touch her, to hold her and

praise her for a plan so well executed. The thought surprised him. No other woman had ever affected him this way. When he was about to raid, he thought of nothing save the adventure. Yet, Dynna was in his thoughts constantly, and now they had escaped together, something he had vowed to himself he would not allow. He did not try to understand it. He just tried to concentrate on getting them as far away as he could by sunlight.

"Will you wear the robe, Dynna? It might slow us down," he told her.

"Oh . . ." She had been half expecting him to announce that he was leaving her to her own devices, and it startled her to learn that he was waiting for her to shed the robe. She quickly stripped off the garment.

"Is something wrong?" Brage asked, seeing the surprise in her expression.

"No, nothing is wrong. Nothing at all," she answered, feeling much relieved to know that he was not going off on his own.

"You looked worried."

She knew he was adept at reading her moods and so answered him honestly. I had thought that you might go on your own from here, since you have your own sword and shield now."

"You doubted that I would keep my part of the bargain?" This time it was his turn to be surprised, and a little disappointed that she would think so poorly of him.

"I was not sure."

"I gave you my word. We have a bargain," he said.

"Then we had better go. We must travel west."

"How close is the nearest stream?"

"Why?" She did not understand the importance. She wanted to cross the open ground as quickly as they could while it was dark, but it seemed he had another idea.

"No doubt your prince will bring the dogs with him when

he tries to hunt us down. It is best to hide our scent early, lose it in water, and leave them hunting in frustration."

Dynna nodded her approval and led the way.

They were skirting the road, staying near but not on it. At the turn that offered the final clear view of the tower, Dynna paused to take one last look back at what had once been her home. It no longer looked welcoming and warm. It no longer reminded her of Warren. Now, it loomed dark and sinister in the night, as threatening as Edmund. She shivered as she thought of him and the horror of being his wife.

"Let us go," she insisted quickly, making the sign of the cross on herself. "I pray that I will never see this place again."

Brage echoed her sentiments as he followed her into the night.

The night grew darker as low clouds blocked any light, making their going difficult. Still, they set a steady pace and kept to it. When they reached the stream nearly an hour later, Brage waded into the knee-deep water first, with Dynna following close behind. The water was icy, but she did not protest. She concentrated only on keeping up with Brage. At his insistence, they waded as far as they could, staying in the middle of the rushing current.

"If the gods are with us, there will be a storm before dawn," Brage told her as he stopped to study the sky. The clouds looked threatening. "A good, hard rain will help to erase our trail and make it impossible for them to find us," he explained.

"And if it does not rain?"

"Then we had better be a lot farther along by daylight. They will be coming after us on horseback."

The thought chilled Dynna more than the water did, and she shivered uncontrollably as she remembered Edmund charging toward her during the first battle. He had chosen only to humiliate her then. He had not hurt her physically, but this time, she could not conceive that he would be so forgiving. She had helped the prisoner to escape and had fled with him. There would be no charity in Edmund's heart if he caught her.

"I can walk faster," she told Brage, glancing nervously behind her and suddenly feeling the heat of the chase. "Let us hurry."

He glanced at her in amazement, for so far he had been walking at a steady, measured speed. He wondered if she could keep up with him if he struck off at his usual pace. "Are you sure?"

At her agreement, they quickened their strides once they had left the stream and headed west.

Dynna had deliberately directed their trek across country this time. She wanted to avoid everyone she could. She could not afford any mishaps this time. She had to reach her parents. Only they could save her from the coming disastrous wedding.

Brage and Dynna traveled on through the night, crossing farmlands and making their way through thick forests. It was about two hours before daybreak when Brage stopped and turned to her. They had been walking for hours, and her breathing was heavy.

"Do you need to rest?" Brage asked.

"No! There is no need to stop now," she insisted. "We have little time left. It will soon be daylight."

Her endurance surprised and pleased him. They did not rest.

Near dawn the thunder began, warning them of the coming storm. Brage and Dynna sought shelter in a copse of trees whose branches grew low to the ground, offering them some protection from the elements and from discovery.

The rains came—a torrential downpour that washed clean the countryside. Lightning crackled brilliantly in the sky above, and thunder rumbled around them. They sat beneath the trees a distance apart, their shoulders hunched against the rain, listening to the power of nature as it swept over them.

"Do you really think this will help us?" Dynna asked. She tried to control the shivering that was racking her body, but with each gust of wind that accompanied the storm, she grew even colder.

"Yes. Any trace of our trail will be gone. The terrain was rugged enough, but this storm has given us extra time."

"Good. Edmund will guess where we are heading, and he will try to find us before we get to my family. But once we are under my father's protection, we will be safe." She shivered more violently at the thought of what would happen to her if Edmund found her before she reached home.

Brage looked over at Dynna and went still. Her gown was soaked, plastered to her body. His throat tightened as he made out the swell of her breasts. They were firm and round, and, coupled with the memory of her kiss, he felt heat settle low within his body. Again, his reaction to her surprised him. They were running for their very lives, yet instead of thinking of her as a partner, he was thinking of her more and more as a woman . . . a very attractive woman. He could see the full outline of her body, and it was then that he realized just how badly she was trembling. "Come and sit closer to me," he said.

She glanced at him, her expression wary as she tried to keep her teeth from chattering.

"You will be warmer here beside me, Dynna."

"No . . . I . . . " She hesitated, wanting to keep her distance from him.

Lightning flashed just then, and Brage was able to see the doubt and mistrust in her expression. He said in a gentling tone, "You will have to learn to trust me. I have never forced a woman to do anything in my life, and I will not start with you."

Dynna knew he was right. If they were going to make this

trip together, she had to have faith in him. He could have left her, but he had held to their bargain. "All right," she agreed, moving nearer to him.

Dynna still tried to maintain a distance between them, but Brage reached out and put his arm around her and drew her into the circle of his warmth. Using his shield to protect them, he managed to deflect most of the rain.

Despite her best intentions, once Dynna was pressed against the hard-muscled warmth of him, she found herself wanting to get even closer. She knew it was ridiculous, but in that moment she felt safe and protected for the first time since Warren had died. Her back was against Brage's chest, his arm around her shoulder. Her shivering slowly stopped as the heat of him warmed her.

"Do you think they are going to catch us?" she asked, needing reassurance.

"Not if I can help it," he said with no hesitation. "We slipped from the tower without being seen, and then the storm came. It seems luck is with us tonight."

"That would be a change for me," she said, thinking of Warren's death and then her capture by the Vikings as she was on the verge of freedom.

She sounded so forlorn that Brage looked down at her in sympathy. "That would make two of us."

Dynna felt his gaze upon her and looked up at him. Their eyes met just as a gust of wind swept rain over them. They huddled even closer together as they both grinned.

"Maybe we will be lucky for each other. Maybe together our luck will change," Dynna said.

"I intend to see that it does." There was certainty in his voice. He had his shield and his sword. He was on his own with Dynna, matching wits against nature and Sir Edmund. He had no intention of their losing either battle. All he had to do was take her to her parents' home and then he would be free to go.

Suddenly, the day's long hours of planning and the night's

march caught up with Dynna. Fatigue swept over her, and in spite of her best efforts, she sighed.

Brage understood how exhausted she was. He had marched her at a warrior's pace, and she had stayed with him without faltering. Even the hardiest of Vikings would need to rest after the trek they had just endured.

"Rest for a while," he encouraged her. "There is no point in our going on until the weather clears."

"But I need to stay alert. What if someone comes?" she worried.

"I will keep watch. Sleep while you can."

"No," Dynna refused, sitting up straighter. She remembered his argument about having her with him, and she was resolved to match him step for step. She would not be coddled. "We are partners in this. I will keep watch, too."

"There is no reason for both of us to stay awake," he countered.

"Either you agree that we will share the time to keep watch, or I will stay awake with you and we will both keep watch."

He saw the determined look on her face that he was becoming used to, the tilt of her chin, the flash of defiance in her eyes, and he knew it was pointless to argue with her. "Very well. You rest first. I will try to sleep when I wake you."

She nodded in acceptance and leaned a little more into him, to get away from the rain. The slow rise and fall of his chest along with the sound of the solid beat of his heart had a calming effect on her, and she dozed.

Brage remained still and at watch, shielding her as best he could from the storm. Dynna felt delicate, almost fragile to him as she lay against him; yet she was smart and quick and endowed with enormous courage, qualities that he had never known in a woman before. Most of the females he had known relied on their feminine wiles to get what they wanted, rather than talk to men on their own terms and deal with them squarely as Dynna did.

Dynna intrigued him. She was a widow, yet there was still an aura of innocence about her. The more he was with her, the more he learned about her, the more he found himself wanting to keep her from harm. He especially wanted to keep her from Edmund.

Brage could tell the moment Dynna fell into a deep sleep. Even lying so close to him, she had held herself stiffly, and when she slept, she relaxed completely against him. He felt a surge of intense protectiveness as he gazed down at her, her head resting on his shoulder. Her skin was luminous in the darkness. He knew a driving need to touch the softness of her cheek, yet he held himself back, not wanting to disturb her slumber. His gaze swept over her, taking in the curve of her hips, and he instinctively tightened his arm around her. She was beautiful, even dressed as she was in the wet, dirty gown. The women he had known always dressed in elegant garments and perfumed themselves and adorned themselves with jewelry to attract him. This one with her spirit and courage stirred him more than any of the others.

His breathing grew tight in his chest as he thought of the kiss they had shared. He wondered if that moment of ecstasy had been just a moment out of time, heightened by the danger of his situation, or if that kiss had truly meant as much as he thought it had. He wanted to know. He wanted to find out. But this was not the time.

Resolved to keeping her safe from the terrors that threatened her, Brage cradled Dynna against him. He kept his sword close at hand, for he would take no chances with her life. He would protect her with his.

"The Black Hawk has escaped?" Edmund stared at the servant named Hammond across his bedchamber. He was enraged. "How did this happen? Where is Perkin? Bring him to me! I must speak with him!"

"One of the other men is helping him down here even now, my lord," Hammond explained.

"Perkin was injured? Was there a fight? Why didn't anyone hear it?"

"Perhaps he can explain it to you. It's all very strange . . ."

Edmund saw the guard come into view in the doorway of the room. He was leaning on Clive, needing his help to steady himself.

"Is what Hammond says true, Perkin?" Edmund demanded. "Has the Viking escaped?"

"Yes, my lord. Last evening, the Black Hawk was not feeling well. Lady Dynna was with him, and he had gone very weak and could not stand. I went in to help get him into bed."

"Dynna was in the room?"

"Yes, my lord. The next thing I knew, it was morning. The prisoner was gone, and I was bound and gagged and locked inside."

"You were duped!" he snarled.

"But he seemed ill and very weak . . ."

"There is no doubt in my mind that the prisoner was doing fine, you fool! He escaped!"

"But what of Lady Dynna, my lord?" Perkin adored Dynna and worried that something terrible had happened to her. "Could he have taken her with him? He might have hurt her . . ."

"I will check on Lady Dynna," Edmund said, his mouth tightening into a grim line. He wanted to tell him what he thought had happened, but held his tongue. It was not for the guard to know just yet. First, he had to make certain that what he suspected was true.

"I will go look for her," Perkin offered, but as he turned to go, he groaned and held his head. "I do not feel so well. My head is paining me . . ."

"Perhaps I should cut your head off! Then it would pain you no more!" Edmund ground out viciously.

Perkin did not doubt for a minute that Sir Edmund might do exactly as he had said if he took a notion to. "I do not understand it, my lord. How could this have happened? How could I not have awakened when he bound me? I have no recollection of being tied at all. The whole night is a blur . . . and then this terrible pain . . ." He rubbed at his temples, trying to clear his thoughts, trying to make sense of it all.

Edmund knew what had happened. When he spoke, the rage that was within him was barely under control. "Find Lady Dynna and bring her to me," he said to Hammond and Clive.

"Yes, my lord." they echoed as they hurried off.

Edmund ignored the ailing Perkin as he paced his chamber, waiting and wondering if Dynna would be found, yet already knowing she, too, was gone. He thought back over the past few days and realized how very calm and almost submissive Dynna had been. He should have been warned by that change in her behavior that she had been plotting something. He was used to her fiery disposition. He was used to battling her at every turn. She had played him for a fool. The thought left him seething.

"Sir Edmund? Lady Dynna was not in her room. I sought out Matilda in hopes that she would know where Lady Dynna could be, and oddly, the maid was still sleeping," Hammond reported, Clive standing nervously behind him.

"Rouse the maid now!' he ordered harshly.

A drugged and sleepy Matilda was all but dragged before him. Edmund faced Matilda and Perkin.

"Yes, my lord?" Matilda asked, frowning and squinting at him. Her head was hurting and she felt lethargic. Her limbs felt as if they were weighted with stones.

"Where is your mistress?" Edmund demanded.

"Abed, my lord?" She answered his question with a question. "Oooh . . . my head is hurting . . ."

"I am not amused by your answer," he ground out. "Where is Lady Dynna?"

"I do not know," she replied honestly. "I saw her last night as she was preparing for bed. It is my custom to leave her then if she has no need for me. Why, my lord?" She gave him a curious, slightly troubled look. "Is something wrong?"

"The Black Hawk has escaped, and it would seem Lady Dynna has gone with him."

Matilda seemed to be shocked by the news, but the truth was, she was thrilled to know her mistress had fled safely.

"She is not in the tower." Edmund closed on the hapless Matilda. He loomed over her as he said, "I want you to tell me what you know about this. You are her faithful servant. I want to hear everything she ever said to you about the prisoner."

Matilda looked up at him, bewildered. "I am merely her maid, my lord. She said little to me about the Black Hawk. I know only that his fever had broken and his wounds were healing. She was trying to get him up and walking, but I do not know if he was doing well or not."

"Obviously, he was doing very well!" Edmund erupted, wanting to throttle the servant within an inch of her worthless life. "He was doing *so* well that he has somehow managed to walk right out of this tower without being seen! A Viking walked through our midst last night and no one noticed! We are fortunate that we were not all slaughtered in our sleep!"

"I was up and around late," Hammond answered. "But I saw nothing unusual, my lord. All was quiet."

"I want the tower searched from the roof to the cellar," he ordered. "Search every corner, every shadow, every possible hideaway! Check them once, then check them again. Have the guard who manned the gate last night sent here to me."

"Yes, my lord." He quickly left the room with Clive following him.

Edmund turned to the guard. "Perkin . . . did you have

anything out of the ordinary to drink last night?" And then he addressed the maid. "What of you, Matilda?"

"I had my usual ale with my meal, my lord," Perkin answered. He concentrated, trying to remember all that had transpired. As his thoughts cleared a bit, he remembered Dynna bringing him the mug of ale.

"No one brought either of you anything different to eat or drink?"

"Lady Dynna . . ." Perkin blurted out, though he hated to believe that the lovely woman would do such a thing to him.

"What about our fair Dynna?"

"She brought me a mug of ale last eve when she came to work with the prisoner."

"Ah, Lady Dynna, our healer who works with potions and medicines, gave you a drink . . ." Edmund smiled knowingly. Hatred gleamed in his eyes as he thought of her conniving. "And you, Matilda? What did your mistress give you to drink?"

"I had a small cup of wine in my mistress's room before I left her."

His expression became even more savage at this affirmation of all he had suspected. "Have you any idea where she could be right now?"

"No, my lord. I slept soundly all night. I did not even realize it was this late in the morning. I am usually up with the dawn."

"Go and search with the others. Find your mistress and bring her to me. If you value her life, it would behoove you to pray that she is found in the tower."

"Where else could she go?"

"Where else indeed with the Viking missing!" he bellowed, red in the face. His father had not been told yet of the escape, and he did not want to say anything until he had the whole story. Only then would he go to his father with the truth.

## Twelve

Edmund stalked to the window of his bedchamber, his hands clenched into fists. As he stared out across the sodden landscape, he cursed the weather that showed no sign of clearing. The sky was heavy with lead-gray clouds that hung low as far as the eye could see. If Dynna and the Black Hawk had indeed managed to flee the tower, it would be impossible to track them. The rains, steady since before dawn, would have erased any trace of their passing.

Edmund's humiliation ran deep, and he ground his teeth in silent fury. He had always known Dynna was spirited, but this time she had gone too far. He would find her, and when he did . . .

His eyes narrowed as he considered what his retribution would be. He had planned to honor her by making her his wife, but no longer. In running with the Viking, she had sealed her own fate. He would keep her and her dowry as his own, but he would not take her in marriage. She had proven herself unworthy of the position of his lady. He would take her to his bed and use her as he saw fit. Where before he had felt desire for her; now he felt only loathing. He had planned to teach her obedience. Now he would teach her pain. He would punish her and shame her before all the land.

Thoughts of his father intruded on his fantasy, and Edmund's rage turned to a sober chill. Lord Alfrick would be furious over the loss of the prisoner. Hereld would be returning soon with word from Anslak. There could be no exchange without the Black Hawk. He would have to find him, and when he did, he had no doubt he would also find his "betrothed."

Edmund was certain his father would not object to his plan for Dynna. She had, after all, destroyed his carefully made plan by freeing the Viking.

Memories of the interest Dynna had shown in the Black Hawk from the very first taunted Edmund, and he wondered if she had been bedding him all the time she had been visiting him, alone, in the locked room. The possibility fueled his anger. He would see the Black Hawk dead yet! He would slay him, slowly and painfully, right before Dynna's eyes. He would have her crawling to him on her hands and knees pleading for mercy and forgiveness, and he would enjoy every minute of her subjugation.

The image pleased him, and he smiled for the first time that morning. It was a smile that had nothing to do with laughter or joy. Dynna would pay for what she had done.

"Has something pleased you, my son?" Lord Alfrick asked as he came into the room with Sir Thomas. He had met a servant on the stairs and asked where to find Edmund.

"I was smiling, for I was envisioning the Black Hawk dead." He turned to greet his father, not looking forward to this conversation at all.

"But remember, Son, the Black Hawk must be alive for the exchange to be made," Lord Alfrick cautioned.

"I understand." He did not like that fact. "I do have some news this morning that you must hear, but it is not good."

Alfrick's expression turned questioning. "I do not know of what you speak. What news? Has Hereld returned with word that Anslak has refused to pay?"

Edmund only wished it were that simple. "No. Hereld has not yet returned from his journey."

"Then what is it that causes you such concern?"

"Word came to me just a short time ago that the Black Hawk has escaped."

There was a moment of silence, then Alfrick roared, "What?!"

"The Black Hawk is gone?" Sir Thomas echoed, completely puzzled.

"How can this be? What of Perkin? Was he not guarding the door? Was he killed in the attempt?"

"Perkin was not killed, Father."

"It would have been better for the man had he been!" Lord Alfrick raged.

"No, Father. It seems that Perkin was drugged—put to sleep by a sleeping potion concocted by my beloved betrothed," Edmund said with savage intensity.

"You say that Dynna helped the Black Hawk to escape?" Alfrick demanded.

"It would appear that way."

"Where is she?" Lord Alfrick snarled.

"She is missing, too." Edmund's answer was flat and hard. "The tower is being searched, but it is my belief that she drugged those who would stand in her way and fled with the Viking some time during the night."

Lord Alfrick was as outraged as his son. "Word of the exchange will be coming any day. Hereld is due back at any time. Find the Viking, Edmund! Use whatever resources you must, but find him." He paused, his eyes glittering dangerously, "And bring him back to me!"

"Yes, Father."

"Sir Thomas." Lord Alfrick turned to his man.

"Yes, my lord."

"Go with my son. Help him in whatever he needs. I must have the Black Hawk back before the Vikings come with the ransom. I want him found!"

Hammond returned just then to report on the search of the tower.

Edmund commanded him to answer quickly.

"I regret, Sir Edmund, that we have found nothing. There is no sign of Lady Dynna or the prisoner anywhere. The only things we found missing were the Black Hawk's shield and blade, and Perkin's sword, too."

The man was dismissed just as another appeared.

"My lord, Sir Edmund, I am Angus. I was guarding the gate last eve."

"Did you see anything unusual? It would have been late, possibly after midnight."

"No, my lord. It was a quiet night. Only Father Corwin and Father Osmar passed me as they went into the village."

"Father Corwin and Father Osmar?" Lord Alfrick said sharply. "What need was there for the good fathers to be venturing forth at such an hour?"

"They said there was an illness in a family. I watched them for a distance as they left. They walked toward the village."

"When did they return?" Alfrick was instantly suspicious.

"I do not know. I did not see them come back."

"You may go." Lord Alfrick turned to his son and Sir Thomas. "Edmund, find the priests and bring them to me. I will meet with them in my private chamber below."

Edmund's stride was purposeful as he left the room and headed for the chapel.

Lord Alfrick looked at Sir Thomas. "There is only one place Dynna would go if she were to run, Sir Thomas, and that is to her parents. We will search in that direction. I want the Black Hawk back."

"But what of Dynna?"

"What of her? She is less than nothing in my eyes. She has embarrassed my son by abandoning her promise of marriage to him."

"Is there no chance the Viking took her hostage?" Sir Thomas asked, worrying about the princess. He could not bear the thought of her being harmed in any way.

"With Perkin and Matilda both being drugged? I think not. She is the one learned in healing herbs and potions. She planned this. She knew exactly what she was doing."

Sir Thomas stared at Lord Alfrick, seeing his very real anger and his desire to punish both the prisoner and Dynna. Sir Thomas wanted to argue Dynna's side, but he said nothing. He could not admit it openly, but he understood Dynna's decision to flee the coming arranged marriage for yet a second time. Lady Dynna had loved Warren, but Edmund . . . Edmund was nothing like his brother. Sir Thomas still mourned the young man's unexpected passing. There were times when he watched Edmund and witnessed the viciousness in him and wondered about the circumstances surrounding Warren's death in the hunting accident . . .

Lord Alfrick and Sir Thomas left the room and went downstairs to await the arrival of the priests in his private chamber off the Great Hall. Father Corwin and Father Osmar soon joined them, accompanied by Edmund.

"My lord, what has happened?" Father Corwin asked, seeing Lord Alfrick's strained expression.

Lord Alfrick revealed the grim news.

"The Viking has taken Lady Dynna along with him as a hostage?" Father Osmar was aghast.

"No. It is believed that she helped to plan his escape."

"Lady Dynna?" Father Corwin appeared shocked. "But how could she?"

"That is what we wanted to speak with you about. Angus was guarding the gate last night when you left to go into the village. I was wondering if you saw anything unusual on your trek there?"

"I am sorry, my lord, but I do not understand." Father Osmar stared at him in confusion. "I did not go into the village last night."

"Nor did I," Father Corwin offered truthfully. "I prayed in the chapel until late and then retired for the night."

Lord Alfrick gave Sir Edmund and Sir Thomas a knowing look as he asked, "Angus, what were the good fathers wearing when they left the tower last night?"

"Their usual dark robes, my lord."

"It is impossible," Father Osmar denied again.

"Tell me, do you have extra robes?"

"I have several more. They are in my room," Father Corwin answered.

"As do I," the other priest responded. "Why do you ask?"

"Angus is certain he saw you, or at least two people dressed like you, leave here last night. Let us check and see if your robes are still in your chambers."

They hurried to the priests' quarters and opened the door to Father Corwin's chamber first. The search revealed that two robes were gone.

"I did not miss them this morning, for I had already laid out my clothes for today," the priest explained.

"And you saw and heard nothing unusual all night long?" Edmund asked sharply.

"Nothing unusual at all. I prayed long into the night and then retired." He did not lie. It was not unusual for Lady Dynna to come to the chapel. She often prayed there. Looking at Sir Edmund, he knew what she had been praying for: deliverance from him. He hoped with all his heart that she made it safely to wherever she was going. She deserved happiness.

"You are certain?" Edmund pressed him, hoping he would remember some odd thing in the late hours of the night.

"Of course, I am certain. Do you think I would bear false witness to you?" he challenged Sir Edmund, detesting him, but knowing he could not show that emotion openly.

"Edmund was not questioning your honesty, Father. He is merely anxious to find Lady Dynna," Lord Alfrick put in. "And you, Father Osmar, what were you doing last night?"

"I retired very early. I was weary from the long day."

Lord Alfrick nodded in acceptance of his statement.

"Do you need anything else from us, my lord?" Father Corwin asked.

"Only your prayers that the rain stops soon so we can find

the Black Hawk before his father arrives with the gold for his ransom."

The priests left the room, their heads bowed in prayerful reverence.

"I still find it odd that her maid would not know of her plan to escape. Perhaps I should question Matilda more thoroughly," Edmund said.

"Why would Lady Dynna have given Matilda the sleeping potion if she had known of the plan?" Thomas tried to deflect some of his suspicion from the innocent servant. He knew how vicious Sir Edmund's temper could be, and he didn't want to see Matilda pay for Dynna's escape.

"True enough," Lord Alfrick agreed. "Do not waste your time on the maid. It is more important that we begin searching for them as soon as possible. It is clear that they left the tower before dawn, and so have a goodly headstart on us. The Black Hawk is armed again, so it will not be easy to take him alive, but we must."

"Dynna will try to return to her family. There is nowhere else for her to go. I will ride out soon as the rain lessens. I am going to bring them back. I will not return until I do." Edmund's tone was harsh. His stride was quick and his manner deadly as he started off toward the stables to prepare for the search. Again, he cursed Dynna and the rains that continued to hamper him.

"I will ride with Sir Edmund as soon as the weather improves. Is there anything else you require of me?" Sir Thomas asked his lord. His offer sounded natural, but there was far more to his motive than just the desire to find Dynna and the Viking.

"No. You may go."

"I will be in the Great Hall waiting out the storm, should you want me."

Lord Alfrick dismissed him. He remained in the private chamber to mull over all that happened and to plan a strategy to deal with Anslak should he arrive to make the exchange before they found his son.

Sir Thomas went out into the Great Hall and saw Father Corwin about to start up the stairs to the chapel.

"Father Corwin..." Sir Thomas called out. "Do you have time for a mug of ale before you begin your prayers?"

"I would like that." His gaze met Sir Thomas's and they shared a look of understanding.

The two men settled in at one of the trestle tables.

"You seem worried, Sir Thomas. Do you have need to talk with me? Is there something troubling your soul?"

"No, Father," Sir Thomas said with a chuckle. "I am in no state of sin. I just enjoy the peace of your company."

"And I, yours."

"Lady Dynna is a favorite of mine. I am fond of her and am worried about what will happen to her now."

The priest glanced around to make sure it was safe to speak openly. When he spoke, his voice was low and for Sir Thomas's ears only. "I am worried, too. Edmund thinks only of his embarrassment. I find I can think only of the pain she would have suffered married to him. He would have been harsh before, but now..."

"I know. She is far too fine a woman to be forced into a marriage with him. Warren was a good husband to her, but this one..." Sir Thomas knew it was wrong to speak so about Sir Edmund, but he could not help himself.

"Warren loved Dynna. He was a good and true husband to her. He would have made her happy—had he lived..." He let the sentence hang, letting Sir Thomas know that he had his own questions about Warren's untimely passing.

Their gazes met, and each knew he had found a kindred spirit in the other. They remained silent in that understanding as they wondered what they could do to help Dynna.

"We will both pray that she is safe," Father Corwin finally offered.

Sir Thomas nodded thoughtfully. "That is what I want for her most . . . safety. I would see her happy again."

"I would, too."

The steady drumming of the rain was hypnotic, and Brage forced himself to stay alert as he kept watch. Time was passing slowly, the gray sky just now beginning to lighten. He would have welcomed rest, but he could not afford the luxury. He would sleep later when the threat of danger had lessened. Now was not the time.

Brage thought of Dynna's insistence that they share the vigil and did not doubt her desire to help in the duty. Certainly, he knew her to be smart enough to match wits with any man. But if they were found out, it would take brute force to stay alive and free, and she was hardly strong enough to wield his sword against the likes of Edmund and his men.

Dynna was nestled closely against him within the curve of his protective arm. Brage knew she had to be exhausted to be sleeping so soundly. He took the time to study her, his gaze caressing the sweet curve of her throat and the delicate line of her cheek. The darkness under her eyes was another testimony to her weariness, and he felt no guilt in letting her rest. To keep up with him, she would need all the sleep she could get. He kept his arm around her, shielding her, warming her, comforting her, and he turned his gaze back to the vigil.

Later, when the rain finally slowed to a light drizzle, Brage knew they had to start moving again. He hated to wake Dynna, but had no choice. If they wanted to stay free, they could not remain in one place too long.

"My lady," he said softly as he touched her cheek. "It is morning and we must move on."

Dynna came awake with a start. She had been dreaming that she was back home with her mother, safe and warm and loved. It was a shock to wake to the reality of the rain and mud and danger. Only the sight of Brage, still so close beside her, calmed her fear. It was then that she remembered his promise.

"You did not rouse me to stand watch," she said accusingly.

"There was nothing to concern you through the night. All was quiet in the rain."

"That was not our agreement."

"I felt no need to rest yet," he answered simply. "Come, let us go while there is still time."

Dynna realized it was useless to argue further with him, and though she hated to admit it even to herself, she had desperately needed the sleep. She was miserable in her wet clothes, but that misery was worth it to be free of Edmund. "I am ready," she announced. "We head to the north and west again."

She saw a flicker of something that looked like respect in Brage's eyes as he regarded her. She did not know what he expected of her, but she had told him she would match him step for step and she had meant it.

They left the safety of the trees together and headed once again across country, away from the tower. The drizzle stayed with them, and it was late morning before the rain finally stopped and the sky started to clear.

"Maybe now my gown will dry," Dynna observed, feeling uncomfortable in the sodden garment.

Brage, too, was soaked, but he was used to discomfort. Her words were a statement, not a complaint, but he realized then that he should try to find her something dry to wear. They had been deliberately staying as far afield as they could, but he now angled their path closer to what looked to be a small farm in the distance.

"Wait here," he ordered as he stopped at the top of a low rise a distance from the hut. He could make out a man and woman working the fields away from the house, and thought it safe to approach.

"What are you about?" she asked, nervous at the thought of being seen.

"Food, Dynna. This looks the likely spot."

Dynna had been starving since she awakened that morning, but had said nothing, suffering her pangs in silence. She took the fault herself that she had not thought to bring food with her. "But what if you are caught?"

Brage cast her an incredulous look. Raiding was his life. Did she so doubt his abilities that she did not think he could find them a meal? "Rest easy. No one will see me."

Leaving his shield with her and advising her to stay down, he moved forward cautiously, sword in hand. He took care to stay hidden, and slipped inside the single-room hut, leaving Dynna watching nervously from the knoll.

He had suspected that the family would have little and he had been right. He helped himself to what food they had, a partial loaf of hardened bread and a hunk of cheese, then went through their few belongings and found what he needed to start a fire. He wrapped everything in a cloth and was starting from the hut when he saw the small chest at the foot of the bed. Opening it, he found a roughly made gown that would be far too big for Dynna and a man's tunic and trousers that seemed smaller. At least they were dry, and he thought no more of it, taking the men's garments, too. Brage slipped away from the hut unseen and returned to Dynna.

"Let us be gone, lest they return to the hut earlier than sundown to discover my raid," he said.

"Did you get food?" Her gaze was fixed on the bundles he carried.

"Enough for a day or so. I will raid again if I must," he informed her.

Dynna realized Father Corwin would be shocked by his deed, yet without Brage's daring, they would have gone hungry. She could hardly wait until they were far enough away so they could stop and eat.

Brage made sure they had crossed quite a distance before

he started looking for a place for them to rest. He finally found a quiet location on the tree-shrouded bank of a small stream. It was just protected enough to provide the haven they needed.

Brage handed her the bundle of clothes. "I do not know how they will fit, but at least they will be dry." His gaze swept over her muddy, damp gown, and he knew she had to be uncomfortable.

"It would be heavenly to be dry. I thank you for the thought," she told him, fighting down the impulse to hug him.

"They are not pretty, but they will keep you warm until your own have dried."

The smile Dynna gave Brage was so engaging that Brage found himself enchanted. Had he presented her with the finest gown and richest jewelry, he doubted she would have seemed more delighted. He had never seen her happy before, and it pleased him to see her so—and to know that he was the cause.

Dynna took the coarse woolen garments from him and hurried away into the bushes. She glanced back at him shyly, knowing that she was not fully protected from his view.

"You have nothing to fear from me, Dynna. I will turn my back to give you the privacy you seek." He made the offer before she could ask, having seen the look of uncertainty in her eyes. Even as he promised, though, he realized it would be difficult for him to restrain himself.

Dynna murmured her gratitude and hurriedly turned her back to him as she began to strip off the damp gown. It clung to her almost like a living thing, and she was thrilled when she was finally freed of it. She stood unclothed for only a moment before drawing the peasant's garment over her head. It was rough against her, chafing her skin, but she did not complain, for it was dry and warm. From the short length of the tunic she realized it was a man's garment and as such, much shorter than a woman's, revealing most of her legs.

Dynna quickly donned the trousers and tied the waist tight. She had never worn pants before and she felt strange in them. Gathering up her wet clothes, she started from the secluded place.

Brage had been waiting as patiently as he could, knowing that she was undressing behind him. He had been fighting a battle to keep his word to her while she undressed. He had heard her toss the sodden garment aside and had known at that moment that she was standing nude in the midst of the forest. An image formed in his mind of Dynna appearing the nymph, a woodland creature, silken and beautiful in the glade.

The fantasy almost brought a groan from Brage. The thought of Dynna unclothed standing so near to him, set a fire deep within him. He remembered her kiss, the softness of her against him as she had slept, and the smile she had bestowed upon him when he had given her the dry clothing. Brage wanted her with a burning hunger that tested his control.

He tried to fight down what he was feeling for her, concentrating instead on keeping watch over the open lands for Edmund and his men. When that did not work, he tried to distract himself with other thoughts. He realized then that his shirt was wet, too. He pulled the offending garment over his head and spread it over a bush nearby. The day was warm, and he would suffer no chill to be bare-chested.

Brage had just finished laying out his shirt when Dynna stepped out into the open.

"I am changed," she announced.

At the sound of her voice, he could wait no longer to feast his gaze upon her. He turned to face her, and they stood staring at each other, each suddenly, breathlessly aware of the other.

Brage would not have thought that seeing her clad in the men's tunic and trousers would be arousing, but it was overwhelmingly so.

Dynna stared at Brage as he stood before her naked to the

waist, and her heartbeat quickened. She told herself it was ridiculous to feel this way. She had bathed him and nursed him for days on end and had not felt this way before, but there was something so appealing about the wide expanse of his muscled chest that she found she wanted to touch him—not in a healing way, but in a loving way as she had with Warren.

"The clothes will do?" Brage managed.

"Yes, thank you. Though I wonder if you have ever seen a woman in a man's trousers before?"

"I have not, but I do not find the view unpleasant," he said in a tone that was rich with meaning.

Dynna blushed at his words. "Your shirt was wet, too?" she stammered.

He nodded. "Give me your things and I will spread them out with mine while we eat."

She gave him her sodden garments. After he quickly laid them on the bushes in hopes that they would begin to dry, they sat down and he brought out the bread and cheese. He tore off a thick piece of the bread for himself and one for Dynna. He then broke off chunks of cheese for them both before rewrapping what remained for later.

Dynna took the proffered nourishment with eagerness. Though the food was of the meanest of fare, Dynna thought the meal one of the most delicious she had ever eaten.

She found herself watching Brage as he ate, and she noticed that he did not favor his wounded shoulder at all. He acted as if he were completely healed, and she marveled at his strength and recuperative powers. "You are feeling well?" she asked.

"Indeed. You are a good healer. I doubt I would have fared so well at the hands of another."

"It is a talent I learned from my mother."

"Then I am thankful that your mother taught you so well."

Their gazes met as he spoke, and neither looked away. It seemed an eternity passed as they stared spellbound at each other. They were no longer Viking warrior and Saxon woman—enemies sworn. They were now man and woman, and the recognition seared their souls.

Brage spoke first. Ever the warrior, he could not forget that danger was just a breath away. While he was drawn to her as he had never been to another, he knew her safety was the most important thing. They had to stay far ahead of Sir Edmund in their flight to safety. He could think of nothing else for now.

"Come, we must move on. No doubt Edmund is already riding the fields looking for us."

His mention of Edmund jerked her painfully back to the present, and Dynna stood up. "You are right. We have rested here long enough."

She took the food and went to gather their damp clothing while Brage carried his shield and sword. They moved off, their pace quicker now that they had eaten.

They walked on through the afternoon, never resting, ever heading toward her home. The sun finally broke through the clouds late in the day.

Dynna was relieved that they encountered no one on the way. She realized now that if she and Matilda had followed this route the first time, she would have long ago been at home with her parents.

At the thought of her maid, Dynna wondered how the young woman had fared in the face of Sir Edmund's fury. She was sure Lord Alfrick and Edmund had been outraged when they discovered she had fled with Brage, and she hoped they had not taken their anger out on Matilda. Once she was home with her parents, she would send for the loyal servant. Until then, she just prayed that things went easily for her and that she could stay out of harm's way.

"You are worried about something?" Brage asked, glancing back at her and seeing her darkened expression.

"My maid, Matilda. I fear that some misfortune will befall her because I left her behind to bear the brunt of their anger."

"Does the wench know where we have gone?"

"No. I told her nothing of my plan. It was safer for her that way, but I know how cruel Edmund can be when he has been thwarted."

"It is you he wants. He will not waste time with her once he is certain she cannot help him."

"That is my hope."

"And that is why we will keep walking until after the sun has set. The next few days will be the most dangerous."

She nodded. "Do not fear that I will fail you. I have said that I will match you and I will."

Again, Brage had to admire her courage, and the look he gave her told her he was pleased with her answer. They trudged on, heading farther and farther away from the demons that chased them.

It was just at dusk when they heard the roar. Dynna knew a terrible sinking feeling as she recognized the sound of the stream flowing fast and deep. She had known there was another stream to cross, but she had not thought it would be running this high. The rains to the north must have been even heavier than the ones they had suffered.

Dynna and Brage made their way to the bank and stared at the rushing water. Brage studied the banks on both sides, trying to pick the safest place to ford the waist-deep stream. The current looked dangerous, and he knew if they lost their balance, it would be difficult to regain their footing.

"Should we camp on this bank and cross the stream on the morrow?" Dynna asked, hating the prospect of getting wet again. As fast and deep as it was, there was no way she could stay dry in the crossing. By the next day, the level should drop and make crossing easier.

"There is still enough daylight left for us to ford now." He answered without glancing at her, so he did not see her concern. He had been born and raised with streams like these. He knew it would not be an easy crossing, but he knew it could be done if they were careful.

# PASSION

He left Dynna standing on the bank as he scouted the stream to find the safest place to ford. It took him a few minutes in the fading light, but he finally found it. The bank was steep, but the current looked less threatening there. He returned to get Dynna and led her to the site.

"Follow me," he said as he slid down the bank and readied himself to enter the rushing stream.

Dynna was dreading getting all wet again, but knew she had no choice. Staying away from Edmund was more important than any temporary misery. She started down the steep slope to join Brage. Dynna had not counted on the bank being so slippery, and she half-slid down the incline to the water's edge.

"Stay there," he ordered as he worked his way across the stream, testing to make sure it would not be too dangerous for Dynna.

He moved slowly and carefully through the rushing current, keeping his shield and sword out of the water. He was glad the water level did not rise above his waist. The opposite bank was not as steep as the one he had entered from. He left his weapon and shield there and went back to guide Dynna across.

"Take my hand and I will help you," he told her as he neared the bank where she waited for him.

He held out his hand to her as he stood in the thigh-deep water. Though it was not dangerously deep here, the current was strong, and he did not want to take any chances with her safety. As she reached out to take his outstretched hand, juggling the bundles of food and clothes, she slipped and lost her footing, almost falling into the water.

Brage reacted instinctively, sweeping her up into his arms and clasping her to his chest, safe and dry out of the water. "Are you all right?" he demanded.

Dynna gazed into his eyes, breathless from his rescue and more . . . "Yes."

He stood there, the cold stream rushing around him, unaware of anything save the precious weight of Dynna in his arms. He looked into her eyes and could see the longing there that matched his own, and he could not stop—not this time. He bent his head to her, his lips seeking and finding hers in a passionate claim.

# Thirteen

The kiss kindled the long-banked fire of Brage's need, and the flame of his desire flared hotly to life. Dynna responded without reserve, linking her arms around his neck and returning his kiss full measure. The heady embrace left them both stunned by its power.

They gazed at each other in passionate wonder as Brage strode across the stream, taking care to keep Dynna out of the cold water. He had little recollection of the fording, for his eyes were only on Dynna. They reached the other bank, and he did not pause but walked straight to a tree-sheltered area where he laid her down upon the bed of soft, sweet grass.

Brage stretched out beside her, his mouth taking hers again in a bold proclamation of his need. Dynna moaned softly. Warren had been a kind and gentle lover, but his kisses had never roused her this way. When Brage suddenly drew away from her, she opened her eyes wondering at his abandonment and ready to plead with him not to leave her.

"Brage?" She said his name in a husky whisper as she held out her arms to him in entreaty.

It was all he could do not to forget his mission, but he stood firm in what he knew he must do. "I will be right back."

Dynna was all Brage wanted and needed, but in wanting her and needing her, he had to protect her. Ever vigilant, he returned to the bank to take up his shield and sword from where he had left them. He quickly returned to her side.

Dynna watched Brage as he returned to her in the dying light of the day, and a thrill of anticipation filled her. He was tall, broad-shouldered, and almost savage-looking as he came to stand over her with his sword in hand. His jaw was shadowed by a new growth of beard, giving him an even more dangerous appearance. Her pulse quickened. Brage was man—all man. His pants, soaked from crossing the stream, clung to his long, powerful legs like a second skin. Learned in the ways of men, there was no mistaking for Dynna the desire he felt for her. Yet far from feeling embarrassment over the proof of his need, she was pleased. As he laid his weapon aside within arm's reach, though, the thought of their danger threatened the building passion she was feeling.

Brage saw the flicker of fear in her eyes and dropped to his knees beside her. "You are safe with me. Nothing will harm you while I have breath in my body," he vowed, his gaze searing hers with the intensity of what he was feeling.

"I know," she said softly.

"I know not what the morrow brings, but we have this night . . ." he began.

She lifted her hand to his cheek. "Let us share it fully."

Brage's breath caught in his chest at her gentle touch. He shed his wet clothing, not wanting to dampen hers, and then groaned in male appreciation of her feminine softness as he drew her near. He stared down at her in the darkness of the hour and could see the desire in her expression that matched his own.

"Tonight you are mine," he said. His mouth sought hers in a hungry kiss.

Dynna welcomed Brage eagerly. Her hands skimmed over him, memorizing his hard-muscled body.

With the threat of discovery ever haunting them, she realized this might very well be their only night together, and she was determined to share her passion with Brage. She had wanted him from the first, though she had not freely admitted it to herself until now. They were from two different worlds and would remain so, but for this moment in time, they were together, and that was all that mattered.

The fire of their need blazed ever higher, and they would not deny themselves. The uncertainty of the future they faced made their coming together all the more poignant.

With gentle hands, Brage caressed Dynna through the coarse woolen fabric of the peasant's clothes she wore. As near as he was to her, though, he wanted to be even nearer. He wanted to touch the silken softness of her bare skin. He wanted to sheath himself in the velvet core of her. He wanted to make her his in all ways. With muttered impatience, he shifted away from her just enough so he could help her to undress.

Dynna was glad to be rid of the clothing. She wanted to press herself against him, to feel the heat of him warming the coolness of her own flesh, to feel his hard chest against her sensitive breasts.

As he lifted her tunic over her head, she arched herself toward him. She was rewarded when he gave a growl of appreciation as he saw her breasts for the first time. His hands claimed the silken orbs, caressing them, cupping them. His lips sought that tender flesh, and she gasped at the sensation that pulsed through her. She clasped his head to her, enraptured by his intimate touch.

When Brage laid her back upon their bed of soft grass, Dynna drew him down with her, holding him to her. When he moved from her, she felt momentarily lost, but the look of burning desire he gave her left no doubt in her mind that it would not be for long. He untied the men's trousers she wore and pulled them from her, baring her slender legs to his view. He caressed her legs, glorying in their supple firmness.

"You are beautiful, Dynna," he told her, his eyes intense

with passion and need and another emotion he could not yet name. He wanted her more than he had ever wanted any woman.

"I am glad you think so. I think you are, too," she said in a husky voice as she reached for him.

"Men are not beautiful."

"You are," she said in a throaty voice.

Brage was glad that the frustrating barrier of her clothing was gone. They came together. Dynna caressed him and kissed him, evoking powerful responses from Brage that surprised him with their intensity. They desperately sought that unity of love with each other, hoping to find solace and peace.

When at last he moved to make her his own, Dynna was ready. She boldly touched him, taking him deep within her as she wrapped her legs around his hips and met him in a passionate mating. She was fire to his flame. Her lovemaking, so freely given, drove him to mindlessness as he sank deep within her and then drew back to claim her again. It was pure ecstasy to be one with her.

Rapture enveloped them as their lips met. Their hands were never still as he moved with her, and she matched him thrust for thrust. She wanted him. She wanted this. She did not know what the morrow would bring, and right then, it did not matter. All that mattered was Brage.

Brage had never known passion so wild and free. He did not know if it was the desperation of their situation or the truth of their feelings for each other, and he did not care. He was enthralled, lost in a sea of sensual enchantment that sent him soaring to heights of excitement he had never known existed.

Brage's possession was so powerful and so thrilling that Dynna gave herself over to it. The heat of him deep within her stirred her to mindlessness, and she clasped him to her, rocking against him, seeking to give him pleasure. Brage's expert caresses and kisses created a hot, coiling need within her, and Dynna pressed herself even more tightly to him. When he sought her breast with another heated kiss, the ecstasy that had been blossoming within burst upon her fully. She clung to her Viking as the sensations of that perfect peak throbbed through her.

Brage saw the look of satisfaction on her face and kissed her deeply. She returned his kiss as he continued to move strongly against her, and he shuddered in pleasure as he reached the pinnacle of his own excitement. He held her close, his breathing a harsh, strangled rasp. Never had he known such bliss.

They drifted back to reality together, clasped in each other's arms, their limbs entwined. Neither spoke. Neither felt the need to. Their bodies had expressed far more eloquently than words ever could what they were feeling.

"I did not know it could be so sweet . . ." Dynna finally whispered when she had her strength back.

"Nor I," he answered as he braced himself on his elbows to gaze down at her in the darkness.

His movement brought his hips even more firmly against hers, and they gazed at each other in knowing wonder. Brage would have preferred to remain lost in the haze of her lovemaking, but with the cooling of his passion, sanity returned. He shifted away from her, positioning himself closer to his sword.

Dynna did not want to be separated from him, and she moved to lie beside him. She did not want this time of intimacy to end. Brage slipped an arm around her and brought her to rest her head on his shoulder. She splayed her hand out on his chest and felt the heavy thud of his heartbeat beneath her palm.

"Now I am the one who is glad that I am a talented healer," she told him.

He gave a soft chuckle. "You may heal me any time."

"It would be my pleasure." Her voice was throaty with promise.

"I do have an ache that pains me, woman."

Dynna immediately thought that he had somehow reinjured himself in their coming together. Her expression turned serious as she sat up and reached for his other shoulder, thinking it was paining him again.

"No, wench. It is not my shoulder that aches, but here," he caught her hand and brought it to his lips. "A kiss should cure it, I think."

Her eyes sparkled as she realized his jest, and she gladly doctored his pain, kissing him warmly.

Brage had not expected that simple kiss to rouse him again so soon, but it did. He thought for a moment that she was a witch who had cast a spell on him, but as she moved over him, taking him deep within her body, he ceased to think at all.

It was much later, when Dynna slumbered beside him, that Brage realized the power of what he felt for her. She had done as she had said she would. She had matched him in all things. He watched her sleep, knowing she was the only woman who had ever shown him such courage and openness. There had been no maidenly shyness in their joining, and it pleased him to know that he had given her pleasure.

Even now, having taken her twice, he felt a desire for Dynna stir in his loins at the thought of tasting her passion yet another time. Unwilling to sacrifice even one minute of the black silken night, Brage kissed her awake and began to caress her once more.

When at last exhaustion claimed them both, Brage held her in the circle of his arms and kept her safe and warm through the balance of the night.

Dynna awoke as dawn stained the eastern sky and the morning birds offered up their song. She kept her eyes closed as she nestled against Brage's chest. It was heavenly to be so protected, so safe in his arms.

Dynna felt no guilt over what they had shared through the

long hours of darkness. She had wanted to make love to him. Though their futures were uncertain, at least now she would have last night to remember. She moved slightly, and Brage came instantly awake.

"Is something wrong?" he asked, immediately alert and reaching for his sword.

"It is dawn," she said softly, still not wanting to leave his embrace.

"Then we must move, and quickly," he said.

Brage started to get up and dress, but somehow the temptation of her sweet body pressed so tightly against his, heated his blood again.

Dynna felt the response in him and smiled invitingly. Warren had been a good lover, but never had he been as passionate as Brage. "Must we leave right away . . . ?"

Her question brought only a growl of torment from him as his logic warred with his physical need. The sense that had always kept him alive told him to fight the passion she roused in him, so he could keep her safe, but it was her safety that gave him the strength to deny himself that which he wanted most.

Brage kissed her, deeply, wildly, letting her know by his embrace that he was not rejecting her. "I cannot take a chance with your life, love," he told her in a voice that betrayed the conflict within him. "We must move while we can."

Tears burned in her eyes as she lifted her hand to caress his cheek. No one else had ever put her safety and happiness first. It touched her that this man, this Viking who had been her prisoner, now was protecting her with his life. "I will be ready in a moment."

She rose up to kiss him, sweetly, gently, then moved out of the haven of his embrace to wash at the edge of the stream. She thought about donning her own gown this morning, but found it still slightly damp. Resigned to wearing the stolen garments again, she dressed quickly.

Brage had tugged on his own clothes as he had kept watch over Dynna. It had been all he could do not to join her at the water's edge and help her with her bathing. There could be no forgetting the satin of her skin and the sweet weight of her breasts in his palms. His body stirred against his will, and he turned his thoughts to food.

He tore them off each a piece of bread and cheese, and they ate as they walked on, leaving their secluded paradise behind. Together, they headed out into the unknown.

It was late that afternoon when Edmund and his men rode into the small farm. After looking about for a while, they finally located the farmer and his wife working the fields. Edmund did not give any thought to the fact that his horse was trampling the crops that they were working so hard to tend. He cared only that he had to find Dynna and the Viking—and soon.

"Tell us, have you seen a man and a woman?" Edmund demanded.

The peasant stared up at Sir Edmund. He wondered why he had come to them. "We have seen no one, my lord."

"And nothing unusual has happened?"

At this the wife interrupted. "Tell him, Dorcas. Tell him about the missing food and clothing."

"Food? Clothing?" Sir Thomas repeated her words.

"While we were working the fields yesterday, someone entered the house and took bread and cheese from our larder," the man explained, "along with my extra tunic and pants. Odd, that. We saw no one and heard nothing."

"There was no trace of a trail? No hint to the direction the thief fled?"

"None, my lord. It was near dark by the time we returned to the house, and by morning, whatever trail might have been there was lost."

Edmund glanced back at his men. "Spread out in all directions away from the fields. Search everywhere. Find them."

Sir Thomas assumed the lead. The men had been riding every daylight hour since the rain had stopped. Their horses were growing weary at the task, but there would be no quitting until the Black Hawk was found.

Sir Edmund knew Hereld would be returning at any time, and no doubt soon after him the Vikings would come to pay the ransom. Time was of the essence. There could be no more mistakes made. They had to find the Black Hawk.

It was near dark when one of the men came to the place by the stream where Brage and Dynna had crossed.

"Here, Sir Edmund!" one man called. "They forded here!"

Edmund's avidness to find them intensified as he studied the bank and then rode his horse across to the other side. For the first time since leaving the tower, he knew they were closing in on them.

His frustration had been great. He had tried to use the hounds, but the scent had been lost in the rain just as he had feared, and they had proved useless. Since then, it had been a matter of searching every possible route to Dynna's parents' home, and now finally, it would be only a matter of time before the Viking was back in his control and Dynna in his bed.

"Do we search on or make camp for the night and begin anew with the morning?" Sir Thomas rode up beside Edmund in the clearing where the lord sat on his mount.

Edmund wanted to continue, but he feared that if it grew too dark they might miss something. "We will stay the night here and ride on at first light."

"I will tell the men," Sir Thomas replied.

Alone again, Edmund dismounted and stared around. Only a short time before, Dynna had passed this way. He smiled a cruel smile. Soon he would have her back. Soon she would be his. The thought gave him respite for the night. Yet, knowing they were so close, he did not sleep well. He remembered his father's stern admonishments to return as quickly as possible with the Viking. He vowed he would not rest easy until the Black Hawk was found.

Dynna and Brage moved rapidly across the countryside, distancing themselves ever more from the tower. Still, no matter how many miles they crossed, they both knew danger could be awaiting them as close as the top of the next hill.

Brage had been hard pressed to keep his mind on their flight. He had never let a woman intrude on his thoughts when he was raiding. Yet he found himself constantly aware of Dynna. Memories of her loving were seared upon his soul and haunted him. No woman who had ever given so freely of herself, and none had satisfied him so completely. He found himself wanting to stay near her, to touch her every chance he could. These new emotions were foreign to him, and he had to battle them down. He could not allow himself to be distracted from keeping careful watch.

Dynna had kept up with Brage as he walked at his fast, long-strided pace. She was exhausted, but understood that he was driven, as she was, by the need to reach safety. She offered no protest to his speed, but stayed with him. Occasionally, he would glance at her to make certain she was all right, and their eyes would meet. It was then that she could see he was remembering what had passed between them, and she would smile at him without saying a word. It was all the communication they needed. Brage would lead on again, taking the most difficult route to throw off anyone who dared to give chase.

Near midday, they stopped to drink from a cool, clear stream and to rest for a while and share more of the bread and cheese. Brage had been thinking of Warren. He wanted to know more about him.

"Tell me of your husband, Dynna," he asked casually, though his feelings were hardly cool on the subject.

"What of him?" she returned with caution, not sure why he was asking.

"What kind of man was he? Surely, he was nothing like Edmund."

"They were as different as the bright sun of the morning is from the black darkness of the night," she said quickly in Warren's defense. "My husband was a good man, kind of heart and generous with those he loved."

"Has he been dead long?"

"Less than a year. A hunting accident took him unexpectedly. It was always my sorrow that I never had the chance to say good-bye to him."

Brage saw the real sadness in her eyes, and asked, "Did you love him?"

"He was good to me, gentle and caring."

"But did you love him? Did you want the marriage to him?" Though he knew not why, it was so important to him to know the truth of her feelings for her dead husband.

Before last night, Dynna would have quickly answered in the affirmative, but having spent hours of splendor sharing Brage's lovemaking, she was no longer certain of anything. Struggling for an answer to his question, she replied, "My marriage to Warren was arranged for the benefit of both of our lands, but I had no objection to it."

Brage listened to her evasive response and still was uncertain of her feelings. It seemed that Dynna would not or could not tell him that which he wanted to know. Had she loved Sir Warren, he reasoned, she surely would have confessed as much. There was no shame in loving your spouse. The thought that she could not answer him straight out made Brage inexplicably happy.

Dynna had suffered Brage's questions, and now found herself wondering about his past. She suddenly worried that he might have a wife waiting for him. The possibility struck at the very heart of her.

"Now there is a question I must ask you," Dynna finally ventured, garnering enough strength to hear the news she expected—that a woman who loved him was keeping his home for him while he was off raiding.

Brage's brows rose at the tightness he heard in her voice. "What do you wish to know?"

She paused to draw a breath before asking the dreaded query.

"This worries you?"

"If you have pledged yourself to another, what has passed between us would be wrong in the eyes of God and man."

He smiled softly at her honesty. "Do not fear, my Dynna. I have no wife to count the nights till my return or to mourn the news of my death."

Dynna did not attempt to hide her pleasure, and the smile that lit up her face sent a surge of desire coursing through Brage. He could not stop himself from going to her right then in the light of day and taking her in his embrace. He gazed down at Dynna for a long moment before kissing her. She responded without reserve, looping her arms around his neck as she clung to him. When at last Brage ended the kiss, they were both hungry for more. Only the knowledge that it was daylight and they might be discovered kept them apart.

"We must go," he said regretfully.

They gathered their few possessions and headed onward toward the haven at the end of their journey.

It was late before they stopped for the night. Darkness was settling its sheltering grace across the land as they finished off the last of their food. An aura of anticipation existed between them as they remembered the promise of the embrace they had shared at their midday meal.

Dynna had been shocked to find herself burning with the need to be one with Brage. All afternoon she had followed his lead, her eyes constantly on him. She had marveled at his strength and endurance, watching the fluid way he moved even over the roughest terrain, watching the play of his muscles across his arms and back as he led the way. Occasionally, when their gazes had met she had seen in the depths of his intense blue-eyed regard the heat that had branded her last night, and knew that it had not been a dream.

Dynna rose and without a word spread her gown out on the grass. Brage was confused by her action.

"Is the gown still wet that you would spread it out again to dry? If so, the dew will dampen it even more by morning."

"It is already dry, my lord Viking."

"You do not wish to wear it again?" He had thought she would put it back on once it had dried. The material was of the finest and would wear far more softly on her fair skin than the peasant's things.

"I have found it is far easier for me to match your steps in these trousers. Matilda, I fear, would not approve of my brazenness, though," she said, grinning at him as she found his gaze focused on her legs.

Brage grinned back at her. Again, she was proving to be far different from any woman he had ever known. She was not the least concerned with her appearance, only with keeping her word to him that she would not slow them down. He closed the distance between them to hold her.

*"I* approve most heartily of your brazenness," he told her as he lifted her chin and claimed her lips in a hungry kiss. He felt complete now that he had her in his arms. "Then what is your game with the garment?"

"I merely make your bed for your pleasure," she told him huskily as she looked up at him.

Hearing her words, passion flared in his eyes and the heat of it consumed him. She felt a shiver of excitement of her own frisson down her spine. He kissed her once more, and, at the touch of his lips, Dynna was lost.

When they lay down together on the simple bed, they came together in a heated rush of desire that had been building between them all day. Their hands were eager as they caressed each other, and they rushed to strip away the garments that kept them apart. When at last all the barriers between them were gone, they became one.

Brage sank within the depths of her body. He knew eventually he would be parted from her, and that realization brought an edge of desperation to their lovemaking, as if each sought that short time to feel free. They clung together, one in spirit and need, until the rapture of their release crested upon them. They collapsed together, spent, yet content, in each other's arms.

Dynna stared up at the star-studded night sky. She did not know how she had come to give herself so freely to a man who only a short time before had been her enemy. Yet, as she lay in the haven of his embrace, she felt no threat; instead, she felt as if nothing could harm her as long as she was with him.

Her heart swelled as she realized they had only a short time left to be together. He would return to his own people, as she would go back to hers.

"I want more of you, Brage," she whispered, feeling more bold than ever before, for she had never before dared say such to a man.

Her words were all the invitation Brage needed. He moved over her, claiming her body with his in one fiercely possessive move. She accepted him fully, glorying in the unity with him. His hands explored her silken flesh, tracing patterns of fire upon her, rousing her once again, until they were moving together in search of that ultimate fulfillment.

Brage longed to tell her that he wanted her, too, yet he could not say it. They would be parted soon. He could not take her with him on his trek home. It would be far too dangerous. Far better that he saw her to her parents, and then left her there knowing she would be protected. It would not be easy to leave her behind, but he had no choice.

They made love quickly and powerfully, and they were

left breathless in the wake of the ecstasy that swept over them. They lay quietly together, their limbs entwined, celebrating the beauty of their loving, their hearts beating as one.

They slept.

When at dawn they awoke, the desire to remain in the quiet woodland, sharing their intimacy was near to overwhelming, but they both knew it was impossible. They could not forget the threat of Edmund.

Brage held Dynna close for a long quiet moment before they gathered their things and started onward.

They crossed several open fields that left them both nervous and watchful. They had no food and soon Brage would have to find more.

It was just past the noon hour when Brage caught sight of the riders in the distance coming their way.

"It is Edmund . . . " Dynna gasped, recognizing his steed from afar. She began to tremble, but knew this was no time to let her fears overrule her reason. They were at the edge of a forest, and Brage grabbed her arm and dragged her into the cover of the thick foliage.

"Did they see us?" she asked, panting from the exertion of running beside him full speed through the tangled undergrowth. It reminded her dreadfully of that first day when she and Matilda had been trapped by Brage's men. She could only pray that the same fate would not befall them this time.

"I am not certain, but I will take no chance."

He ran on, never looking back, heading for the thickest brush. He knew it would be hard to track them there and difficult for the horses to maneuver. A ledge rose ahead of them, and though it did not offer much in the way of real protection for them, at least it would shield their backs as he made his stand against those who would attack them from the fore.

"In here!" Brage ordered.

Dynna was nearly exhausted, but she would not give up.

Edmund was right behind them, and the terror of being taken by him again gave her the strength she needed.

Brage pushed her into the protected area and stood staunch and ready before her. He held his sword in a death grip, his knuckles showing white as the tension of the coming battle filled him. He wondered how many men would come after him. He would not go back just to be slain. Better that he die here, weapon in hand and go to Valhalla than to be offered up in sacrifice to the Saxon's devious and deadly plan.

"They are near," he warned Dynna in a whisper. "Hold your tongue. Any sound will draw them . . ."

As they stood poised together they heard the sound of a horse's hooves as the steed made its way through the woods in their direction. Twigs snapped, leaves rustled.

Dynna held her breath as she watched and waited. She beseeched God to keep them safe, pleaded for protection from Edmund's cruelty and cunning.

Brage had little time for prayers to his gods. He concentrated on the sound of the horse's tread. He waited, every muscle tense. His senses were screaming a warning, and he let his gaze sweep the vista before him for a sign of the one following them. He would attack first if he could. It would be his only chance to survive. If he killed one of Edmund's men, he could take his weapon and horse. He would be equal to the others then, and perhaps could draw them away and give Dynna time to escape. He heard the horse stop. He waited. He heard the sound of the mount start to move again . . . closer . . . ever closer . . .

Brage lifted his weapon as he knew the horse and rider were nearly upon them. He heard the horse's wheeze and knew they would be seen by the Saxons. The one who had followed them had known what he was about. There would be no escape, no safe haven, no return home.

Brage readied himself. He was about to do mortal combat.

Dynna was quaking in terror as their pursuer closed on them. Edmund's man was near . . . so very near. She wished they were invisible. She wished they had wings so they could fly from this place that had become a death trap and not a hiding place. She longed for safety for herself and Brage. She did not want him to lose his life protecting her.

The thought of him dead tore at her, and Dynna almost reached out to touch him, to reassure him. Just as she was about to, though, the horse loomed into her line of vision and she had to bite back a scream of terror.

Brage's nerves were stretched taut. All their running had been for naught. All their planning had been pointless.

He heard the steed stop before their hideaway, and he raised his sword ready to slay the one who had found them. If he had to die, he would not make it easy for them.

# Fourteen

It all happened in an instant. Brage was ready to deliver a death blow to the one who had ventured too near them when Dynna launched herself at him and grabbed his sword arm. Brage shook her off. He was fully ready to do battle with this man, but when he looked up at the one on horseback, he stopped. There before them was Sir Thomas, and he was staring straight at them.

Brage stood, sword poised at ready, as he met the other man's gaze in challenge. Sir Thomas kept his expression benign, yet his eyes flashed a stern warning. He looked pointedly at Dynna and saw that she was unharmed.

Dynna met his questioning regard evenly, letting him know by the look that she was there because she had chosen to be.

Sir Thomas was caught between a smile of relief over finding her and a frown of concern for their situation. He was pleased to see that Lady Dynna was unharmed, but worried by Sir Edmund's proximity. He wanted to see her freely away from Edmund, but was honor bound to maintain his loyalty to Lord Alfrick. Sir Thomas glanced away, keeping his expression from revealing anything of his discovery.

"Were I of a mind to leave this place, I would stay to the hollow till I came to the headland." He spoke under his breath, his lips barely moving. "From there, it is a straight trek along Woodford Way to Brightwell's Spring. That would seem the safest path to travel this day."

"Brightwell's Spring?" Dynna whispered.

"It is north and to the west. And were a man a friend to another, he would try to lead those who would harm his friend in the opposite direction."

Dynna felt tears burn in her eyes at his quietly offered help. "Thank you, Sir Thomas," she said for his ears alone.

"Any sign of them?" came Sir Edmund's call as he rode close by.

Brage and Dynna froze. Their every nerve was stretched taut as they awaited Sir Thomas's answer. Their gazes were locked on him. He could save them or see them slain.

They did not have to wait long for his answer.

"No. I thought I saw something moving here, but it turned out to be nothing," Sir Thomas answered in a normal voice.

"My lord! Look what I found running in the woods!" another of the men called to Sir Edmund from afar.

Brage and Dynna could hear the horses moving in a direction away from their shelter.

"It would seem that we did see someone heading this way after all," Sir Thomas called out as he watched the man herd two young boys toward Sir Edmund. Then, as he readied himself to join the others in his party, he muttered in a low voice to Brage, "Be warned, Viking. See that no harms befalls her. I would hate to spend the balance of my days tracking you down."

Brage was shocked by the man's threat, and he had enough respect for him to know that he meant it. Sir Thomas made a good friend, but he would also make a relentless enemy. Brage had no time to respond as Sir Thomas immediately whirled his horse around and rode away.

Knowing their danger had not lessened, Brage pressed Dynna farther into their hiding place. He stood with his back to her, shielding her body with his as they waited to see which way Sir Edmund and his men would ride.

Edmund was muttering a vile curse as Sir Thomas rode up. He had thought he had cornered the Black Hawk and

Dynna. His spirits had been high, for he had believed he would be returning to his father with the Viking captive in plenty of time to make the exchange. But his hopes had been dashed. He had merely wasted time hunting down two peasant boys in these woods. He glared at the youths as they were dragged before him.

"Have you seen a tall, black-haired man and gray-eyed woman traveling together on foot?" Sir Edmund demanded of the two. He might not have found the pair he sought, but maybe he could get some information from the ones they *had* found.

"No, my lord," the taller of the boys answered nervously. "We have only seen our own people, no one else."

"How far is your village?" Sir Edmund asked.

"By the river."

"We will take you there, so that we can see if any other has encountered the ones we seek." Edmund was disgusted, but not defeated. He would not stop until he had Dynna and the Viking back. He gestured to the boys. "Bring them along," he ordered two of his men. "Let us ride."

Brage waited tensely for the sounds of the horses to fade away. He was relieved that they had ridden in the opposite direction. Still, neither he nor Dynna moved for what seemed like an eternity. Their hearts were pounding and their breathing was strangled, but they remained still.

Finally, when the sound of the hoofbeats could no longer be heard, Brage spoke. "Stay here while I make certain it is safe."

"Be careful . . ." Dynna said, and she began to tremble.

Brage ventured forth cautiously to survey the forest around them. He stood there, his piercing gaze searching for some sign of Sir Edmund or his men, but all was quiet. They were alone in the woods.

He turned to look back at Dynna, and it was then that he saw how white-faced she was with fear. She had been so brave for so long, that to see her so frightened struck at the very heart of him. He called to her, "It is safe."

At his words, Dynna hurried forth to join him. She wanted to touch him, to make sure he was all right. He could have been killed! It had been close . . . too close. For those few moments, she had lived in horror of seeing Brage struck down before her very eyes. The possibility had left her shaken and drained.

"Had any other of Edmund's men found us, he would have killed you . . ." The terror of the thought still filled her.

"He would have tried," Brage said with a fierceness that reminded her he was a Viking warrior—savage, determined, unafraid.

"Sir Thomas saved us both."

"The man must care for you deeply."

"He is truly a man of honor. He was a friend to Warren and is now a friend to me, and I value that friendship. He is a kind man whose heart is good. I trust him with my life."

"It was not the first time he defended you against Sir Edmund," Brage remarked.

"How did you know?"

"I was watching you that night in the tower when Edmund would have beaten you had not Sir Thomas intervened."

Dynna shuddered visibly at the memory of that horrible moment and at the thought of how close she had come just now to being back in Edmund's power again.

The fear that shone in her eyes stabbed at Brage, and he felt an unusual surge of tenderness. He went to her and touched her hair in a gentling caress.

"It was hard for me to watch, chained as I was." His gaze caught and held hers as he spoke. "I was glad when he came to your aid."

"Edmund is a cruel man. He would have taken great pleasure in beating me."

She trembled again, and Brage drew her close and held her sheltered in his arms.

"There is no need to worry. No one will ever hurt you as long as I am with you."

Dynna drew renewed strength from Brage's confidence, and slowly, the fear that was haunting her eased. As she gazed up at him, she knew she would ever be protected by his side. "There was a time when I thought you hated the very sight of me. You pushed me away and declared you wanted no Saxon hands upon you."

Brage smiled as he thought of the pleasure her hands now gave him. "It was your people I despised, not you, my lady. From the first time I saw you with Ulf, I sensed you were no ordinary maid. Then when I learned from my brother that you had taken a blade to him, I knew what a fearless vixen you were."

"Matilda and I were desperate. We had to get away . . ."

"You are courageous and intelligent and beautiful. I have never known another woman like you." He bent to her and very gently kissed her.

Dynna's heart soared at the touch of his lips. "I feared you at first," she whispered.

"And now, sweet Dynna?" he asked, his voice low and sensual.

She answered him with a passionate kiss. They stood together, wrapped in each other's arms, silently celebrating the fact that they were alive and together and safe—for now.

Finally, reluctantly, they moved apart. Had he his way Brage would never have let Dynna go, but Sir Edmund might still be near. They could take no chances.

"We must move while we can."

She nodded. "If Edmund has followed us this far, he may suspect where we are heading."

"Is it much farther to your home?"

"On foot, if the weather holds, it will take us four days."

"And if we ride?"

"Two days at the most. But we have no mount."

He slanted her a glance. "Then not only do we need more

food, we need a horse as well. We must travel quickly if we are to reach your parents before Edmund."

Dynna cringed inwardly at the thought of stealing a horse in addition to the food, but knew this was a crucial matter. She hoped they would be forgiven.

"Near Woodford Way there are a few small farms. We might find a horse there." She hated planning such, but there was no helping it.

They shared one last embrace before moving away toward the hollow.

"I hope Sir Thomas succeeds in keeping Edmund away," Brage remarked.

"He will do everything he can to help us without betraying his own honor."


Sir Edmund's frustration was growing ever stronger. They had just passed an hour in the village questioning all who were there about Dynna and the Black Hawk, but it had proven a wasted effort. No one had seen them. It was as if Dynna and the Viking had vanished completely. Yet Edmund knew that could not be.

"They must be here somewhere close. There is nothing else for her to do but run to her family home," Edmund said heatedly as he stood with Sir Thomas at the edge of the village staring out across the bucolic countryside. He knew she was there somewhere.

"Perhaps we have been wrong all along, my lord. Perhaps Lady Dynna did not come this way at all."

"What do you mean?"

"This is different from the first time she ran from you. This time she has the Viking with her. He wants to return to his homeland. Surely, they would reason that the first place you would look for them would be at her family home, so that would be the one place they would avoid." Sir Thomas tried to divert Sir Edmund's thoughts from going to Dynna's true destination.

Sir Edmund glanced angrily at the other man. It infuriated him that Sir Thomas had reminded him that Dynna had run from him before. He wondered at Sir Thomas's loyalty, and he made up his mind that when his father died and he took over, the man would be gone. "And I say it is the first place they would head," he insisted. "Where else could they receive the help they need to aid him in an escape to his homeland?"

"But you must remember, my lord, that he is a Viking, a raider adept at living off the land. The Black Hawk would not be foolish enough to accompany Dynna there. Remember, too, that she is not his hostage. She is smart and knows where you will search. We will not find them with her parents," he argued.

"You could be right, and were my father here, I am sure he would follow your counsel. But my father is not here. I am, and this time I will follow my own instincts."

Sir Thomas was frustrated, but could say no more. Had he continued to try to convince Sir Edmund to go elsewhere, he would have drawn unusual attention to himself. He dropped the argument and resigned himself to following Sir Edmund wherever he led. He would try to protect Dynna if she were found, but otherwise there was not much more he could do.

"Come, Sir Thomas. Rally the men. We ride for Dynna's home."

Sir Thomas did as he had been bid. He only hoped as he gave the men their orders that Dynna and the Black Hawk had followed his directions and stayed safely out of their way.

Under the cover of darkness that night, Brage left Dynna in hiding once more and crept in alone to the small farm house. The light within had long ago gone been extinguished, and it was time for him to lay claim to the horse they so desperately needed.

The horse remained still and quiet as he approached. He was relieved that it was a broken, well-trained mount. And when the mare offered no protest as he put the halter on it, he was even more relieved. He did not try to ride the animal, but led it away as slowly and as silently as possible.

Dynna had been waiting for Brage's return. Each moment they were apart seemed an eternity, and she was thrilled when he came back to her leading the horse.

"There was no trouble?" she asked.

"None. All was quiet. She came with me willingly," he said, as he stroked the mare's powerful neck.

Her respect for him continued to grow. "Then let us ride. Though it is dark, the trek along Woodford's Way is not dangerous here."

They both mounted the steed bareback, and Brage held Dynna before him as they started on their way. He kept their pace slow for the time being, not wanting anyone to hear them.

As much as he tried to concentrate fully on the ride, he could not help but take pleasure in their riding double. Dynna fit perfectly against him, her thighs resting against his, her back against his chest, her hips fitted tightly to his loins. Had they not been fleeing for their lives, he might have allowed himself to be completely distracted by her closeness. Instead, he forced himself to concentrate on the trek.

As Dynna rode before Brage, her back pressed against the hard support of his chest, she thought of Warren again. Brage was nothing like her husband, and yet she found herself drawn to him in some elemental way that defied all logic. They had only known each other a fortnight, and still it seemed as if she had known him all her life. Dynna had never felt this way about Warren. She had cared for him. He had been a good husband, and they had gotten along well, but there had never been this tension between them . . . this passion that grew even more powerful with every touch and every kiss.

Brage kept their pace steady as the night aged. He did not stop until the terrain became more difficult. He had kept their conversation at a minimum, wanting to take no risks with their safety. When at last he sought a place to rest, it was once again in a grove of trees that would shield them from view.

After sliding from the horse's back, he lifted his arms to Dynna and helped her down. Her body grazed his as he lowered her to the ground, and the contact was electric even after so many hours in each other's arms. Their weariness was forgotten as they came together, hungry to be one.

Later, when the wildness of their passion had been tamed for the moment, they lay together, treasuring this stolen time of quiet and resting.

"Tell me of your family, Dynna," Brage asked. He knew he would face them soon, and he wanted to be prepared.

"I have but my mother and father. I had a younger brother, but he died as a child, many years ago."

"You loved him." It was a statement, not a question, for he could hear the sadness in her voice.

"Very much."

They were silent for a moment, each reflecting on their own losses.

"And you, Sir Viking? What of your family?" Dynna ventured, needing to know more about him. "I know only that you are the Black Hawk, son of Anslak, and little else, save you have a brother named Ulf."

"Ulf is my half-brother," he answered easily, "by my father's mistress. He is older than me."

"And you are friends?"

"You sound surprised."

"It has been my experience that ofttimes the sons of mistresses are treated badly by the legitimate heirs."

"Ulf and I fought in our youth. We each wanted to impress our father with our strength and prowess, but now he prides himself on protecting me. When I see him again, though, I shall tell him what a poor job he did this last time." Brage stopped suddenly as an ugly thought occurred to him. He frowned, trying to deny the possibility to himself, yet finding it impossible to dismiss. He and Ulf had fought over everything in their youths, trying to establish who was the most favored with their father. Could it have been that Ulf's laughter when he had lost to Brage had merely covered what he had really been feeling. It broke his heart to think such, but . . .

"And the rest of your family?" Dynna was asking.

"My mother died when I was but a babe," he answered.

"Was she the one who gifted you with your dark hair?"

"She was Irish, a slave until my father freed her and married her. It was through her that I come by the 'black' in the Black Hawk."

"So it was not your heart but your hair that earned you the title," Dynna jested sensuously.

"You thought my heart black?"

"The tales of your pillaging are known throughout the land. Many thought your soul and heart were of the blackest pitch. Many claim you are beyond redemption. You are the Black Hawk, fiercest of all the Viking raiders."

Brage pulled her into his arms. "Shall I raid your port, princess? Shall I pillage your most treasured possession?"

"You have already laid waste to my resistance, Sir Viking. I can only surrender to the power you wield over me." She slipped her arms about his neck and kissed him. "It must have been difficult for you, growing up without a mother to see to your needs."

Brage shrugged as she nestled upon his shoulder. "I did not notice. I had my father. Then later, my father married Tove, and they have a son, Kristoffer."

"So you have two half-brothers. Does Kristoffer sail with you, too?"

"He just started. He is young and eager to earn his own glory." Brage smiled as he thought of the enthusiasm Kristoffer had shown before going on this raid. He had been excited to be sailing with him and Ulf. Brage grimaced at what the youngster must have suffered, seeing the mighty Black Hawk defeated that day. He was glad that the inexperienced youth had been unhurt in the fighting. Memories of the battle turned his thoughts back to the betrayal and the suspicion that had come to mind.

Lying as she was against Brage, Dynna felt the change in him as he tensed.

"Is something troubling you?" she asked.

"I was thinking that a traitor is in the midst of my men," he admitted.

"I remember that you spoke of such while you were feverish. Do you know who it is?"

Brage did not answer right away. He went over in his mind all that had transpired. He tried to recall any conversations he and Ulf had had while at sea. He fought to remember any subtle remarks or actions that might have revealed Ulf as the betrayer. The memory of Ulf saying *Ah, but for a few words spoken before the gods, I could be the one planning and leading this raid. Instead, I am relegated by our father to protecting your back . . ."* came to him.

Pain jolted through Brage as he heard the words being said not by one speaking in humor but by one who envied the other and wanted his position in life. Ulf . . . It could not be Ulf, and yet . . . who else?

"I fear I do," he ground out. "And I live for the day when I can exact my revenge on the niding!"

"What is a 'niding'?" She had never heard the term before.

"It is a Viking term that means someone who is disloyal, someone who is a coward, and this one is both." As he said it, though, he was sickened by the thought. Ulf, the man he had trusted for years, his brother and his friend . . . a traitor?

"Why would someone betray you? Do not your men all share in your spoils?"

"They do."

"Then why betray you?"

"I wondered that myself. Why, indeed? I will have the answer before the man lies dead at my feet. My men were the finest of warriors, and now numbers of them are slain because of him!" He would have his revenge. Soon he would be home again, and he would discover the truth of his betrayal.

"I am sorry you have suffered so. The one who has done this must truly hate you. Why else would someone cause such pain and misery to others?"

"I do not know. All my life I have lived by my honor, and I thought those who followed me did, too."

"Sir Edmund and Lord Alfrick knew about your attack for weeks ahead of time. That was why they had time to get help from the neighboring lands. Whoever revealed your plan to Lord Alfrick got word to him early on."

Brage thought back over the weeks before he sailed. Many of his men had been at their farms away from Anslak's village. Ulf had been gone for a while, as had several others. Even young Kristoffer had been off, trading at Hedeby. There was no condemning proof to be found there.

"I wish I could have watched when the news that I lived was delivered to my father. It would have been telling to see how each man reacted."

"Perhaps you will never learn who the real traitor was."

He shrugged. "Perhaps, but I think I know. Time will show me the truth. I will rush to no conclusion without proof."

Brage realized then as he confided in Dynna that he had never talked to another female this way. All women had always been distant to him. He loved them for the softness and physical relief their bodies offered him, but he had never cared deeply for one, never had an intimate conversation with one—until now—until Dynna. He had spoken to her as he would speak to his father. The realization came as a revelation to Brage, and he wondered at this abiding sense of trust she inspired in him. They had begun this adventure together at odds with each other—he not trusting her, she forcing him to her will, and now . . .

The thought that the attraction between them might be more than just a physical coupling dictated by their mutual desperation intrigued him. It seemed as if he were looking at Dynna in a whole new light of a sudden. Not only was she courageous and intelligent, she was gentle and sensitive, too.

Drawn to her, Brage could not resist the temptation as she lay against him. The soft roundness of her breasts against his chest and the sweet curve of her thigh where it rested against his was all the enticement he needed. He lifted her up to him and kissed her with a passion that surprised them both. She met him kiss for kiss, caress for caress, and he took pleasure in knowing that she desired him as much as he desired her.

Dynna was thrilled that Brage wanted her again. She had felt the pain in his soul as he told her of the betrayal, and she had wanted to ease the torment somehow. Though her words had seemed to have helped a little, it was her body he sought now in his solace, and she offered herself up to him freely.

They melded in exquisite pleasure and shared the true depth of their need. When they slept, they held each other close, sated and content.

Anslak stood at the helm of his ship, staring out to the western horizon. Soon, they would reach the lands they sought. Soon, they would have Brage back. They had sailed with five ships, each carrying at least fifty warriors. They would be ready, should deceit reveal itself while they went to claim Brage.

# PASSION

Anslak glanced to where Kristoffer rode at the fore of Brage's craft. Kristoffer had been so intent upon celebrating news of his brother's rescue that he had had to be carried onto the ship when they set out. Now, as they sailed closer to the coast, though, he was steady of hand and eye, directing his men well and ready to do whatever was necessary to ensure his brother's safe return.

Looking to where Ulf commanded a third longship, he saw his oldest son speaking to his men. Ulf was a fine leader and a fierce fighter. He had been Brage's closest friend, and Anslak knew he had suffered when his brother had been thought dead.

Tove had been excited by the news that Brage lived, too, and had promised them an endless feast upon their return.

It would be good when Brage was back at the helm of his own ship where he belonged. Anslak only hoped his son had not suffered over much while in the hands of Lord Alfrick. Soon they would know. If he had, they would repay in kind.

---

Hereld was immediately given audience with Lord Alfrick.

"What word do you bring from the Viking Anslak?" Lord Alfrick demanded.

"He set sail a day after I left him," Hereld answered, quickly telling him where the Viking would meet with them.

"A wise choice," Lord Alfrick said thoughtfully. "There is little chance for betrayal there."

"He will be there at dawn, the day after tomorrow. He expects to see that his son is alive and well before the gold will be paid."

"Fine." Lord Alfrick spoke curtly.

"I have done as you bid, my lord," Hereld said, subtly letting him know that he expected his payment as promised.

"Yes, you have," Lord Alfrick replied, signaling to one of his men to come forth with the small coffer. "And you shall be rewarded. I will pay you half now and half when the ransom has been paid to me."

Lord Alfrick took the coffer from the servant and handed it to Hereld.

"A fair and honest man is what you are, my lord," Hereld groveled appropriately as he felt the weight of the small chest. "I am honored to have carried your message to Anslak for you. I will sing your praises to all I meet. Not only are you a fierce and mighty warrior, but you are a man of your word." He bowed before him.

"You will find that you will be even more honored once all is done. You may go, but do not venture too far. I would have you with me on the morning that Anslak arrives."

"Yes, my lord. I will be there," Hereld answered, thinking that all would go smoothly now as he clutched the coffer to him and left the room.

Alfrick watched him go, almost amused by his ways. Hereld was completely driven by profit. At least, with one so blatant, one knew where one stood.

He turned his thoughts back to the Black Hawk and the ransom. For not the first time, he cursed the situation he found himself in. In another day, the Vikings would be landing on his coast expecting to reclaim one of their own. Alfrick could only hope that Edmund would have returned with the captive by then. If he had not, Alfrick knew he was going to have to think of some way to encourage Anslak's trust and prevent bloodshed. Hereld had said that the Viking leader was not a forgiving man. If he chose not to believe that the Black Hawk had escaped, there might be a terrible battle . . . one that he himself would lose. Alfrick knew he had to come up with some way to prevent a confrontation. He only hoped he could.

## Fifteen

Hereld sat with Sir Roland and several of his friends in the Great Hall enjoying a cup of mead. He was feeling good about everything that had happened and was eagerly looking forward to the exchange being made so he could get the rest of the payment owed him.

"Where are Sir Edmund and Sir Thomas?" he asked Sir Roland. He had not seen them since returning to the tower.

Sir Roland shot him a surprised look. "You mean you do not know? Lord Alfrick did not tell you?"

"Tell me what?" Hereld was suddenly worried, judging from the sound of the man's voice.

"About the Black Hawk? Did you not know he escaped?"

"He what?" Hereld repeated, his eyes widening in shock. Lord Alfrick had said that he wanted him at his side when he met with Anslak in a day and a half, but Hereld knew that would be suicide if they did not have the captive to make the trade.

"It would seem that Lady Dynna helped him escape and then went with him to avoid marrying Sir Edmund. It has been days that Sir Edmund has been out combing the countryside for the two of them. We have heard nothing so far. When are the Vikings due?"

"They will be here the day after tomorrow. A meeting place has been set. They are ready and more than willing to pay the ransom to get the Black Hawk back."

"And what will they do if the Black Hawk is not there?" one of the other men asked.

"It is hard to say," Hereld lied, not wanting them to know how scared he was of just that prospect. "They might be pleased that he has escaped and saved them the ransom price."

"It would be good if that came to pass," Sir Roland said.

"It would be very good," Hereld agreed, drinking down the rest of his mead in one long gulp.

Hereld looked around at the men gathered there and wondered if they realized what a short time they had to live. Anslak would be furious if the Black Hawk was not there, and what came next would not be pretty.

Suddenly faking weariness, he stood up. "It has been a pleasure to see you again, but it has been a long day's journey and I must retire for the night. I will see you on the morrow."

They bid him an indifferent good night.

Gathering up his coffer, Hereld made his way as nonchalantly as possible from the Great Hall. Outwardly, he maintained a casual air as he headed back to his ship. When he reached the boat, however, he started issuing orders and shouting at his men to get ready to set sail.

His men looked at him as if he were crazed. They had thought they were there to stay for a while. One by one, they sought answers.

"What is it, Hereld? Why have you returned from the tower so quickly?"

"We must head south, now, tonight."

"But why?"

Herald explained the grim situation. "The Black Hawk is no longer held here by Lord Alfrick. I do not want to be anywhere around when Anslak learns what has happened."

"Did you get all the reward Lord Alfrick owed you?"

"Half, and I can be happy with the half as long as I am still alive to enjoy it. Let us sail now, before dawn. I want to be out of Lord Alfrick's reach before he discovers that I have flown."

As they sailed away, Hereld counted his one hundred pounds of gold and the amount in his coffer from Lord Alfrick as worthy payment. He did not think he owed Lord Alfrick his life.

Brage and Dynna rose at dawn and rode all day. They were hungry and the horse was tired, but they kept on. What rests they took were short, and they did not linger overlong. Her parents' tower was within reach, and they would ride all that night if they had to, for they were desperate to reach it before Edmund.

It was just at sundown when they topped a low rise and Brage saw her father's tower and extensive estates for the first time.

"We are here . . ." Dynna cried, tears streaming down her cheeks as she saw her family home.

"True, but Edmund might be here as well," Brage pointed out, not ready to let his guard down just yet.

"I do not see any sign of him or his men."

"They could be within the hall already. We must still be careful. It would be foolish to rush in."

Dynna knew he was right. "We can wait until dark. There is a secret entrance in. I can go first and make certain it is safe for you to come inside."

He nodded in agreement with her plan. "Your father's holdings are vast?"

"They are, but not as vast as Lord Alfrick's. That is why my father approved and encouraged my marriage to Warren. It was a wise diplomatic move, for the alliance strengthened us."

"How will your father feel about you returning home?"

"He will understand. While he approved of Warren, he

had made it known long ago that had Edmund been the one to approach him for my hand, he would have refused."

"A wise man, your father."

She agreed warmly, and added, "Now we will be safe." Here she had known love and complete acceptance. Here she had spent the happiest days of her life. She was home.

"You are certain that your parents will welcome me?"

"They trust my judgment. You have helped me, Sir Viking. They will help you."

Brage hoped she was right. He realized then just how much his trust in people had been shaken by the traitor's betrayal. He looked at everyone with a jaundiced eye now, looking for deceit and treachery. He wondered if he would ever trust again.

"Come, I will show you where we can hide until it is dark enough for me to go in."

She directed Brage to a wooded area at the back of the tower. They remained there, out of view, until the night covered the land.

"It may take me a while, but do not fear, I will come back to you," Dynna promised.

They gazed at each other in the darkness, and then Brage pulled her close. They shared one poignant kiss before parting, both sensing their relationship would change the moment she passed through the tower's portal.

"Be careful, Dynna," Brage cautioned.

"I will." With that, she was gone, making her way unnoticed to the small, hidden gate.

As Dynna had suspected, her family's oldest retainer, Sir Eaton, was there standing guard.

"Lady Dynna!" he said her name in surprise, shocked as she appeared out of the darkness before him. He stared at her in confusion. She was there for certain, but she was dressed as a boy.

"Sir Eaton! It is so good to see you," she greeted the older man with a warm smile.

"It is good to see you, too, my lady. But what are you doing here? Coming in like this?" He couldn't stop himself from asking, for it was so unusual for her to enter the tower this way. On her visits home, she always rode proudly through the front gate.

"It is a long story and one I do not have time to relate right now. Tell me, Sir Eaton, has anyone come to the tower today?"

"There were all manner of people here today, as usual," he answered, still confused.

"The ones I am concerned about are my dead husband's brother, Edmund, and a group of his men. Did they arrive here today?"

"Oh, no, my lady. Those I would know for certain. There has been no sign of the likes of them."

"Thank heaven," Dynna said in relief. It was safe for her to go back for Brage.

"Lady Dynna . . . where are you bound? You cannot leave so . . ."

"I will be right back. Please inform my parents that I have returned and have brought a trusted companion with me. Tell them it is important I meet with them right away."

"Yes, my lady." Sir Eaton stared after her for a moment, then rushed away from the gate to do as she had directed.

Dynna hurried back to where Brage waited with the horse.

"It is safe for us to enter. Edmund has not arrived yet."

"We have Sir Thomas to thank for this," Brage said as they started toward the tower, leading the mount.

Brage held out hope that Sir Thomas had been able to direct Sir Edmund completely away from the tower. If he had managed that, it would give him all the time he needed to head for home. However, if they arrived here in the next day or so, it would be difficult, but not impossible for him to still get away. Either way, it did not matter to Brage right now. What mattered was they had reached the tower without being taken and that Dynna would be protected by her parents.

Brage followed Dynna through the narrow gate and into the protection of the stronghold. At her call, one of her father's men quickly ran to take charge of their horse.

Sir Eaton met them as they neared the hall. When he saw the tall man carrying the Viking shield and sword, he almost drew his own sword to defend against him. Dynna saw his nervousness, and she stepped between them.

"Have no fear, Sir Eaton. This is Brage. He has been my protector since leaving Lord Alfrick's lands."

"But he is a Viking, my lady!" Sir Eaton protested, still not relaxing as he eyed Brage.

"He is that, but he is here with me as friend not foe."

"As you say, my lady," he said, stepping back to let them pass. "Your parents await you in their private chamber."

She ushered Brage inside, her head held high as she ignored the curious looks of her father's men who were in the Great Hall. "This way."

Dynna moved regally, and Brage followed closely. He took the time to look around the Great Hall and found that while it was spacious and clean, it was not nearly the size of Lord Alfrick's.

Dynna stopped before a closed door and knocked only once before being bid to enter. Opening the portal, she saw her mother standing beside her father across the room. Unable to resist the love she knew awaited her, she ran to them and all but threw herself into her mother's arms.

"Mother!" she cried, tears streaming down her cheeks. "I am home! I am really home!"

"Oh, my darling daughter, I have been so worried about you." Lady Audrey hugged her daughter near as she shed her own tears of joy. She had seen Dynna only once since Warren's death, and that had been right after the accident. She had wanted to take Dynna home with her then, but Lord

Alfrick had stood firm and had prohibited it. "I had thought I would never see you again."

"Nor I you, Mother," she said. "There were moments when I did not know if I would ever get here."

Lord Garman, Dynna's father, cleared his throat to distract the two women he loved most in the world from their crying as he eyed Brage. "You have brought a visitor with you, Daughter. Who is this Viking who stands before us?"

"Father, Mother, this is Brage. He helped me escape Lord Alfrick's tower.

"What? You had to escape and with a Viking, no less? What nonsense is this? Were you not cherished and cared for as Warren's grieving widow?" Lord Garman demanded in anger and confusion.

"Nay, Father. It was horrible. Lord Alfrick ordered that I be married to Edmund. The priest had arrived and the marriage was to take place in a matter of days," she explained. "I am sorry, Father, but I could not do it. Edmund is not the man Warren was."

"We both know of his character, but surely you did not have to flee the place."

"I did. There was no saving myself any other way. Matilda and I tried to run away several weeks ago, but we were caught by the Vikings when they landed to raid."

"Word had come to us of the raid and of how Alfrick defeated the Norsemen and captured the . . ." Garman's eyes narrowed in suspicion as he turned to look at Brage.

"Yes, Father, he is the Black Hawk."

"And you brought him here?" He was outraged.

"He has come as friend. Alfrick set me to healing him after the battle. I learned by accident that Edmund planned to ransom him back to his people and, once the gold was paid, slay him before he could return home. It was then that I knew what I had to do." As she spoke, she looked at Brage. He was standing silently, listening as she explained all to her parents.

"You had to escape and take the Black Hawk with you . . ." Her father finished the sentence for her incredulously.

"Do not be angry, Father. I could not suffer the thought of Edmund's touch. I would have chosen death over the horror of a marriage to him. He delights in cruelty."

Garman had had dealings with Edmund in the past and knew what kind of man he was. "It is all right, my child, I understand." He went to her and put an arm around her.

"I entreated Brage to help me escape the tower. I promised him that in return for seeing me safely to you, we would help him get back to his own homeland."

Audrey and Garman both studied the Norsemen. He was tall, darkly handsome, and fierce-looking as he stood proudly before them. It was no wonder his reputation was so terrible. He was an intimidating presence.

"We thank you for bringing our daughter to us, Brage," Audrey said, then introduced herself and her husband to the Viking.

Brage nodded in response to the older woman's thanks. He understood where Dynna got her beauty. Her mother, though her hair was silvering, was a lovely woman, tall, slender and endowed with gracious charm. "It is good that we arrived here safely, and I thank you for your welcome."

"Dynna is a fine judge of character. You shall be treated as one of us," Lord Garman said.

"What is it you will need to make your journey home?" Audrey asked.

"A small ship, and help to man it. I, too, must escape the fate Lord Alfrick and Edmund had planned for me."

"It is done," Garman responded. "We will travel to the coast and arrange for your transport on the morrow."

Dynna smiled up at Brage, thrilled that her parents were being so understanding of the situation. Audrey saw the look her daughter gave the Viking, and understood far more than what was being said aloud.

"There is only one more thing . . . A crucial matter, Father."

"What, my child?"

"Should Edmund come here, our presence must be kept from him. There is no telling what he would do if he learned we were here."

"We will keep the secret, Dynna. Now, come, let us have a meal and talk of what must be done so Brage can set sail," Garman said.

"While you men confer, I am going to take Dynna abovestairs, so that she may bathe and change into a more appropriate gown. I will also lay out fresh clothes for you, Brage."

Brage watched Dynna climb the tower steps, his gaze following her every move until he was sure she was out of sight. Garman did not miss his interest.

"I am thankful for your help," Brage told Dynna's father as he turned to him. "I was not sure what welcome I would get here."

"Any man who keeps my daughter from harm earns my lifelong gratitude. Come, let us share a mug of ale while we await their return. You may leave your weapon and shield here. You are in no danger while you are within my tower."

Brage wanted to believe him, but could not give them up again after having been without them for so long. Besides, there was always the threat of Edmund. "I will keep them with me." His tone brooked no argument.

Lord Garman nodded. He led the way to a trestle table in the Great Hall. Brage placed his sword and shield within reach.

Lord Garman noted his actions, but said nothing. He could tell the Viking was a fine warrior, and he wished he had several men like him to help protect the tower. His own defenses were not good. His men preferred farming to fighting. They were not located near the coast and so had not suffered the devastating Viking raids the others had. Garman knew should they ever be attacked or sieged, they would not be capable of putting up much resistance. That was why he had agreed to Dynna's marriage to Warren in the first place. Lord Alfrick could mount a strong force, and, with Alfrick as an ally, few would dare attack them.

"Thank you, Mother," Dynna said as they entered the bedchamber that had been hers in her youth.

"For what, dear?"

"For understanding my need to flee."

Finally, Dynna was beginning to relax. Being with her parents provided the security she had longed for. Here with her family, no harm could come to her.

"So tell me all that has happened, Daughter." Audrey pressed her for the details of her unhappiness and her escape.

Dynna told her all, starting with Lord Alfrick's announcement that she marry Edmund whether she wanted to or not, and ending with her decision to escape with Brage.

"But where is Matilda? If you took her with you that first time, why is she not with you now? I cannot conceive that she would let you out of her sight." She knew how devoted the servant was to her daughter.

Dynna explained how she had escaped, and how she had deliberately kept the secret of their plan from Matilda to ensure the woman safety.

"And what of this Brage?" She remembered the way Dynna had looked at him. "What is the Viking to you?"

"Why, he is nothing to me, Mother." She felt color flush her cheeks. She had never been able to lie to her mother.

Audrey went on as if she had not heard her denial. "You have feelings for him. What manner of man is he?"

Dynna was not surprised by her mother's perceptiveness. She always seemed to know what was in her daughter's thoughts and in her heart. "I do not know what I feel for him, Mother. I have seen him fierce and savage, and I have seen him as a tender, caring man." Her expression was thoughtful, then turned almost sad.

"Yes?" Audrey asked, knowing there was more Dynna had not revealed—not to her and perhaps not even to herself.

"I am afraid that when he leaves here tomorrow, I will never see him again." She lifted her gaze to her mother's. "I do not know if I can bear that."

"So he *does* mean something to you." She could easily understand why. The Viking was very handsome, and they had been alone together for days on end.

Dynna turned tormented eyes to her mother. "He does, but I do not understand it. What I feel for him is so different from what I felt for Warren . . . The power of it is almost frightening. Sometimes, there are moments when I think I have imagined it all. But then . . ."

"Then what?"

"Then he touches me again, and I know it is no dream—these feelings I have for him."

"When he leaves here in the morning, it is almost assured that you will not meet again. You are from two different worlds."

"I know." Dynna was filled with anguish at the thought. Yet she knew she had to let him go. "But I can not hold him."

The older woman nodded her agreement. "Do you have any idea how he feels about you?" she then asked.

"He has declared nothing, save that he believes me to be brave and that he has met none other like me." She sighed painfully. "I do not feel brave when I think of being parted from him forever."

"Then let us see what happens tonight. Perhaps he will come to see that you are important to him, also."

"That would be a wonderful thing . . ."

Audrey only smiled. Her daughter deserved happiness, and if a union with this Norseman would bring her such, then so be it. A truce between his land and theirs would be a good thing, too—for trade and for an end to the threat of warfare. Not to mention the joy that shone in her daughter's eyes at the thought of the warrior.

Audrey decided she would speak to Garman about the matter later, when they were abed alone.

Dynna bathed quickly, scrubbing her body and hair clean of the dirt of the many days' travel. With her mother's help, she quickly combed out her thick, tangled mane and then donned one of her mother's tunics and embroidered overgowns. The color was a soft rose that lent a sparkle to her gray eyes and enhanced the flush of color in her cheeks the days in the sun had left.

"There, you look lovely. Come see in the mirror," her mother encouraged as she drew her to stand before the polished bronze mirror.

Dynna was pleased with her appearance and gave her mother a quick impulsive hug. "Shall we return to the hall?"

"The men await us," she answered.

They left the bedchamber and started down the steps to the Great Hall.

It was as if Brage could sense the moment Dynna drew near. He lifted his head and looked toward the steps to find that she was descending with her mother. He said nothing. He could only stare. Dynna looked more lovely to him than she ever had before, and he took the time to appreciate her. The realization overcame him then that he truly would be leaving her. It would not be such an easy thing to sail from her.

The women joined them at the table, and Garman signaled for the servants to bring food. Dynna and Brage ate hungrily, for there had been very little for them to eat for the whole day.

"We will travel to the coast in the morning," Lord Garman announced. "Weather permitting, I should be able to arrange for Brage to sail within a day."

Dynna managed a smile she did not feel. She turned to

Brage. "It is good that you will be returning to your home. I know how much you must miss it and your family."

"It will be good to see them again, though I will not rest until the traitor has been revealed."

Revenge was what drove him. Revenge was what had kept him alive when lesser men would have died from their wounds. She said no more, her heart heavy.

They passed the balance of the meal in easy conversation, and when at last it was time for them to retire, Dynna needed to have a few minutes alone with Brage.

"It would be safest for Brage to take the high tower room. It is secluded and few know of it," Garman said. "Should there be trouble, he would be hidden there."

Dynna almost wished her father had given him a room closer to hers, but for her own sake it was best that their rooms were far apart. Whatever they had to say to each other would have to be said now, this night. The next day, he would be gone.

"I will see him to the chamber then," she told her parents.

"I will send maids with a bath and with the fresh clothing," Audrey said.

Brage thanked them again, then rose, picked up his sword and shield and followed Dynna.

Dynna and Brage walked together to the stairs and mounted them slowly with measured tread.

"It will be over soon. You will be on your way," Dynna said softly.

"I did not think it possible that I would leave here without a battle."

"Perhaps there are times when things do go as they should. Perhaps there is such a thing as a happy ending." She did not look at him as she spoke. The pain she was feeling over parting from him was too great.

They reached the high tower room and stood together, alone.

"Will you be there in the morning to see me off with your father?"

"I could not let you leave without saying good-bye."

Brage went to her and held her, his mouth slanting across hers in a hungry exchange. At the sound of the maid's knock, Dynna pulled away. She stared up at Brage, her gaze going over his beloved features as if memorizing them, etching them upon her heart. The second knock and a call sent her to the door to let them in.

"I must bid you good night, Sir Viking," she said as the maids hurried to prepare his bath.

"Good night, Dynna," Brage replied, and he watched helplessly as Dynna slipped away. . . . out of his room . . . out of his life. He thought he saw a tear on her cheek, but he could not be sure.

When the maids had finished their duties and departed, Brage sank down in the tub and began to wash away the grime from their travels. His mood was not good. Another knock at the door distracted him and one of the maids came back into the room.

"I was wondering if there was something else you needed," she asked, offering more than just her maidly services. He was a fine specimen of a man, and she was not adverse to comforting him should he want it.

"No. Be gone. I want only solitude." He wanted no quick tumble with a servant, and it surprised him that he actually found the thought distasteful. There was only one woman he wanted in his bed, only one woman who fired his blood, and that was Dynna.

He cursed under his breath. Revenge was sending him home to his people to find the one who had betrayed them. But even as he tried to focus on his need to bring the traitor to justice, thoughts of Dynna kept intruding.

Dynna . . . A vision of her floated through his thoughts. Dynna the brave . . . Dynna the healer . . . Dynna the lover . . . He cursed again. Could not this attraction he felt for her be put aside and forgotten, as what he had felt for all the other women in his life had been?

Brage stared off into space thinking of her courage and beauty, of how she responded to his touch and kiss. He found himself longing to hold her again, to caress and make love to her that night in a real bed, not on a bed of nature's pleasure, but one of soft comfort. He wanted to go to her chamber, but knew he could not, not that night in her parents' home.

He finished bathing, then sought sleep, but it would not come. He had become accustomed to slumbering with her beside him. The more he thought of Dynna, the greater the ache within him grew to be with her. He thought of returning home, of seeing his family again, but he felt little joy in the prospect unless Dynna would be at his side.

Unable to rest, Brage rose and began to pace. What manner of woman was this vixen that she could haunt him even as he was preparing to sail for home and freedom. He stopped before one of the narrow tower windows and stared out at the cloudless night sky. The stars were bright and the moon was silver. It was a lovers' night, and yet he was alone, as was Dynna.

Somehow, in that moment, Brage knew. It was a lovers' night. They had been lovers. They were meant to be together—he, the fearless Black Hawk, and she, the brave Saxon who had tamed him. He finally admitted it to himself then. He loved Dynna. He had never said the words to a woman. He had never declared himself before, but he would now, for he did love her. He wanted no other.

Impulsively, Brage wanted to go to her that minute and tell her of his love. He wanted to ask her to go with him to his land and be his wife. He wanted her with him every day and every night. He paused in thought as he imagined her round with his child. To his amazement, he found the thought appealing. They belonged together, and he could not bear to be parted from her.

A great sense of relief filled him along with a feeling of great anticipation. On the morrow, before he left the tower with her father, he would declare his love to Dynna. On the morrow, he would ask her to be his wife.

Finally, Brage was at peace. He lay back down and drifted off to sleep, eagerly awaiting the dawn so he could see Dynna and tell her of his feelings. He would take her home with him for he could not imagine a life without her.

Dynna tossed and turned in her own bed. After leaving Brage, she had come to realize just how powerful her feelings for him were. She loved him as she had loved no other. Her heart was breaking at the thought of losing him. She had lost Warren to death. But Brage . . . Brage was alive! She had nothing to fear, save him leaving without learning the truth of her love.

It did not take Dynna long to decide what to do. It would not be easy for her. She had never brazenly proclaimed her love to any man. With Warren there had been no need, but this was not Warren. This was Brage, the man whose very touch set her soul ablaze, the man she wanted to spend the rest of her days loving. She could not bear to see him leave her in the morning. She did not know what he would say when she told him she loved him and did not want him to go, but she could not let the moment pass without speaking of her feelings.

As she had learned upon Warren's death, life was too short, and it often had cruel twists and turns. Dynna knew she had to seize what happiness she could, while she could. She would be up before the dawn, and she would tell Brage that she loved him. She could not let him go. So determined, she went to bed. Peaceful sleep claimed her, for at last she knew what she wanted and how she was going to get it.

\* \* \*

There was no warning before disaster struck. One moment all was peaceful at the tower, and the next Edmund's men were surging through the gates. Sir Eaton was slain along with several other of Lord Garman's men when they tried to block their way.

"It was as easy as I thought it would be," Sir Edmund gloated as he led the way into the Great Hall. The entry had been so quick that no alarm had been sounded.

Sir Thomas managed to stay in control, but he longed to strike down the bloodthirsty man who led him. He had tried to convince Edmund not to force his way into the tower. He had tried to tell him that it would have serious consequences if Dynna and the Viking were not there. But Sir Edmund had been so intent on believing they were there, he had been beyond reasoning. Now, all Sir Thomas could do was keep watch for Dynna and try to keep her out of danger.

He followed behind as Edmund took the stairs two at a time. It was a simple thing to find the main bedchamber, and they burst into the room, shocking Lady Audrey and Lord Garman from a sound sleep. Lord Garman started to rise, but one of Sir Edmund's men blocked him, his sword pointed at the center of his chest.

"Where are they?" Edmund demanded as he stalked to the foot of the bed.

"Where are who?" Lord Garman asked. "And what is the meaning of this?"

"Do not play the innocent with me. I want to know where your daughter and the Viking she helped escape are hiding."

"I do not know what you are talking about."

"Do not lie to me, Lord Garman. It will not go well for you, if you do . . ."

"Do not threaten me!"

"I will do more than threaten you," Edmund snarled, his hand moving to rest on the hilt of his sword. "I want the Viking and Dynna, and I want them now."

When Lord Garman did not respond fast enough to satisfy

him, he nodded at his man. The man pressed his sword harder against Lord Garman's chest forcing him flat on the bed.

Lady Audrey's eyes were wide with terror. She turned to Sir Edmund. "Why are you doing this? We are your father's ally. Why have you raided our home? All you had to do was ask for permission to enter, and you would have been invited in."

"I care not about your invitations. While you would have detained me with ale and wine, the Viking and Dynna could escape by another route. Nay, I know they are here."

"I do not know what you are speaking of," Lord Garman denied.

Sir Edmund gave him a disbelieving look. "I will take this tower apart stone by stone if I have to until I find them. It would be much simpler should you just tell me where they are."

Audrey and Garman shared a look, but did not speak.

"Search every room."

They raced off to do his bidding. Sir Thomas made certain that he went first. If Dynna was to be found, he was going to be the one bringing her to Edmund. No other's hands would touch her.

They searched only three rooms before they found Dynna. Sir Thomas threw her door wide and confronted her.

"Sir Thomas!" Dynna sat up in bed, clutching her covers to her breast.

"You must come with me," he told her sternly, lest the men with him doubt his loyalty.

"But why? What has happened?"

"Edmund is here with your parents, and he wants you and the Viking brought before him. You must come with me, or I will have to drag you to him." He hated saying the words, but had no choice. Better he should take her than the others.

Dynna nodded and rose from the bed with all the calm she could manage. Her knees were weak as she donned her wrapper and regally walked ahead of Sir Thomas. She knew he would help her as much as he could.

Sir Edmund was still standing over Garman and Audrey when he heard the loud, triumphant calls of his men in the hall. He watched the door and he smiled broadly when Dynna entered the room, followed by Sir Thomas and the others.

"So you know nothing of your daughter, Lord Garman? My father will be most interested to learn that you lied to me."

"How dare you enter my parents' home this way and abuse us!" Dynna demanded as she was brought to stand before Edmund.

"As I told you once before, sweet Dynna, I would dare much with you. Where is the Viking?"

"I do not know."

"Somehow, I find that I do not believe you. I want to know where he is. I have no time for riddles. If you value your parents' lives, you will answer me quickly and with the truth. Once more I ask you, where is the Viking?"

"He is gone," she answered tightly, praying that Brage had heard the invaders and had somehow gotten away.

"Gone? When did he leave?"

"Tonight. He left just before midnight. I am sure he is well on his way home."

"You lie!" Edmund erupted, enraged. He slapped her viciously. "He has to be here!"

"I tell you he is gone," she repeated, wanting to convince him, hoping to convince him. Her cheek was stinging from his assault, but she did not cower.

Edmund's expression was one of pure hatred. "I still do not believe you." He turned to his men. "Bring her mother to me."

As one of them dragged Audrey from the bed, Edmund drew out his dagger. His man held her while Edmund pressed the sharp-edged dagger to her throat.

"You go too far!" Lord Garman started to rise to go to

his wife's rescue, but the other man's sword held him fast on the bed.

"Now, my lovely betrothed, be it known that it will not pain me overmuch to end your mother's life. I know she is the one you love above all others. Will you watch her die for the Viking? Will you have her death on your hands because you would not return the Black Hawk to me."

"You would not . . ." she gasped.

"Ah, but I would." He drew blood. "It matters not to me if I must slay everyone within these walls. I will do so and claim it was the act of the Norsemen. Who would be alive to contradict me?" He laughed at his own cunning as he saw the very real distress on her face.

Audrey whimpered in terror. She had always known that Edmund was crazed, but she had never known he could be this barbaric. Lord Garman watched helplessly from the bed. He was used to protecting his own. It filled him with fury that he could do nothing to rescue his wife or daughter from Edmund's vicious possession. He thought perhaps he might try to move slowly and position himself to make a move against the one who held the sword on him, but as he did so, Edmund saw him.

"Should you move another inch, Lord Garman, I will see you run through—after you have watched me slit your wife's throat!" He turned his gaze back to Dynna. "Now, Dynna, where is the Viking."

Dynna was helpless. Two people she loved were about to die because she would not reveal Brage's whereabouts. Yet, if she told where he was hiding, Edmund would eventually see him slain. She clasped her hands together to stop the trembling. How could she sacrifice Brage for her parents? What was she to do?

"I will tell you what you want to know!" Lord Garman offered, knowing there was no way out. As they had gone to bed, Audrey had disclosed to him how much Dynna loved Brage and how terrible it was going to be for her to be parted from him in the morning. He could imagine her suffering, having to choose between saving their lives or saving Brage's life.

"Ah, a man with good sense. I like that. Perhaps I will spare you, should your daughter tell me where he is. I want the words from Dynna. I want her to be the one to tell me of the Black Hawk. Well, beloved?" he sneered. "Will your parents die or will you tell all?"

Dynna felt sick under the weight of her decision, but there was nothing else she could do. She told him what he wanted to know.

Edmund shoved Audrey roughly aside. "Keep watch over them until I return!" he commanded his men.

He raced from the room, intent on finding the Black Hawk. Audrey was sobbing as she collapsed in her husband's arms. Dynna ran to join them. Two men remained behind to keep watch over them.

Sword drawn and ready, Sir Edmund raced to the tower room. Sir Thomas and the rest of the men stayed right with him. They found the room with no difficulty and exchanged powerful, triumphant glances before breaking down that final barrier. Sir Edmund kicked in the door with an explosive crash.

## Sixteen

As the door burst open, Brage awakened instantly and bolted from the bed. His hand closed around the hilt of his sword he had kept by his side as he prepared to do battle. He saw Edmund coming toward him and was filled with fury. As quickly as he realized they had been found, worries of Dynna consumed him. Was she safe? Had she eluded Edmund?

Brage attacked, slashing violently at Edmund, but the Saxon held his own against his ferocious assault. Had they been in the open, Brage would have had little trouble slaying him, but trapped as he was in the confines of the small room with more of Edmund's men pouring in behind him, death looked to be his only escape.

As he continued to fight, Brage's thoughts returned to Dynna, and he grew even more determined to kill Edmund before he himself was felled. If he could do nothing else for her, he could save her from Edmund.

The men who entered the room were armed and ready for this confrontation. They had chased the Viking endlessly and wanted to take him. They looked on as Edmund fought his greatest battle.

"I want to kill you, Viking!" Edmund growled. He came at Brage another time, slashing and thrusting as he attempted to drive him back and trap him against the wall.

"Try, Saxon," Brage challenged, their swords crashing together.

Sir Thomas stood in the doorway watching them. He saw the bloodlust in their eyes and knew both men would fight to the death. As much as Sir Thomas would have liked to see Brage win, he could not let the battle come to that. There was little time left. They needed to return to Lord Alfrick immediately.

"Sir Edmund, you forget your purpose! Cease this battle!" Sir Thomas ordered as he stepped into the room, his own sword drawn. He knew Edmund would not appreciate his interference, but he did not care.

Edmund ground his teeth in frustration at Sir Thomas's words, for he knew he spoke the truth.

Brage did not want to end the fight. He was prepared to battle to the death, but Sir Thomas positioned himself before Sir Edmund, his own sword in hand. "Drop your weapon, Viking."

Brage clutched it even tighter.

"Perhaps our friend wants to die," Sir Edmund remarked. "If so, I will be happy to oblige."

"You speak foolishness. We must leave the tower at once to return to your father."

Again, Sir Edmund chafed at being so chastened by the older man. Still, he knew he was right. He lowered his sword.

Sir Thomas turned back to Brage. "Give your weapon to me."

Brage's gaze met his, and slowly, cautiously, Brage handed it over.

Two of Edmund's men grabbed him from behind then and started to drag him from the room. As they passed by Edmund, Edmund ordered, "Do what you must short of killing him to see that he causes us no trouble."

When they had agreed and gone, Edmund stalked toward Sir Thomas, his eyes glowing with an inner fervor, his breathing ragged. "I will only say this once. Never again chastise me before my men!"

"I only advise you as your father's counsel," Sir Thomas

responded. He saw the fury in his eyes and had his own sword ready just in case. "Your father told me to be sure that we brought the Viking back alive for the ransom exchange. I was merely following my lord's orders."

Edmund saw the unyielding look in Sir Thomas's regard and his aggressive posture. There was only one way for him to save face, and he took it. He smiled easily, banking the fire of his fury for another day. "You are right. The Black Hawk is worth far more to us alive than dead. Let us return to my father's lands and claim the gold."

He strode past Sir Thomas without a look. He returned to Dynna's parents' bedchamber. Some of the men had gathered outside the door to await his return.

"Four of you, come with me. The rest of you wait with the horses, we will be leaving soon." So ordering, he entered the room to find that the two men he had left there were still standing guard over Lady Audrey and Lord Garman.

"The Viking is ours," Sir Edmund announced as the four others followed him inside.

"Is Brage alive?" Dynna asked, unable to hide her torment. She awaited news of what had happened with terror in her heart, and she had to know the truth. Tears clouded her vision as she faced Edmund.

"How is it, sweet, that you are so concerned about the life of one miserable Norseman?" Edmund snarled, seeing the truth in her expression and detesting it. Sarcastically, he went on, "Do not fear, my dear, the Black Hawk lives, and I will see that he remains alive long enough to bring us the ransom we have demanded."

He turned to his men. "You six stay here and act as guards until I return. Keep the Lord and his Lady locked in here for the day, then release them to the tower grounds. I would have two of you remain with Dynna in her chamber to 'protect' her day and night. I do not ever want her to leave that room. I do not want her left alone with just one of you. Do you understand?"

"Yes, Sir Edmund," they chorused.

"Good. See that you follow my orders exactly. I will know if you fail to do what I have said. Once our dealings with the Viking have been concluded, I will return to claim Dynna."

The men were suitably fearful. They had seen what happened to those who did not obey him, and they were not about to join their ranks.

"Now, Dynna, come with me. I would speak with you alone." He did not wait for her to reply, but grabbed her arm in a bruising grip and all but dragged her from the room. He shut the door behind them.

Dynna controlled her anger and did as he bid, for she did not want to cause her parents any more trouble. When they reached the hall, she finally spoke. "What do you want from me? I ran from the tower because I did not want to marry you. Nothing has changed."

"Ah, but everything has changed, and we have much to talk about."

"We have nothing to talk about."

"Know this, Dynna . . ." His voice was savage as he pulled her closer to him. "You are mine. I own you." His gaze was cold and threatening as it held hers. "When all is done with the Viking, I will be back for you. But do not think that I will grace you with my name and my title. Your worries about marrying me are over. I will not take you as my wife. You will now be my slut. You will service my needs and you will cater to my desires. You will be lower than the lowest slave. I will make good use of you, for you do have a lush body, but you will never have the honor of my name or position."

"I will die first. I would welcome death before dishonor at your hands," she replied. Her heart was pounding and her thoughts were racing.

Edmund struck her, backhanding her as hard as he could and driving her to her knees. "You will have no such pleasure. I will make certain that you suffer as long as it pleases me. Perhaps after I tire of you, I will be the one to give you that surcease you would welcome." He snarled his words, staring down at her as she knelt unrepentant before him, her gray eyes shining silver, her lips bloodied and swelling. He would have liked to throw her down and take that which he had so long desired from her. He wanted to beat the defiance out of her. He wanted her with a hunger that would not be sated even in a hundred years, but there was no time now to act upon it.

"Death would be a pleasure compared to sharing your bed."

He laughed coldly. "There are many women who would disagree with you . . . many who would gladly trade places with you."

"I have known a man's touch. You are an animal. Brage is ten times the man you could ever hope to be!"

He grabbed her wrists, dragged her to her feet and crushed her against him. He was beyond fury now that she had affirmed what he had suspected all along. "Pity I do not have time to show you how very wrong you are!"

Dynna was beyond caring what he might do to her. Her world had been destroyed. "There is not enough time left in your life to prove me wrong!"

His hands tightened on her even more as he ground himself against her, letting her know just what he intended to do to her when he returned. "No one else could ever have said the things to me you have and lived. You have fought me at every turn, but no more. I will tame you and train you. I will see you docile before me. You are mine. The reprieve you have is only for me to see the Viking brought to my father. Were things otherwise, I would stay and show you that your days of defiance are at an end."

Dynna felt the hardness of him and was repelled by it. Where Brage's manly strength had thrilled her, Edmund's left her filled with disgust. "I hate you!"

He smiled. "And you will hate me even more before I am through with you. I will be back. I expect to find you ready for me when I return."

He pushed her away from him and opened the door to the room for her to enter. He called two of the guards to come out into the hall. After giving them further instructions on how to handle Dynna while he was gone, he walked away without a backward glance.

When Edmund reached the grounds, he found that the Viking was unconscious and tied on a mount.

"He was resisting going along with us," one of the men explained, and Edmund only smiled. He ignored the ugly look Sir Thomas was giving him. He liked the Viking just that way.

All were ready to ride. Sir Edmund glanced up at the tower to find Dynna standing in a window watching them. He smiled up at her and gave her a triumphant wave as he mounted his horse.

"Let us head for home. There is little time. We must ride like the wind."

They guided their mounts from the tower leaving death, destruction, and desperation behind them.

"Come, Lady Dynna, we must go now," Balder, one of Edmund's men, said as he motioned for her to follow him.

She gave a curt nod as she turned away from the narrow window out of which she had been staring.

"Dynna . . ." her mother asked, worriedly. "Where are they taking you?"

"We have been instructed to keep her secluded in her chamber until Sir Edmund returns," he answered.

"I would go with her," her mother stated firmly. She feared for her daughter's very life and did not want to leave her alone with Edmund's men.

"No. You are to stay locked in your room until tomorrow. Only then may you leave."

"How dare you?" Lord Garman thundered, angry and humiliated by the treatment they were receiving at the hands of his supposed ally's men.

"We have been so ordered by Sir Edmund, and we will not disobey."

Lord Garman saw the fear that drove them and knew it was pointless to argue. One day would seem an eternity, but it would eventually pass. The guards left the room and locked the door behind them.

"Garman?" Audrey said his name questioningly.

"We will bide our time, my love," he said, as he went to her and took her in his arms. "Tomorrow, you will be able to visit Dynna freely."

"But will Dynna be all right? And what about Brage?"

"I am certain that Edmund wants no harm to come to Dynna. But I do not know about the Viking. As devious and vicious as Edmund is, I know not if Brage will live out the week."

They fell silent as they settled in their room to await the dawn. They were captives in their own home, prisoners of Edmund's vengeance and hatred.

Dynna entered her room and started to close the door, but two men followed her inside.

"What is the meaning of this? Am I to be allowed no privacy?"

"No, my lady. Lord Edmund has directed that we are to stay with you constantly. We are not to let you out of our sight."

"But that is ridiculous!"

"It is what he wishes. We will do as he has ordered." The men did not understand his concern, either. What could she do that would cause Edmund to be so distrustful? Still, they knew better than to question him or his motives. They would do as they were told, for they had no desire to suffer the consequences of Edmund's anger.

"But . . ." she began.

Balder cut her off. "There is no discussion of the matter. It is decided. We will remain here with you until he returns. You may as well adjust to the order, it will not be countered."

Dynna stared at the two determined men and knew she was trapped. Perhaps later she could figure out a way to help save Brage.

The door was locked. Balder took the key and then the two of them sat down across the chamber.

Dynna climbed back into bed. Pulling the covers up to her chin, she tried not to cry as she thought of all that had transpired. Brage had been taken away, helplessly bound. She had watched as the men had tied him onto the horse's back. She could only hope that Sir Thomas would somehow aid him, and she prayed fervently that Brage would be spared the fate Edmund had planned for him. There had to be something she could do . . .

Dynna did not sleep the balance of the night, but lay silently abed, trying not to notice that she had two hulking men guarding her closely, and trying to think of a way to save Brage.

Brage came awake to find himself bound and hanging helplessly over the horse's back, its pounding gait jarring him to the bone. He remained unmoving for a time, trying to gather his wits. Sir Thomas was leading the horse and saw that he was stirring but said nothing. One of the other men though, called out to Sir Edmund.

"Sir Edmund! He rouses!"

At the call, Sir Edmund brought the riders to a halt. He dismounted and approached the horse Sir Thomas was leading. He reached Brage, grabbed him by the hair and lifted his head so their gazes could meet.

"So, you are finally with us . . . The famed and dreaded Black Hawk is awake." A cruel, taunting smile curved his thin lips. "Know this. You tried to escape me, but you failed. I found you, Viking, and you are my captive once again, thanks to the lovely Dynna."

"Dynna?" Brage could not stop himself from asking. "What of her? What have you done to her?"

He saw the questioning look in Brage's eyes, and he smiled even more confidently. Keeping his voice low, just for Brage's ears, he went on, "Ah, yes, Dynna was the one who told me where you were hidden. She was most cooperative. We struck a bargain, she and I."

Until that moment, Brage had not believed anything Edmund had said, but at the mention of a bargain, he cursed himself for being seven kinds of a fool.

"A bargain?"

"Information about you, in exchange for being allowed to stay with her parents. I coaxed it from her while we were abed. She pleaded and begged to be allowed to stay there, so we came to an agreement. She will remain with her parents as long as she comes to my bed whenever I want her. So, you see, she got what she wanted, while you are right back in my safekeeping."

Anger surged through Brage. Everything Edmund was saying fit. Dynna had told him at the outset that she would do whatever was necessary to save herself, and she had. Why had he thought there was anything more between them than just convenience? Once she had reached her parents' home, she had no more need of him.

Edmund saw the fiery flash of emotion in Brage's gaze and knew he had struck a nerve. It pleased him.

"Dynna has always been quick to see the way of things. She has always had the ability to use people to her advantage, and so she has with you.

Brage silently cursed Dynna. To save herself, she had betrayed him. Brage knew he should have left her at the gate of her father's tower and gone on his way alone. He had been betrayed twice by people he had come to trust, and he could only hope that one day justice would be his . . .

"Sir Thomas," Edmund turned away from him, and called out to the older man, "Give the Viking his seat, but keep his hands tied behind him, and you continue to lead the horse. I want no trouble on the trek back. We must move quickly, without delays."

Sir Thomas hurried to untie Brage and pull him off the horse. He then retied his hands and aided him in mounting again. He had no opportunity to speak to him with Edmund standing nearby.

Once Brage was settled, they rode on. Edmund was determined to reach his father's tower as quickly as possible. He knew time was of the essence.

Anslak studied the landing site with a critical eye. He was expecting trouble. He did not trust the Saxons to keep to their word, yet he could see no sign of a trap. He gestured to Ulf and Kristoffer to bring their longships in closer to his.

"Ulf, I want you to go ashore with me. Kristoffer, you take Brage's ship and two others and stay at sea. We will signal you by dropping the sail on my ship should there be a problem."

Anslak and Ulf made for shore, while Kristoffer kept the ships under his command at bay.

Kristoffer stood on the raised front deck of the Black Hawk's longship watching their every move. He wanted to be ready in case his father needed him. Though his brother's men had followed his orders on this voyage, Kristoffer knew they would be glad to have their leader back. He just wondered how badly his brother had suffered at the Saxons' hands and how soon he would be well enough to put out to sea again. He knew he would soon have his answer.

The moment for the exchange was near as Anslak and

Ulf's longships pulled into shore. The men following them were ready for a fight. They remembered the last time they had landed here and were more than willing to shed some Saxon blood for the losses they had suffered that day.

"There will be no fighting unless I give the order," Anslak told them. "We will make the exchange and see Brage safely away. That is all we came for, and that is all we will do."

The men grunted in agreement. They understood his desire for caution, but they still would have preferred a fight.

He directed two men to bring the gold to the front of the ship but not to unload it until they saw that Brage was with them. "Half of you stay with the ship, the rest follow us, but not closely."

The men knew the plan and were ready.

"Come, Ulf. Let us find Brage and take him home," Anslak said to his son, and the two of them started up the shore to the open field beyond with the rest of the men staying back a distance.

"They have landed, Lord Alfrick! The Vikings are here just as they said they would be!" shouted one of the old men who was keeping watch.

Alfrick girded himself for what was to come. He hoped Anslak was a man of patience and intelligence, a reasonable man. The army he had put together to fight them during the Black Hawk's raid had disbanded, and the bulk of his force had ridden with Edmund to search for Dynna and the Viking. As it was, the tower had its usual force of men to defend it, but if a fight came, their numbers would not be enough. Anslak did not need to know that, and to that end, Alfrick had stationed whatever old men and youths he could find at strategic places to make it look as if his men were truly there in full force.

"Where is Hereld? Bring him to me at the gate," Alfrick ordered as he started down the stairs to the Great Hall.

The servant ran to do as the lord had asked, but returned quickly with news Alfrick did not want to hear. "I am sorry, my lord, but Hereld left the tower yesterday and has not returned. One of the men told me that he sailed last night with the tide."

"He *what?*" Alfrick repeated, stunned. He had told the merchant that he had wanted him with him today to face the Vikings. The merchant was due another payment after the meeting and so he had believed he would be there. Had the merchant fled because he feared Anslak and his men so greatly?

"Hereld is gone, my lord," he repeated.

"Bring three guards, and we will go forth to meet with Anslak and the others without him."

Alfrick led the way with his few men. He wore a sword at his hip as did the others, but there were no archers in the woods to slay the Vikings from cover and no men mounted and armed with broadswords ready to ride from the safety of the tower. He wondered where Edmund was as he ventured forth to deliver the message he dreaded giving.

Anslak walked steadily without fear toward the place where he had agreed to meet with Alfrick. He was as excited as he was cautious. They were about to free Brage . . . He could imagine his son's fury at being imprisoned for so long, but now he was being released and that was all that mattered. Soon, he would have his son back.

"I see nothing unusual," Anslak remarked to Ulf as they neared the appointed place.

"Nor do I. All is quiet—perhaps too quiet."

"We shall see. If they are planning to attack us, we will answer blood for blood. But there is no need for vengeance this day. All I want is my son returned alive and well. That is what Hereld promised and that is what I expect."

"The Saxons are coming now," Ulf announced, his hand going automatically to his sword.

"Easy, Ulf. Make no threatening gestures. We want your brother back alive," Anslak warned.

"I do not see Brage."

"Let us stop here. It is open and the ground is flat." Anslak stopped and waited for Alfrick and his men to walk to him.

"Hail, Anslak," Alfrick called out in greeting.

"I have come for my son as the trader Hereld bid. I demand to see him now!" Anslak's voice was loud and powerful.

Alfrick stopped and remained where he was a short distance away from the Vikings. He said to those who accompanied him, "Without Edmund's return, there is no avoiding this moment. I must tell the truth."

"Is there any way we can stall them? Get them to wait another day or two?" one man asked under his breath.

"And then, when Edmund does not return, what should we do?" Alfrick countered quietly. "No, it is time for the truth. There is no guarantee that Edmund will even find the Black Hawk, let alone bring him back in time for the ransom to be claimed."

Anslak could see that he was talking with his men. "What say you, Saxon? I await your reply. Where is my son?" he demanded again.

"I am Lord Alfrick. I am the one who sent the trader Hereld to you with word of the terms for the exchange."

"Aye, we know of you. We have the gold. Present my son, and the exchange will take place," he called out, sensing something was not right.

Alfrick drew a deep breath. "I must explain what has happened."

"What are you saying? What has happened?" Ulf asked, suddenly angry at the man's evasiveness. It bothered him that Brage was nowhere to be seen. "Where is my brother?"

"I do not know."

"What?" Both Anslak and Ulf were furious. They had been assured that Brage was there, recovering from his wounds, and now . . .

"The Black Hawk escaped the tower several days ago. We

have not seen or heard of him since. I have men looking for him, but with no success. He has fled."

Anslak did not believe a word the Saxon was saying. "I believe you not. Has my son died at your hands? Where is his body? I would see it before I strike you down."

"There is no need for bloodshed. He is not dead."

"Where is Hereld? Bring Hereld before me. I trust not the word of a Saxon."

"Hereld is gone. You must take my word that—"

"I take nothing from you," Anslak growled as he drew his sword. "I believe nothing you say. Hereld made claims and promises in your name. My son was here, alive, awaiting my arrival, and he would be turned over to me with the payment of six hundred pounds of gold . . ."

"Payment of what?" Alfrick was shocked.

"Six hundred pounds of gold. One hundred in good faith and the rest now."

"The demand was only for five hundred pounds of gold!" No wonder the double-dealing trader had fled.

"That only proves what liars you are! All that he told me you said were lies, and all that he said to me were lies, too! You shall pay for your deceit!"

"Do not act so hastily! You can have your men search the tower. Then you will see that I bear no false witness."

"We will search your tower! We will tear it down if we have to, but we will find my son!" Anslak's eyes narrowed dangerously as he regarded the lying Saxon dog.

"Were he here, I would turn him over to you, but I cannot give you that which I do not have."

Anslak was livid. Brage had to be there somewhere, and he was going to find him. He did not bother to order Ulf to give the signal to attack, but gave it himself.

Those on the shore saw him and relayed the signal to Kristoffer. Kristoffer immediately set the longships in toward land.

The fierceness in his father's voice matched Ulf's own

emotions. Brage had to be there. They would take this Lord Alfrick hostage and hold him as they searched his tower.

The fighting erupted as Anslak and Ulf charged Alfrick and his small escort. Alfrick put up a valiant fight but was no match for the furious Vikings. Anslak quickly disarmed him, as Ulf did the others.

Multitudes of Norsemen were swarming toward them from the shore.

"Now, Lord Alfrick, we will search your tower and see if you are lying." Anslak was furious. He would find Brage alive or he would find the ones responsible for his death!

They started toward the tower, and when those inside saw that Lord Alfrick had been taken by the Vikings, they knew not what to do.

"Leave the gates open," Lord Alfrick ordered. "The Vikings are to search the tower."

Inside, terror reigned. With Lord Alfrick and his men taken captive, and Sir Thomas and Edmund away, there was no force to defend them and no one to lead them. When the Vikings came through the gate, the Saxon defenders laid down their weapons. They were herded away and imprisoned with their lord, while the search began for Brage. The Vikings had come to find the Black Hawk, and they would not be satisfied until they searched every inch of the tower and learned the truth of his fate.

Anslak led the way into the Great Hall with Ulf and Kristoffer close behind. "Ulf, take some men and check the tower rooms. Kristoffer, gather your men and search the grounds. I want every inch gone over. I want to know what happened to my son," he thundered, his blue eyes glowing with a fervor that spoke of anger and worry. He would not leave this place until he had the answers he sought.

"And treasure, Father? What shall we do with any bounty we find?" Kristoffer asked.

"Bring it here before me. Perhaps instead of paying out

gold, we will take some instead," Anslak answered. "I will wait here for your return. If you find anyone with any knowledge of Brage, bring them to me. I will question them about his absence."

They divided into two groups and began the search. The Saxon servants huddled in corners, terrified of the Norsemen. Having heard all the tales of the Vikings, they feared for their lives.

Ulf was tense as he kicked in the door of a tower room and ransacked it looking for some sign of his brother. But each chamber revealed nothing. As he reached one door, it was barred heavily from the inside, and he knew a moment of hope that this might be the room that held Brage. With the help of two of his men, they smashed the door open, sending pieces of wood flying about the chamber as he strode inside.

The room was darkly shadowed, and at first he could see no sign of life.

"Tear the room apart," he ordered gruffly.

Three of the men quickly did just that and dragged a hiding woman from beneath the bed. The female began to fight the moment their hands were upon her, and in the process her clothing was torn, revealing the tops of her breasts. The men, encouraged by her resistance, began to paw at her.

"Enough!" Ulf ordered suddenly. "Be gone! I will question this one!"

The men were puzzled by his reaction, but quickly quit the room, leaving Ulf alone with the woman.

Ulf was staring in disbelief at the prey they had flushed from hiding. There was no mistaking the flame-haired female who now stood before him, trying to cover herself with the torn top of her gown. He was face-to-face with one of the Saxon wenches they had captured just before the ill-fated raid.

"What are you doing here?" he demanded, closing the

distance between them. He gazed down at her, thinking she looked most beautiful with the flush to her cheeks and the sparkle of defiance in her eyes.

"Hiding from you and your men," she retorted haughtily, giving a lift of her chin as she regarded the giant she remembered oh so well from that first failed escape attempt.

"And once again, I have found you. Perhaps you should practice your hiding."

Matilda glared at him. "It would be a peaceful life here, if Vikings stayed in their own lands where they belong."

"Where is the Black Hawk?" he demanded, forcing his gaze away from her bosom and remembering why he was there.

"I wish I knew," she replied. "Then I could send you on your way."

"Have caution, woman," he growled threateningly.

"My name is Matilda."

"Do not push me. We have come to claim my brother, yet your lies abound. Your lord is our prisoner, your tower taken. Now, tell me of my brother, and perhaps I will let you live."

"You do not frighten me, Viking. Kill me if you must, but I will be no use to you dead."

"And how can you be of use to me?" he returned, marveling at her bravado in the face of such overwhelming odds. Most women cowered before him—his height, weight, and scar frightening them. This one showed no fear. He had known that she and the other woman they had captured that day were no ordinary peasant women.

"It would seem your brother and my lady fled the tower some days ago. I do not know where they are at this moment, but I do know where my lady planned to flee."

" 'Your lady'?"

"Aye, Lady Dynna, widow to Sir Warren, son of Lord Alfrick. I am her maid servant, have been such since she was a child. She was the one who was with me that day you took us captive. She is also the healer who nursed Brage."

At the mention of his brother's given name, Ulf knew she was speaking the truth. "Go on."

Matilda told him everything about Dynna's role in arranging her and Brage's escape from the tower. "Though she did not tell me, so to keep me safe from the wrath of Edmund," she concluded, "I believe there is only one place she would have run."

"And where is that?"

"She would have returned to her family."

"You know the way?"

"Aye."

"Then you will direct me and my men there. We will leave now."

"But it is far—many days' walk."

"There are horses in the stables here. We will ride. We will find my brother. Where are the rest of your defenders who attacked us that day?"

"Most were from neighboring lands, and they have returned to their homes. Sir Edmund and Sir Thomas led the rest in search of Brage and Dynna."

"Have you knowledge of their recapture?"

"No word has come. All were waiting to see if Sir Edmund would return with the Black Hawk before you arrived. He failed most severely, and his father has now paid the price."

"Let us hope he has failed in all ways. Let us hope we find my brother free and unharmed. Come, you will tell my father, Anslak, all you have told me, and then we will ride to find them."

Ulf reached out to take her by her upper arm. She expected his hold to be painful, a restraining vise meant to subdue her and she was surprised when his touch upon her arm proved to be gentle. She glanced down at his big hand upon her and then up at his face and saw the pride mirrored in his features. When first she had seen him that day when they had been running, she had thought his scar fearsome. Now she found it intriguing. This Ulf was an interesting man.

# Seventeen

"And why would you tell us these things? Why would you go against your lord?" Anslak asked after listening to Matilda's story.

"I am but a lowly servant. My loyalty is, and always has been, to Lady Dynna. I seek only my lady's happiness, and she will not be happy with the likes of Sir Edmund," she responded forthrightly. She had nothing to lose.

"Then let us go now in search of them. You will lead the way." Anslak was anxious to find Brage, especially now that he knew the Saxons were hunting him as well. "But be warned, woman. If you try to trick us in some way or lead us into a trap, you will be the first to die."

Matilda faced him proudly. "I do not fear your wrath, for I will not betray you. I want Sir Edmund's defeat as much as you. He is a cruel man, not worthy of the honor of being lord to his people."

Servant though she might be, Anslak regarded Matilda with a dawning of respect. She was as brave as some Viking women. He glanced over at Ulf and was surprised to find him looking at the woman with the same emotion mirrored in his expression.

"Find Kristoffer," Anslak told Ulf. "Have him prepare mounts from the stables. We will ride this hour."

When Ulf had gone, Anslak looked at Matilda. "You say Brage was recovering?"

"He had been wounded in the shoulder and had a minor

head injury, but he seemed to be doing well. He must have been stronger than he pretended, to have escaped with Lady Dynna as he did and to have managed to avoid capture by Sir Edmund this long."

Anslak was pleased with her answer, but grunted in response, unwilling to let her know how important it was to him. Now, if his son had only managed to elude this Edmund while he was running, all would be well. The hardest part was going to be finding him themselves. Brage had always loved the wilderness, and Anslak knew he could hide in a forest and live off the land for some time if forced to do so.

Within minutes, Ulf was back with the news that Kristoffer would have the horses ready for them as soon as they were prepared to leave. Anslak went out to meet with his youngest son, while Ulf remained with Matilda.

"I must know something, Matilda," Ulf began.

"What is it?" she responded cautiously.

"What were you and your lady doing, dressed as you were, out in the countryside the morning we found you?"

Matilda decided total honesty would serve her best. "Lady Dynna was being forced to wed Sir Edmund, her dead husband's brother, against her wishes. She had hoped to return to her family home and seek the protection of her father. To that end, we disguised ourselves as peasants and escaped the tower the night before your raid. As it was, though, Sir Edmund found us just after the fighting began, and we were returned."

"So Brage was right. He had thought your lady was more than just a serving girl," Ulf mused.

"Serving girls sometimes have more freedom than ladies. She was a virtual prisoner after Edmund brought us back. Lady Dynna risked all to get them both free. I only hope they are safe."

"There will be hell to pay in this land if Brage has been harmed in any way."

"Then let us hope that we find him uninjured, so the innocent do not pay the price for Sir Edmund's deeds."

Anslak stood aside with Kristoffer. "I do not know how long we will be gone, but I am entrusting the tower to your keeping," he informed his son. "Hold it in our name. We have claimed it for our own. I will leave a third of the men with you to guard it. Can you do this?"

Kris was thrilled to have been given such a vast responsibility. He finally felt as if he had earned his rightful place. His father was actually entrusting him with keeping watch over Lord Alfrick and the other prisoners. He would do his job well. "I regret that I will not be riding with you, but I will hold the stronghold for you until you return."

Anslak clapped him on the shoulder. "You will one day match your brothers for feats of daring. Pray to the gods that we find Brage alive and well."

"I will," he answered solemnly.

"Go now and gather your men to secure the tower. We will return as quickly as possible."

"Good luck, Father." Kristoffer hurried away to see to the challenge assigned him.

Ulf and Matilda heard Anslak's call from the grounds and went to join him and the others as they prepared to leave.

"Kris does not ride with us?" Ulf asked, looking around for his younger brother.

"I have left him with a third of the men to keep the tower."

"I am sure he is pleased with the task," Ulf said with a smile, thinking of how Kristoffer longed to be a leader among men and how he wanted to follow in his and Brage's footsteps.

"It would seem so. Let us hope he does as fine a job as you or Brage would do."

"He will. He is your son," Ulf told him.

"Now, let us find the one who is missing and bring him home."

"We ride!"

The number of horses had been limited, so those who had been given a steed mounted, while the rest followed on foot.

The force that left the tower that day was a fearsome one. All those in the countryside who saw them coming quaked in terror and ran to hide. None were foolhardy enough to try to stop them. The Vikings traveled until dark, then camped for the night in a clearing that provided them with a good view of the surrounding area. They did not build campfires, wanting to keep their location hidden, should Edmund's force be near.

Ulf returned from a meeting with his father to find Matilda sitting by herself. She had drawn her knees up and wrapped her arms around them. Her shoulders were hunched against the night's chill that was settling over the land.

Ulf spread his cloak on the ground near her and gestured for Matilda to lie down. "There is your bed. Seek rest while you can."

"You would give me your own cloak for my comfort?" His thoughtfulness touched her—for a moment.

Ulf grinned at her assumption. "No, woman, I need my rest, too. I would share the cloak with you."

Matilda had spent most of the day in close companionship with Ulf, riding beside him, talking with him, and she had no objection to this, for he had been as kind as he could be to her considering the circumstances. But she was not about to share a bed with him.

"I will sit here, then, to pass the night, and you, Viking, can seek your rest alone."

Ulf again was amazed by her audacity, but this time he would not allow her to get away with defying him. He wanted her within reach in case she changed her mind about leading them to Brage and tried to slip away in the night. That way, too, if it turned out she had been lying to them, she could not escape their wrath. Not that he did not find her attractive. He did. But finding Brage alive was the most important thing to him. Later he would think about her as a woman. For now, she was their guide, and he would keep her with him as his father had ordered.

"It would be a simple thing to agree to your plan, Matilda, but it will not work. My father has bid me to watch over you, and I shall. Come join me willingly or I will be forced to bring you to my side," he told her in a tone that left no doubt he would do it. "What do you fear? That I will force myself upon you?" he taunted. "Know this, Matilda, there are many women in the world. You are only one. I have no need to take what is not freely given."

"But Vikings are known for their brutish ways . . ."

"Have I treated you such today?"

"No, but . . ."

"It was your lord who lied and deceived. We came in good faith to pay the ransom and claim my brother. Had rape and pillage been our reason for taking the tower, it would have been simple to do, for there was no resistance. But you are here, safe and unharmed, as are the others in the tower. Tonight, I merely offer you this comfort to protect you, nothing more. Join me now and put an end to this senseless debate. The hour grows late, and we must be up and gone with the dawn."

Matilda could have continued to argue with him, but he did outweigh her by at least seven stone. She did not doubt for a moment that he would pick her up and deposit her there beside him if he chose to. Certainly, she was no match for his strength. Deciding to make it easy upon herself, she rose and went to sit on his cloak.

Ulf was pleased that she had given in to his order without forcing him to a fight. He did not want to anger her. He only wanted to keep her near. He gave a grunt of satisfaction at her decision and then sat down beside her.

"Lie down, woman. Do not be so tense."

Ulf turned on his side and drew the cloak up over them as he slipped an arm about Matilda's waist and pulled her back against his chest.

Matilda stiffened at such intimacy with the big man, but when he made no further moves, she slowly began to relax. The day had been a long one and she was exhausted. Ulf's warmth soothed her, and his quiet closeness gave her a sense of security. Eventually, she slept.

Ulf felt the skittishness slowly go out of Matilda and thought of how much she reminded him of the fine filly he had at home. He knew that a gentle touch, a soft word and a constant, steady hand nurtured trust. It had taken him weeks to train the spirited horse, but her ride had been worth the wait. If it had worked with the filly, he would try the same on this Matilda. Certainly, her fiery hair and intelligence appealed to him. As he enjoyed the feel of her slender curves pressed against him, Ulf decided that she was definitely worth the effort. When Brage was rescued and they returned home, he would take Matilda with him. She might fight him for a while, but he would make sure that she changed her mind once they were there.

Matilda awoke just before dawn to find that Ulf had already gone from her side. It surprised her that she had slept so deeply as not to have noticed when he left her. The thought was discomforting. She did not understand why she trusted this Viking warrior, but she instinctively knew that no harm would come to her while she was with him.

Standing, Matilda shook out Ulf's cloak and went in search of him. She found him deep in discussion with his father. They both looked up at her as she neared and their conversation ceased as they waited for her to join them.

"Tell us, maid, from this point how distant is the tower we seek?" Ulf asked.

"A three days' hard ride from here."

"And where would this Edmund be, if he were seeking your lady and my son?" Anslak asked.

"I am certain he would have ridden there first, but after that . . ." Matilda wanted to be of more help, but could only guess at Sir Edmund's moves. "Perhaps he is already on his way back toward us with Brage, or perhaps he reached the tower and they were not there. I do not know."

Anslak stared off in the direction they were headed. "Let us go now. Each minute we wait endangers Brage more."

Ulf called out the order to the men, and all were soon ready to begin the hard day's search. The hours of travel proved fruitless. A farmer was questioned, and it was learned that Edmund and his men had passed that way several days before. Even so, there was no sign of them now.

That night they camped near a stream, and planned to move out again at first light the next morning.

"Ulf, you take several men and scout the area ahead of us before we break camp," Anslak directed. "I do not know if we are closing on him or not, but it is always best to be careful."

"I will take Parr and Upton. They are good men who know what to look for."

Again Ulf sought rest with Matilda, wrapped in the protection of his cloak. She awoke this time when he roused before dawn.

"Where are you bound?" she asked, worried that something had happened.

"I am to scout ahead and make certain of what we will face this day."

"Take your cloak. I will be fine without it." She knelt and held his garment out to him.

"You keep it. I will be back soon. Stay near my father. He will protect you."

She looked so beautiful to him as she gazed up at him from on her knees that he could not resist reaching out and touching her cheek.

"You are lovely, Matilda."

Matilda was so surprised by his words and his caress that

she could only stare up at him. He gave her a slight smile and then turned and hurried off, leaving her looking after him.

Parr and Upton were waiting for Ulf. They rode away from the encampment at a ground-eating pace, determined to scour the area ahead.

They came upon the Saxon men by accident. Two of Edmund's scouts were checking the route for danger just as they were, when Ulf spotted them. Ulf and the others tried capturing them in order to question them, but the two drew their swords. The fight was fierce. When all was done, the Saxons lay dead.

"They were Saxon and they were armed. Edmund must be near," Ulf said, disappointed that they had not taken the two alive. "Let us see just where they are camped and what their strength is. If the gods are with us, we might be able to attack them at daylight."

The sky was only beginning to brighten in the east as they continued on their way silently. They were starting up a low rise when Ulf reined in.

"Stay here with my horse," Ulf ordered Parr and Upton. "I will go on foot to take a look beyond. I would not want them to see us now."

Staying low, Ulf made his way to the top of the hill to survey the scene before him. He stood immobile for a long moment, staring at Sir Edmund and his men spread out in the valley below. He pressed himself close to the ground, wanting to stay hidden as he tried to estimate their numbers. As his gaze swept over the area, he caught sight of his brother, tied at the far end of their campsite. Ulf scrambled from his hiding place and raced back to where Parr and Upton waited.

He related what he had seen, then gave his directions to the men. "We must take them by surprise before they start out for the day or there will be no way to protect Barge."

He practically threw himself on the horse's back and the three galloped back to where Anslak waited.

"We found them!" Ulf bellowed.

Matilda heard him shouting and rushed forth to see what he had learned. She was standing with Anslak when Ulf reined in and dismounted.

"What about Lady Dynna? Was she with them, too? Did you see her?" Matilda ran to Ulf's side, desperate to know her lady's fate.

It had not occurred to him to worry about the Saxon wench. All he cared about was finding his brother alive. "I did not see her, but that does not mean she is not there. It was still quite dark."

Matilda did not feel better. She worried that something terrible had happened to Dynna.

"Let us go now, while they are still encamped and not suspicious." Anslak called to his men as they gathered around to hear what Ulf and the others had discovered.

Eager to free Brage, those with horses raced for their mounts. The rest picked up their weapons and prepared to move out.

Ulf turned to his father. "What shall we do with Matilda? I do not want her harmed in any way."

Anslak showed surprise as his son's concern, then turned to the young woman. "You will remain here until we return."

"No. I cannot. What if Lady Dynna is with the others? What if she needs me?"

"We will see to her. You stay here away from the bloodletting," Anslak repeated sternly.

"But . . ."

Ulf silenced her protest with a severe look. "I will come back for you as quickly as I can."

"Ulf . . . There is one thing . . ." She clutched his arm. At his questioning look, she continued, "There is one man who is friend to Dynna and who was kind to your brother.

His name is Sir Thomas. Please . . . if you can, see that no harm comes to him."

The warrior felt a sting at her words of concern for another man, and he wondered at the emotion. "You care about this man?" he asked harshly.

"Very much," she answered, knowing how Sir Thomas had defended Dynna.

Ulf gave a nod, then walked away from her, donning his helmet as he went.

Matilda watched him go, and realized then that he might be injured or even killed in the upcoming fight. She found herself following him, wanting to speak to him once more, but his pace was too fast for her. She could not catch up. At last, she had to call out to him. As he was about to mount, he heard her voice.

"Ulf!"

He glanced back, wondering what she wanted.

"Be careful . . ." she told him.

He nodded again, but felt oddly pleased. He wheeled his horse around and rode toward the front of the force. He would ride by his father's side into battle. Today, he would save his brother.

Brage sat in silence watching the Saxons in the camp around him and wondering what would happen when they reached the tower in another day. He wondered if his father was waiting there with the ransom they had demanded. He wondered, too, if he would live through the exchange.

These times of helplessness had taught him to forge his anger into determination. There was much revenge to be wreaked, and he would act upon it as soon as he was freed. The difficult thing would be surviving Edmund's treachery. Somehow, he would have to find a way to warn his father about it.

The night just passed had seemed endless. He had sought

sleep on the hard ground, but none had come. His thoughts had been too fierce, too disquieting. He could not dismiss memories of Dynna's betrayal, and he had been filled with a burning need to avenge himself. One day he would find her again, and when he did . . . Brage had deliberately tried to distract himself with thoughts of home, but still his mind returned to betrayal and the need for revenge. The first thing he would do when he returned was find the traitor who was responsible for the deaths of so many of his men.

Brage had tossed on the hard ground, seeking the final answer to the riddle that haunted him. Again and again, he went over everything he could remember that would point out the one who had turned against him, and again and again he was faced with the fact that there seemed to be only one person who would have or could have done it. Ulf. Ulf with his advance knowledge; Ulf who was supposed to protect his back.

As children, they had waged an almost savage competition against each other in their effort to win their father's favor. Many times their boyhood battles had ended in draws, for Ulf had met him equally in all things. Yet he himself was the one who had earned most of his father's praise, for he was the son of his father's most beloved wife. Ulf had not been ignored, but he had been less favored than Anslak's two sons by marriage, and now that one thing seemed the most damning thing. Where had Ulf been during the battle? Where was he now? Taking over his longship? Leading his men on raids?

Brage thought of his younger brother and began to worry about him. If it had been this easy for Ulf to get rid of him, he could only imagine how simple it would be for Ulf to dispose of Kris. If that were his plan, Kris's death would leave Ulf the sole son and heir, legitimate or not. Though Kris would be a fine warrior one day, he was still young and inexperienced. He was no match for the ferocious Ulf.

Brage stared up at the sky and noticed that the eastern

horizon was brightening. Soon it would be dawn. Soon they would be arriving at Alfrick's tower once again. He did not look forward to it.

The first hint that something was amiss was when a panicked shout went up.

"Vikings!"

At the cry, chaos erupted in the camp. All eyes turned toward the rise, and it was then that they had their first view of mounted Viking warriors, topping the rise and thundering toward them.

"Turn your back!" Sir Thomas ordered Brage as he drew his knife from his belt.

Brage heard the urgency in his voice and did as he had said. He was grateful when the Saxon cut his bonds. Sir Thomas was truly a man of honor.

"There, Viking. You are free again. Save yourself!" Sir Thomas told him.

Brage turned, and for an instant their gazes met. Each saw respect mirrored in the other's eyes.

"Go!" Sir Thomas repeated.

Brage ran as Sir Thomas turned toward the battle. Brage started hunting for a weapon, wanting to join the fight.

Sir Thomas picked up his sword, ready for the battle. He charged forward toward the fighting prepared to die with his own men. But it was too late. The rest of the Saxons were not ready to ride or to fight. The battle was swift, and the outcome was deadly. It was over almost before it began.

Sir Thomas was almost immediately surrounded by four large, angry-looking Vikings. They all stood with their swords pointed at him.

"Drop your weapon," Ulf ordered as they closed on him.

Sir Thomas thought of attacking, but thought better of it. He quietly laid his sword on the ground.

"Where is he? Where is the Black Hawk?"

"I freed him."

Ulf stepped forward and pressed the point of his blade to Sir Thomas's throat. "Speak the truth or I will kill you now."

"Ulf! Wait!! Stop!"

Ulf recognized the voice immediately and looked around to find Brage running toward them. Relief and great joy filled him.

"Brage lives!" he shouted for all to hear, dropping his sword from Sir Thomas's throat and turning to welcome his brother.

"Do not harm this man!" Brage insisted as he came to stand before them. He saw what looked like happiness in Ulf's expression, and he wondered when his brother had become such a good actor.

"But he is the Saxon who held you prisoner," Ulf argued. "I saw him from the rise when I was scouting."

"He is also the Saxon who saved my life," Brage countered. He turned to Sir Thomas. "My debt to you is paid. We are even now, Sir Thomas . . . a life for a life."

Sir Thomas nodded in response, but said nothing. Ulf eyed the other man with interest.

Around them, the last of the weak resistance was wiped out. The battle was done. The bodies of the dead and dying Saxons were scattered about the encampment. Edmund lay facedown where he was slain as he tried to run away.

Anslak finished fighting and looked up to see Ulf standing with Brage as he rode toward them, his gaze met his son's. Brage saw his father coming and went to him. As soon as Anslak had dismounted, they embraced warmly. Anslak did not attempt to hide the depth of his feeling over finding his son alive. Tears burned in his eyes as he held Brage away from him to look at him.

"You are well?" he asked, his voice gruff with emotion.

"Now that you are here," he replied, smiling at his father. He had wondered if this moment would ever come, and he was thankful for it.

"We did not know what to believe when we landed and you were not there for the ransom."

"I learned that Edmund planned to kill me, even after the gold was paid, so when the chance came to escape, I took it. What of the tower? What did you find there?"

"Nobody but the maid, Matilda. She is the one who told Ulf the truth of all that had happened. She led us here, but is waiting back where we camped."

"So you took Alfrick's stronghold?"

"We did. Alfrick is imprisoned. The tower is ours. Kristoffer holds it for us even as we speak."

"Kris is there and he is well . . ." he repeated, relieved to find his younger brother was unharmed.

"He is growing into a fine warrior. He has proven himself well these last weeks, though he still has a long way to go to match you and Ulf."

Brage looked around the campsite again and saw that Edmund lay dead. It pleased him to know that the man would never torment anyone again. "It is right that he was struck down while running away from a full-fledged battle. He was a coward and is deserving of a coward's death."

"Let us go home now. We have what we came for," Anslak said, ready to return to the longships.

"Nay, Father, there is one more thing I must do before we sail."

"What is that?"

"I must go back . . ." He stared in the direction of Dynna's home, his jaw tight with anger. "There is someone I must confront."

"Who is this person who is more important to you than returning to your own home?"

Brage gave a vicious laugh. "I return there not for any tender emotion, Father. I return for revenge." As he said the word, he looked pointedly at Ulf. "These last weeks I was betrayed not once, but twice. I will see that the deceivers pay for their treachery."

Ulf was the first to look away. "I must return for Matilda. I will join you soon." He turned back to Brage and embraced him. "I am glad you are alive and safe."

"As am I," Brage replied.

When Ulf had gone, Brage and Anslak continued to talk.

"Father, this man, Sir Thomas, saved my life. He is a good man, fair to all. He would command respect should he be placed in authority at the tower."

"You think he is friend and not foe?"

"I know he is a friend. Perhaps it would be a good thing to trade with this land."

"We will speak to him of such. A Saxon ally would be unusual, but profitable."

Matilda had waited what seemed an eternity for Ulf's return. The place where she sat was shaded and comfortable and secure enough, but the fear that something terrible was happening haunted her.

Matilda's emotions were torn. These were the Vikings, the dreaded invaders, yet they seemed more civilized than Edmund ever had. And Ulf . . . She smiled in spite of herself as she thought of him. He was a big man, a gruff man, but despite his size, he had surprised her many times with his gentleness. She tried to tell herself that she did not care what happened to any of them as long as Lady Dynna was all right. She loved Dynna and needed to know that she was safe. She could not imagine that Sir Edmund let her go, not after the feverish ways he had been pursuing her all these months. She prayed fervently that her lady was unharmed. She wanted to be reunited with her at her parents' home and live there for the rest of their lives in peace. Still, as she waited, she could not help but wonder if Ulf had survived the battle uninjured and would return for her . . .

The sound of a lone horse galloping her way drew her from her thoughts. Matilda was not sure whether she should run to meet the one who was coming or attempt to hide until she could see who it was. She chose the latter and hid among the trees there on the bank of the stream. Crouching low, she watched anxiously as the horse came over the nearby hill. Only then did she breathe a sigh of relief, for it was Ulf returning to her.

"You are well! The battle is won?" she called as she forgot all caution and ran out to him.

When Ulf had ridden over the hill and had seen no sign of Matilda, he had been deeply worried. For a moment, he had feared that she had fled, but then he saw her emerge from the woods and he urged his horse in her direction. As he neared her, he did not rein in, but reached down with one arm and scooped her up to seat her before him.

"My brother lives!" His happiness knew no bounds. Then, unable to stop himself, he kissed her.

Matilda was shocked by his kiss, but did not fight him. He was the victor returning with the good news of their glory. And besides, she admitted faintly to herself, his kiss was not unpleasant.

When Ulf ended the exchange, he gazed down at her seeing the glow in her eyes and the slight curve of satisfaction to her lips. He wanted her. He had since the beginning. He would take her back home with him. Before he could say a word, though, she began to question him.

"What of Lady Dynna? Was she there?"

"No. Your lady was not with them. Brage did not speak of her. But we ride to her family's home now."

"I will go with you," she stated. "I must find out what has happened to my lady."

Ulf nodded, and they went to rejoin the others.

After learning how poor the defenses were at the other tower, Anslak ordered half his men to remain behind with Sir Thomas and guard the survivors of the battle until they returned. He saw Ulf riding back in with the maid and ordered the men to prepare to leave.

Matilda pleaded with Ulf as they neared the place where Brage and Anslak stood. "I must speak with your brother for a moment. He will know about Dynna."

Ulf nodded and rode up to him.

"Brage . . ." Matilda called out to him as Ulf helped her to dismount.

When he turned toward her, his expression was stony and his eyes cold. She shivered in spite of the warmth of the day.

"I am glad you are well, but I must know. Where is my lady? Did she get away safely or did Edmund harm her?"

Brage's answer was terse. "Your lady," he almost spat the words, "is at her father's tower. She is awaiting my justice."

## Eighteen

"Your justice?" Matilda was staring at him in confusion. "I do not understand. Has she not been hurt enough already by Sir Edmund? Did she not save your life?"

"Only to forfeit it again in exchange for her own comfort?"

"What are you saying?"

"I tell you, your lady is as deceitful as Edmund ever was. It is a shame he is dead and they did not have time to marry, for they would have gotten along well together."

His words were sharply spoken and took Matilda aback.

"You are wrong about Lady Dynna." She started to protest, but Brage cut her off.

"Enough! I will hear no more about it. Let us return to Lord Garman's tower. It will be yet another day's ride."

Brage was given one of the Saxon's horses, and Matilda got her own mount back. Many of the men who previously had been walking were now riding, and the pace was much faster. Brage rode at the fore with his father while Ulf rode a short distance back beside Matilda. They had been traveling for some time before Matilda spoke.

"I do not understand what could have happened between them," she said, glancing over at Ulf. "He spoke of deceit, yet I cannot fathom how she could have deceived him. Had she wanted to see him dead, she had but to leave him behind when she made her escape."

"True enough. There is naught to do but wait. Neither of us have a say in it anyway."

"I will not stand by and see my lady hurt," Matilda declared, knowing she would do whatever was necessary to ensure Dynna's safety.

Ulf shot her a sidelong glance, seeing the strength in her profile and the determination in the set of her jaw. She was a fighter, this one. She had a headstrong way about her, and he was certainly enjoying her spirit.

Dynna sat in her bedchamber ever aware of the two guards, Balder and Ives, sitting across the room from her. She had had no peace since Edmund had ridden away with Brage as his prisoner once more. Guilt consumed her, though she knew there had been nothing else she could have done.

Each day, Dynna prayed fervently that Brage was all right, that his father would be waiting for him at Alfrick's tower with the ransom, and that the exchange would be made without incident. But knowing that Edmund was as treacherous as a snake, she did not put any trust in him. She despised being this helpless, and she chafed at the restrictions on her. Had she had a moment's freedom, she would have found some way to help Brage, but she was entombed in her chamber, with only a single daily visit allowed by her parents.

Dynna was glad that her parents were unharmed. Lord Garman and Lady Audrey had been given free rein of the tower the day after Edmund had left. But not Dynna. The guards were following Edmund's orders to the letter, for he had terrorized them with the threats of what would happen should she turn up missing. They were not taking any chances with her, and she was suffering from their dedication.

Often, Dynna found herself imagining that Brage would be ransomed back to his father and then return here for her. She loved him. She would never love another. She wondered if they would ever be together again. In her mind's eye, she was back on the bank of the stream with Brage, and they were . . .

A sudden, frantic pounding at the chamber door jarred her from her reverie, and the two guards raced to answer it.

"What is it?" Balder demanded as he threw the door wide.

"Riders! And they are coming this way!" the other Saxon told him excitedly.

"Could it be Sir Edmund returning already?" Ives asked.

"No, it is too soon. There is no way they could have reached Alfrick's stronghold and ridden back in just these few days."

"Then who?"

All three knew a moment of dread.

"How many did you see?" Balder asked.

"Over a hundred . . ."

"The Vikings . . ." Ives stated out loud what they did not want to consider.

"If they are the Vikings, then what can we do? Six of us cannot hold this place!"

"And if they are the Vikings, then what of Sir Edmund? What of Lord Alfrick?"

The men exchanged looks of terrible understanding.

Balder bravely fought off the fear that threatened to cow them all. He straightened his shoulders as he glared at the other two. "We are bound by honor to Sir Edmund and Lord Alfrick. We must hold to our duty. We must keep Lady Dynna from harm until Sir Edmund returns."

"But what if . . ."

Balder shot him a quelling look. "We must defend this stronghold as best we can. Have you ordered the bridge drawn?"

"Yes. I have done all I can with just the six of us. I have locked Lord Garman and Lady Audrey in the tower room and if we lock Lady Dynna in here, we will have that much less to worry about."

"Should one of us stay with her?" Ives asked, remembering how Sir Edmund had insisted they keep constant watch over her.

"I think there is little need."

All understood his meaning, and they left the room and locked the door from the outside.

Dynna ran to the door and tried to open it, but it was useless. She was trapped in her chamber, unable to help anyone and unable to escape. The total futility of her position infuriated her, yet she knew a glimmer of hope. If Vikings were coming, then perhaps Brage had survived . . . perhaps Brage was returning for her. She clung to that chance as she went to the window and kept watch.

It took Brage little time to breach the pitiful defenses of Lord Garman's stronghold. Brage had not been sure how many men had been left there to hold it, but the number had not been large. Upon arriving at the tower, he had sent the bulk of the men to the front to keep Edmund's remaining guards busy, while he, his father, Ulf, and a small group of the others attempted to enter through the secret gate he and Dynna had used. As Brage had suspected, there was only one man standing guard, and it had been a simple matter to battle their way inside. Once they had disarmed him and entered, they engaged the others quickly. Balder, of all the guards, had presented himself the most bravely, but it had all been for naught. He had been outnumbered and overpowered, and in the end, every one of them had been taken captive. The bridge was lowered for the Vikings to enter.

Matilda knew Lord Garman's stronghold well, for it had been her home. As soon as they had crossed the bridge, she dismounted and ran through the hall to the stairs.

Brage followed. He did not know where Dynna and her parents might be hiding, but he intended to find them.

When Matilda reached Dynna's chamber, she found the

door locked. "Lady Dynna, are you in there?" she cried as she pounded on the door.

"Matilda?" Dynna's voice was filled with promise. "Thank God it is you! Get me out of here! What has happened? Is Brage here? Is he all right?"

"There is no key, but I will . . ."

"Move, woman."

At the sound of Brage's voice so near, Matilda jumped. She hastened to get out of his way.

Brage stepped forward and with one powerful kick, shattered the lock. It took only another forceful shove to push open the door to Dynna's bedchamber.

Dynna had been terrified for an instant, but when she saw that it was Brage who stood there, a look of joy shone upon her face. He was alive and well and he had come back for her! Her heart ached with her love for him as she gazed at him. He looked so incredibly handsome that she could not wait to kiss him and hold him.

"You are here!" she cried. "You are alive!"

Happiness filled her. She cast all her fears aside as she ran to him. She was going to declare her love for him. She was going to pledge her undying devotion. She was going to explain to him the horror of the choice she had been forced to make and how glad she was that he was uninjured and free!

Brage stood unmoving as she came toward him. Memories of her, warm and willing, assailed him for a moment, but then thoughts of her lying betrayal returned and pain surged within him. He saw her smile and happiness and wondered how she had managed to become such an accomplished liar. She had turned him over to Edmund in exchange for her own ends and now was pretending that she was glad he was alive! It enraged him.

Brage did not move until Dynna was almost to him. As she was about to throw her arms around him, he snared her wrists in a powerful grip and forced her to her knees before him.

"Brage . . . ?" Shock and confusion sounded in her voice and showed in her expression.

"True, I am alive, but it is no thanks to you," he ground out, hatred echoing in his every word.

"I do not understand . . ." Dynna was shocked by his words and tears quickly filled her eyes.

He ignored her as he went on, "I should be used to cunning and betrayal by now. But thanks to you, I have learned another lesson in trusting. I will no longer believe anyone who uses sweet lies in their treachery."

Brage glared at her, despising her and despising what she made him feel. For though he hated her, he found he still desired her, and the emotion only added to his fury. Dynna went deathly pale as he spoke, and he knew he had been right.

"You sold me to Edmund for the cost of your own freedom, Dynna."

"No! I did not!"

"You came to my bed to rid yourself of Edmund, and you went to his bed to rid yourself of me!" he snarled, tightening his grip on her.

His hold was brutally painful and she cried out softly in protest, but he did not ease his hold.

"Brage . . . you must listen to me . . ."

"No, I will hear no more lies from your lips!"

"But there was a reason . . ." She had to tell him the truth—that Edmund would have killed her mother if she had not told him of his hiding place.

But Brage gave her no opportunity as he countered coldly, "The betrayer always believes he is justified in his treacherous ways."

Dynna was crying. His coldness stabbed at her heart. Why would he not listen? If only he would let her explain, he would understand . . .

Crystalline tears traced paths down her pale cheeks, but they did not touch Brage's heart. He had hardened himself against her.

"Save your tears for someone who will believe them, Dynna. You bought your freedom with your body, and you think to buy it again with your weeping. It will not work. You have wasted it all. No longer will I treat you as one to be treasured. I now make you my slave. Get up and let us be gone from here. I have had enough of the Saxon lands, and of its people."

He stared down at her as she quietly sobbed, then turned away from the sight of her. He found Matilda standing in the doorway watching them, and he spoke to her sharply.

"Bring her. She can ride with you."

Matilda nodded and hurried to her lady's side as Brage stalked off to rejoin the others.

"Lady Dynna . . ." she said softly as she went to her and wrapped her arms around her. "Do not cry so. It will be all right."

Dynna looked up at her friend, her face tear-ravaged. "Oh, Matilda . . . What am I to do? He believes I am as deceitful as the one who betrayed him to Lord Alfrick."

"We know it is not true, my lady."

"Edmund was going to kill my mother. He was holding a knife to her throat! He would slay her unless I told them where Brage was hiding . . ."

Matilda saw the horror of Dynna's position and understood the dilemma she had faced.

"But Brage thinks . . ."

"Brage knows only what Sir Edmund told him, my lady."

"Sir Edmund lied. But will Brage ever listen to me? Brage knows Sir Edmund. Does he not understand his deceptions? If Brage will not listen to my side, my life with him will be as barren as a life with Sir Edmund would have been. There will be no love between us, no trust. There would only be hate . . ."

"There is nothing you can do right now to change his mind. He is blinded by anger. Perhaps with time . . ."

"But what if he never listens?"

"You cannot think of that now, my lady. He is waiting for us. We must go. Just remember that you did what you had to, to save your mother's life."

Dynna slowly got to her feet. She knew Matilda was right, yet it did not ease the pain of losing Brage's trust. "I will give it time," she said sadly. "That is all I can do."

As they started off to join Brage, the future stretched bleakly before her.

Before leaving her family home, Dynna managed a short visit with her parents.

"You go with him willingly, Daughter?" Lord Garman asked, staring at Dynna.

Dynna wanted to burst into tears, she held herself together and looked her father in the eye as she answered, "Yes."

Audrey hugged her tearfully. "You will take care, my daughter? I will miss you terribly."

"I will be safe from harm, Mother. Do not fear."

As they were embracing, the call went out that it was time to leave. Matilda came for her.

"We must leave, my lady. Brage awaits us."

"Take care of my daughter, Matilda," Audrey told her.

"I have these many years, and I will continue," she promised.

Dynna hugged her father one last time and then hurried off with Matilda.

"You lied to them?" Matilda questioned.

"I had no choice. If my father knew of Brage's anger toward me and of his plans to make me his slave, he would have fought and died to save me. It is better this way."

Matilda's silence told Dynna that she agreed with her decision. Soon, Dynna was mounted behind Matilda and was riding away with her, leaving her family and former life behind forever.

* * *

The long hours of travel were tiring and monotonous. During the day, Brage completely ignored Dynna, but at night, he insisted that she sleep beside him. He made no attempt to touch her, yet even so, Dynna did not sleep well. Brage, however, had no such difficulty. And so the days and miles passed. Dynna only felt at ease when she was with Matilda or when she managed an occasional word with Sir Thomas, who was among the Saxon prisoners marching with them as they returned to Alfrick's lands.

When at last they reached Lord Alfrick's tower, all were glad that the trek was over and that the outcome was a triumphant one. They reached the stronghold at midmorning and made plans to set sail for home before dark that night. They were eager to be home.

Matilda stared at the tower as they rode ever nearer, and wondered what was going to happen next. "Lady Dynna, I do not know if I will be allowed to go with you or not, but I will speak with Ulf. I do not think Brage is the one to ask at this moment."

"Nor do I," she agreed, looking over to where the warrior rode proudly before them with his father and brother. She had thought him magnificent before, but now in victory, he was the conqueror—powerful, invincible. He had survived all, and to his reasoning, no thanks to her. "I pray Ulf allows you to come."

"As do I. It would be no life for me here without you."

They fell silent in understanding, knowing that the next few hours would determine the rest of their days. When they had reined in at Alfrick's tower and dismounted, Brage came to Dynna.

"You may go to your room and gather a few of your things to take with you," he directed. "We will sail soon. I expect you to be here waiting for me when I am ready to go."

As Dynna went to gather her personal belongings, Matilda

sought out Ulf. "I must speak to you," she said, as she found him with his father.

When he had finished talking with Anslak, Ulf turned to her.

"I do not know your plans," she began when she had his complete attention, "but I beseech you to take me with you. I must stay with Lady Dynna. I have cared for her since she was but a small child, and I cannot bear to be separated from her."

Ulf saw the very real depth of emotion in Matilda's imploring gaze and smiled inwardly. He had had no intention of leaving her behind, but now knew he could use the situation to his benefit. "And why should I care about Lady Dynna's comforts?"

"I ask this for myself, Ulf. There is nothing left here for me without my lady."

He smiled down at her in a gentle way, remembering the wildness of the filly and knowing that kindness earned much trust. "You will sail with us."

She smiled brightly up at him, the first true smile of happiness she had ever given him. She touched his arm as she thanked him.

He was startled by the effect her smile and simple touch had on him. He wanted to take her in his arms and kiss her, to make love to her all day and night, but was too smart to act on his desires just yet. He would give it time. He did not want a quick tumble with Matilda. He wanted more . . . He wanted her by his side.

"It was a fierce fight, Father, but we won," Kristoffer told Anslak as he faced him upon his return.

"You say Lord Alfrick and all those who were imprisoned were slain?" his father repeated, stunned.

"Somehow they had escaped and we trapped them as they were about to leave the tower."

"You did well," he responded. "You have proven yourself again, my son."

"Thank you, Father. If you wish, I will stay and keep the stronghold for you," Kristoffer offered. "Give me a strong force of men and I will hold this land for you forever."

Anslak knew Kris was going to be disappointed, for he had already decided on another way of handling it.

"Nay, Son, I would not leave you here. I want you to sail with me. As Brage has suggested, we will leave the stronghold in the charge of the man named Sir Thomas."

"Brage would give what you won to one of the conquered?" Kris stared at his father as if his sire were daft.

"He would give that which we conquered to a friend, Kris," Brage chided gently, not wanting to insult the boy, but wanting him to know the reasons behind the decision.

"After all the men who have died at their hands, you believe a Saxon is friend to us?" Kris challenged.

"Sir Thomas commands respect from all who know him. He saved my life when all others would have seen me dead," Brage said as he came to join them. "Far better we leave one of their own here to lead them. Sir Thomas will be an ally in a land where we have no other. We will be trading with him now, instead of raiding."

Kris could see that his father and Brage had already made the decision without asking him and that he had little recourse. He would have to accept it, but he did not have to like it. "Then I shall gather the men and prepare to set sail."

"I will take my ship. It will be good to be back with my men again," Brage told him.

"Kris, you can sail with me," Anslak said. "I will join you as soon as all is settled here."

Brage and Anslak sought out Sir Thomas where he waited for news of his fate along with the other Saxon captives.

"Sir Thomas," Brage said as he approached him. "We would speak with you."

Sir Thomas was cautious, but he got up and came to stand

before them. He was ready for whatever they were about to pronounce. He did not expect mercy. He had fought the Vikings. He had spilled their blood. Vikings were renowned for being thorough in their revenge. He had tried to guess with the other men what would be done to them, and the best they all were hoping for was to be sold into slavery.

"We have reached a decision, my son and I," Anslak told him as he studied him closely. "Brage seems to think that you would be a far better ally than enemy."

"I do not understand," Sir Thomas said as he looked between them, puzzled.

"He thinks that you would rule well here at Lord Alfrick's tower. What do you say?"

"Rule here?" He was truly puzzled.

"Sir Thomas . . . By my son's own testimony, you risked all to keep him alive. I now give you the gift of this stronghold and these lands, along with the lives of the other captives."

"You bid me to take Lord Alfrick's place?" He stared at Anslak and then at Brage in disbelief.

"That we do. We would seek trade with you now, not war. What do you say to our offer?"

"I will do it! And with great thanks!" He thought of the misery everyone had suffered under Sir Edmund's presence and knew he could make life better here.

"Good. Then the lands are yours. Rule well and fairly, friend," Brage told him.

"We sail for home now. See that these lands prosper," Anslak said.

"I will, and again I thank you."

"Thank you—for saving my son." His words were heartfelt.

Anslak moved off, leaving Brage and Sir Thomas alone.

"And what of Lady Dynna? Does she stay?" Sir Thomas asked, worried.

The warmth Brage had been feeling chilled at the mention of her. "Dynna goes with me."

"You will be good to her?"

Brage turned an icy glare on him. "Do not push our friendship. It was Dynna who turned me over to Edmund."

Sir Thomas heard the hatred in his voice. He knew what had happened in the room that night with Sir Edmund and Dynna's parents and it was obvious that Brage did not know the whole of it. "I fear you are misjudging her." He started to explain what had happened. "Lady Dynna would never have—"

Brage cut him off, not wanting to hear a word of his defense of her. "I would expect as much from you. You defend her always, but do not champion her to me this time. There is no defending what she did."

"There are times when one should use his heart and not his head when making decisions."

"If I thought your way in my life, I would have been dead long ago." Not wanting to listen to any more of Dynna, Brage stalked away. He knew her for what she was.

"Think on my words, Viking." Sir Thomas called after him as he watched him go. He hoped that Brage would recognize the truth and learn the power of forgiveness.

Sir Thomas went in search of Dynna then, wanting to tell her of all that had happened and to bid her good-bye. He found her just as she was leaving the tower with Matilda.

"I knew one day I would leave this place for good, but I had never thought it would be to travel to the north lands," she was saying as she passed through the gate for the last time. She had already said her farewell to the priests and servants and was on her way to begin a future that held no promise of happiness.

"At least we go together," Matilda said.

Dynna paused. Her eyes were filled with warmth and tenderness as she gazed at her loyal companion. She touched her hand. "You are a true friend, Matilda. You, alone, are the reason I can bear what is about to happen."

"Lady Dynna . . ."

Both women glanced around to find Sir Thomas coming toward them.

"Sir Thomas!" She dropped what she was carrying and threw herself into his arms. She hugged him to her as she had never done before. "What has happened to you? I feared what the Vikings would do once we reached here."

"Brage is a fair and generous man, as is his father." At her surprised look, he explained what Brage and Anslak had done for him. "And they have given the rest of the men their freedom, in return for future trade," he added.

"Oh, Sir Thomas, that is wonderful! I cannot think of another who inspires more honesty and devotion from their men than you."

"I am grateful to be worthy of their trust."

Dynna wished she had Brage's trust again, but she knew it was too late. "I am glad you will be happy here, my friend."

"I want happiness for you, too, my lady."

"I do not think that is possible anymore."

"Do not fret," he said, seeing the sadness in the depths of her gaze. "Brage seems a hard man at times, but I believe there is hope."

Dynna gave a soft, despondent laugh. "If only you were right, Sir Thomas, *I* might have hope that my life had some meaning. But he hates me now. His heart is poisoned against me, and nothing will change that."

"Have faith that time heals all. Do you love him?" he asked, having seen that emotion in both of them and wanting to confirm he had not been wrong.

She looked up at him. "I had planned to tell him the truth of my feelings that next morning before he was to leave to return to his home. But then Edmund came and the chance was forever taken from me."

"He is an angry man right now, Lady Dynna, and rightfully so. He was betrayed by one of his own, and many of his men were killed. He seeks revenge for the wrong. I understand his need, but I doubt that he will ever learn the traitor's identity."

Sir Thomas thought of that night that seemed so long ago, of how the betrayer had spoken in a hushed, hoarse voice and how he had never been allowed to see his face. He himself would not be able to identify him now, even if he were face-to-face with him.

Sir Thomas continued, "And then just when he thought himself free to return home, he found himself believing he was betrayed by you."

"But I had to save my mother's life . . ."

"Who knows what lies Edmund told him? Only Brage knows now, and he will not talk about it or listen to any explanations."

Dynna felt the sharp bite of Edmund's cunning. Even in death, he had managed to cause her misery.

"I will do as you say, for there is naught else I can do."

He hugged *her* this time. "Go now, they await you."

She glanced to where everyone had gathered.

"I will miss you, my lady." He spoke from the heart.

"And I will miss you, my friend. For always," she said, as she kissed his weathered cheek.

Sir Thomas watched as she moved off with Matilda to make the trek to where the longships awaited them. He prayed that she would find happiness with Brage. She was a kind and beautiful woman. She deserved to live the rest of her life surrounded by love.

When they reached the longships, Dynna and Matilda were helped on board Brage's ship. They sought what comfort they could find away from where the men manned the oars and settled in. They had heard the Vikings discussing the return trip and learned that it would be nearly a week before they reached Anslak's village, Brage's home.

As the longships pulled away from the shore, Dynna and Matilda watched the land fade from view. Neither spoke, for their emotions were in turmoil. They silently prayed that they would find peace, if not some kind of happiness, in their new lives far from the land of their births.

The days passed slowly as they headed ever northward. Dynna found herself watching Brage as he moved about the ship, comfortable in his command. She saw how the men responded to him and respected him. He was truly a trusted leader, a man among men.

Whenever Brage glanced her way, she always lowered her gaze, for she did not want to see the cold hatred she was certain would be in his eyes.

At night, Brage sought her out. He slept beside her, but did not touch her. One night, he awoke to find her nestled against him. He had ached to touch her, to caress the silk of her hair and bury himself within her, but he fought against the desire. He would not fall into her trap again. When he took her the next time, it would be coldly, without emotion, a quick tumble without the heart involved. He had gotten up and passed the rest of that night pacing the ship.

Several nights, Dynna found herself aching to reach out to Brage, to be in his arms and know his kiss again, but he made no overtures to her, barely speaking to her except in passing each day. Every morning when she awoke, he would already be gone to resume his duties, and she would feel a terrible emptiness inside, as if something vital was missing from her heart.

It was the third day out that Dynna noticed Matilda watching across the sea in the direction of another ship. "What about the craft interests you so?" she asked.

Matilda blushed a little as she glanced back at her lady. "Why, that is the longship that Ulf commands, Lady Dynna."

"Ulf? You have feelings for him?"

She nodded.

"And how does he feel about you?"

"I do not know, but he was the one I begged to let me accompany you, and I am here."

"Remind me to thank him when we finally make landfall."

"I will. I think I will thank him once more myself," she said as her gaze drifted back to the tall, broad-shouldered man who stood at the fore of the distant ship guiding it toward home. A slow smile curved her lips.

"I am glad you are finding some happiness in our situation."

"I had worried that you and I would be separated. I could not have stayed behind and watched you sail away."

"I only hope that in time I find happiness, too. You heard what Brage said that day in my chamber, that I am to be his slave when we return to his homeland."

"Perhaps he will change."

"I fear, Matilda, that my life is over. I would have lived in misery with Edmund, and now, it seems, I will be living in misery with Brage. I will keep trying to make him understand the situation and pray that one day he will listen."

Dynna caught sight of Brage out of the corner of her eye and turned to watch him moving among his men. He was smiling and laughing. How she longed for that smile to be directed her way!

Dynna dragged her gaze away from him to stare out to the open sea again. Somehow, she would find a way to prove to him that she loved him.

# Nineteen

Brage stood at the prow of his ship, gazing at his homeland. From the high mountains to the clear waters of the fjord, its beauty never failed to touch him. He would have been celebrating the joyousness of his return had his thoughts not been focused on the driving force that had obsessed him all these weeks. The time had come. Soon, he would name the traitor.

For most of the voyage, Brage had been watching his men, hoping for a clue or hint that might help identify someone other than Ulf. But he had learned nothing new. Though there had been talk among the men of the treachery on the first raid, none of them had any idea who would have betrayed them to the Saxon lord.

Brage looked over toward Ulf's vessel and saw his brother standing on the foredeck. Ulf looked the great leader. Ulf looked the proud Viking. Ulf looked the fierce warrior. But could he have been the conspirator? Had he been the one who had sacrificed Brage's men?

As if sensing Brage's gaze upon him, Ulf looked his way. Seeing that his brother was indeed watching him, he lifted his arm in salute of his return. Brage could see that Ulf was smiling, and he wondered how much it had cost him to pretend such happiness.

Brage looked away and glanced toward Dynna. He found her standing with Matilda near the stern, watching the passing scenery. Though he had slept each night by her side, he had deliberately treated her with cold indifference during the voyage. The memory of the passion they had shared would not be forgotten, and the knowledge that he loved her and had been about to declare it to her stung him. He had been a fool, mesmerized by her lovemaking and her lies. He still wanted her. There was no denying that, and once settled back in at his home, he would not deny himself the pleasure of her body. But he would never trust her again, because each kiss, each caress could be another betrayal.

The echo of the horns sounding their arrival came to Brage, and he looked toward the village. They were nearing the landing area. He could see the people hurrying down to meet them. It became real to him then that his weeks of torment were really at an end. It was over. He was free. He was home!

"What do you suppose will happen to us now, Lady Dynna?" Matilda asked a little nervously. The ships were slowing as they prepared to slide into shore, and another whole way of life was about to begin for them. The thought was frightening.

"I am to be Brage's slave," she responded sadly, looking up at Brage where he stood at the fore. Her heart ached as she watched him, and she knew he no longer felt any tender emotions for her.

"The outcome could have been worse," Matilda said, trying to cheer her.

Dynna was puzzled.

"Sir Edmund could have been victorious. You could be facing a lifetime of living hell with him."

Dynna managed a wan smile. "What you say is true. Perhaps being Brage's slave will not be as terrible as it seems..." Dynna thought of how just his touch had once made her body sing with pleasure. She remembered his warmth and his caring. She would never know them again as his slave. Each day would bring new heartbreak as she struggled to live with her love for him.

As Brage's longship pulled into shore, the two women stood close together, ready to face whatever the future in this foreign land held for them.

A roar of excitement went up among the villagers as they saw that Brage was at the fore of his own ship. He was alive! Anslak had brought him back as he had vowed to! Word spread quickly, and the throng increased as more and more poured forth to welcome Brage home.

Brage started to leave the ship, then thought better of it and turned to Parr. "Take the women to my home. I will be there shortly after I speak with my father."

Brage left the ship and met his father and Kristoffer on the shore. As they started through the crowd, he heard a woman call his name.

Inger had heard the call of the horn and was one of the first to reach the hilltop overlooking the fjord. When she had seen that it was Anslak returning, she had raced to the shore to learn Brage's fate. Now, seeing that he was alive, she could hardly control herself. Without a thought to those surrounding them, she launched herself at him.

Brage found the beauteous blond woman in his arms, her lips on his before he could say a word. He allowed himself to enjoy her embrace, then tried to free himself from her clinging presence. "Inger . . ." he said gently, "it is good to see you."

"Oh, Brage! Thank the gods, you are back and you are safe!" Her hands went over his shoulders and trailed down his chest as she gazed up at him adoringly. Her spirits were soaring. Brage had come back to her, just as she had hoped he would. "We will celebrate tonight!" Inger told him, her eyes warm with promise.

"There will be a fine celebration at my home!" Anslak

interrupted, saving Brage from the embarrassment of having to extract himself from Inger. "But for now, Brage—come with me. I am sure Tove wants to see you . . ."

Inger was left pouting, but still thrilled that he had returned. She would plan much for that evening. She wanted Brage for her husband and she would do what she could to entice him. She watched as he moved off to greet Anslak's wife.

Tove had been busy and was one of the last to hear of the ships' arrivals. She rushed down the slight embankment toward her husband and natural-born son, and Brage.

"You have returned, and with the Black Hawk!" She was smiling broadly as she greeted them, giving her husband a welcoming kiss as well as Kristoffer. She turned to Brage and regarded him proudly. "I am glad you are well. There has not been a moment's peace since that dreadful day when Ulf and Kris returned with the news of the defeat at Alfrick's hands. It is good that you are home."

Her reminder of the lost battle pained Brage, yet he managed to smile at her. "It is good to be home."

"Come to the house. We will begin the preparations now for a feast in your honor tonight. Mead and ale shall flow, and perhaps your father will open the fine barrel of wine he brought back from the east last winter." She took Brage's arm and led him off.

He went easily along with her, his father, and Kristoffer. He was glad to have been rescued so smoothly from the possessive Inger.

The men were pouring off the ships now, as the rest of the boats landed. It was a far happier time than the last time Ulf and Kristoffer had returned. Ulf's ship was the last to pull in, and many had already moved off to rejoin their families before he came ashore. He stood on the beach staring after his father and Brage and the others, then turned away to find Inger behind him.

"You have done a fine job in returning him to me, Ulf. I

thank you." She was smiling at him, pleased with the day's events.

"I did not return him just for you, Inger," Ulf chided with a chuckle, seeing the gleam in the woman's eyes and wondering how safe Brage was now that he was home.

"It matters not. He will be mine soon enough. You will see." She started to move away when she caught sight of Parr bringing the two women from Brage's ship. She stopped cold to stare at them. One woman was tall, dark-haired, and lovely, and though her clothing showed the wear of long days at sea, the quality of the garments declared her well-born. The other woman had hair the color of a fiery summer sunset. Inger recognized that she was dressed as a servant and so immediately dismissed her as unimportant. The dark-haired woman troubled her, though, and Inger called to Ulf.

"Who are these women aboard the Black Hawk's vessel?" she asked, not taking her eyes off them.

Ulf knew Inger well and was not about to tell her more than she needed to know. "Two slaves Brage has claimed as his due."

"Slaves?" Inger laughed in relief. Still, it did bother her that they were going to be living in Brage's home. She went forth to speak to them and to make certain they understood their place.

Dynna and Matilda were carrying their few possessions and following Parr inland when Inger approached. Dynna had seen the other woman throw herself at Brage and kiss him hungrily in front of everyone. She had been hard put to control the jealousy that reared up within her. Parr had ordered her to come with him just then, and so she had been reminded that she was no fine lady now. She was to be a Viking's slave. Had she been possessed of lesser willpower she might have cried, but instead, Dynna stood even prouder as she followed Parr toward Brage's home. Now, though, she was not sure what this woman wanted.

"Parr, I would speak to Brage's slaves," she announced, standing before him.

"Brage has told me to take the two to his home, and I must do so," he countered.

"It will not take long," she assured him, giving him a sweet smile.

He shrugged, knowing that she did have some favor with the Black Hawk.

Inger walked up to Matilda, looked her over as she would inspect a horse she was about to buy, then moved on to do the same to Dynna. As she eyed this one who was obviously a lady and was returning her regard with equal measure, she sneered, "You are slaves now. You are subject to Brage's every wish and want, but remember—he owns you. You are pieces of property to him, nothing more."

"We are aware of our positions here," Dynna replied with a dignity and grace that amazed even her, considering the state of her temper right then. She had watched this woman kiss Brage and now was being forced to suffer her insults.

"Just in case you should need to be reminded, let me tell you that you are less important to Brage than his shield or his sword. You are of less value to him than his horse or his ship."

Dynna gritted her teeth as she listened to the lecture from the arrogant Viking woman. "I suspect no woman could mean more to him than his ship."

"Ah, there you are wrong. It will not be long before you must do my bidding as well as Brage's, for once we marry, I will be your mistress," Inger said, flaunting herself before this woman whose confidence annoyed her.

Dynna smiled coolly. "When the day comes that you are Brage's wife, I will respect you. Until then I will do only as my master bids, and I have been instructed to go with Parr." With her head held high, she walked regally past her.

Parr had been looking on with something almost akin to amusement. All in the village knew Inger wanted to wed

Brage, and when Dynna refused to be cowed by her, he was impressed with her courage.

Inger felt the sting of her dismissal. She was about to reach out and grab the Saxon wench by the hair when Ulf's voice boomed from behind her.

"I would think twice before harming any of my brother's property, Inger," Ulf said. He had finished his business and had been on his way to see Matilda when he had overheard the exchange between Inger and Dynna.

"She was arrogant with me," she charged.

"She is a lady."

*"Was* a lady," she insisted. "She is but a slave now."

"But she is Brage's slave." He turned to Dynna and Matilda. "Come. I will take you to my brother's house. Parr, you can go on about your way."

Parr went off to see his own family, and, red-faced, Inger quickly disappeared, infuriated by Ulf's interference.

"I will show you the way to your new home," Ulf told them as he started off toward the village.

"Is it far?" Matilda asked.

"No, it is just on the other side of the village," he said, and the two of them talked on of the voyage. "It is close to the forest."

"And what is beyond the forest?" Dynna asked.

"Never mind, Lady Dynna. You will run no more," Ulf replied, thinking she was already considering escape.

Dynna fell silent. Her thoughts were on her life to come, and she wondered at the hell her existence would be were Brage to marry Inger.

Brage drank ale with his father and Kristoffer at the table in Anslak's house.

"Ulf and Kristoffer thought that you were betrayed on the raid. Do you believe this?" Anslak asked.

"I do. Alfrick was ready for us. His battle was planned.

There was no element of surprise. Somehow, he knew we were coming."

Anslak scowled, hatred for the betrayer showing on his face. "But who? Who would do this thing when all who sail with you profit?"

"I am not certain."

"Who does not sail with you but would like to see you dead? Do you have such an enemy?" Kristoffer asked.

"I had thought not, but I must be wrong."

"Then who?" Anslak wondered.

"I have suspicions, but must know more. Perhaps tonight at the celebration, the betrayer will give himself away. I will not rest until I find the one responsible," Brage vowed. "But for now, I will return home to see to my slaves."

He rose to go, and Anslak followed him outside. They stood together in the sun.

"Speaking of your 'slaves,' do you really think it was wise to bring Lady Dynna with you? By your own words, you said that she turned you over to Alfrick's son. Why would you bring her here, to your home? Would you not have been better served to sell her away at the slave market?"

"I trust her not, and yet I cannot bear to be parted from her."

"I do not understand."

"Nor do I. I had thought for a time that I loved her. But now, I only know that I want her, even as I despise what she did."

"What do you know of what she did?"

"Edmund told me that she had given me over to him."

"And you believed this man? Your sworn enemy?"

"I had all the proof I needed," Brage said heatedly. "I was his prisoner again, taken while in Dynna's father's tower."

"Go see to your slaves, but be back by sundown. There will be no celebration without you," Anslak said, wisely avoiding saying any more. He remembered a time when Brage's mother, Mira, had been a slave. He remembered the passion they had shared. He had bought her freedom, just so he could take her to wife. Though he cared deeply for Tove, he had loved no other as he loved Mira.

Brage crossed the village slowly, deep in thought. For the first time since gaining his freedom, he realized that he had believed everything Edmund had said to him. He went over in his mind all the things the other man had said, and tried to sort the truth from the lies. Again and again, he replayed his words in his mind: *Dynna had always been quick to see the way of things. Dynna had always used others to her advantage.*

Brage tried to reconcile those statements with what he knew of her. He had seen Sir Thomas's devotion to her. She had gone into the village to tend the wounded and dying. She had tried to tend his own wounds, enemy though she knew him to be. He frowned, confused.

Brage was still frowning as he entered his house, and his scowl deepened even more when he found Ulf there in the main room with Dynna and Matilda.

"Parr is gone?"

"He had family to see. I offered to bring them here," Ulf explained. "I did not know which room would be theirs. So I leave that task to you. I will see you tonight."

Ulf could tell Brage was troubled. He wanted to say something to him, to offer to talk about whatever was bothering him, but there was a reserve about Brage he had never known before. He left without speaking of it.

Brage's house was a large one for a man living alone as he did. It consisted of the center room where all the cooking and visiting was done, and three smaller chambers off it.

"Matilda, you may take the room to the back," he directed.

She went to look at the chamber that would be hers, leaving Dynna facing Brage alone.

"And Dynna," he began, his gaze inscrutable upon her, "you will sleep here."

He led the way to his own room. It was sparsely furnished,

but comfortable with a wide bed, small table beside it, and a large chest for storing things.

"So I am to share you chamber and your bed," Dynna remarked, startled that he would want her with him.

"You are."

"And what happens when you marry Inger and bring her here to your marriage bed?"

"I have no plans to marry Inger."

"You do not choose to believe me, so I do not choose to believe you.

Brage closed the distance between them and pulled her into his arms. He told himself he did not want her. He told himself his father was right. He should sell her in the market. It was not too late to send her to that fate. But as her breasts grazed his chest, he felt the surge of power that settled in his loins and knew the truth. Damn her! Despite everything she had done, he still loved her!

His mouth claimed hers in a heated brand that told her he desired her, and she returned his passion full measure. This was the first time he had touched her since that fateful day at her father's tower. She ached to be close to him, to feel him against her, to hold him to her and savor his kiss. If he wouldn't listen to her words, maybe he would listen to her heart.

Brage lifted her up and laid her upon his bed. He stood over her, his eyes glowing with passion. His body demanded that he take her. His heart ached that he be one with her. But he could not put her treachery or Edmund's words from his mind. He stopped and stood there looking down at her, frozen by her lying ways.

"Brage?" Dynna looked up at him and shivered when she saw that the desire in his eyes had disappeared. His gaze was cold upon her.

"I can take you whenever and wherever I please. But I do not choose for it to be now." He moved away from her. "Prepare yourself to go to my father's home. Tonight there is to be a celebration there in honor of my return. You and Matilda will help my mother's servants." He turned his back on her and left the house.

Dynna lay there staring after him. She was torn between anger at his cold, heartless treatment of her and feeling lost and lonely. At the sound of Matilda's call, she got up and left the room.

"Where did Brage go?" Matilda asked.

"I do not know. He spoke to me for only a few minutes and then he left." Dynna told Matilda of his plans for them that evening.

"Would you like a bath then? I found a tub we can use in the other room."

Dynna's eyes lit up at the thought of blessed cleanliness after all the days at sea. "Please. It may be the last time I am ever allowed to indulge myself."

"Surely you do not think Brage will object to our bathing?"

"Right now, even if he did, I would not care. Even the lowliest servant must wash. Surely if he wants us to serve him this night, he will want us to be clean."

Matilda went to get the water while Dynna sorted through her meager selection of garments. She chose a long, dark-violet tunic for the underdress and one of a lighter hue to wear over it. When Matilda called her, Dynna was more than ready to soak the many days' grime from her body.

Dynna stepped into the partially filled tub and sighed. "It feels wonderful. She sank down in the heated water, leaned her head back against the side of the tub and closed her eyes.

"The soap is on the stool beside you, as is a towel. If you need me, I will be in the main room," Matilda explained, then questioned, "Do you know how much time we have?"

"Brage did not say, but I would think that we have at least a few hours before we must see to his needs."

"Good. That will give me time to bathe when you are

finished." Matilda felt sure that Ulf would be at the celebration tonight, and she wanted to look her best for him.

Matilda left Dynna then, closing the door as she went to give her privacy. Dynna took the time alone to savor the sweet warmth of the water and to pretend, for just that little while, that none of this had happened, that she was owned by no man and that her life still stretched ahead of her. She began to wash as the heat of the water faded, then she slipped beneath the water to rinse the soap from her hair. She reveled in how refreshed she felt.

Dynna had just stood and was wrapping her hair in a towel when she heard the door open behind her. She turned, expecting it to be Matilda. She stood unmoving as she found Brage standing in the doorway staring at her.

When Brage had returned to the house and not seen Dynna, he had feared that she had run away. He had angrily asked Matilda where she had gone, and when he had discovered she was merely in the other room, his relief, to his annoyance, had been great. He had stalked across the room and thrown the door wide, not bothering to listen to the maid's further explanation of what she was doing. He was mesmerized by the sight of Dynna standing in naked splendor before him.

"Even a lowly slave should be allowed some privacy," Dynna said.

His gaze was like a flame as it swept over her body, and Dynna could almost feel the heat of it. She picked up another towel and wrapped it around herself. When she looked up at him again, she lifted her chin proudly.

"We will be leaving within the hour," he ground out scowling.

"I will be ready."

"Clothe yourself." He turned away and shut the door behind him.

Brage stood on the other side of the closed door, fighting down the driving need to tear the door open again and claim

# PASSION

Dynna as his own. The sight of her standing there unclad before him had ignited the blaze of his passion for her, and he was hard put to bring it back under control. Finally, drawing a ragged breath, he stalked from the house.

Matilda knocked on the door a few minutes later, and went in to help Dynna comb out her hair and to dress. Then Matilda took a quick bath of her own.

"We are ready to leave, if you are," Dynna announced to Brage, who had returned and was sitting in the main room.

Brage looked up to find Dynna and Matilda coming across the room. He had been trying to come to understand what he was feeling for Dynna. There was no denying that he wanted her, for his body reminded him regularly. But having her here in such close proximity was already proving pure torment. On the ship, there had been the buffer of the men to keep him from dwelling on her nearness, but now they were in his house and she was to sleep in his bed. The memory of her looking up at him, willing and warm, just a short time before and then standing naked before him, made him swallow tightly. He did not understand how he could still feel this way about her knowing what she had done.

"Let us go. It promises to be a late night," he said gruffly as he stood and walked from the house, leaving them to follow.

The noise coming from Anslak's house could be heard a distance away. When Brage, Dynna, and Matilda arrived, they found it filled with people, the crowd even spilling outside onto the grounds.

"Here comes the Black Hawk now!" one of the villagers called out, and a rousing cheer went up.

"Make room! Brage is here!"

The crowd parted, and Brage entered his father's home. He was clapped on the back and welcomed home warmly by all who knew him. Dynna walked a short distance behind. She saw the genuine affection everyone had for him and watched the way he seemed to honestly like all those who spoke to him. She and Matilda followed him inside and were aware of the questioning stares of the Viking people.

"Tove!" Brage called out to his father's wife as he finally reached the crowded main room of the house. "I have brought these women to help you serve. You may use them as you see fit."

Tove had heard the tale of the dark-haired one's betrayal and she knew exactly where she would put them to work.

"Come with me," Tove ordered, motioning for Dynna and Matilda to go back to the kitchen area. It would be hot and tiring back there, tasks suitable for slaves such as these. Ladies though they might appear to be, they were ladies no more.

Ulf was already there, sitting off to the side with some of the men, drinking ale with gusto. He was glad to have his brother home, and he was even more glad that Matilda was here tonight. He planned to buy her from Brage, and he would speak to his brother about a price later. He wanted her for his own. He had thought of little else during the voyage, and now that they were settled in, the time had come.

His gaze followed Matilda as she passed through the room. As if she felt his eyes upon her, she looked his way and smiled at him. Ulf was surprised by the unexpected feeling of happiness that filled him. He smiled back at her as she disappeared into the kitchen with Tove and Dynna.

Brage was waved to the table at the center of the room to sit with his father and Kristoffer. A mug of wine was pressed into his hand and the drinking began.

It was almost an hour before the food was brought out. Dynna, Matilda, and several of Tove's slaves carried heavily ladened platters of venison and roast duck. When those were served, they followed with heavy pots of steaming soups and trays of hot bread. It was a feast fit for a returning hero, and the mood in the room was joyous.

Brage sat at the table while the food was being served, conversing with those around him. He could not, however, stop himself from watching Dynna's move around the room. He had thought to humble her by forcing her to serve, but she was handling the duty with ease, bantering with the men who made comments to her and cleverly eluding those who grabbed at her as she passed them. Brage grew angry as he watched the others, and as she moved by the table, he called to her.

Dynna stopped before him and gave him a quizzical look. She had been wielding the heavy tray with care and had thought she was doing a good job. She did not know what she could have done to anger him.

"From now on, you are to serve only this table," he ordered tersely, gaining a curious glance from his father.

"If that is what you want," she replied submissively, then nodded and went off to the kitchen to tell Tove of his order. Brage's gaze followed her until she was out of sight, and then he took a deep drink of his wine, draining the glass. As another servant passed by, he claimed a mug of ale from her and started to down that.

Anslak was watching them together. "The wench is treacherous, but beautiful. Will you keep her?"

"I will keep her until I tire of her," Brage answered, but as memories of her lovemaking played though his mind, he wondered if the day would come when he would ever tire of her—betrayal or not. He could not forget that Dynna had saved his life when he was first taken captive. She had kept the secret of his identity and had tried to nurse him until Sir Edmund had stopped her. She had helped him to escape, though it had suited her purpose to do so. He shook his head to push thoughts of her from his mind.

"And the other? It would seem Ulf wants her."

Brage shrugged as he looked toward his brother, his gaze hardening as he saw Ulf snare Matilda around the waist and pull her onto his lap. The girl offered no resistance, but laughed and threw her arms around his neck, kissing him boldly. Ulf seemed to be enjoying himself, and Brage felt the spark of suspicion he had harbored for so long burst into full flame.

At that moment, Ulf glanced his way, and across the crowded room, their gazes met. Ulf had been laughing, but his laughter died and he frowned in response to his brother's regard.

"What shall we do about the traitor? Do you suspect someone?" Anslak asked.

Brage tensed even more at the mention of that which was troubling him so greatly. "Perhaps I should thank the betrayer," he said, drinking the ale. "He is the reason I am still alive, for the need to find him was what kept me fighting to live. I want to see him suffer for his treachery."

"Revenge is a powerful emotion," his father agreed.

"Indeed," Brage ground out, his gaze swinging back in Ulf's direction.

Ulf was deep in conversation with some of the men.

"Look at him," Parr was saying to Ulf. "Sitting there beside Anslak as if nothing had happened to him at all."

"And here he has been wounded, chained and imprisoned, and yet now he is fine," another added in awe of Brage's strength and ability.

"He is the Black Hawk," Ulf answered simply. He had always known how brave and strong his brother was. Even as children when he had stood a full head taller than Brage and outweighed him by at least two stone, Brage had matched him effort for effort in most things. There had even been times when Brage had beaten him.

"We should never have doubted him, but, Ulf, that day of the raid . . . I saw him go down, too. I thought he was dead. It is a miracle that he is with us." Parr's expression was troubled as he thought of that day.

Ulf looked toward Brage to find his brother watching him again with a strangely blank expression. "It is truly a miracle that he lives," Ulf agreed.

When the food had been served, the women were sent out

with trays of ale, mead, and wine to walk among the guests. Dynna brought her tray of ale to Brage, and he took another mug and drank thirstily from it.

"I am enjoying your celebration, Brage," Inger purred as she appeared before the table, smiling coyly at him.

"I am glad," Brage answered simply. He had seen her making her way to him through the crowd and had been wishing for some way to avoid her. She was an alluring woman, but he did not love her and had no real interest in her and her clinging ways.

After she had served Brage his ale, Dynna remained standing beside him as he had instructed her to. Inger was annoyed at her presence.

"Woman, go fetch me a glass of wine," she ordered imperiously.

"She stays," Brage said quickly. "If you want wine, fetch it for yourself."

"She is but a servant!" Inger's face turned red at his callousness.

"She is my servant," he replied, "here to do as I bid."

Inger was humiliated. She knew Anslak and Kristoffer were staring at her, and she knew that the others who had heard his terse comments knew he was deliberately shunning her. She hurried away, her hope to marry him shattered.

Brage's mood was tense. He had had little patience with Inger's prattle and fawning attentions. The more he thought about Ulf's betrayal the angrier he became. When he saw Ulf crossing the room toward them, he readied himself for the confrontation. He had waited a long time for this moment. He was going to face his deceitful brother down right there in front of everyone. He was going to reveal him for the treacherous bastard that he was.

"My brother, I would know why you seem so solemn this night?" Ulf asked as he stopped before him at the table. He had carried his own ale with him and took a drink.

"Is it so difficult to understand when I know that a traitor shares the celebration?"

Ulf looked pointedly around the crowded room. "You are thinking of the betrayal tonight when you should be celebrating your return?"

"I have thought of little else since the day I saw my men slaughtered and I was taken prisoner by the Saxons."

Anslak and Kristoffer could not ignore the exchange, and they listened intently.

"What do you think? Do you know the one? If you know who it is, I will help you take him."

"I have had many hours to consider it. I have thought long and hard about it. And I know who would stand to gain the most were I dead." Brage's expression was steely as he slowly rose to stand eye-to-eye with Ulf across the width of the table.

"Who is it?" Ulf asked, seeing his fury and fully understanding it. His men had died because of this traitor, and Brage was not a forgiving man. "I will seize him for you."

"It is you."

# Twenty

Ulf's color faded as he stared at Brage in disbelief, stricken by his accusation. "You question my loyalty to you? You think I could betray you? You are my brother! I have fought side by side with you, and now you accuse me of this! How could you suggest such a thing?"

"I more than suggest it," Brage countered angrily, rounding the table to stand before him. "I say it *was* you!"

A shocked silence had fallen over the crowd. All eyes were riveted on them in disbelief.

Dynna was still standing back behind the table, watching as the two men confronted each other.

"You cannot mean this," Ulf said.

"You had knowledge of all my plans," Brage charged.

"So did others," he offered in self-defense.

"You stood to gain the most with me gone. You would command my men; you would have my ship. With me out of the way, Father would look upon you with even more favor," Brage accused.

Brage glanced around and saw his father's and Kristoffer's swords against the wall. He strode furiously to them and picked them up, tossing Lord Anslak's weapon to Ulf. It was a beautiful sword with a golden hilt. Each legitimate son had been given a sword with a golden hilt, too. Brage wielded Kristoffer's now, its hilt a bejeweled dragon's head.

"There is our father's sword. You have wanted it all your life. Use it now!"

Ulf was astounded by all he was saying, and he stared at his brother in astonishment. He had caught the weapon and held it in his right hand, but when Brage came at him, ready to fight, Ulf knew he could not risk harming the one he had sworn to protect. He stood tall, his head high, as he said, "I will not fight you, Brage."

Ulf took the sword and stabbed it into the tabletop so it stood upright for all to see.

Brage advanced on him, the sword he held at ready. "Pick up the sword. Fight me like a man."

Ulf merely stared at him. "It is true, I knew guilt after the battle when I thought you were dead. But the guilt came from my failure in my sworn duty to protect you. I had allowed harm to come to you and to the other men. I would have welcomed death on the battlefield myself that day. I would have preferred Valhalla to living with the knowledge that I had failed you. So kill me now if you must. Pierce my heart with the sword, as you have already pierced it with your words, but know this. I would die, here, now, a death without honor, before I would allow you to go on believing that I betrayed you. It would be worth the sacrifice of my life for you to know the truth, Brother. I was not the one who betrayed you to Lord Alfrick."

Brage was even more furious at his denial. He closed on him, murder in his eyes. He wanted the traitor. He wanted him now. He looked as if he were going to run Ulf through.

Matilda had been in the kitchen when she realized things had gone suddenly silent in the main room. She came to the doorway to see Brage confronting Ulf. As Brage seemed to be about to attack him, she cried out, "No! Wait! Ulf was not the man!"

Everyone in the room gasped at her cry and turned to look at Matilda. She ran forward and stood before Brage, putting herself between the men.

"Do not do this, Brage. I know Ulf was not the one. I was there that night!"

"You were what?" Brage demanded.

"Matilda, what are you saying?" Dynna asked from where she stood.

"I was in the Great Hall the night the Viking came with news of your coming raid."

"You know who the traitor is?" Anslak had risen and was coming to join his sons.

"I watched and listened, and when the man left, I followed him," she quickly explained.

"Who is the betrayer?" Brage demanded. "Name him!"

"I do not know who he is exactly, I only know that he was not Ulf. He was smaller than Ulf, more slightly built. He wore a beard, full and blond, and . . ."

She looked around the room, trying to match the glimpse of the face she had seen in the moonlight that night with one of the men there, but to no avail. And then her gaze fell to the sword Brage was holding, and she gasped.

"The sword! That is the one the man was carrying! I saw that dragon's head in the moonlight, and I remember thinking how wicked it looked with the jewels gleaming in its eyes!"

A totally stunned silence fell as Brage stared down at Kristoffer's weapon. He turned slowly to find his brother getting to his feet and backing away.

"She is daft!" Kris said. "What has she to gain by telling such lies? Is not her mistress a liar, and she has now proven herself to be one, too?"

"Kristoffer!" Anslak pulled his sword free from the tabletop.

Kris glared at his father, hatred gleaming in his eyes.

It was then, as she caught a glimpse of his profile, that Matilda realized it was Kristoffer. "It was him! I recognize him now! He is the one who visited Lord Alfrick that night!"

Kris started to bolt from the room, but Ulf went after him as did Lord Anslak and Brage. He got no farther than the center of the room, when several of the men grabbed him. They dragged him back before the others.

Brage looked at Kristoffer in shock. Hurt and anger filled him. "Why, Kris? All those good men dead . . . They were your friends . . ."

"Friends!" Kris spat at him venomously as he thrust himself forward and slammed his hands on the tabletop. He glared at all three of them—Brage, Ulf, and his father. "Your ship! Your sword! Your shield! Your friends! Everything was yours, Brage! The only person anybody cares about around here is the famous Black Hawk. You can do no wrong."

"What are you saying?" Anslak bellowed, barely able to keep his hands from him. "You did this thing? You turned traitor. You warned Alfrick of your brother's raid?"

"Yes, I did it! And if it had worked, I would have been your sole heir. Both Ulf and Brage would have been killed, and I would have had Brage's ships and his men. Then I would have been even more successful than the Black Hawk!"

Anslak could not stop himself from hitting Kris. He backhanded him. "You are a niding, the lowest of the low, a coward among men. I would kill you myself right now, but you do not deserve anything so honorable as death! I would not honor a coward so! I sentence you to banishment for the rest of your days! Be gone from my sight. I do not ever want to see you again. You are no longer of my flesh and my blood!" he finished in disgust.

"Do you think I care now? Having lived in the shadow of the magnificent Black Hawk for all these years, it matters not to me to be sent from here! Never did I do anything to earn your praise! Never did I please you as Brage did!"

His hatred, unleashed now for the first time was a vicious, consuming thing. Anslak never before had suspected that young Kris harbored such violent emotions. Never before had he believed the boy capable of such madness.

"Take him from my sight! I have only two sons. I have only Ulf and Brage."

Brage turned away from Kris and went to Ulf. He stood

before his brother, his friend, his ally. His expression was grave. "I have done you a great wrong, Ulf."

Ulf looked Brage straight in the eye, respecting him for his courage in admitting he was wrong. All this time, he had been feeling guilt over his inability to have saved his brother's life that day. It had weighed on his soul and had haunted his every waking hour. "And I did not keep my vow to protect your back. I thought you were dead. In the beginning, I would rather it had been me slain on the field of battle. Then when we learned you were alive, it was almost worse for me, for I had sentenced you to imprisonment by abandoning you in your time of need."

"No, it was never of your doing. You did not fail me. I failed you. To doubt you as I have after all these years . . ." Brage put his hand on his shoulder. "It was wrong. I am sorry."

"Treachery and hatred conspired against us. You are my brother. You are my friend."

"To show you my thanks, I would give you anything I have. You have but to name it, Brother, and it is yours," Brage offered.

"There is no need to make such an offer. This was a misunderstanding, nothing more. All is well between us."

Brage had been prepared to hand over his longship, his sword, his home. His refusal to take anything just reinforced all the good things Brage had always known about him. They embraced.

As they moved apart, Ulf grinned and said, "There is one thing I would ask of you."

"Yes?"

"Would you sell the slave Matilda to me? I want to free her so I can take her as my wife."

"Sell her? Nay, I free her now. It is done. I announce before all that Matilda is freed. I think you must be the one to make her your wife. I have no such power."

Ulf and Brage embraced again. Peace was restored between them.

Ulf turned toward Matilda and gestured for her to come to him. She was blushing and her heart was beating a frantic rhythm as she flew into his arms and hugged him.

"I was so afraid something was going to happen to you. I knew you could not be the traitor. Your heart is too pure." She gazed up at him, loving his scarred face, loving his kind spirit and good heart.

Ulf was touched by her words. "What of it, woman? You are free now. Will you marry me?"

Matilda looked up at her fierce warrior and smiled gently. "I will marry you, Ulf. I will make you a good wife."

A cheer of happiness for him went up around the room. But Kristoffer, who was still being held by the others, broke into the festive spirit abruptly. "You sicken me!" he said coldly, having listened to Brage and Ulf as long as he could. "There were always just the two of you. I was tolerated only because we shared the same sire, never for myself! Remember this, my plan almost worked!"

"You are a fool, Kris!" Brage turned on him. "Neither of us sought to take anything from you. We sought to give to you, to teach you the ways of honor and battle."

Kristoffer glared at them. "You sought to keep me out of your way so you could claim all the glory and riches for yourselves!"

"Enough of your ugly words and viciousness!" Anslak bellowed. "Take him from this house. See him bound overnight. In the morning, we will take him into the countryside and release him to his fate of wandering with no family or friends. Perhaps then he will realize what he has lost."

Two of the men started to lead Kristoffer from the room. He went easily, not fighting or protesting their hands upon him.

Dynna had been afraid that Brage was going to be injured. She watched him now, knowing that she loved him. As she had watched him reconcile with Ulf, she knew for certain that she had never met a better man. She only wished that there was some way she could prove to him that she had been forced to betray him.

It was then that she saw Kristoffer jerk forcefully away from the two men who were holding him and trying to escort him from the house. It was then that she saw him grab one of the men's daggers from his belt and turn, ready to throw it at Brage.

"Brage! No!" she cried as she ran toward him, wanting to push him out of the way, to save him from harm.

As she called out her warning, the others did, too. Brage heard the urgency in her cry and pivoted, ready for trouble. He turned just in time to see Dynna take the knife that was meant for him. It struck her in the back, as she had thrown herself before him.

"Brage . . ." Dynna gasped his name as her eyes met his and she collapsed toward him.

"Dynna . . ." He caught her as she fell and lowered her gently to the floor as around them chaos broke loose.

The Vikings subdued Kristoffer by force and dragged his unconscious body from the house to leave him bound and gagged and locked in a storage room nearby.

Brage was cradling Dynna in his arms as Matilda came running to kneel beside her.

"Lady Dynna . . ." Matilda was crying as she stared down at her.

Brage drew her across his lap, and it was then that he saw her blood staining his hands. He pulled the knife from the wound and cast it aside like a hated thing.

"You are bleeding . . ." His voice was choked with emotion. "You saved my life . . ."

Dynna opened her eyes to gaze up at him as he hovered over her. "Far better it be my blood that is shed. I would give my life for you. I would have that night in the tower, but I was given no choice. My mother would be killed if I did not tell Edmund of your hiding place."

Brage stared down at her, the dawning of horrible understanding showing in his eyes as he realized the terrible choice she had been given. Edmund had lied and manipulated them both. "I am sorry . . . I did not know . . . I have been a fool not to believe you."

"I love you," she whispered, and then her eyes closed.

"Dynna?" Brage stared down at her, terrified for one moment that she had died, there in his arms. He held her to him, close to his heart. "Dynna . . . no . . ."

It was then that he realized she was still breathing, and he vowed, "I will not let you die, Dynna. I want you with me . . . always."

Brage ordered that the healing woman be brought immediately as he lifted her in his arms and carried her through the crowd that parted for him to his father's bedroom. He laid her upon the bed, then knelt beside it, taking her hand.

"I love you, Dynna. If you live through this, I will never let anything hurt you again. I swear it."

Brage remained there until he was forced to abandon the bedside when Olga, the most skilled Viking healer, appeared. He refused to leave the room, and waited, watching all that was happening. He looked up once and saw Ulf in the doorway. He went to him.

"She will be fine," Ulf said reassuringly.

"She has to be. I knew I loved her, but I did not know how much until now . . . Now that I fear I might lose her." Brage raised his tormented gaze to his brother.

"Edmund was a vicious man. He would have stopped at nothing to take what he wanted, and if he could not have it for himself, he wanted to make certain that no one else could claim it either. It is good that you know your heart now."

"It is very good. Where have they taken Kristoffer?"

"He is locked in the storage area, and Father has posted

a guard at the door. In the morning, he will see to his banishment himself."

"I have always thought I was a good judge of men, but I never suspected that Kristoffer hated us so."

"Nor did I. He was a good actor, hiding his true feelings from us all these years."

"If Dynna dies . . ." Brage's unspoken threat to Kristoffer was understood by Ulf.

"Brage . . ." Matilda came to him.

"How is she? Will she live?" Brage asked quickly.

At last a smile softened Matilda's expression. "It was a mere flesh wound. Lady Dynna will live."

"Thank the gods . . ." he breathed.

She nodded in agreement, and he smiled, relieved. She looked up to see Ulf there. When he held out his arms to her, she went to him. As she rested in the haven of Ulf's powerful embrace, she said a prayer of thanks that everything had turned out so well.

Brage walked silently to the side of the bed, passing Olga, who was on her way out. He stood over the bed, gazing down at Dynna as she lay unmoving. He thought she might be asleep, but then she opened her eyes to look up at him.

"Dynna . . ." He dropped to his knee beside the bed and took her hand again, pressing a devoted kiss to her palm. "They say you will recover."

"I know I will be up soon." Her voice was soft and a bit weak.

"There is something I have to say to you." His grip on her hand tightened, just enough to let her know that powerful emotions were driving him.

"I give you your freedom now, Dynna. You are no longer my slave. You are free to return to your parents. I will arrange safe transport for you." The last thing Brage wanted was to lose her. He wanted to marry her and spend the rest of his days loving her, but he would not force her to that choice.

Dynna gazed up at him, tears in her eyes. "Is this a reward for saving your life?"

"No. It is because I love you and cannot bear to see you unhappy. If returning to your parents is what you want, then it is what I want for you, too." Brage girded himself for her to say that she was leaving him.

"Did you say that you loved me?"

"I love you," he repeated solemnly.

"If I am free now, then I am free to make my own choices, and I do not choose to return to my parents. I wish to stay here with you, if you would have me." She lifted her hand to touch his cheek.

Brage gazed down at her, all the love he had been fighting now shining in his eyes. He bent to kiss her. It was a kiss of adoration, a kiss that told her just how much he cherished her. "I want no other. I love you, Dynna. Will you marry me?"

"I think I have loved you from that first time Ulf brought me before you. I know no other man like you. You are strong, but you are not afraid to be kind. You can be a fierce warrior, but you know the power of gentleness. You are a tender lover. I think my future with you is filled with many days of happiness and love. I will marry you, Brage. I will be your wife."

Brage's lips met hers again as they sealed their pledge to wed.

"As soon as you are healed," he vowed, "we will have the celebration. I cannot wait any longer than that."


Tove stood before Anslak as she told him of her plans. "I must do this. I have no other choice."

"Your son is a niding. He has proven disloyal and is not worthy of your devotion," Anslak argued with the woman who was his wife but who was now telling him that she was going to leave and follow Kristoffer when he was banished. "You are foolish to do this. Kris will be released, but word of his deeds will precede him, and he will have no peace for the balance of his days."

"He is but a boy . . ." Tove defended Kristoffer.

"He is a niding! A coward! A fool! Join him in exile if you wish, but know that he will never be welcomed here again."

"I understand," she said icily. "But *you* need to understand. While you have many who love you, Kristoffer only has me."

"You are the one who wishes to leave. You are the one who wishes to travel with your son. So be it. He is your son now, not mine. I do not claim cowards as kin. Kristoffer has done the unpardonable. He cannot be forgiven for his treachery."

"Then I must do what I must do," Tove insisted. She did not approve of what her son had done, but she understood it. He had lived in the shadow of Brage and Ulf all his life. Just as she had always lived in the shadow of the long-dead Mira. She could not allow Kristoffer to leave forever. Her love for her son was more powerful than her love for Anslak.

"The choice is yours, but know that you will always be welcome here."

She nodded brusquely and walked away. In the morning, she would leave the village with her son. Together, they would seek a new life elsewhere.

A week passed before Dynna was fully recovered. Brage had stayed by her side as much as he could, never wanting to be parted from her. She and Brage pledged themselves to each other before all, and then celebrated with a wedding feast long into the night.

When at last they were alone in their home, Brage took her hand and drew her with him to his bed. They lay upon it, pledging their bodies as well as their lives to each other. They made love tenderly, caring for each other, gently vow-ing their unfailing devotion, promising to never doubt each other again.

"I am sorry I did not listen to you that day at the tower. Had I listened and believed in you then, I would not have lost all this time in loving you," Brage said as he caressed her silken curves.

"What matters is that we are together now, sweet husband," she said, drawing him down for a hungry kiss.

"Yes, Wife, and we will be together forever."

They came together in a blaze of passion, joining together as man and wife, knowing their love would last for always. As they sought the heights of love's perfection, they knew peace and contentment would be theirs for all the days of their lives.

# Epilogue

The old woman cast the runes and then stared down at the prophetic stones where they lay on the table. She selected three with great care and studied their inscriptions. After a long moment, she looked up at the warrior and his woman where they sat before her.

"It is as they predicted, my handsome one," she said cryptically as she looked back down at the runes. "The treasure of great value is yours. You have defeated all. You have survived the danger. You have seen through the deceit and false words and have claimed the prize and made it your own."

Brage remembered her prediction from the last time he had been to her. He was sitting beside Dynna now, and he slipped his arm about her, knowing the treasure of which the old woman spoke. "You were right. The prize was more precious than any I had claimed before."

Dynna cast him a questioning sidelong glance, but he ignored it.

"Tell me then, what of our future? What do the runes say?"

The old woman stared down at the stones again, seeking an answer, seeking the secrets of the future. "A son . . ." she said quickly. "A fine strapping son, to be followed by girls who will prove a challenge to their father."

Dynna and Brage looked at each other as Dynna's hand strayed to rest on her still-flat stomach.

"And there will be peace in our lives?" Dynna asked, for she could not forget the ugliness of Kristoffer's hatred.

"The peace you have long sought is found. Your warrior will protect you and love you. Go now. And know that your days will be filled with sunshine and laughter."

And they were.

## SURRENDER TO THE SPLENDOR OF THE ROMANCES OF ROSANNE BITTNER!

| | |
|---|---|
| CARESS | (3791, $5.99/$6.99) |
| COMANCHE SUNSET | (3568, $4.99/$5.99) |
| HEARTS SURRENDER | (2945, $4.50/$5.50) |
| LAWLESS LOVE | (3877, $4.50/$5.50) |
| PRAIRIE EMBRACE | (3160, $4.50/$5.50) |
| RAPTURE'S GOLD | (3879, $4.50/$5.50) |
| SHAMELESS | (4056, $5.99/$6.99) |

Available wherever paperbacks are sold, or order direct from the Publisher. Send cover price plus 50¢ per copy for mailing and handling to Penguin USA, P.O. Box 999, c/o Dept. 17109, Bergenfield, NJ 07621. Residents of New York and Tennessee must include sales tax. DO NOT SEND CASH.

## *WHAT'S LOVE GOT TO DO WITH IT?*

*Everything . . . Just ask Kathleen Drymon . . . and Zebra Books*

| | |
|---|---|
| **CASTAWAY ANGEL** | *(3569-1, $4.50/$5.50)* |
| **GENTLE SAVAGE** | *(3888-7, $4.50/$5.50)* |
| **MIDNIGHT BRIDE** | *(3265-X, $4.50/$5.50)* |
| **VELVET SAVAGE** | *(3886-0, $4.50/$5.50)* |
| **TEXAS BLOSSOM** | *(3887-9, $4.50/$5.50)* |
| **WARRIOR OF THE SUN** | *(3924-7, $4.99/$5.99)* |

*Available wherever paperbacks are sold, or order direct from the Publisher. Send cover price plus 50¢ per copy for mailing and handling to Penguin USA, P.O. Box 999, c/o Dept. 17109, Bergenfield, NJ 07621. Residents of New York and Tennessee must include sales tax. DO NOT SEND CASH.*